Previous books by Christodoulos Moisa

Blood and Koka Kola

"This collection of short stories … is everything such a book should be. The author has put his artist's eyes and poet's ear to good use. The stories have the sparseness of Hemingway and resonate with an understanding of the human condition – a prerequisite of the genre. They make compelling reading and the subject matter ranges from the macabre to historical, from the mythical to the quirky, some enigmatic, others rich with humour and irony; all written with perfect pitch. The mix of New Zealanders and Cypriots reflects the author's own history and lends authenticity to the stories. It is a treasure." *JOAN ROSIER-JONES* – author of Waiting for Elizabeth

"*Blood and Koka Kola* is a mix of tales … Some are told in the traditional manner; with a beginning, middle and end; others are short staccato bursts of poetic energy, gorgeous in their use of language and satisfying as a good story should be … None is disappointing. Each story is a good read, and the variety of construction adds to the interest and encourages further exploration … For your average Kiwi, it adds an exotic touch and extra interest … Some stories make you wonder where they come from, how they arrived in the author's imagination, but they're so good you'd be pleased they did." *PAUL BROOKS* – Midweek

"Moisa doesn't disappoint. His stories are wide-ranging, both in subject matter and character portrayal, and his wit and his perception of human frailty reflect a life lived in several manifestations. This collection covers stories from New Zealand scenes as well as echoing the six years spent as a child in Cyprus in the late 1950s and as a young man in 1973 and 1974. … Several of Moisa's stories have the surprise ending which is imperative for a good story, and this is one of the strengths and delights of his book … *Blood and Koka Kola* … is a very interesting, insightful and appealing collection of short stories …" *MICHAEL O'LEARY* – Landfall

The Hour of the Grey Wolf

"… is a crime story … in many ways, it defies the genre. It is literary fiction as well, experimental in form, so experimental that, simply linked together with logic, the parts should not work together to form that coherent whole. And yet they do. … a compelling page-turner, a classic whodunit. … I kept turning the pages and am certain other readers will too. The overall effect of *The Hour of the Grey Wolf* cannot be denied: the setting and characters are still resonating with me …"
ANTONY MILLEN – Crime Watch

"… is for those who like comedy, tragedy, a murder mystery, and romance along with a wide range of cultural and historical references, conservation ethics and political insight. The New Zealand/Cypriot narrator can offer both an insider and an outsider view of the situation in Cyprus when tensions between Greeks and Turks, as well as factions within the Greek community, were at their height. Surely, something for everyone." *NELSON WATTIE*

"… I recommend it on two levels – a literary experiment and a ripping good yarn." *PAUL BROOKS* – Midweek *and* NZ Herald

"… is a handsome book and something to be really proud of. A real achievement – and a remarkable work in broadening the range and the depth of inquiry of the New Zealand novel." *KEVIN IRELAND* – NZ poet and novelist

"… Moisa takes the readers on an exciting journey influenced by his roots with this compelling literary page turner …Moisa delivers a unique and atmospheric whodunnit that is richly textured with history, philosophy and labyrinthine politics. Pleasingly it's the first in a series." *CRAIG SISTERSON* – New Zealand Books

Overcast Sunday

The Desert (long poem)

Wolves in Dogs' Clothing

Thrown
to the
Wolves

Christodoulos Moisa is an award-winning poet and artist. Born in 1948 in Lower Hutt, New Zealand to Cypriot immigrant parents, Moisa spent five years of his childhood in Cyprus and a further 18 months there in 1972/73. He has published six volumes of poetry and the critically acclaimed long poem *The Desert*. In 2010 his first book of short stories, *Blood and Koka Kola*, was published. The first of the Wolf Trilogy novels, *The Hour of the Grey Wolf*, was published in 2016, followed in 2017 by *Wolves in Dogs' Clothing*. Moisa lives and works in Whanganui, a river city on the west coast of New Zealand.

Thrown to the Wolves: In this final volume of the Wolf Trilogy, New Zealand journalist Steve Carpenter is eking a precarious existence on the Mediterranean island of Cyprus. Suffering from "battle fatigue," he keeps busy writing about the coup de d'état and the Turkish invasion of the previous summer. He also, at times, travels to conflict zones in the Middle East, filing profile features for the London press. A casual phone call to his cousin Inspector Zimaras finds Carpenter been driven to the Red-Villages of southern Cyprus, where a body has been discovered. Meanwhile, another murder scene is unfolding in an upscale hotel in the new beach resort of Agia Napa. To the dismay of the local police, both crimes involve tourists which have serious implications for the coming holiday season. However, to the intrepid Carpenter, they present an opportunity to delve into the murky world of sex-tourism, forged passports and international terrorism.

A gripping whodunit with colourful characters; *Thrown to the Wolves* explores kinship and conflict on an island scarred by political skulduggery and violent extremism. A thrilling and thought provoking read.

Thrown
to the
Wolves

Christodoulos Moisa

ONE EYED PRESS

To the people of Christchurch, New Zealand,

who have suffered

three calamities in one lifetime:

The 22 February 2011 earthquake, the 15 March 2019

terrorist attack and the 2020 Covid-19 Corona Virus outbreak.

May all the victims find peace.

Note to the reader

Case is a grammatical category whose value reflects the grammatical function performed by a noun or pronoun in a phrase, clause or sentence. Unlike Greek, English has largely lost its case system, although case distinctions can still be seen with the personal pronouns. In Greek, there are four cases in the singular and four in the plural: the nominative, the genitive, the accusative and the vocative. Case also exists in names. It is difficult sometimes to translate written Greek or Greek speech into English without using the Greek case system. The author takes total responsibility for trying to invoke the richness, complexity and the essence of the Greek language, and it is hoped that by latching on to the stem of a noun, the reader can navigate this linguistic difficulty without much hindrance.

Acknowledgements

First and foremost, I would like to thank Wikipedia, the modern Alexandrian library-like repository of knowledge, for enabling me to research the factual elements of this novel from the comfort of my writing room. I would also like to thank the authors whose books are listed in the bibliography for their fleshing out of the background to the Cyprus conundrum and their dedication to the truth. Thanks to the following for their help and advice: Kevin Ireland, Robert Irlam, Eleanour Barricoat, George Georgakakos, Frank Gibson, Sophia Sparks, Myrto Kenny, Iraklis Kanarkotis, David Pate, Nelson Wattie, Lynda Barrett, Neove Christoforou, Caroline M. Simpson, Chrystalla Thoma, Niki Thoma, Helen Ridley, Alexander McCowan, Georgina Christensen and Andy Economou.

I am particularly thankful to: Sara Esam for helping me to get to Cyprus to research some aspects of this novel; to my dear friend Paul Morris for his encouragement and advice on all things religious; to my friend Artemis Poulos for his help in discussing Cypriot slang and his help in researching factual Cypriot elements of the novel; to my friend Bruce Miller for his beta reading of the novel and for his honest opinion and encouragement; to Andy Hynds for his help in analysing the complexity of the British Sovereign Bases in Cyprus; to Mac McCallion and Wi Taipa for their invaluable help on the deployment of the New Zealand army in Vietnam and their friendship; to my guardian angels in our family, my cousins Angela Duthie and Maria Evangeli for their encouragement and help; to my brother-in-law Giannakis Costantinou Toulounge who toured with me the battlefields that he fought in during the Turkish invasion and I also thank him for his generosity and loyal friendship; to my godfather, Panagiotis Pauvlides, and godmother, Anthoula Pavlides, who have always had time for me and extended to me their unconditional love; and finally to my sister Kleanthi and her family in Cyprus for their generosity, love and understanding.

Glossary – Translation

Agia – *female saint*

Agios – *male saint*

Alpha – *first letter of the Greek alphabet, can also denote first*

Asihtir – *"fuckin' hell" in Turkish.*

Béta – *second letter of the Greek alphabet, can also denote second*

Briki – *a small copper galvanised pot in which Greek or Turkish coffee is made*

Demotic – *language of the common people*

ELDYK – *The Hellenic (Greek) Force in Cyprus*

Giagia – *grandmother, can also be an honorific for someone who is older*

Hajji – *one who goes on a pilgrimage to Mecca. In reference to Greeks, it is an honorific denoting one who has gone on a pilgrimage to Jerusalem and been baptised in the River Jordan*

Kafenio – *coffee shop*

Kafkala – *crust*

Kara – *black*

Kyria – *mistress, madame or missus (slang)*

Kyrie – *master or mister*

Kaliméra – *good morning*

Kali sou mera – *good day to you*

Kapilé – *Turkish, derogatory word for vagina*

Katharévousa – *a fomal form of modern Greek which was replaced in 1976 by the "demotic".*

Kleftikos – *stolen meat cooked in a sealed oven.*

Koumpáros – *best man or groomsman*

Koumpára – *best woman or bridesmaid*

Maláka – *wanker*

Marangós – *carpenter*

Muktar – *village headsman*

Pappou – *grandfather*

Papa – *prefix indicating a priest or, in a non-priest's surname, that they are the child of a priest. Also diminutive of father*

Pentadactylos – *Five-finger Mountain*

Pommie – *Prisoner of Mother England, slang for an Englishman*

Poustis – *poofter*

Shísto – *arshole*

Sheitánis – *The Tempter, relating to the Devil or Lucifer*

Sketos, Medrios, Gligos – *in reference to coffee: plain, middling, sweet*

Souvláki – *pieces of meat cooked on a skewer*

Thios – *uncle, can also be an honorific for someone respected*

Thia – *aunt, can also be an honorific for someone respected*

Victor Charlie – *Vietcong*

Zimarás – *someone who kneads bread*

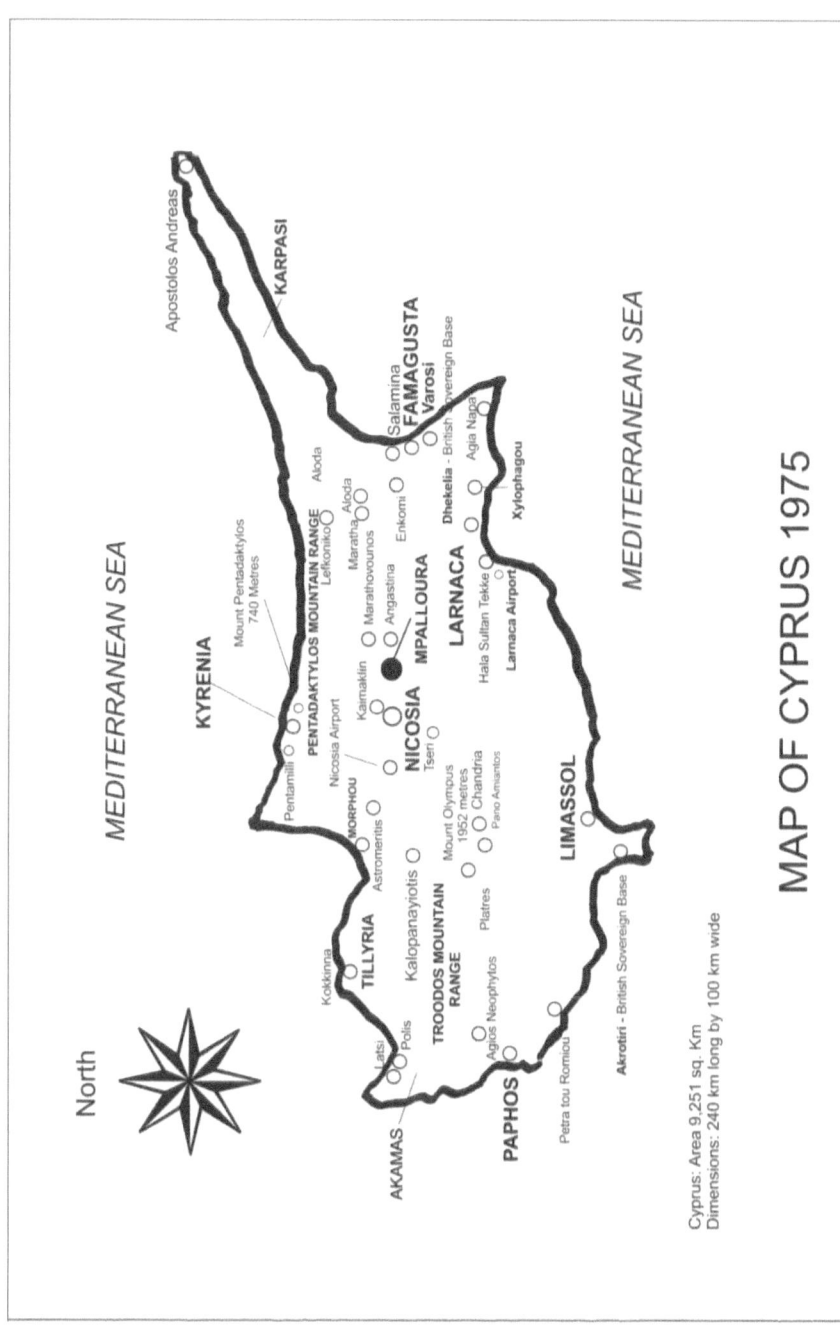

MAP OF CYPRUS 1975

MEDITERRANEAN SEA

North

Apostolos Andreas

KARPASI

KYRENIA

Mount Pentadaktylos
740 Metres

PENTADAKTYLOS MOUNTAIN RANGE

Pentamili

Nicosia Airport

Lefkoniko

Aloda

Aloda

Maratha

Marathovounos

Kamakin

Angastina

Enkomi

Salamina
FAMAGUSTA
Varosi

Dhekelia - British Sovereign Base

Agia Napa

Xylophagou

MPALLOURA

NICOSIA

Tseri

LARNACA

MORPHOU

Astromeritis

Hala Sultan Tekke

Larnaca Airport

TILLYRIA

Kalopanayiotis

Mount Olympus
1952 metres

Chandria

Pano Amiantos

TROODOS MOUNTAIN
RANGE

Platres

Kokkina

Polis

Latsi

AKAMAS

Agios Neophytos

PAPHOS

Petra tou Romiou

LIMASSOL

Akrotiri - British Sovereign Base

MEDITERRANEAN SEA

Cyprus: Area 9,251 sq. Km.
Dimensions: 240 km long by 100 km wide

Prologue

From the ridiculous to the sublime.

The phrase *From the sublime to the ridiculous* was first coined by American philosopher Thomas Paine in his 1794 treatise *The Age of Reason.* In this three-part publication, he provokingly challenged institutionalized religion and the legitimacy of the Bible as a sacred text. He also, like other deists, demanded that debate rests on reason and rationality and that – like Isaac Newton – all things in the universe, even God, must obey the laws of nature. What Paine meant, when he came to conjure the phrase, was that two positions can be so closely related that it is but one small step from one to the other.

From the ridiculous to the sublime, intoned under my breath – **Paines' construct** reversed – was I suppose, my take on the phrase. It seemed, at the time, to succinctly sum up my self-inflicted impasse after a convoluted mulling over of the principle of the Coriolis effect on the earth's winds.

I came across the theory when I was researching the source of the Boreas – the north wind – and stumbled over the name of Gaspard-Gustave de Coriolis. He was a French scientist who, in 1835, produced a paper on the energy yield of machines with rotating parts – such as waterwheels. Although Giovanni Battista Riccioli already described the effect in 1651 and Claude François Milliet Dechales in 1674, de Coriolis was the first to publish the mathematical explanation of the theory and, as sometimes happens in science, was bequeathed the privilege of the effect being named after him.

The Coriolis effect describes a natural phenomenon caused by the rotation of the earth, which spins from west to east. According to the theory, if a wind starts descending towards the equator from the polar Arctic, the spinning earth will deflect it to veer eastwards rather than travel directly south. The same happens in the southern hemisphere, producing the westerlies named after the latitudes they

17

occur in and aptly known by their intensity as the roaring forties, furious fifties and screaming sixties.

It was just after this that I was struck by a rather ridiculous notion – out of left-field, as they say. Could this left to right trajectory somehow also affect the prevailing rise of right-wing governments? And, if true, could left-wing governments be predestined for failure?

Too much time on my hands?

Perhaps.

Absurd?

Absolutely!

However, in all honesty, I do have to admit pondering this counter-intuitive notion for more than a few moments. Fortunately, just as quickly, the editor in me dismissed it as I had also garnered from the same source that the band of trade winds between the Tropic of Capricorn and the Equator travel from right to left. So the proof that the concept could be applied to politics should have been the existence of a plethora of left-wing governments in Central Africa and Central America … Of course, instead, as we all know, there are a plethora of nasty dictatorships ... and, as it always happens with hindsight and some reflection on such things, I denied myself the, keenly anticipated, opportunity of contrasting and comparing the attributes of the pathological extreme-left with the pathological extreme-right ... Not that I was, by then, even slightly persuaded that there was a difference.

And now, to the sublime ...

Chapter 1

1

The Boreas – which was not only the ancient Greeks' name for the north wind but was also their name for the god of winter – was depicted by them as a bearded, purple-winged, bad-tempered old man with feet in the form of wings or snakes. The ancient Greeks thought that this child of the Keeper of the Winds, Aeolus, came from Thrace in northern Greece. However, they were only partly right.

In actuality, the Boreas begins its long journey – further north than Thrace – at the belly button of the North Pole, as a descending, cold, but dry band of air sweeping over the permafrosted, treeless Arctic. If – in the first instance – one puts aside the intrinsic aspects of the atmospheric Polar, Ferrel and Hadley convection cells, the course of this icy polar blast is southwesterly. However, at the 60° north parallel, it is picked up by the Coriolis effect and gently deflected in a southeasterly direction, where it dumps snow over the forests and grasslands of Russia. Soon after, it also dumps snow on the mountain ranges of Ukraine, the Rhodope mountains of Bulgaria and the undulating highlands of Romania, and northern Greece.

Morphing into a screeching and chanting Sophoclean, dark-robed chorus, the Boreas mercilessly dispenses thunder, lightning and hail and also a staccato of ominous black, snorting waterspouts the length of the Aegean before dumping more snow on Turkey and its southern Karamania mountains.

Still going strong, the Boreas, now pushing a black cumulonimbus curtain, skims the forty-six miles over the now wine-dark waters of the Mediterranean to the island of Cyprus – where more thunder is clapped and bolts of lightning are cast on both plain and hill – to slam into a wall of rising, warm African air over the 6,000 foot high Troodos massif. Here, finally, with a tired, expiring sigh, the Boreas transmogrifies and falls as pure white snow on the highest peak of Cyprus, Mount Olympus – one of seven or so similarly named mountain peaks in the Ancient Greek world named after the home of their capricious, ambrosia-feasting gods.

So strictly speaking, in Cyprus, the Boreas – from the Greek verb *boraô* meaning *to devour* – is not a northerly but a northwesterly.

Or at least I hope so.

Loudly from offstage right: What I am absolutely certain of is my uncertainty.

From offstage left: Who said that?

From offstage above: Why?

*

Sometimes, the Boreas also speckles a dusting of snow on the northern Pentadactylos mountain range and the fertile alluvial lowlands of the Mesaoria before it storms and breaches the Venetian-built ramparts of Nicosia – the capital – battering and tearing at its houses and cobbled narrow streets, sapping them of any residual summer warmth; to remind me, if I ever forget, of a bone-chilling April, Antarctic southerly battering New Zealand's capital, Wellington, where I was born and raised.

On such an occasion, between the odd report to Reuters or a newspaper assignment to a Middle Eastern or African country, there is only one recourse. Hole up at the reading rooms of the British Council in Nicosia reading the latest English periodicals, researching my latest book on my experiences of the coup d'état and the Turkish invasion of the previous summer, or go and find a quiet corner at *Kyriou* Louizou's *kafenio* to read the Greek newspapers.

I had started to frequent *Kyriou* Andrea Louizou's establishment ever since my move within the walls of old Nicosia, known by Cypriots as Lefkosia, derived from the Greek phrase *leuke ousia* – white estate – perhaps something to do with its gypsum-white topography. The *kafenio* was close to my apartment and I liked its atmosphere. Not too trendy – like those new cafés on Makarios III Avenue outside the walls – but in the village tradition, easy-going and friendly. As a favour to me, *Kyrios* Louizos also subscribes to the Sunday edition of *Kathimerini,* an Athenian centrist newspaper, which I pay for, and when I finish it, I take it back for his other customers also to read. Sometimes after a brisk walk, which since I started helps me sleep at night, I go to the nearby Turkish baths, now renamed Greek baths. I'd discovered the baths, where I take a sauna, just south of the Green Line demarcation border that splits Nicosia in two. The baths not only cleanse but also warm me, especially my old leg injury, which aches when there's a cold wind. The injury was a present from my Vietnam sojourn, although that is a bit of an understatement as I was actually there on and off for nearly three years.

Some days, around lunchtime, I ring my friend and cousin who is now also a senior inspector in the Cyprus police, Petros Zimaras. The kinship with Petros is to some degree tenuous as third cousins rarely acknowledge each other beyond a nod in the village, let alone the city. However, for Petros it is important, and over the last couple of years, it has become important for me too. Although, because of my New Zealand sensibilities, I see him more as a very close friend, even if *friendship,* the Cypriot kind, is still an evolving concept for me.

"You are now through to Inspector Zimaras' office, *Kyrie*," the Central Police Station telephonist intoned in Greek, as if she was imparting some saucy secret.

"Zimaras," boomed the voice of my cousin.

"Have I woken you?" The opening gambit to one of our friendly, reciprocal put-down banters.

"Stauvro!" Petros cheerily answered back in his accented English, ignoring the bait. "How are you, cousin?"

"Bored and freezing my balls off. How are you? How's Eleni?"

"Thanks to God, fine. We are all fine."

"How about lunch?"

"I am sorry, cousin. I wish I could. But I have to go to Dhekelia," the cheery tonality evaporating.

"Pity. What's in Dhekelia?"

"Work."

"What work?"

"Police business."

"What? Another bird poacher?"

"No."

"Cyprus mafia?"

"No."

"Smugglers?"

"No."

"A matricide?"

"No."

"A uxoricide?"

"What the hell is that?"

"A man killing his wife."

There was a brief silence and then, "Not exactly."

Jesus, cousin! Like getting blood out of a stone.

"Come on, Petros. Stop pissing me around."

"Okay. Okay. A killing."

"What? A patricide ... a parricide ... a prolicide ... a sororicide ...?" I rattled off.

"No. No."

There was a brief silence and then. "Not exactly. Well ..."

A longer silence.

"What?"

Then, finally, "They've found a *neanitha* ..." he said in Greek.

"A young girl? A teenager?" I tried, clarifying it in English.

"Yes, a teenager. She's dead. God rest her soul. She was killed."

"Oh? I am sorry to hear that, cousin."

A silence hung between us.

Maybe an opportunity beckons.

I take a deep breath and squint my eyes. "Is there a story in it for me?" I ask in trepidation as I know this can go either of two ways.

And the way it goes is the one where Petros explodes. "God, Stauvro, you're like a stray dog always looking for a bone!"

"I have to make a living cousin," I managed.

More silence. Then, "You are right, Stauvro. But, no." Then, again, "Actually … I don't know."

As always, I was reluctant to press Petros too much for the heads up to a story as one can push friendship or, it also seems, kinship, too far, and although I was getting desperate of late for something to pay the bills with, I decided to let it go.

"Don't worry about it …"

"Wait a minute, let me think …"

More silence.

"Stauvro … Where are you?"

"At the telephone booth outside Louizou's *kafenio*." I used the booth rather than the telephone inside. This was to avoid the usual entrapment of being shouted a coffee and out of politeness having to sit down, inevitably to be drawn into a lengthy and multifaceted political discussion by *Kyrios* Louizos or his customers.

"Can you ring me back in ten minutes. I need to check something. Ten minutes, no more."

'Sure, ten minutes," I said and hung up.

I stood in the telephone booth twiddling my thumbs and watching the world go by. I zipped up the leather World War II British bomber jacket that I bought in one of London's second-hand shops, just off Piccadilly Circus, and lifted the collar up against the icy wind. The jacket replaced the duffel coat that I lost in the Turkish invasion – it was either still warming a former Turkish soldier or some shivering refugee from the south.

It was a normal, cloudless Nicosia winter's weekday. The contrail of a military jet, perhaps Turkish, etched a white line across the northern azure sky. The lottery sellers were calling out, hawking their wares, as were bucket, *koulouria* and roast-chestnut sellers. The smell of the roasting chestnuts tempted me for a moment to abandon my post, as did the smell of coffee wafting out of Louizou's *kafenio* every time a customer opened the door.

Everyone was dressed in winter garb, plus the odd cap and umbrella. There were several pigeons with two sparrows picking over the remnants of something thrown for them from the *kafenio*.

If you were blind to the bullet holes dotting the walls around you and if anyone told you that those streets were a bloody battlefield a year ago with some of the worst street-to-street fighting of the war, you would have laughed at them. I couldn't be more amazed at how quickly life got back to normal – if there is such a thing – after a coup d'état and a war.

For some reason, the nearby *Panagia Phaneromenis* church bell began to toll.

A baptism? ... Not for that time of the day. Maybe a funeral.

Ten minutes later, I rang back.

"*Yia, kai pali* – hello, once again – Stauvro, I needed to touch base with the boss and get his okay. How would you like a trip to Dhekelia? ... Actually, Xylophagou. You can come here, leave your car in the station car park and we can go in the Alfa Romeo."

I didn't even have to think about it. "Sounds good," I said. Any excuse, really, to get out of Nicosia. Maybe it was my troubled mindset at that moment as living in the city induced a certain amount of claustrophobia in me. Initially, I thought that it must be the rampart walls that enclosed the city's narrow streets or something similar but more convoluted that I had not figured out as yet. That was why I loved my parents' village, Mpalloura: after a two minute walk, I would find myself out in the countryside taking in the fresh air, smelling the newly ploughed earth or spring flowers and squinting my eyes against the setting sun to view what was an inexplicable and unique landscape – a combination of an endless plain, rolling hills and the backdrop beyond of the reassuring presence of the Pentadactylos mountain range. But Mpalloura, the village of my parents and my ancestors, was ostensibly no more. It was now occupied by the Turkish army. They even renamed it.

"As long as you put your car heater on full," I said.

"I'll even get you a hot water bottle," said Petros, laughing as he hung up.

2

Petros was sitting in the dark blue Alfa Romeo waiting for me on the side road that led to the Central Police Station, at the beginning of the Limassol to Nicosia highway. The Alfa Romeo was a hand-me-down to the police department from the presidential detail.

I parked my Morris 1000 convertible in the police station's car park and then walked back to the side road and got in.

"I see you had *to saravalo* – the old bomb – patched up," said Petros, by way of a greeting.

I ignored the snide remark. "Yeah, one of the boys from our village has opened up a panel beating and motor repair workshop near the Green Line, just down from the Turkish baths. I came across him last month, and he promised he'd give it a tune-up and fix the bodywork as good as new." I reached into my pocket and took out an Il Moro cigar packet and then removed and halved a cigar. I offered it to Petros, but he shook his head. "It's about time," I continued pensively, in reference to the Morris 1000, "Now that our wounds are healed it's about time that the cars do too. You don't think cars have nightmares do you, cousin?"

"What do you mean?"

"It's a rhetorical question. I am being silly. Don't worry about it," I said, looking into the far distance.

"You decided to keep it the same dark green colour. It looks good."

"Yeah, I feel good with green. There's so little of it around here ... well, other than in spring ... and if it rains."

We were waiting for a gap to turn left into Limassol Avenue.

"My God, Stauvro! You are not still bitching about the lack of greenery. If you want greenery, go to Troodos," said Petros as he put the car into gear and pushed into the southern traffic.

"I am telling you what I feel," I said, trying to put my heart into it but not sure if I was succeeding. "Here on the plain, it's like a bloody desert, and lush greenery is what I miss most about New Zealand."

"You are just homesick, cousin. You see, that's why spring is so spectacular here. The golden-wheat of summer, the earthy, umber browns of winter and then that spectacle of rebirth ... that sudden burst of lush green ... Spring!" Wonders will never cease. My cousin was waxing lyrical, a quality that usually eluded him.

"You are probably right ..." I reluctantly conceded. "That's something that we don't get much back home in Wellington ... seasons ... that sharp transition, but it does happen in the South Island ..." Giving up on inflicting on Petros another New Zealand climatology and geography lesson, I changed tack. "So, what's all this about?"

"This girl ..." Petros searched his overcoat pocket for his cigarettes with his left hand, "... is a foreigner, we think. A tourist. Someone raped and killed her ... and then he buried her outside Xylophagou ... the part that is near Dhekelia, the British base."

I knew Xylophagou as that was near where Petros' family and I spent some time taking refuge under the trees of an orchard with *Giagia* Androutsou, her niece Melani and her young son Christos during the Turkish invasion. Petros' family joined us soon after. It certainly was a summer that we all would never forget.

"So, what is so important about this case?"

Petros, giving up on finding a cigarette packet in his pockets, indicated the glove box compartment. Finding a packet of Peter Stuyvesant, I withdrew one, put it in my mouth, lit it and stuck it in his mouth. He took a long drag and then, withdrawing the cigarette between his nicotine-stained fingers, he perched it on the wheel and exhaled the smoke slowly.

"God forgive me, and I know it's a terrible thing to say, but if she's a tourist, it could be really bad for us. Tourism is our lifeblood now, cousin. Imagine what will happen if the press in Britain picks it up and blows it out of proportion. Already the base's military police think it's one of our boys that has done it, and to be honest the way things are nowadays I wouldn't be surprised if one of our horny, war-damaged little bastards did do it."

I resisted the impulse to point out to Petros that the little Cypriot bastards he was referring to were damaged well before the war. All the war did was prove the fact.

"So why me?"

"Well, you are a journalist. I need your help to … how do you say it in English, 'phrase things.' "

"Phrase things … For whom?"

"For us."

"To whom?"

"To the press."

"What do you mean the press? I *am* the press."

"I know. But …"

"So, there's no story for me?" I said, perplexed.

"No story … This is friendship. No, I don't mean it that way. Look, I need your help. If there is a story … at the appropriate time, fine, write about it."

I turned and glared at him. "Listen, *Kyrie Mustaki* …" I began venting. Petros had kept the moustache after he shaved off the beard that he grew for his mother-in-law's forty-day mourning period. She had died the previous November. For Petros, like most bereaved men, staying unshaved was a sign of respect. Eleni said that her mother died from a broken heart after the damage that she witnessed being inflicted on her village by the war. Her death wasn't needed to convince me that people can die from a broken heart. "… I have to make a living. I have to work. You know what work is? That thing that brings money in and pays the rent and food for me and … Scipio." I just threw Scipio's name in to show that I had dependants … even if he was a cat. "Tell your fat boss that next time he needs my services he has my permission to think about what he can pay me. But as we are sitting here and I am starting to feel cosy, I'll help you this time, pro bono."

"First of all, my boss is not fat ... well, not any more ... Like many of us, he's lost weight in the last year or so ... and what the fuck does 'pro bono' mean?"

"It's Latin. It's short for pro bono publico. It means for the public good ... I don't get paid. But if ..." I wasn't letting Petros off so easily, "... it turns into something that is of interest to the British press, I get the scoop ... that is if there is something of interest, I get to write it first."

"Okay, okay keep your toupee on ..."

"No toupee, cousin. Genuine, thick and curly chestnut hair. You're just jealous that yours is falling out," I goaded him. "You're becoming old before your time ... speckles of grey ... even in your moustache ... and you, cousin, unlike your boss, are not losing weight but actually putting it on."

For some reason mentioning Petros' weight seemed to upset him as he squinted his eyes, a sign of his irritation. So I did not push my luck.

"My God! Okay, okay ... We have a deal ... Jesus help me, you truly are the great-grandson of *Sheitánis* ... slippery as a bloody eel," he vented in turn.

The perfect Cypriot put-down for the great-grandson of the Tempter.

3

When we were near the British base in Dhekelia, Petros stopped the Alfa Romeo and used his new radio to ask for directions to the murder scene. But instead, he was told to wait at the eastern entrance of the base, near the pillbox, where a British military policeman would meet us.

There are two British military bases in southern Cyprus. Dhekelia and Akrotiri. The British refer to them as East Base and West Base. The bases were something the British exacted out of the Cypriots and incorporated in the London and Zürich agreements when they allowed them to secure their independence in 1959. They are 'sovereign bases', which means that they are British territory. The areas have their own legal system, distinct from the United Kingdom and the Republic of Cyprus. The laws of Dhekelia and Akrotiri, though, are closely aligned with, and in some cases identical to, the laws operating within the Republic of Cyprus. The Court of the Sovereign Base Areas deals with offences committed by any person within Akrotiri and Dhekelia, and the Sovereign Base Areas police uphold law and order. The Cyprus Joint Police Unit (the Royal Military Police and the Royal Air Force Police) deals with offences involving British Forces Cyprus and the military law. It has complete authority over military offences committed by service personnel on British military sites in Cyprus, including the radar station on top of Mount Olympus. Bizarre, really, when you consider that Cyprus must be the only sovereign country in the world to have a foreign country's radar station on its highest peak.

We drove through Dhekelia, and it was still strange to see limestone, terracotta-tiled, two-storey English bungalows with leaf green shuttered windows and manicured lawns. When I first saw those suburban apparitions emerging from the haze in Akrotiri it was midsummer, and those doll-like, perfect houses on their manicured green lawn setting stood out in what to me was a surreal and clashing counterbalance to the sunbleached yellow ochre, desert-like landscape that surrounded them.

The soil in the Dhekelia area is red because it is rich in iron. That is why they call the villages outside the base the *Kokkinochoria* – the Red Villages. The soil, watered from artesian aquifers, is not only excellent for growing lawns but also for growing potatoes and carrots and for years this district used to supply the British vegetable market. After the Turkish invasion though, many farmers gave up working the land and turned to the building trade as the government was financing housing projects to accommodate the 200,000 Greek refugees who were displaced to the south by the war. Although some refugees had moved into the houses of the Turkish Cypriots, who moved north in the disproportionate population exchange, multi-storey apartments were filling the suburbs of Nicosia and other cities. To the farmers, the building trade was a surer thing and it did not depend on the vagaries of the weather or the market.

Petros parked the car on the Republic's side of the pillbox. We sat there for a while and Petros lit another cigarette. He was wearing his long, well-cut English overcoat over his usual dark suit and black tie. I had to admit that the thick, upturned moustache suited him. It gave him gravitas.

"So, why are we waiting for the Brit?" I asked.

"It's just good form. I need to get on their good side. I need to have some control over this … so when he arrives, watch, listen and don't say anything unless you are asked a direct question …" Switching to Greek, "You hear me, *mikre* – child?" He was joking.

"*Nai, Pappou* – yes, grandad." So was I.

"Good lad. Keep it up and your respect will be rewarded with a blessing … a Zimaras' blessing is to die for …"

"God! If I have to die for it what fucking use is it to —"

What was rapidly becoming a disassembled repartee was interrupted by the arrival of a military Land Rover. It stopped next to us and a tall, uniformed, impressively built man in his mid-thirties got out and approached us. Petros got out and moved forward to meet him. I followed my cousin.

"Good morning ... Inspector Zimaras?" asked the British policeman in a clipped Stanford accent.

Petros threw his cigarette on the ground, stomped on it and nodded. He offered his hand.

The man took Petros' hand, giving it a short, perfunctory shake.

"Ellery ... Detective Inspector Ellery ... of the Royal British Military Police," said the six-foot-two representative of the Queen of England. He was dressed in suitably tailored military winter garb and a red beret. "Call me John."

"Well, in that case, you can call me Petro," reciprocated my cousin. He didn't bother to introduce me.

"Petro it is. If you follow me in your car, Petro ... We don't have far to go."

He walked back to the Land Rover and soon we were following him through some rough, sandy dirt roads. The loamy soil was now a dark reddish umber as it had rained, and the lush green vegetation, like in Vietnam, contrasted sharply against it.

After about ten minutes, we arrived. The sky had cleared. A canopy of ultramarine blue, even at the end of winter. We could see that the murder scene was next to an orange grove, not far off the road. The orchard where we had found sanctuary the previous summer was somewhere to the northeast.

We parked, and followed by the British Military detective, we walked over to where a dozen policemen, both British and Greek, were assembled. The recent downpour released a heavy, earthy smell from the soil.

One of the plain-clothes Greek policemen turned and when he saw Petros, he made a beeline for him.

"*Yiasou, Kyrie* Zimara. Thanks for coming. My *Anglezika* is crap …"

"*Yia*. No problem, Phantis," said Petros. Obviously, he knew the detective and had seniority over him, even if Phantis seemed older. I estimated that he was well over fifty and carried quite a bit of extra weight. He barely made the minimum height restriction and wore a rather bedraggled dark suit with a stained white shirt and black tie, partially covered by a fluttering grey plastic-looking raincoat.

"Tell me what you have got."

"Well, *Kyrie* Zimara, the farmer of that *pervoli* – orchard – over there," he said indicating north, "was going past on his tractor and his dog took off. It wouldn't follow him and so he backed up and went to have a look. He thought it might be a hare in a hole. Imagine his surprise when he saw his dog tugging on a hand. The farmer went back into Xylophagou and rang us. We have a full team here. The pathologist, *o Kyrios* Hatzimichaelis, came and watched the exhumation, then did a preliminary examination and has just gone back to Larnaca. He described her as Caucasian, probably English, but he said she could be Scandinavian. Nineteen or twenty, with trauma to the head. In fact, he is understating that. Poor thing, God rest her soul … the front of her skull is savagely beaten in. I think that not even her parents would recognise her. He reckons she's been here one or two days, but he will be more exact when he gets her to the morgue. I have already put several men to check with the

Larnaca and Agia Napa hotels to see if they have a guest missing. Unfortunately, it rained last night, so there are no footprints left around. What you'll see under the sheets of army tarp is the farmer's and his dog's footprints. Also, the photographer's, two of our men who dug her up and the pathologist's footprints are outside the perimeter. I kept the approach diagonal to the burial just in case there's something that we may find. Our boys are wearing gumboots."

"Anything else?"

"No, that's it for the moment."

Petros nodded at one of the policemen, and in English, he explained to Ellery what was said. Then he asked Phantis to bring one of the shovels. Taking it, he looked towards the pile of dug earth and the rectangular shape formed by the tarp, moved to the right where Phantis had pointed to the tracks already made, stuck the shovel in the ground and then stomped on it, burying it to the top of the blade. We were about ten yards from where the body was found.

"Continue to walk the same path, eh?" Then Petros stepped carefully from the spade directly towards the shallow grave, looking in front of him for anything of interest and stepping over them by extending his stride. I stayed where I was.

Petros was approaching the body from the south. I could see he was having difficulty walking as the wet soil clung to his shoes. However, he ignored it and moved on slowly, still looking before his foot went down then moving either to the left or the right, as required, until he reached the overlapping tarp sheets. Then he took another three steps.

He stood before the grave and then, after a minute or two, turned around.

"Stauvro," he called out. "I want you to go back to the road and walk on this side east and see what you can find. Phanti, send one of your boys to go with him and to do the other side and send another two to do the same, south towards Dhekelia. Anything you find, mark its location," he said, indicating a pile of short-flagged bamboo sticks, "get the photographer to photograph it and then bag it. Do a map and position the objects on the map. Pace things out and write it down, working from there." He indicated the upright shovel. "Then do the other side of the road about a stone's throw in."

Having delegated the tasks, Petros continued with the job at hand. He caught Ellery's eye and indicated to him to follow and walked forward. When he got to the edge of the tarp that enclosed a rectangle around the body, I saw him standing still, looking at what was before him, for a long time. Ellery took one long look and turned around and walked back to his men. Then Petros slowly began to walk around the body.

Phantis' policeman and I finished our task twenty minutes later.

"What did you find?' asked Petros.

"Couple of beer bottles on the other side of the road and one on this side," I said, indicating towards the village. "All KEO," I added. KEO is one of the three major beer brands produced in Cyprus, the others being Leon and Carlsberg.

"Also, an empty packet of cigarettes in the road drain next to the culvert on that side," said the policeman.

"Good. Get some more pegs for anything else you might find. Then get everything photographed in situ before you bag them. Send them to be checked for fingerprints. Stauvro, you stay with me."

"Phanti, send someone to talk to the locals in Xylophagou and see if there is some sort of Casanova among them who prefers tourist girls." Then he paused, "Actually, there may be more … from the damage done to her, I got a feeling there was more than one," he said thoughtfully.

"What, you mean a pack?" I said.

"Could be."

"What … a sort of gang rape?" I said, switching to English.

"Could be."

"Would our boys do something like this?"

'Why not? Look what happened with the war. You of all people saw it, cousin: rape, murder, you name it … and we found out that, like everyone else, we could do it … yeah, even some of our boys who went *sto Katihitiko* – to Sunday School." Petros' candidness again surprised me somewhat. It's something that Petros, like other Greek Cypriots, found very hard to admit. Then, exasperated by keeping it all in perspective, "Go now and sort out what was war and what was personal. It's just that with the fighting and then the mess afterward, we haven't caught up with them yet to sort it out." Then, as if it left a bad taste in his mouth he added, "They may have developed a taste for it."

Looking around for the Larnaca inspector and spotting him, "Phanti," Petros called out, "can you ask the photographer to take several shots of the area around here? General shots. Tell him to place the frame number of the camera on the map with an arrow where he is photographing from so that we can then have them as a reference. Once the body is taken away, look for anything that's left behind in the grave. Then put a grid down and get your men to walk it to see if there's anything else that we missed."

"Stauvro," he called out, "Listen, I have been thinking. I need to talk to the boss. But first, please come closer."

He indicated the path that he wanted me to take. I walked carefully towards him. The smell of the wet, upturned earth was overwhelming, but as I moved forward, something more pronounced was taking over.

"Look at the poor girl. Have you ever seen anything like this?"

When I looked at what was before me, I admit I nearly threw up. It was probably the sweet smell of putrefaction that did it. I managed to hold it together. What shocked me, despite the warning, was the ferocity of the damage to the face. Her mandible was just hanging on and teeth were missing from the upper jaw. The eye sockets were also shattered. The girl was in a frilly white blouse that was pulled up around her throat, exposing her small breasts, and her blue shorts and undies were wrapped around her feet. She was covered with red, wet earth that seemed like curdled blood around her head. Then I suddenly realised that it was not just blood. Her hair was actually red, ginger red.

"Yes, at Santalaris," I finally said. "But they were shot. This is something else, eh?" I took a deep breath.

"*Theos kai Panagia* – God and Holy Mary – protect us," muttered Petros sombrely and crossed himself. "Yeah, the poor girl … the poor parents."

We stood there before I broke the silence. "I know now that the same has been done to our side Petro, but isn't it dreadful that we already dismiss those as *war* and forget about them. She is but one. And yet for some reason, I feel more for her than I did for all those hundred or so bodies."

"Yes, we do … and no it is not. It's a default mechanism, cousin … a blessing … provided for us by Mother Nature. It's the way she protects us against all the shit that life throws at us," said Petros quietly. "Or so I hope," he added, as he reached into his pocket for his cigarettes.

He lit one and then withdrew to the Land Rover, and I saw him talking to Ellery, who had been conferring with two other British Red Caps. They were pointing at a map and after a few minutes they seemed to have made a decision. Then Petros went to the Alfa Romeo and used the radio. After five minutes he came back.

"They agreed. It's in our area, so we have jurisdiction. So, change of plan. The boss has made a suggestion and I agreed. I am going to give you a formal interview. I want you to write it down and then send it to Rogers in London when we go into Larnaca."

"Rogers? … oh, you mean Reuters."

"Yes, that's it. I want to be in front of this story before anyone else gets it. Then all the papers, including ours, can and will write whatever they want."

We walked back to the Alfa Romeo. I took my notebook out and after five minutes I got enough together to be able to write a bona fide press release that could be read or translated for European readers.

Dhekelia-Cyprus. 15 January 1975. This morning the body of a young woman was discovered buried in a field in southern Cyprus. A farmer's dog dug up the body on the border between the British Sovereign Base of Dhekelia and the district of Xylophagou village. Officers of Cyprus CID are working closely with British Military Police investigators to identify the body and to catch the perpetrator ...

Petros said that it was not wise to say there was a possibility of more than one perpetrator until they had conclusive evidence.

The police suspect the victim may be a tourist. Already the local police from the Larnaca Police Prefecture are canvassing local hotels for a missing guest. With the hostilities of last year over, tourists are starting to return and now this happens ...

I finished my report and read it to Petros.

"The bit about the tourists is a bit off, but I suppose if you don't say it someone else will. Come on ... You and I are going into Larnaca. I want to attend *tin nekropsia* – the post-mortem – and see what else those scumbags have been up to. Have you seen the archaeological museum in Larnaca?"

"Yes, very briefly when I first arrived."

"Well, I recommend another visit. I'll drop you off to send your article, and then while I am with the pathologist, you go to the museum. We'll meet," he said, looking at his watch, "at four o'clock at the entrance."

4

Petros dropped me off at the Larnaca Telephone Exchange where I rang through my report. I couldn't help but share some banter about the weather

41

with the desk jockey who took my call at Reuters and about what else was happening in London. "Cloudy and drizzly," he said. That somehow cheered me up.

Then ambling like a carefree tourist, I made my way along to the waterfront.

This seafront district of Larnaca is called *Phinikoudes* – small palms – as once the tall palms that now line the sea's edge were small. Larnaca's name was derived from the Greek *larnax* – coffin – probably because of the thousands of *sarcophagi* that were found in the area.

The port of the city goes back to prehistoric times when it was called Kition. It was re-established by Achaean Greek colonists – after it was abandoned by the Mycenean Greeks – around 1300 BC. Then the Phoenicians established a naval base there. Island-wide earthquakes in AD 322 and 342 that destroyed Salamis and Paphos also saw Kition razed to the ground. The new city was rebuilt closer to the seafront. A castle was built by the Byzantines in the fourteenth century and the area west of that was developed as a port by the Ottomans. That part was known as *Skala*, which in Greek means ladder … possibly the ladder that one needs to climb to get on a ship.

I walked through some back streets, trying to remember where the Larnaca District Archaeological Museum was.

I enjoyed regularly visiting the archaeological exhibits in the Cyprus Museum in Nicosia, ambling through its austere white corridors, looking at all the finds that stretched from the Neolithic to the Roman period. At the smaller, poorer cousin, the Larnaca Museum, there was a similar array of exhibits as well as the bone remains of prehistoric pygmy elephants and hippopotami. I was astonished by the latter on my first visit, and on this occasion, after paying and entering the quiet rooms, I paid more attention to where they were found and their dates.

The pygmy hippopotami and pygmy elephant bones were first found in the *Agios* Georgios cave grotto near the chapel of *Agios* Phanourios on the northern coast of Kyrenia in 1902 by palaeontologist and pioneer of archaeozoology Dorothea Bate, whose name had now been appended to the findings.

Apparently, these mammals were hunted to extinction like the moa, the ostrich-like bird back home in New Zealand. The hippos stood at about two and a half feet tall and four feet long and were estimated to have weighed 440 pounds, a weight reduction of ninety-five per cent from their ancestors that weighed ten tons. Their remains were dated around 9,000 years ago, and with the pygmy elephants, they were thought to be the largest mammal to have existed on the island. They were excavated at several other sites including *Aetokremnos*, a sea site promontory within the Akrotiri British Sovereign Base, to the west of Limassol. The elephants, too, weighed around 440 pounds but were about four and a half feet tall. It is thought that they were stranded on Cyprus during the ice age and lived there peacefully until the arrival of passing sailors and early Levant Semitic settlers, who hunted them to extinction.

Later I found out that those mammals' petrified bones were mistaken by Christian believers for the bones of *Agios* Phanourios, who fell and died in the area. Apparently, they ground them into potions and took them for various ills. According to a recent newspaper report I came across, a chapel dedicated to *Agios* Georgios still stands on the coastal site west of Kyrenia but was extensively damaged during the beach invasion by Turkish troops. The nearby cave grotto, down some steps and just above sea level, is dedicated to *Agios* Phanourios and is said to be respected by both Turkish and Greek Cypriots.

I moved from display case to display cabinet, looking closely at different findings. Looking at the small, austere, semi-abstract granite-figurine sculptures of the Neolithic, I stopped and wondered how those so-called one-eyed Greek nationalists managed to rationalise those Henri Moore-like sculptures' existence into a cultural limbo. For them, it seems, Cypriot history started with the arrival myth of the Mycenaean Greeks after the Trojan War about 1300 BC. Those Greeks, it was said, were led by the famed Greek archer Teucer, the son of Telamon, the king of Salamis Island and the brother of Ajax the Great. Ajax committed suicide near the end of the Trojan War as he lost face when he was beaten in a competition by Odysseus for the armaments of Achilles. Teucer was tried, disowned and banished by his father for not bringing his brother's body and armaments back to their home. As a result, Teucer sailed for Cyprus, arriving at the Gulf of Famagusta, where he founded a city that he named after his homeland, Salamis. There are 7,000 years, or maybe even more, of human history before Teucer's arrival in Cyprus that the nationalists ignore, or if they don't, they understate.

Once again, I came across sculptures of different gods that can be traced to pre-dynastic Nile Valley cultures, like the ugly dwarf war god Bes. Bes was brought to Cyprus by the Phoenicians – and various examples were excavated at the ancient city of Amathus near Limassol. Soon Bes and gods of his Asian kind were pitted against the more feminine, athletic and psychologically more complex ancient Greek gods like Apollo, the god of music, truth, prophecy, healing, the sun and light, plague, poetry … and the list goes on. It seemed to me that the indigenous people of Cyprus were at one stage confronted by a stark choice: either choose the minimalist, seafaring Phoenician culture or the more flamboyant and sophisticated Greek culture. The Greek culture won,

44

and they were converted to it to the degree that they embraced its mores and religiosity hook, line and sinker, as they did at other times as different imperial powers took Cyprus over. As far as mores go, during the more recent Ottoman period, you couldn't tell a Christian Greek from a Muslim Turk if you looked at their attire ... as once again, the Cypriots chose to dress like their powerful and more sophisticated rulers.

In prehistoric times, just like the present, Cyprus was a strategic island. It was renowned for its readily available copper – as apparently copper nuggets were strewn on the surface – and myriads of cypress trees for shipbuilding covered its plains and hills. According to the Greek historian and geographer Strabo of Amasia, the Greek mathematician Eratosthenes had said that shipbuilding was the reason for the deforestation of the island, for the sea was a traffic route, sometimes for whole merchant fleets.

Cyprus was then, as it is now, the crossroads of East and West. At one stage all this Eastern world spoke Koine Greek, just as English is spoken around the world nowadays. With the arrival of Jews from Syria-Palaestina touting a new religion, Christianity, the Cypriots, to the surprise of their Jewish immigrant compatriots, embraced it from its early stages and very quickly made it their own.

The Jews had escaped Syria-Palaestina to avoid the direct tyranny of Rome. In Cyprus, they found a compliant and open-minded population who welcomed them and allowed them to prosper, despite the cursory supervision of the Roman administration. In AD 112 insurrections against Roman rule broke out all over the Middle East by Jewish zealots who despised their polytheistic masters. Such a zealot was the leader of the Cypriot Jews, Artemion. The bloodied carnage that ensued in Salamis and spread throughout Cyprus did not spare the indigenous Cypriots. In turn, the massacre brought rough justice from the Romans, who wiped out the troublemakers and then banished all the Jews from the island under the penalty of death if they returned. That the rebellion must have had an impact on the island's population is obvious. If Dio Cassius correctly recorded the 240,000 Cypriot casualties dead in Salamis, it is conceivable that the island could have had a population of around three-quarters of a million at that time. Now, the whole island has half a million inhabitants. That is without the 200,000 or so of expat Cypriots who live as immigrants around the world.

During achaic times, the population consisted of indigenous Cypriots, Roman centurions, Phoenician and Egyptian traders, Jewish and Greek immigrants. One wit of a British historian once said that Cypriots can almost guarantee that every one of them has royal blood in their veins due to the existence in archaic times of ten kingdoms. However, although there must have been intermarriage, Greek paganism, which was absorbed by Christianity, ensured that during its post-historic period the Cypriots retained their homogeneity as a race.

In the 1930s, the British came up with the term *Eteocypriots*, a term to describe the pre-Greek Iron Age Cypriots. By coining the term, they were hoping to exploit ancient history and archaeology to counter Greek nationalism. By this subtle method they tried, as only the British could, to deny the prevailing Hellenistic character of ancient and modern Cyprus. One can see how this got the Greek Cypriots' backs up. However, for the nationalists to proclaim that all Greek Cypriots were ethnically just Greek was really stretching the truth and hopefully, sometime in the future, this will be somehow proved. It will take a brave soul, though, to challenge that right now. One does not get a prize for challenging historical or religious orthodoxies.

Don't get me wrong, I didn't go to the museum to connect with some sort of pagan past. What did happen was that I became more acutely aware of how complicated Cypriot history was and that the simple slogan of *ENOSIS* – union with Greece – that drove the Greek Cypriots to rebel in an armed struggle against the British in the fifties and the thousand or so EOKA B's renegades to near self-destruction the previous summer, was not satisfactory to me. I was still trying to understand where the Cypriots went wrong after gaining their independence – led by their own equivalent of Artemion: Nikos Sampson, the *enosis* zealot.

There are many examples of countries gaining independence from a tyrannical ruler and, after, falling into the folly of a civil war. The American Civil War after the American War of Independence from Britain, the Indian subcontinent's post-independence civil war that gave rise to Pakistan, and the Russian civil war after the fall of the Russian monarchy are but a few examples. Some of those civil wars lasted for many years. In that context, Cyprus was very fortunate that its recent civil war only lasted eight days.

I didn't see myself as a historian and I still don't, but history does inform, or more accurately has to inform, whatever a journalist writes in this part of the world. Not only here. Everywhere.

5

True to his word, Petros arrived at four o'clock on the dot, a remarkable feat for a Cypriot.

I got into the Alfa Romeo and he drove towards the south, weaving through streets that I didn't know until we got to the waterfront.

47

"Ground rules," he said. "I'll tell you what we found, but please tell me if and when you decide to write it up. I don't want to be blindsided by you."

"There is no story for me," I said, "unless the girl is English. So don't worry."

"Well, that is the problem, cousin. She is English. So, ground rules?" "Ground rules" was an ethical demarcation line that we came up with the previous year, similar to "off the record".

I reluctantly nodded.

"She was reported missing by a girlfriend of hers," he continued, "who thought that she took off with a boy after they went for the night to a Larnaca nightclub. When she didn't come back the next day, the friend began to worry and reported it yesterday to the police in Agia Napa." Agia Napa was a newly established tourist trap. It replaced the former Miami-like tourist trap of Varosi, which was now a no-man's-land enclosed with barbed wire. It was mainly British tourists who frequented this rapidly growing, overrated town. They didn't mind its exorbitant prices as long they were getting drunk on the cheap alcohol, getting laid and having a good time.

"They wrote it up but didn't forward it to Larnaca until today. Her name is Tracy Baxter. She's nineteen and is from North London. If you want me to, I will wait at the Telephone Exchange until you send this information through. We have informed Scotland Yard and they have contacted the parents."

"Thanks," I said. "Anything else that I can say?"

"Repeat that the British Military Police and the Cyprus CID are working hard on the case and expect a breakthrough soon."

"Do you have a breakthrough?"

"Yes, but I'll tell you after you have sent your report. Remember, *ground rules*."

I reluctantly kept my mouth shut and my cousin continued to the Telephone Exchange.

Petros double-parked and I ran in and rang through the update to London. Twenty minutes later I was out.

"We are going down to the police station," he said in English. "We have got a lead. A very good lead. The pathologist confirmed that the girl was raped. She will be hard to identify because her head is such a mess. He thinks she was killed with a spade. He also said he found so much semen in her that it must have come from three or four different men. The contents of her stomach indicate that she was killed three hours after she ate at what he thinks is a local restaurant. The boys have been doing the rounds showing an identikit photo to all the restaurants. I am sorry I didn't give you this information for your report. However, and I take no pleasure from this, you will now watch how Cyprus' finest solve a crime … and by the way, the commissioner has agreed to the *quid pro quo* for helping us, Stauvro," said Petros, proud to be able to remember the Latin phrase.

6

At the Larnaca Police Station, Petros flashed his warrant card at the guard and I handed over my New Zealand passport.

The guard looked up from my passport to Petros.

The passport was the replacement that I had got on my way through to Cyprus from London, after Vietnam and my time in a hospital in Auckland. In London, I had inadvertently put it through a wash at the bed and breakfast I was staying at in Earl's Court. This newer version did not include the passport owner's profession any more, something that made it very useful in situations such as this.

"*O Kyrios* is from New Zealand," said Petros, as a way of indicating that my presence was fine.

We walked down a long corridor to Phantis' office.

Petros knocked and we both went in.

Phantis was standing up in front of a blackboard and there were several plain-clothes and also two uniformed policemen sitting down. Another uniformed policeman was giving his report. Phantis gestured for us to go to the front.

"… the restaurateur said that he recognised her from the holiday snapshot that the girlfriend gave us. He said that she stuck out as she had red hair and freckles. She was at the Larnaca tavern with four young British soldiers. They ate mezes and drank a lot of beer. They were all very drunk when they left, but they paid the waiter and left a handsome tip. Lakis and I got a full description of them."

You could hear a pin drop in the room. Also, the relief of the possible perpetrators being British soldiers could be clearly seen on everyone's face.

Petros stepped forward and stood next to Phantis.

"You didn't say anything about us finding her, Phanti?" he said looking at his perplexed colleague.

"No. We just said that she was missing, *Kyrie* Zimara."

"Good … We have to tell the *Bretanos* policeman. We need his help to bring those soldiers in for questioning. It was outside the base, but she was almost on the line between the two sides. But it does not matter. We have jurisdiction as it's a full-blown murder investigation. Phanti, you carry on. I'll wait until the *Bretanos* comes in, then I am going back to Nicosia to brief the boss and the chief commissioner. You *pethia* – lads – have done really well … *bravo*. Nothing to the press, eh, until we arrest them and they are in jail."

He looked around sternly, slowly, getting a nod from each person in the room, including me, even if I was the very manifestation of the fraternity that he instructed no contact with.

"Right, keep up the good work." Then turning to me, "Come on, Stauvro, let's go to the canteen and have a coffee."

When we were seated, Petros lit a cigarette. He drew on it deeply, holding the smoke for several seconds and then exhaling.

"Well, that was fast," I said.

"It usually is here. We probably would have solved the whole fiasco of those serial murders faster if it wasn't for the *praxikopima* – coup d'état – and the invasion. I told you before, Cyprus is a small place. It's only idiots and hotheads who commit crimes here."

The *kafetzis* brought the coffees to our table with glasses of water. Phantis came into the canteen, and seeing where we were seated, he joined us but did not take a seat.

"*Kyrie* Zimara … can I have a word with you, please?" Phantis looked at me.

"Sit. *O Kyrios* Marangos is working with us on this, Phanti. So, what is it?"

Phantis pulled up a chair and sat down.

"I got word from Agia Napa that one of our *neous* – young men – was found shot dead in bed with a tourist woman at a local hotel, and they need me to go over as there has been a very serious accident on the Protaras road. A DISI politician got killed and there are only two of our lads at the hotel. Can you deal with the *Bretanos* detective and keep an eye on things until I get back?" DISI was a centre-right party. A dead politician ranks higher than a shot couple in Cyprus.

"No problem, Phanti … Go."

7

On the way back to Nicosia late in the afternoon, Petros and I discussed the day.

"Did you see the shock on the Englishman's face when I told him?" said Petros. "I sort of felt sorry for him. I think he was absolutely sure that it was one of our lot that did it."

"What do you expect, Petro? Of course, he was shocked. If I were in his shoes, I would be too. I still think he took it in his stride, though, once he recovered. Don't forget the British once ruled the world, cousin, and they didn't do it by being thin-skinned. Do you think they'll hand them over?'

"If they did do it, yes. It's in the Sovereign Base agreement. They will be tried by a court of the Cypriot republic."

"So, when can I write about this?"

"You have already written about it."

"I mean more in-depth, mentioning names, etcetera."

"As soon as they are arrested and charged. By then, the cat will be out of the bag. I will ring you and leave a message at your *kafenio* as soon as that happens."

"Okay. Thanks."

"No problem. Thank you … for your help."

Unable to resist the possibility of a jibe, "So, now I can apply for a job in the Government Press Office?" I said.

Petros laughed. "In your dreams. No. I told you … You are not allowed."

I already knew why but I feigned … "What! Why not?"

"You are not a Cypriot citizen and to be one you have to have done your military service. You have to be a citizen to join the public service."

"Oops! I forgot that small detail. How silly of me!"

"Anyway, the republic has every right to arrest you, cousin, and stick you in uniform, even if you were born in New Zealand. Your father is a Cypriot and you have to serve … that's the law. What's saved you so far is your profession and that English Carpenter name. But you wait … someone will spill the beans."

"You?"

"No. Not me, but one of those *sarandasportous* – forty seeds – you have been pissing on. One of them will turn you in."

I didn't say anything, but in my mind I started to add up my enemies. I had made a few since I arrived.

"How many times have I told you that I am putting my head on the block having you work with me?" Petros reminded me.

"Even Karageorgis can see that I give quality and insight to everything that I have helped you with." Karageorgis was Petros' sergeant and offsider and he trusted him with his life, and I am sure Karageorgis with his.

"Well, not everyone is as forgiving as Karageorgis. Why don't you sign up? Two years will go by fast. As you've been to university they may even make you an officer."

"No thanks, cousin. I've seen what politicians do with officers … officers of all ranks … and also to their poor, hapless underlings … Remember, I was in Vietnam."

"Well, you'll have to do those six-month stints – toing and froing to other countries – until you do your army service." What Petros described was something that I got in the habit of doing to extend my visa as a New Zealand citizen in Cyprus. My R & R in Greece and Italy. Doing stories in nearby countries also helped me in this subterfuge when needed.

"No problem."

Petros thought for a while.

"Well, I don't blame you, cousin," said Petros reflectively. "You are right. The problem is those fucking politicians. Our National Guard was solely created to protect our new republic. But those *pezevenkides* – those men who prostitute their sisters – had other ideas. They wanted to be heroes, show what they were made of. If the Turks hadn't landed, then we would have had an even bigger *adelphoctonia* – fratricide. EOKA B had lists of all they wanted to get rid of, the same as in South America." I was told about the list by someone who was on it on the first day of the coup, but it was compiled by AKEL, the communist party of Cyprus, comprising so-called atheists, who ironically were ready to stand and fight for Makarios, a religious leader. Makarios turned them down as he was afraid of what the Americans would say. Unfortunately, the list was found in the ruins of the Presidential Palace after the coup.

"Now all those fanatics are licking their wounds. I know that most were blindly led by the patriotic blind, who in turn were led by the Greek junta, but I think they should be held accountable for breaking the law. But with the full amnesty that Makarios granted them … they have got away with it. The problem is all the others got away with it as well … the rapists and child killers," he said with heartfelt bitterness.

He ran his left hand over his eyes as if he was washing the thought off. He searched his jacket pocket for his packet of cigarettes, took one out and I lit it for him with the car cigarette lighter.

"You won't believe it. Sometimes I feel sorry for those extremists, from both sides, the same way that I feel sorry for people who belong to *latries* – cults. I know that sometimes I rave on, but many were really just brainwashed. Right from the time they were young. With the *dexious* – right-wingers – most of their families were in the original EOKA against the British. A lot of them were true believers in their cause, but others formed an alliance of convenience for later benefits like a government job. The Church helped to get them prepped and ready to go: for God, kin and Mother Greece. All that was needed was for someone to take control – like the Greek junta – stoke up their patriotism, challenge their honour, get them foaming at the mouth, give them a gun and a mask and point them at someone and let them off the leash. Then the old traditions of family and fidelity to kinship disappeared.

"Well, to be honest, not entirely ... I have heard stories where members of EOKA B refused to arrest their left-wing father-in-law or cousin. I think that with the breakdown of tribe, and now family, we are all too ready to join and belong to something. Look at the football clubs, the different political parties." Then Petros recited the list of political parties. "Once committed, it is very hard for those people to change allegiances. Some would rather die than change. Sometimes in a family, you get one who is a rightist and another who is a leftist. The communists can be just as fanatical. A recipe for a disaster and life-long conflict ... of the worst type. That's what *adelphoctonia* is, cousin. A fraternal war."

He drew heavily on his cigarette and with the smoke he exhaled a sigh.

"So how did you manage to stay out of it all?" I asked cautiously as I could see that my cousin was getting really upset.

"I think it was my father ... he was somehow responsible for keeping me on the straight and narrow. When EOKA started, it was the orphan boys who joined up first. No father, you see. Grivas became their father … I think it was because I loved my father so much and respected him that I signed up as a policeman, just before the revolution broke out. I liked the idea of being a keeper of the law, and I never wanted to do anything that would bring shame on him or our family. That was why I resigned from the police when the British appointed all those *epikourikous* – Turkish police specials."

Petros had never talked of this before.

"You resigned? Why did you do that?"

"Well, you probably know that there was a lot of hanging of captured EOKA fighters during the revolt …"

"Yes, I've read about it."

"Well … some were just kids, and all the Greek policemen couldn't stomach it any more. Many resigned because we became the meat in the sandwich. Then the British appointed the *epkourikous*. They basically ignored what their own people did … I was a young detective constable working mainly on minor crimes, domestic disputes and civilian homicides by then. Because of my good grasp of English, I had been sent to London to study the forensic science approach to a crime scene, which I admit I enjoyed, but I missed Eleni and Maria when I was there. However, the hangings made my continuing as a policeman untenable. I also realised, despite the status and salary, we policemen were helping Imperial Britain subjugate our own people. There was a rumour that they were going to get me to join Special Branch, which basically concentrated on EOKA. Most were British, but there were quite a few Greeks and Turks in it. They were really just thugs … So, I resigned. Maybe I was naive.

"Instead, I helped my father in the fields and the bakery. With independence, because of my experience and qualifications, I was reappointed. Then in our wisdom, we created our own army ... our so-called defence force. The government introduced compulsory military training. I was in the first intake. We had it easy because of it. Nowadays, it's so hard ... they kill some boys in training. Especially in the *Lokatzithes*. The fucking army has done a lot of damage to the fidelity of kinship, Stauvro. They beat it out of one ... well not everyone. Leonidas managed to stick out everything they threw at him and he still kept his moral compass." Leonidas was Petros' son-in-law.

He took another puff of his cigarette.

"You probably won't know this, but in 1964 three Greek policemen were killed by the Turks. Our police kidnapped seventeen Turks and executed them by a firing squad in Famagusta. Not long after, another eleven Turks were kidnapped and the same fate befell them. I nearly resigned again, but my father talked me into staying. I found it hard not to be able to bring all those murderers to justice. Ethnic murders became an expediency after that, just as now.

"At least in Greece the Greeks have imprisoned Papadopoulos and he is now serving life in jail, as is Ioannidis." Georgios Papadopoulos was the leader of the junta that overthrew the democratically elected Government of Greece in 1967, and Dimitrios Ioannidis was his co-conspirator and replacement before the junta imploded.

Petros knocked the cigarette on the edge of the car ashtray, breaking the ash. "Did you hear there's talk that they'll let all the Greek civil war ex-patriots who are living in the Eastern bloc and Russia return? Greece has a chance to put things right and map a positive future for itself … that's if the big powers let it."

"Well, the Americans, despite all the palaver, have lost the war in Vietnam, and they are going to be keeping a low profile for a while," I suggested.

"From your lips to the ears of God."

I looked at my friend. I was about to come back with a smart-arsed retort on the confirmed deafness of God … but I held my tongue.

8

The next day I half-heartedly cleaned up the apartment and did some shopping at the *agora*. On my way back home, I came across my friend Father Sosimas sitting on a bench in front of his church, the Church of Archangel Michael Trypiotis, warming himself in the sun. George Dalaras was blasting out of a nearby upstairs apartment. It was the *Asia Minor* album he and Charis Alexiou had released. The lyrics were by Pythagoras and music by Apostolos Kalderas. It was a popular hit as it invoked the friendly coexistence in the Bosphorus between the Greeks and Turks and the military adventurism of Greece, France, Italy and Britain that led to the enmity between the two communities, Greece's military defeat and the massacre and burning of Smyrna. After what happened the previous summer, it seems history had repeated itself.

I had met Father Sosima soon after I moved to Nicosia, and he helped me when I tried to get a handle on something that Petros and I were working on at the time.

"*Kalimera, Daskale* – Good day, Teacher." Teacher is an honorific interchangeable with Father when addressing a priest.

"*Kalimera*, Stauvro *mou*. How are you today my son?"

He was dressed in his usual black cassock and his long hair was tied at the back into a tight knot. His face looked more gaunt than when I last saw him, but it could have been because someone had tidied his long, white beard. He now had one of those long, ascetic faces that could be found in an El Greco painting.

"Fine. Can I sit with you a moment?"

"Sit and rest. I was just looking at the sparrows. I am their devoted student," he said, chuckling. "Those sparrows have taught me much over the years, Stauvro. When one thinks of all that has happened the past year, they are the only ones not displaced from their homes, eh?"

"That's true, Father. They know no borders, eh?"

"As it really should be. But we … we humans are different, eh? First, we say we want to divide the land so that we have a patch that we can call our own. Then, not satisfied, we try to buy or steal someone else's patch and join it to our own … and before we know it, those that we hurt in doing so declare a vendetta or war against us. Even us Cypriots."

Then the old man squinted at me.

"I have a story for this," he said. "You want to hear a story, a wise story, Stauvro, *mou*?"

I gave a slight nod.

"Yes, I think you will like this story," he continued and nodded to himself. "It was told to me by a holy brother at Stauvrovouni, may God rest his soul, not long ago. I think it may help you understand what I mean."

Father Sosima ran his tongue over his parched lips. "Well, Jesus Christ our Lord," began the old priest crossing himself, "is high in heaven and he begins wondering how the people left behind by him on earth are doing. He goes to God and says, 'Father, do you mind if I take a few days off and go down to earth and visit Cyprus, the island that first embraced my teachings, the Christian faith.' God looks at him and seeing that his son is roused, in fact excited, by the possibilities of this mission, grants him permission. 'And when you are there, my son, would you kindly bring back for me a bottle of that firewater the Cypriots make, that *zivana*. It makes the days go by easier.' The holy brother had added that to make the story more interesting. Imagine God chucking back a *zivana*, eh?" Father Sosimas chuckled and coughed. Clearing his throat, " 'No problem, Father,' says Jesus and packs a small bundle and sets off."

"So, Jesus descends from heaven, and the first city he decides to visit is Limassol. He is walking around downtown along the promenade next to the sea and comes across a well-dressed man. 'Hello, my son,' he says. 'How are you?' 'I am fine, Your All Holiness,' says the man. 'Things are settling down. As you probably heard, we've had a coup and a war, but fortunately, we here in Limassol weren't affected that much.' 'So you are happy?' asks Jesus. The man thinks. 'To tell you the truth, Your All Holiness, actually I am not happy.' 'Why not, my son?' 'Well, there is something that is bothering me.' 'And what is that, my son?' asks Jesus. 'Well, my neighbour has an Austin car and he can drive his family to weddings in other towns, and in the summer he takes them up to the cool of the mountains for picnics. It would be great, Your All Holiness, if I had a car as well, but a little bigger, preferably a Mercedes Benz, and if you grant me this wish I will be grateful and I will give a prayer of thanks to you every day for the rest of my life.' 'That's not a problem, my son,' said Jesus. 'Go home and you'll find a Mercedes Benz parked in front of your house.' 'Oh, thank you, Your All Holiness,' gushes the man, crossing himself with a modest perfunctory gesture in our Greek Orthodox way.

"Next, Jesus decides to come to Nicosia. He walks along the ramparts of the old city and finally finds *Makridromos*. Halfway down that street, he comes across a woman. 'Hello, my child,' says Jesus. 'How is life treating you?' 'Great, Your All Holiness, we have our health and we all have jobs, but there is something that bothers me.' 'What is that, my child?' 'Well, Your All Holiness … my neighbours have built a house next door and it is bigger than mine. Ever since then, I can't sleep at night because I wish for a house that is as big as theirs, but two storeys high.' 'Oh, that is not a problem, my child,' says Jesus. 'Go home and you'll find your wish fulfilled.' 'Oh, thank you, thank you, Your All Holiness,' babbles the woman, crossing herself from her forehead to her knees and with a joyful smile she skips off to her home.

"Next, Jesus decides it is about time to go to the Troodos Mountains. He is walking along a rugged road and comes across an old shepherd tending to his goat herd. 'Hello, my son,' he says to the elderly shepherd. 'How are you doing?' 'Oh, well enough, Your All Holiness,' says the shepherd. 'And how's the flock prospering?' 'It's all right, thanks to God your father,' says the man, crossing himself from the brow to the ground. 'It has rained this year and there's plenty of feed, but I am still unhappy,' said the old shepherd. 'Why is that, my son?' asks Jesus. 'Well, Your All Holiness, I only have 100 goats, but my neighbour has 200, and it has been bothering me and because of it I can't eat and sleep and I am losing weight.' 'Well, my child, that's not a problem,' says Jesus and immediately produces one hundred goats out of thin air."

Father Sosima smiled and I knew the punch line was coming. "But instead of thanking him, the old man does what?"

I shook my head.

"He starts screaming and berating Jesus. 'No, Your All Holiness. No! That's not what I want. What I want is all his goats and I want them all dead!' "

I couldn't help but chuckle, mostly because I was expecting a joke instead of a parable.

The old priest chuckled again too. "You see, Stauvro, that story sums up us Cypriots and everyone else really. Utopia is beyond the grasp of us humans. Even the communists. We are driven by envy. But don't look at the wider world, look at any village. It has been going on since the beginning of time. Did you know that Cyprus, although a very small island, once had ten kingdoms?"

I nodded my head.

"Now we have two left. The Turkish side and the Greek side. What brought us to this situation? Envy.

"You see in the beginning, Stauvro *mou*, there were huge forests that separated each of those ten kingdoms. Here, where we are sitting, is Ancient Ledra. Like on Mount Athos where the monasteries are ranked in importance, the ancient kingdoms here were also ranked. Ledra was ninth. It was a small town then. You had to cross it to go from the northern coast to the southern coast. Where that small sparrow is taking a dust bath, every conquering power of the world stomped its foot. You name them, Assyrians, Egyptians, Greeks, Romans, Franks, Venetians and the list goes on. They all left something behind to have their transience remembered by. Just like our soldiers who in the fourth-century BC engraved their names on the temple of Aghori in Karnak in Egypt. Imagine my surprise when as a young man on my travels I saw each Cypriot soldier's name carved into the stone, each inscription ending with their city of origin, Ledra."

"What, they were from here?"

"Yes, from here. You see we are like dogs, Stauvro. We have to leave our scent wherever we go. If you dig under my church, you'll probably find some old temple to this or that god or goddess. We had a deity for everything." He coughed again to clear his throat. "Why I mentioned Mount Athos, Stauvro, is that I was highly amused when I was there. When I found out that the monasteries are ranked. A sort of pecking order. And some monks take it seriously. Have you been to Mount Athos, Stauvro?"

I shook my head.

"You should. It is a stunning place. However, after I visited there, I was surprised to find on my return that what I was searching for by hiking all over that rugged peninsular was actually back here in Cyprus. We Cypriots have a long history and tradition in mysticism, but we largely ignore it. Those, what do you call them ... Beatles ... who are of our Christian faith ... they go to India to find spiritual enlightenment in Hinduism ..."

"Well, they did not last long," I interceded. "I read somewhere that Ringo left after ten days and John Lennon dragged Paul and George out of the retreat after two months. But they did write thirty songs there."

"Well, that may well be, but we Christians have a whole tradition of our own that goes back to the birth of Christ … all over the Middle East … From the Black Sea to the Sinai Desert. Every so often, throw a stone and there'd be a church or monastery … unfortunately, many have been pillaged and destroyed by war and invasion. Here in Cyprus we have even more. Now they are being pillaged by the Turks and their icons and other treasures are sold on the black market. But we still have our living treasures. Our wise men. People come now from all over the world to see and speak with those holy fathers, and other wise people like my friend Delphinidis the *Daskalos* of Tseri."

"You mentioned him before."

"He now, with a handful of old monks, represents the accumulated wisdom of our past here on this rock we call Cyprus, Stauvro *mou*. Delphinidis, God protect him, has a way of opening doors to people's inner self. He is also a healer. He refuses to take credit or payment for his healing as he sees himself as an extension of the very mystical tradition that began with our Lord Jesus Christ and is a continuum to the present day, the lighting of the torch on the way to the spirit.

"Delphinidis is an exceptional man. Our Church demonised him for a while, calling him a magus, but eventually they came to their senses. You should go and see him. It will do you good … He is a good man to talk to … also, it will broaden your understanding of what it is to be a spiritual man."

The old priest scratched his beard and looked straight at me.

"We should all search and find what our essence is, Stauvro. Something greater than us. Even I, although I may sit here, I meditate, I think. You see, I am still searching. *O Daskalos* teaches that it is not until we are at peace with ourselves that the past reveals itself to us. He sees it as past lives. I see it as the continuum …"

He coughed and brought up some phlegm that he captured with a clean handkerchief.

"When was the last time you went to confession, my son?"

"A long time ago … when I was young."

"Please forgive me if I am presumptuous, Stauvro *mou* … but if you wish to confess, I would be honoured to hear your confession."

"I think it will take weeks, Father," I said, laughing off the invitation but knowing that what I said was probably true.

"It may help relieve your burden, my son … people underestimate the power of letting someone share their load. You see Stauvro … I sense you are troubled. Maybe you are searching for something." Then looking at me with his kindly, green-grey eyes. "What are you searching for, Stauvro?"

Chapter 2

1

Like every year, over the first two weeks of February with the first blooms of the almond trees, the skies above Cyprus come alive with mesmerising, pulsating, multi-hued, dancing clouds as millions of twittering birds on their spring migration fly cross the island from south to north.

This breathtaking spectacle and symphonic cacophony starts with the arrival of the first swallows and house martins and the wheateaters, with their black and red markings. Soon after, the grey capped and winged great spotted cuckoos – with a yellowish face and upper breast and white underparts – arrive as well. The pink flamingos already have interrupted their journey north in November by stopping off in the *Alitzi,* the salt lake near Larnaca. Apparently, those elegant creatures, whose tongue was considered a great delicacy by the Romans, acquire their pink plumage from the alpha and beta-carotene pigment of the brine, algae and shrimps they eat. In March, the flamingos, fully fortified and their plumage at their brightest pink, continue on their journey and the first hoopoe with their distinctive crown of feathers and colourful orangey plumage arrive. By the end of the month, the spring migration is under full swing with the arrival of pallid harriers, wrynecks, larks, pipits, wagtails, black-eared wheatears, Sylvia warblers and Cretzschmar's and ortolan buntings. The birds are allowed to pass on to their hatching destinations which for some it is as far away as the Arctic.

The bird migration continues into early April with the additional arrival of various herons, egrets, waders, rollers, bee-eaters, olivaceous warblers, shrikes, golden orioles, and black-headed buntings. Towards the end of April, the perching bird migration drops off, but the wader migration continues as they take over the seashore, wading in mud and water.

Then in autumn, the whole process repeats itself in reverse. That is when the hunting season opens – in autumn. Lime sticks, nets and pellet shotguns are used and a virtual slaughter of game species ensues. The ortolans are caught with nets set during their return migratory flight to Africa. They are then kept in covered cages or boxes. The birds react to the dark cage by gorging themselves on grain, usually millet seed, until they double their bulk. Roman Emperors stabbed out ortolans' eyes to make the birds think it was night, making them eat even more. The birds were then thrown into a container of Armagnac, which both drowned and marinated them. At one time, Cyprus formed a chief depot for the export of ortolans, which were pickled in spices and vinegar and packed in casks containing from 300 to 400 each. In the early twentieth century, between 400 and 500 casks were annually exported from Cyprus.

While this majestic epiphany of life was exploding around me, things were catching up with me mentally and they were going from bad to worse.

It is difficult to know precisely when I first became aware that I was falling into what I later referred to as *the abyss of troubled minds*.

A bit cuckoo?

Maybe, Stevo.

The only person who ever called me Stevo was Johnny Spears, an Australian mate of Frank's who was also in the SAS but in the Australian contingent. He and the other Aussies had this way of twisting a name to make it their own. We'd come across him now and then in a bar, and without any inhibition or restraint he'd yell, "At long last, Frankie and Stevo … c'mon cobbers, get your fuckin' marmite-covered arses up to the bar!" Or, "Whores and Gentlemen, Stevo and Frankie, the sheep-shaggers, have arrived."

So, my id threw *Stevo* into the mix.

No maybe, Stevo, mate.

What?

Come on, Stevo. Face it.

Face what?

Come on, mate … face it. You are out of your fucking tree.

Okay. Okay. But …

But … But what? C'mon, Mister Carpenter … aka Kyrie Marange … don't be a fuckin' wuss.

I tell you …

Tell me what?

I …

Face it! Mate!

Okay! OKAY.

C'mon, get it off your chest.

Okay … For fuck's sake, give me couple of seconds, will you?

One, two … Your time's up … Mate! Come on …

I ...

Come on ... Don't hold back ...

"I ..."

Your seconds are up, Stevo ...

I am ...

C'mon! ... Do it!

I am lost in a ... convoluted ...

That's it, Stevo ...

I am lost in a convoluted ... labyrinthine ... mind-fucking cuckoo land

...

That's it, Stevo. That's it, get it off your chest!

I am lost in a convoluted ... labyrinthine, mind-fucking cuckoo land ...

But?

... but, with a Carpenter twist.

That's it, Stevo. Don't you feel better now?

Yeah.

Yeah? ...What a wanker.

*

After arriving in Cyprus, and as soon as I established myself in my parent's village Mpalloura, I started having recurring dreams that I would wake out of in sheer and utter terror. Sometimes I'd wake up after crashing on the floor. I would be fighting someone or running towards or away from something, and tangled in the sheets, I would inevitably fall off the bed. Only a kitten then, poor Scipio, who'd liked sleeping curled up in my armpit, would wake up on the floor with me.

Around last Christmas I also began getting blinding migraines that made me incapable of doing anything important except draw the curtains, swallow a couple of Aspros and go to bed and hope that they would go away.

Violent mood swings were not my thing, but in a period that lasted a week they also began to occur. Noise started getting to me and my hearing became so acute that someone walking down the street would wake me, let alone the cars and motorbikes that never seemed to stop. Barking dogs and crowing roosters and the twittering of the passing migratory birds that I use to find easy to ignore were also getting to me. The music directed towards the south from the Turkish sector was achieving what it was intended to do: disrupt one's sleep and get under one's skin. I would have flashbacks of Vietnam … or of Elizabeth lying in the bath, her veins slashed open. I would constantly swear to myself that Elizabeth's solution to end her hidden misery was not an option and that that was not going to happen to me. But I found that I was becoming more unkempt, and the dry baths or the wet showers I use to take daily got incrementally reduced, to the degree that after the regular turning off of water from the Turkish side began I couldn't remember when I had last had a proper wash. The water for Nicosia was still piped from the *Kephalovrisos* spring on the Pentadactylos, but the Turks would turn it off every so often. Probably some sort of power play. Also, my confidence, my greatest asset, what got me through Vietnam, the coup d'état and the war here, simply evaporated.

Suddenly I was second-guessing myself and undergoing self-flagellatory, self-indulgent self-analysis.

Sure ... I argued ... I vent against the corrupting influence of rusfeti and yet I, the paragon of incorruptibility, hit on Petros and Karageorgis to breach confidentiality for a lead on a story ... which is hypocrisy of the highest order ... in anyone's book ... And as for journalism ... what sort of fuckin' human am I, turning one person's misery into another person's entertainment? ... And on top of that, I have the gall to misrepresent myself in certain situations and, to be frank and really honest, blatantly lie, merely to get a pithy quote ...

That description that I once used of journalists being whores going from trick to trick also caught up with me. As a result, I went through about a week of more self-critique ending with me being totally disgusted with what I had become and browbeating myself with pithy little irrational sayings I feel ashamed to repeat.

As I said, cuckoo land.

I think the last straw was when I screamed at Scipio for doing something that one would normally expect from all cats ... he caught and played with a mouse. The poor bugger ran off and hid under the bed and wouldn't come out until I collapsed drunk on the sofa. I was awakened by him licking my face. Shows you how forgiving some animals can be.

But the tirades wouldn't stop.

Anyway, who the hell do you think you are, Stevo? … You are only a two-bit reporter … a crippled, fuckin' journalist, a third-rate scribbler, nothing else really …

A pompous stuck up prick who thinks that your views on world events matter … are important … and for Christ's sake, you even have the audacity to compare yourself to whores, you fuckin' prick. How dare you? … You've no shame.

For fuck's sake, Steve … Whores! What the fuck have you got against whores? … What have whores done to you, you arsehole? … At least whores have a purpose … They give relief, comfort, listen to peoples' problems … So, what's your fuckin' problem with whores?

I'll tell you what your problem is, Steve…The problem is, that you are worse than a whore. You are a SHIT, a worthless piece of slimy excrement … You give no joy … You are incapable of joy … You are a leach … A fucken parasite … You just suckle on the tit of other people's misery.

And the tirades continue …

Yeah, a journalist … What, fuckin' journalist? What, fuckin' foreign correspondent? What, roving eyewitness? What, steady thumb on the pulse of society? … A collector of misery, that's what you are.

And so, I would berate myself, again and again, as if it was some sort of fuckin' mantra – *If you can't stand the heat in the kitchen, Steve … get out! If you can't stand the fuckin' heat, get out … GET OUT!*

Yeah! Fuckin' cuckoo land. Right?

As I already have said, I started walking. I still had the self-awareness to realise that something serious was happening to me. I started stopping off at the Turkish baths in answer to the Turks cutting the water from the north more regularly. I increased the walks from once a week to every second day after recognising the benefits. Half of the walk was undertaken within the old city and the other half outside. Sometimes I'd walk it clockwise and sometimes anticlockwise. I soon found it relaxing and sometimes it enabled me to think through what I was going to write, whether a piece of journalism or a piece of fiction.

I knew I needed someone to talk with about it. I didn't have a doctor and I never trusted psychiatrists. American soldiers that I got to know said to me that although they were declared unfit for service by one shrink, the army would find another to sanction them to go on missions that sometimes ended up with them doing things that they were ashamed of and never thought themselves capable of.

Battle fatigue was something that was glossed over in Vietnam and now here in Cyprus too. I saw many people walking the streets, talking to themselves or screaming at each other, despite Cypriots being inclined to loudness anyway. One could see the difference, though. It was visceral.

I had thought that I was tough, but I wasn't. I nearly confided to Petros one evening about what was happening to me, but for some reason, I stopped myself. Maybe it was because his presence drew out a joviality that brought me out of myself … out of what was becoming a sort of a living hell, and I didn't want to risk losing it. Knowing Petros, he would become concerned, mollycoddle me and treat me with kid gloves. Then I remembered what Father Sosimas told me about the man dubbed *o Daskalos* or, as I learned later, the Magus of Tseri.

74

Being the typical cowardly male, as far as health issues are concerned, as usual, when cornered, I fabricated in my own mind an approach that instinctively protected my self-esteem and my ego, which was becoming increasingly more fragile. He wouldn't have been my first choice but he would have to do. Seeing myself as a sceptic, the concept of a magus, a magician, was hard to swallow. But swallow it I did. As much as I tried, I couldn't see a problem in just visiting him. He was supposed to be a sort of healer. If he couldn't heal me, maybe he'd recommend someone who could.

I looked around on my desk for the *Daskalos'* phone number, but I could not find it. For some reason, I thought that Father Sosimas had given it to me. If he had, I had lost it. So I decided that on my next walk I would stop off and ask him for it.

2

So the next day, as planned, after posting a letter to my parents and some shopping, I eventually headed down Solonos Street, where I saw Father Sosimas whitewashing some new graffiti that someone had painted on the walls of his church.

I stopped at the wrought-iron boundary fence and read some of the messages that were written in red, blue and black paint. Red for the left, blue for the right and black for … well, I didn't know. Some were simply the names of football teams and others anti-Makariorite slogans that someone had resurrected. However, there were several circled As and football slogans and another slogan that I did not understand with a swastika underneath.

Father Sosima sensed me watching and turned and shouted a greeting.

"*Kalimera*, Stauvro. How are you, *pethi mou* – my son?"

"*Kalimera, Daskale*. I am fine."

The old man looked at me carefully, but whatever he saw he decided to let it go.

"Someone's giving you work to do?" I asked, smiling to show I was joking.

"Well, if I don't clean them up no one will. My parishioners are afraid they'd fall out with whoever wrote them."

I saw that the old man was struggling somewhat, so I went through the metal gate and took the brush from him without saying anything.

"You have my blessing threefold, my son," said the old man, flinching. "My back is killing me."

"Why don't you go and sit down," I said "I'll finish and wash up then come and join you. When you get your breath back, can you please find *Kyrios* Delphinidis' telephone number. I've lost it. I have decided to take up your advice and go and meet with him."

"Sure, Stauvro *mou* … as soon as I have a little rest," said the old man.

I continued whitewashing the wall until all the graffiti was covered.

After I washed the brush and the bucket at an outside tap, I went and found Father Sosima sitting in the afternoon sun, having moved the bench from the church veranda to the side of the church. A piece of paper was next to him.

"So, how are you, *Daskale*?"

"I am well, thanks be to God. Nowadays, I take it one day at a time," he said with a twinkle in his green-grey eyes. Just greyer today.

"So how often do you do this," I asked, indicating the whitewashed wall and picking up and folding the piece of paper with Delphinidis' phone number and putting it in my shirt pocket.

"Whenever one of the local football teams wins or whenever there is a political demonstration." He stroked his beard to a point and scratched his temple. "You see, graffiti is not new ... it has been around for thousands of years, Stauvro *mou* ... It's one of those conundrums of history. Ancient Rome was covered with it and the Romans didn't mince their words. Even the early Christians used to graffiti their fish symbol all over the pagan temples and in the catacombs. I really don't mind it. When I was a kid, I used to go around our village and paint anti-British slogans. Harmless enough, or so I thought at the time."

"Why? What do you mean, Father?"

"Well, graffiti to me is a sign of courage, but unfortunately courage does not discriminate."

I didn't understand, and from my blank look, the old man decided that he had to elaborate.

"Courage is a two-edged sword, Stauvro *mou*, as someone who has courage can be good or bad. That's the dualism that we use to understand things. We humans are strange creatures, Stauvro. Either because of some slight or a self-perceived wrong, we begin to vent and brood ... and in brooding, we think we are thinking ... and we think our garbled thinking is important, and then we search and find like-minded thinkers and we are embraced by them … They become our friends, a sort of a family and we talk and talk … and then we are given some leaflets to scatter and after we boast of our deed and are smothered with effusive praise ... and then again we talk and talk ... and then we paint slogans on walls and again we boast and get more efusive praise ... and then again we talk and talk … and then we punch some poor sod because of their beliefs or because of the way they look and again we talk and talk … and then we throw a stone and we boast and it's again affirmed and praised, and then we talk even more … and then … instead of a stone, we finally throw a bomb … That is when we stop talking. That is when, like a sleepwalker, we take the next step … We shoot someone and we don't say a word … and by then we are too far gone … we have become a fully-fledged killer committed to killing.

"Very rarely do we just *do*, act spontaneously like when we were a child. It's conditioned out of us. It's called civilisation. I know! … This graffiti is a form of talking out our thoughts, a precursor, a sort of a practice run and an indication of what may be coming. Do you remember the graffiti before the *praxokopima* – coup?"

"Actually, I do."

"Well, it was, if you excuse the phrase, a pissing contest really, to see who could paint more and bigger slogans. Everyone marked out their patch and covered it with their own garbage. Passers-by saw it and were encouraged or intimidated. Then there was the end of the talking and then came the doing and in doing many did a lot of bad things. It takes courage to do bad and good things. A conundrum, really ... God protect us."

The old man crossed himself, maybe to avert the evil that he spoke of.

"What did that piece '*MARKA TOY KAIN*' mean, Father? It's just that it had a swastika underneath it." Then, speculating, "Is '*MARKA*' the feminine of Marcus and is '*KAIN*' a local football team or something?"

The old man smiled. "No. *Marka* is an Italian word ... it's their word for *symbolon* – symbol – Stauvro. It's a word absorbed into the Greek ... you hear it used when someone marks someone in football. I think the word also exists in French."

I nodded.

"Yes, you are right ... it exists in English as well ... to *mark* someone or something. But the *swastika*, though, is the *marka* of the German fascists."

"That is true. But it was actually stolen. It was appropriated by the Nazis, the German fascists, and because of its meaning has been tarnished and now it's associated with the genocide of the Jews and all the other poor souls that the Nazis wanted to get rid of. But you see, Stauvro, the swastika as a symbol has been around for a very long time. It's an auspicious sign and means good luck. The Indians, both Hindus and Buddhists, still use it ... on special occasions, they paint it on themselves. But as for *KAIN*, well, it may stand for Cain from the book of Genesis in the Old Testament."

"You mean the one who killed his brother?"

"Yes, that's the one. The son of Adam and Eve. Their first born. Their second son was Abel. As you may know, Stauvro, Abel was a *georgos* – a tiller of the soil. When both of the brothers brought gifts of obeyance, God acknowledged Abel's gifts but not those of Cain. You see, Cain was a *voskos* – a shepherd. He gave his best first lambs as gifts to God, but his gifts were not considered good enough by God. Cain felt a great injustice was done, so

79

seeing this reaction, God said to Cain, 'Why are you incensed, and why is your face fallen? For whether you offer well, or whether you do not, at the tent flap sin crouches and for you it is longing, but you will rule over it.' You see, Stauvro, God was testing Cain and had faith in him that he would make the right choice.

"However, Cain could not control his jealous rage and killed his brother. Then God marked him and banished him to wander in the wilderness until he found a wife, married and had Enoch, one of four children … one of those inconsistencies that exist in the Old Testament if you consider that Adam and Eve were supposed to be the first humans. We say that Cain committed the first murder and Abel was the first man murdered.

"When we say, 'so and so has the mark of Cain on him', we mean he is cursed for he is a murderer.

"And regarding the swastika … as I said, the Nazis appropriated it from the ancients … If you go to our museums, you will see the symbol on our old pottery, sometimes from as far back as 3,000 BC."

"Yes, I've seen it at the museum in Nicosia."

"Well, in ancient India and up to modern times, it is a positive symbol. Apparently, the Navajo Indians and other tribes of North America have it, but to them it has a different meaning. The Nazis, Stauvro *mou*, perverted it and made it synonymous with racism, hatred and mass murder. Now it has become a symbol for people who don't like Jews or whoever. I think what our scribe means is that the swastika, the mark of Cain, is upon us. Why the swastika? I don't know."

"And the alpha with the circle?"

"That circle around an alpha is the *symbolon* of anarchy. It has just started to appear in the last few years. One of the boys in my Sunday school class says that it stands for 'Anarchic Order', and apparently, they are saying that they are seeking order through anarchy. But it is not new … I came across this symbol in Spain during the Spanish Civil War."

"What, you were in the Spanish Civil War, Father?"

The old man looked down at his hands. He crossed himself.

"For my sins. Yes, Stauvro … I don't mind admitting now. That's why I said, *I know*. For no real reason, I became a killer. I have the mark of Cain on me. I don't mean a state-sanctioned killer, a soldier who defends himself, his family and his homeland. I mean someone who does it for a dubious reason. Anyway, I was ashamed of what I did. I went to fight the communists on the side of Franco. I was brainwashed by our Church that the atheistic communists were going to wipe out the Spanish Christians … Or at least our village priest thought so. You see, Stauvro, every village has its own Holy Trinity: the *Muktar*, the Teacher and the Priest. The Priest is the most important. Well, he was to my family. I was clay in his hands from the time he selected me as an altar boy until as a young man I left for Spain. On reflection, it was very strange when you consider that we Orthodox Christians hate the Catholics because of what the Venetians, who were Catholics, did to us. As well, of course, there was the attraction of seeing foreign lands, having an adventure. So, like a lamb to the slaughter I travelled to Italy, and General Franco's emissaries arranged for us to be taken to Spain. As I said, like a lamb to the slaughter. A stupid decision that, after what I experienced, I have forever regretted.

"Never provoke the beast in man, Stauvro *mou* ... I saw things there that I hope no one gets to see ... There is nothing worse than a civil war, although as we saw last year, all types of war are abominations."

"Were there any other Cypriots there, *Daskale*?"

"Yes, there were and Greeks too, but from what I learned they were mostly communists who lived in London. They went along with other British communists to defend the republic. You see, what I didn't know at the time was that the republic was a legitimately elected government and that Franco was a fascist. As for Cypriots, I didn't come across any who fought on Franco's side."

"How long were you there?"

"Two years, and when I came back I spent three months in Egypt, working for an uncle of mine in Alexandria selling carpets. But it wasn't me. So I returned home. I married, took my vows, had children and worked in the fields. I tried being a good priest, seeking repentance for my foolishness. I stayed out of the next war. I'd had enough of war. The nearest I came to any fighting in the Second World War was when the German and Italian planes came all the way here to bomb us. What goes around comes around, though. I lost two of my three children to disease and my wife to childbirth."

"You don't blame God for that, do you?"

"No, but I believe that eventually, we pay for all the evil we perpetrate on people ... but, unfortunately, most of the payment is usually paid by our progeny."

"So why the swastika? There are no Jews in Cyprus after that thing that happened in Salamina in Roman times. Or if there are, they are very few."

82

"That is true, but it does not stop people still using the image to beat anyone they don't like on the head. What the Jews did in Salamina was not a nice thing. In fact, what they did in Canaan wasn't either. Isn't it an irony of history, Stauvro, that the Jews ended up in a British concentration camp in Karaolos, just a stone's throw from Salamina, after the Second World War? There was another camp in Xylotympou ... Those were Jews that the British intercepted on their way to Palestine. I remember the camp in Karaolos well as we smuggled food to the poor souls. One of my uncles even dug a tunnel from his well into the camp, and for a small fee, he'd allow them to roam outside at night or others to enter the camp ... They were mainly couriers from Israel. It wasn't until the end of '49 that the camps were closed."

The old man paused, ran his hand over his beard and continued.

"You see, Stauvro, both the Catholics and we believe in what is called deicide, the killing of God. So we blame the Jews for killing Jesus Christ, although at the same time we believe that the death of Jesus was necessary as it took away the collective sin of the human race. A paradox really. The crucifixion is seen by us as an example of Christ's eternal love for mankind and as a self-sacrifice on the part of God for the whole of humanity. But really, Jesus Christ was killed under Roman law, although he was first indicted for heresy by the Pharisees, a Jewish political party of the time whose constitution demanded the death penalty. I think, though, our Church here in Cyprus still holds some sort of grudge for Salamina. Although most Cypriots then were pagans ... a wave of Christian conversion had just begun and our Church, for some unfathomable reason, distorts history until we even forget that Jesus was a rabbi, an Israelite and, most importantly, a Jew. A Jew who led a Jewish religious renaissance that our forefathers were drawn to.

"Fine ... Artemion and his followers butchered everyone who they could get their hands on in Salamina and the rest of Cyprus, but it was no different to what Joshua and the Israelites had done in Canaan. It amazes me how some Jews would preach the Old Testament and quote it as God's word of their history and ignore Israel was founded on the destruction of another nation through an act of mass killing."

"Who, the Palestinians?"

"No, the Canaanites. Of course, as people always do, the Israelites demonised the Canaanites first, like the Germans did with them centuries later – an even greater irony really. They say in the Old Testament that the Canaanites were sinners ... God warned them, gave them a chance but they had perverted practices, etcetera. Joshua ordered them all killed except for a Rahab, a whore, and her family who helped them take the city. But we Greeks are no different. We did it to the Trojans in Troy and to the Ottomans in Greece. In Tripoli in the Peloponnese, during the Greek revolution, the troops under Kolokotronis killed every man, woman and child – over 30,000 people. Read his autobiography. Kolokotronis says when he entered the city, his horse's hooves never touched the ground because of the bodies, and one soldier boasted to him that he had killed ninety Turks. But it wasn't just Turks, it was also Jews and Greeks who lived there. Of course, the Greeks say they were exacting revenge for when Albanian troops – under orders from the Ottomans – killed 3,000 people there at the start of the revolution. So, as you see all the time, you know ... the usual tit for tat, eh? No one forgets an ill done to them and years later they see an opportunity and they exact their revenge."

The old man raised the fingers of his right hand and counted them off. "The Belgians in the Congo, the Turks with the Armenians, Greeks and

Assyrians … the Australians with the Aborigines ... the German Nazis with the Jews, the Freemasons, the communists, the Gypsies and all the cripples of their society. And here those fanatics the Greek nationalists say that the Greeks replaced the Phoenicians and the first settlers of Cyprus. Phut! Nations rise and fall … there are always remnants of bloodstock and culture left. Look at the Romans … they became a pastiche of the Greeks, although they were crueller. In western Italy, where we landed on our way to Spain, you come across streets named in Greek and their inhabitants look very much like they are from the Peloponnese. And even here our hands are not clean, Stauvro *mou*, from what I have experienced and have been told about last year … I hate to say it, but I don't think there is a nation on earth that has not done atrocious things. If there is, may God forgive me." Again, he crossed himself.

I must have looked perplexed or something.

"What is the matter, Stauvro?"

"Sorry, Father," I said, trying to clarify what he was saying to me. It was difficult to keep track of everything. "Can you please go back a little bit. You see, unlike here, we did not have serious biblical studies at our schools in New Zealand. So … I don't get it. I am sort of puzzled. Why did God want to destroy the Canaanites?"

"Because," said the old man without hesitation, "He was a jealous God, Stauvro. He wanted the Canaanites to worship only him and obey his laws. You see the Canaanites were multitheistic like the ancient Greeks. Remember the first commandment brought down from Mount Sinai by Moses, what it demands? 'Thou shalt have no other gods but me.' It's a demand, an order: 'No other gods but me.' You see, the Old Testament concerns only the Jews, Stauvro, while the New Testament embraces all of humanity. Both books are starkly different: death versus life, worldly versus eternal, servitude versus

85

freedom, physical versus spiritual and perpetual guilt versus eternal pardon. The Old Testament God, Stauvro, is a wrathful, demented God and his acts throughout the Old Testament are still the acts of a vengeful and very savage God – although one could easily say that all of the Jews' contemporaries did the same. We Greek Orthodox believe in Jesus Christ, the Holy Ghost and God as one entity. This was decided at the Council in Nicaea under Constantine I in AD 325 under the guidance of one of our very own compatriots, *Agios* Spiridon. He was the one who came up with the wonderful metaphor of clay, water and fire that he saw encapsulated in an earthen pot to describe the Holy Trinity. This god, our God, is the god of love, forgiveness and hope. The Old Testament God was tempered by Jesus, his son, to become a more compassionate god than the one that emerged from Egypt with the Israelites, where strangely, according to my friend Delphinidis, one of their pharaohs, like Socrates, promoted the existence of one god."

The old man was in full flight. But the veracity of all that he was saying needed checking. That would have to wait.

"You see, myth, like history, is a strange thing, Stauvro *mou*. Sometimes you find parallels in them. If you read the origins of the ancient Greeks' Olympian gods, you will see that the father of Zeus was Kronos and his mother was Rhea, two of the original Greek gods, the Titans.

"Kronos was told by his mother Gaia and father Uranus that he would be supplanted by one of his children, so in his jealous rage, he swallowed them all after birth. Interestingly, the first manifestation of humans in the Greeks' creation myth was Gaia, a woman, and her husband Uranus was born to her without a father. The reverse of the biblical creation story. Fortunately for Zeus, after Rhea gave birth to him, she hid him. When he grew up, he gave his father some emetic potion that made him throw up his brothers and sisters …

Poseidon, Hades, Hera, etcetera. So, a patricide occurred, a sort of civil war. After the conquest of the Titans, Zeus imprisoned them in Tartarus. Zeus did not forget or forgive what his father did to his siblings and was planning to do to him. It is not an easy thing to do, forgive, but it is, above all, what I believe in. Forgiveness.

"Look at the parallels ... Kronos, a Grecian father who sacrifices his children ... Our God, a Jewish father who sacrifices his only son. Zeus, a Greek son that rebels and gains the upper hand and rules, in the ancients' terms, more justly ... Jesus, a Jewish son who rebels against his father and modifies his father's laws – like, 'an eye for an eye' – preaching forgiveness and the turning of the other cheek and, as a result, drawing the enmity of many of his co-religionists, especially the ruling class of Judea, the Pharisees. You see, Stauvro, the writers of the gospels played down the role that the Romans had played in the death of Jesus because their doctrine was trying to coexist in a world that did not tolerate anti-Roman sentiment. Even Jesus would not be trapped into attacking Caesar. Remember what he said? 'Render therefore unto Caesar things that are Caesar's and unto God things that are God's.' "

I could see that Father Sosima was now finally exhausted. I stood up. But the old priest was not finished yet.

"Forgiveness is what gives me hope, Stauvro. And so ..." Father Sosima smiled and the kindly glint reappeared in his eyes "... I forgive the graffiti scribes for desecrating our church, as I hope I will be forgiven for my sins."

That afternoon I went back to Larnaca, with the blessing of Petros and his boss, to tidy things up by interviewing some of the main characters of the investigation.

I then took notes for a more detailed report on the arrest of the British soldiers by the Royal Military Police Provost Office, who had handed them over to the police of the Cypriot republic as required by the British base agreement. I looked at the black and white photo of the girl that was issued to the press by the police. She certainly was a looker.

Petros took a back seat in the court except when he had to give evidence, Ellery, his British colleague, explaining whenever he seemed to be at a loss by the turn of an English phrase. The trial was carried out entirely in English.

I remember once, out of curiosity after I first arrived in Cyprus, visiting the courts in Varosi and being shocked to see that not only were all the procedures carried out in English, but the hapless accused did not even have an interpreter. This was twelve years after independence. The accused in the dock just had to trust that his lawyer was doing a proper job. It was explained to me at the time that this misalignment was because the Cypriot judicial system is based on British common law and most lawyers tend to be trained in English universities. Glafcos Clerides, who had been acting president last year during President Archbishop Makarios' absence, was such a lawyer, as was the current Turkish leader Rauf Denktash.

Petros rang Eleni to say that he and I were eating out in Larnaca, and after our tasty fish meal at a seaside restaurant that night, he dropped me off at home.

I had bought a new paraffin heater at the beginning of winter. I lit it and sat down and typed out a feature article of my overview of the arrest and the trial. I mentioned no names other than that of the victim. I thought I'd send it to my friend Vaughn's paper as they already knew me from the investigative piece we did together on a carjacking ring in Cyprus and Britain.

4

The following morning, a Wednesday, I was awakened by a knock on the downstairs door. I pulled on my jeans and a jersey, and half asleep, I stumbled down the stairs to open the front door. Imagine my surprise when I saw Inspector Phantis standing at the door.

"*Kalimera, Kyrie* Marange."

"*Kalimera, Kyrie* …" I then I stopped as I realised that I didn't know Phantis' surname.

He sensed it and added, "Apostolou."

"*Kalimera, Kyrie* Apostolou."

"May I come in, please?"

"Sure. Please. Watch your step. Let me go first."

I thought he was visiting to run past me something to do with the British soldier's case.

I led him upstairs.

When we entered the apartment, he stood looking around.

"Nice place you have."

"Yes, it is. I like it. I am renting it. The owners are elderly and have moved in with their son's family outside Limassol. They have stored their possessions in the shop downstairs. Like many people, they are apprehensive about living near the ceasefire line. It's the gunfire and the loud music that the Turks keep blasting us with. It can grind people down. Anyway, Inspector, what can I do for you? Would you like something to drink ... a coffee?"

"No, thank you, I just had one."

Phantis took out his notebook.

"It will not take long, *Kyrie* Marange. You don't mind if I call you by your Greek name?"

I thought for a moment. "Is this something official?"

"Yes"

"Then, *Kyrie* Apostolou, if it is all right with you, I would prefer Carpenter. My official name is Steven Carpenter. That is what is on my passport and it is also the name on my Reuters byline." One doesn't have a byline in Reuters, but Phantis did not know that.

I could see immediately that Phantis did not like this, but if you give an inch, he might take a mile. And I also had to keep in mind Petros' warning about people trying to get me.

"Fine. Carpenter it is. So, *Kyrie* Carpenter, can you please tell me if you know a boy called Michalis Sketos?" he asked.

"No, I don't think so."

90

"He is nearly eighteen, five eight … a Greek … a Cypriot."

"No, *Kyrie* Apostolou, I've never heard of him."

"Well, this Sketos boy was found dead in Agia Napa. He was with a French woman. She too was shot."

It was the murder that he attended after leaving Petros in charge.

"I am sorry about that, but I never heard of him."

"Then how do you explain your name being found in his wallet, *Kyrie* Carpenter?"

I was taken aback by the revelation.

"I have no idea, Inspector."

The inspector reached into the inside pocket of his jacket. "Well, this may help. It's a photograph. I am afraid he is not a pretty sight."

He stretched out and I took the black and white photograph from him.

I recognised the boy instantly. He had a small calibre wound to the left temple. He looked younger than eighteen despite the stubble.

"Oh, him," I said, nodding. "Yes … yes, I recognise him. I know him as … Mikis. That's it, Mikis … He and a friend of his approached me to be a translator for them."

"Oh, yes. To translate what?"

I went to the bench to get some water. I indicated to the inspector to see if he wanted a glass. He shook his head and stood there waiting until I drank the water and put the glass down.

"They saw some advertisement by a German woman in the *Cyprus Mail* and they wanted me to ring her up and arrange a meeting for them."

"A meeting, for what?"

"To go out with her. She had advertised that she wanted a young Greek man to accompany her during her visit to Cyprus, all expenses paid. I think, if I remember right, it was for two weeks. It was a job with benefits if you understand what I am saying. They saw themselves up for the job."

"Both?"

"No. The offer was for one, but they were going to give her a choice," I said. "He was shot?"

"Yes. So, did you ring the woman for them?"

"No. I made some sort of joke or other to discourage them and they got the idea that I was not interested."

"Did you see them again?"

"No ..."

"I see. Is there anything else that you remember?"

"No. Not really."

"You are sure?"

"Yes."

"Well, thank you, *Kyrie* … Mar … um … Carpenter," he said, folding his notebook. "If you do remember something, please ring me at the Larnaca station."

"I will. By the way, how did you get my address, Inspector?" I asked.

The inspector smiled. "I rang Inspector Zimaras."

"Oh … right."

"Anyway, sorry for disturbing you."

"No problem. I am only sorry that I couldn't be of further use."

He turned to go. Then he stopped. He turned to look at me again.

"You don't happen to remember his friend's name, *Kyrie* Carpenter?"

I stopped and thought for a minute.

"Wait a minute … I think it may have been … Andreas … no, Antónis. Yes, that it. Antónis.

"A surname?"

"No, neither told me their surnames."

"All right. Well … again, thank you. I'll let myself out."

Then the journalist in me finally kicked in. "Inspector … is there something I can report? If the woman is French, the French papers may be interested."

"No. I am afraid we are at an early stage of our investigation … but ring the station at Larnaca and maybe there will be a press release."

Obviously, Inspector Phantis Apostolou was not going to be a new bosom buddy and tell me everything like Petros.

5

That evening, around seven, Petros came around. He flopped himself on the couch. He was already smoking a cigarette. Scipio came out of the bedroom and jumped on his knee and Petros absentmindedly stroked him until he curled up and fell asleep.

"He looks content," I said, surprised at how affectionately my cousin treated the cat. He had proclaimed on many occasions that he hated cats but just made an exception of Scipio for me.

"If you don't watch out, you may become a committed ailurophile," I said.

"What's that?"

"One who likes cats."

"Oh, yeah … *ailos* for cat," Petros scoffed, mainly at himself as he had studied Ancient Greek like every other Cypriot secondary school student.

"Anyway, what's this I hear? You've been trying your hand at pimping." He said this with a crinkling forehead and a big smile, as always more than capable of pricking the thought balloon that I was preparing in reply.

I laughed. "Yeah … and I am good at it … I take forty-five per cent commission … so are you interested? … I have a vacancy now. However, I must warn you that some of my clients have the misfortune to end up with a bullet in their head." I moved to the kitchen sink. "Would you like a coffee?"

"No, but if you have a brandy …"

"As it happens, I have … or would you prefer a whisky?'

"No, a brandy is fine."

After I poured each of us a forty-five-year-old Anglias brandy in small glasses and assembled a plate full of peanuts and dry figs, I placed everything on the table and sat down.

Petros stamped out the butt of his cigarette in the ashtray.

He raised his glass, said *seegeea mas* – to our health – and downed it in one swallow. He took a handful of peanuts and munched on them.

"So, Phantis came and saw you?"

I poured him another brandy.

"Yes … *o Kyrios* Apostolou did come to see me, but he played his cards close to his chest."

"Well, he probably heard what an untrustworthy sod you are," he said, chuckling. "Seriously, though, cousin … it's a big case. Who would believe it, eh? Two murders in a week." He took out another of his cigarettes and lit it. He held my eyes. "Ground rules?"

I looked at him in mock surprise, but I knew that we had to go through this charade as it kept things tidy.

"Ground rules."

"Well, they found two bodies. One was the boy, the other was a twenty-eight-year-old French woman. Her name is Claudine Auguste."

"Yes, Apostolou said she was French. I must say I was surprised. From what I know, I thought that the woman was German."

"No, she's French. Maybe the German one is a different woman. Come on, tell me what happened … You know, when you first met the boys."

I quickly told him what had happened several months before. Then I finished with my pithy parting comment to the boys that I was not as proud of now "… that journalists are *poutanes* – whores – going from trick to trick and so, by that definition, I must be a *putana*. Then I told them to listen when an experienced *putana* tells them to avoid the shackles of servitude and work without a pimp."

"You said that to them?" Petros chortled.

"I was being an arsehole … I was trying to shame them. Put them off."

"It didn't stop them, did it?"

"On reflection, I realise that the analogy wasn't entirely right … You know … we journalists still need pimps … the newspapers," I replied absentmindedly. "And no, it didn't."

"My God, you do over-think things, cousin." Petros wrinkled his forehead again and, lighting another cigarette, "So, that time it was a German woman."

"Well, that is what the advertisement said …"

Petros sipped his second brandy.

"Well, this woman's passport is French. And Claudine Auguste is a French name."

"So, what happened, Petro?"

"We are not sure yet. But it seems they were both shot with a small calibre pistol. Two shots. One to the chest one to the head …"

"Yes, Phantis showed me a photograph of Miki."

"Well, it's a twenty- two. Possibly an automatic. Neither stirred. They were shot where they slept. It looks like a professional did it as there were no cartridges left behind."

"Phantis said Agia Napa. Where?"

"The Helenis."

"I heard of it. It's expensive, isn't it?"

"It is. It's small, discreet and very elite. Only for politicians and their girlfriends … and the rich."

"So, this French woman was loaded?"

"Indeed, she was. Phantis reckons her jewellery alone was worth several thousand. She had just over two hundred Cypriot pounds and three thousand American dollars in the lining of her bag. Of course, one has to ask why she had so much cash with her. What was it for? After all, she was on holiday. Cyprus is not that expensive."

"So, it wasn't a robbery, then?"

"Nope. Well, for the moment. Whoever did it only had one thing in mind. Kill them and get out."

"So, how did the killer get into the room?"

"We don't really know yet. The cleaning girl says the door was locked when she entered the room."

"Who would a boy like him piss off?"

"Well, it may not be the boy. It may have something to do with the woman. The boss wants me to go to Agia Napa as the French ambassador is going over and he wants me to show him around. I am not very happy about it, so I asked the embassy for the ambassador to meet me at the police station in Larnaca. Are you doing anything this afternoon?"

"Why?"

"Well, I need someone who speaks French. I have been told that the ambassador speaks English, but it would be good to have you there to pick up if he and whomever he brings along, lapse into French."

"You got the wrong guy," I said. "The last time I spoke French …" I stopped myself. I remembered that it wasn't Vietnam but with *Giagia* Androutsou, my neighbour in Mpalloura, and then the kids from Egypt caught up in the fighting at the Presidential Palace during the coup. Then I also remembered that Petros had seen me reading *Le Monde* that I had picked up at the Hilton while waiting for one of our meets.

"Look, I won't be of any use to you. My French is terrible," I tried. "Haven't you got someone who can do that for you?"

"Not someone that I can trust."

"Why would you need that?"

"Well, this may have to do with something serious …"

"What?"

"Terrorism."

"You are joking."

"No, I am serious."

I thought about what Petros said for a while.

"Well, don't blame me if I get the wrong end of the stick," I finally said.

"You won't. Anyway, your French is still better than mine, which is virtually non-existent. Come, we'll have a quiet trip … stop somewhere and have a *souvláki* and take in some fresh sea air."

6

By the time Petros and I arrived in Larnaca, it was after two o'clock. I was tired because of the previous sleepless night and had drifted off to sleep. Petros parked the car and that woke me. We were at the police station.

"We have tried to contact the dead boy's parents," explained my cousin, "but they were in Greece visiting his elder brother, who is studying at Athens University. Apparently, afterwards they went on a pilgrimage through the Aegean. We would appreciate it if, for the time being, you identify him, Stauvro. It will help with getting the investigation up and running."

That was probably the real reason Petros wanted me to come with him as it did occur to me that most French diplomats appointed to Cyprus would not only be very proficient in English but maybe even Greek.

"No problem. But you owe me," I said lop-smiling to let him know that I saw through his ploy.

*

The boy was lying on a gurney and was covered with a sheet as white as his protruding pale feet. Petros walked up and drew the sheet back for me to see the face. There was light stubble on the boy's chin. A muzzle imprint could be clearly seen around the rather large entrance wound. Petros reminded me that the mark was usually left if the gun was under three feet from the victim. He also reminded me that a silencer usually leaves an irregular, larger hole – something that I initially learned from the murders of the previous summer. In order to see for himself, Petros lifted the sheet high to see the other shot to the heart. He also revealed several fading brownish bite marks, mainly around the neck and chest area.

"Well?"

"That's him. Mikis. It looks as though whoever shot him knew what he was doing. So you think he was killed by a professional?"

"That's the MO," said Petros in English. "The woman was killed the same way."

"What for?"

"Nothing that we can find. All her traveller's cheques, money, jewellery, passport, etcetera, as said, were still at the crime scene. Whoever killed them had only one thing on his mind. Our pathologist, Hadjicostis, thinks that the boy was killed first and the woman second. Don't ask me how he knows that. Possibly because the boy was the nearest to the killer. They were killed just after midnight according to their stomach contents. He also confirmed that the killer used a silencer, which was why no one heard anything. Hadjicostis thinks she may be a couple of years older than the passport indicates, but she was a good-looking woman and very fit. She's over there," said Petros, indicating a covered body parked on a gurney against the back wall.

"The woman seems to be just an ordinary tourist on vacation. According to the hotel receptionist, she arrived three days before and she brought the boy back with her on the second night. We just found out that they stayed at the same hotel last year, which is probably just after the boys approached you. The woman and the boy got tipsy and were happy. He stayed with her all that day, lounging next to the swimming pool. They dined in the hotel restaurant that night. Room service found them the next day. It was a local girl who works there as a cleaner. She's been with them for five years. No one had heard the shots, so as I said, a silencer was probably used. Also, the hotel is on a pretty noisy thoroughfare."

"So have you got any leads."

"None, really, except the boy's friend. Thanks for remembering his name … it helped us to eventually trace him. I'll be interviewing him tomorrow in Nicosia. I've sent Karageorgis to get a preliminary statement from him."

"This sort of thing is pretty heavy for Cyprus … isn't it?"

"Well, yes, when it comes to civilians … but the Cypriot mafia kill each other in various ways. Mainly bombs. Everyone in this fuckin' place knows how to make bombs. It's the conscription. They have nothing else to do except learn how to make the bloody things. The mafia usually keep families out of it, but this is something more, I think. Come on … Let's go upstairs and see the French ambassador …"

He nodded to an orderly who was standing nearby to take the body away.

"Tell *Kyrio* Hadjicosti I want a copy of the post-mortem as soon as he has done, eh?"

7

We left the pervading odour of formaldehyde, alcohol and death behind and climbed upstairs where the main corridor led to an office. Petros knocked and we both entered.

"*Ah, Monsieur l'Ambassadeur* – Ah, Mr Ambassador," Petros said in halting French. *"Vous êtes si aimable de faire le trajet jusqu'ici.* – How kind of you to come all the way to here. *Je vous présente M. Carpenter. Il m'aidera si ma connaissance de votre langue me fait défaut.* – This is Mr Carpenter. He will help me if I get myself in a tangle with your language."

A tall man wearing a smart grey suit, pale blue shirt and dark blue, impeccably knotted tie moved forward and put his hand out. He was clean-shaven with thin black grey-speckled hair combed straight back. He exuded some sort of cologne. Behind him, there were two men, one short and the other tall, also dressed in dark suits and black striped ties. The ambassador did not bother to introduce them.

102

"It's fine, inspector. Maybe it will help if we can speak in English. So, have you got something to tell me?"

I could see that Petros had shut the French down quickly by indicating that he could speak it. I wondered why, since he did say he wanted me to eavesdrop. Maybe he realised, as I thought, that with the two men accompanying the ambassador, the Greek and English proficiency might be well covered.

"Well, it is too soon, sir. However, what can you tell us about the late Madame Auguste?"

"So far nothing. She did not register with us at the embassy in Nicosia. But usually, short-term tourists don't. Paris will contact you soon with whatever they may find. May I see her passport, inspector?"

"Her passport? I am sorry, sir, but it's held with all her belongings downstairs."

"Oh. When can I have her belongings?"

"Why?"

"Well, it will help identify her and also to pass on to her relatives."

"We still need them, but we will certainly let you know when they will be available, Ambassador."

The ambassador seemed a little put out by Petros' comment, but I thought at the time that I might have been reading too much into the exchange.

"Well, if there is nothing else, Inspector, I shall take my leave."

The two men shook hands and the ambassador left, followed by the short and then the tall man.

Petros stood looking after them, then he turned to me. "If you were an ambassador, would you want to look at a victim's belongings, Stauvro, unless you had a very good reason? And if you had a reason, why wouldn't you tell a policeman about it?"

"I don't know. He just probably wants to trace her relatives as soon as possible."

"He knows her name and all her details. He was already told that nothing was stolen and it wasn't a robbery. So, he knows that all her belongings have been left intact. It just seems odd to me. It may be his tone."

"You are reading too much into it."

"Maybe I am and maybe I am not."

8

When we arrived back in Nicosia from Larnaca, it was late. Petros invited me to a late dinner. I accepted but said that I first needed to feed Scipio and that I'd make my own way from there. He dropped me off outside the city's Venetian walls and I walked to the apartment.

By the time I drove to Petros and Eleni's, it was eight o'clock. Their daughter Maria and son-in-law Leonidas were there with little Petros and the evening passed quickly. Maria and Leonidas kept referring to me as their *koumparos* as I was a best man at their wedding. But so were thirty or so other men – and, incidentally, women as well for the bride – at the time. However,

104

the term gave me a strange comfort. It made me feel as if I belonged. After Maria and Leonidas left, Eleni excused herself and went to bed. Petros and I sat for a while chatting and listened to the late BBC news on the radio. At about one o'clock I was ready for bed. I stood up and Petros accompanied me outside and to my car. Petros asked if he could pick me up to identify Miki's friend, Antónis, who was being brought into the Central Police Station in the morning. As I wasn't doing anything until late in the afternoon, I agreed.

On the way home, I stopped at a kiosk to pick up the early edition of the *Cyprus Mail*. On the front page was the picture of the murdered woman and the boy Mikis. There was very little new information about the woman, but there was a reasonable profile on the boy. Apparently, he was to join the National Guard at the next intake. He was a top student at the English School with a liking for football and he was an APOEL – Athletic Football Club of Greeks of Nicosia – fan. His friends said that he was hoping to study law. His family was from Nicosia. As Petros said, his parents, after visiting the brother in Athens where he was studying medicine went on a pilgrimage, to Tinos in the Aegean visiting the famed Marian shrine site of the Church of Panagia Evangelistria and apparently they were contacted and were on their way back. His uncle said that he was a good boy who tried to make his family proud of him. I wondered if that included his prowess with women. There was no mention of the way he was found except to say that he was shot.

I got back into the car and drove to the parking building. Then I walked to the apartment.

Scipio was pleased to see me. Like an idiot, I had forgotten to replenish his water dish, so he was thirsty. As always, he forgave me my misdemeanour, and after he had a drink, he came and sat on my knee. I sipped a brandy I poured and lit up an Il Moro.

Although I had dismissed Mikis as a cocky little ratbag when he and his friend approached me with their proposal for me to ring up the German woman, I had to admit at his age I was probably worse. Cypriot culture generally prohibited young men from going out with young Cypriot women, especially in the villages, so horny young men either went to the many whorehouses that prospered, thanks to the UN, or to the tourist resorts where young tourist girls were hankering for a holiday romance. A societal option was to marry young. What Mikis and his friend were doing was meeting another demand imported with western European mores. What it was actually doing to Cypriot society – one could only wait and see. Drugs were not a problem in Cyprus as they were everywhere else, but I was sure that would change soon. Although topless bathing was the norm among many tourist women, so far young local women had kept their attire on. I was also sure that wouldn't last long as the '60s hippie revolution showed those behaviours had a habit of spreading like wildfires.

Chapter 3

1

When a young policeman led Antónis into the interview room, I was shocked to see the impact his friend's death had had on him. He was gaunt and wild-eyed. His brown, blonde-tipped hair was dishevelled and he had stubble above his mouth and on his pointy chin. He wore a simple, open brown sports coat over a buttoned-up black shirt and flared black trousers for mourning. He also wore black socks and shoes.

"*Kalimera*, Antóni," said Petros, taking a paternal tone. "I am Inspector Zimaras. *Ta silipitiria mas* – our condolences. We are sorry about your friend Miki's death."

Antónis remained silent.

"You know *Kyrion* Marango?"

Antónis registered me. "I thought you were a journalist," he said in a hushed voice.

"He is, but like you, he is helping us with our inquiries."

"Oh?" said Antónis, but his facial expression said that he wasn't satisfied.

"There's a French component to the investigation and *Kyrios* Marangos is helping me as an interpreter."

"What French component?"

"The woman that Mikis was found with was French."

"What? No, she wasn't. She was German."

Petros looked at me and I at him. So, it seemed that we had already got served a curveball, as the Americans use to say in Vietnam.

Not showing any reaction to the revelation, Petros continued as if nothing happened.

"Fine. Why don't you start from the beginning and tell us everything you know?"

Antónis sat for a minute, gathering his thoughts. "Well … we saw this advertisement in the *Cyprus Mail* and went to see *ton Kyrio* Marango to help us with our English to make contact with the woman."

"How did you know about him?'

"He goes to our friend Photis' father's *kafenio*. Photis Louizou told us about him."

Petros raised his chin nodding in acknowledgement.

"Anyway … *Kyrios* Marangos sort of refused, but Mikis said that he would give it a go anyway. So, he rang the hotel and was put through to her. The next day we caught a taxi to Larnaca and then Agia Napa. She was younger than we thought she'd be, I'd say in her mid-twenties. She liked Miki, maybe because he was bold enough to ring, so I came home. He spent the whole two weeks with her and was full of himself when he got back home. She had bought him new clothes and a watch, and they dined out every night. That was last year. Then about a week ago he got a note from her saying she was back in town and would he meet her at the same hotel. I saw him to the taxi service … that was the last time that I saw him."

"So what makes you think she was German?"

"Other than her advertisement, she spoke English like a German. We had a German teacher at the English School and he talked the same way. If she was French, she might be from the border region with Germany, but I don't think so. I studied French at the *gymnasium* and I am sure she was not French."

"I believe you," said Petros, to reassure him. "Is there anything else that you can remember?"

"The previous time … Mikis said that sometimes she'd go out at night for a walk by herself and she wouldn't allow him to go with her as she said that she wanted to be alone. He said that sometimes she became quite distant, but she was great in bed. At the end of the first time, he said he was glad for the break as she was very aggressive. He showed me his chest and neck. It was covered with bite marks."

"Is there anything else that you can remember?"

"No, that's it."

"You are sure?"

"Yes."

"Well, if you do remember, please ring me at this number, eh?"

Petros pulled a little pad towards him and wrote down his name and number.

"We are very grateful to you for coming in, Antónis, and also for your help. I know it will be hard for you for the next few weeks. One of my men will be going to see Mikis' parents to pass on our condolences. Please keep everything we discussed confidential. We want to catch whoever did this and the only way we can do it is if he doesn't know what we know. So, no press. Please."

"What about *Kyrion* Marango?" asked Antónis recovering his composure.

"Well, he has given an undertaking not to write about it until we solve it."

Antónis nodded his head, shook our hands meekly and was escorted out by the young policeman.

After he left, Petros took out a cigarette, rang for two coffees from the canteen and lit up.

"What do you think?' he asked.

"Could he have done it? Jealousy or whatever, for missing out?"

"I did think about that, but according to Karageorgis, who interviewed him at home, he said that he was at a soccer match in Larnaca and he and his friends didn't get back to Nicosia until late. No, young Antónis is a very shocked boy, and I s'pose he's glad that it wasn't his little dick in bed with the woman."

"What is this about her being German now?"

"Um, that is a very good point and it explains the uneasiness of the ambassador."

"What do you mean?"

"Well, there was something the good ambassador wasn't telling us. I knew there was something wrong. I bet you Interpol will be coming up with something very interesting …"

"Interpol? Isn't it based in Paris? I thought the ambassador contacted Paris."

"We also contacted Paris. But not *Police Nationale*, the French civilian police. I didn't tell him we contacted Interpol for a reason … hopefully, they'll be allowed to do their job properly."

"Who is going to stop them?"

"Strange things happen when there are cases like this."

"Well, I don't see anything strange. Maybe the woman is married and she used another identity to throw her husband off her trail. Maybe her husband caught up with her …"

"Could be … it's not the first time a husband has killed a wife and her lover or vice versa. Even in Cyprus. No! There's something wrong. Things are not well in this house of Denmark, Stauvro …"

"What! You are quoting Shakespeare at me now? It's supposed to be 'Something is rotten in the state of Denmark.' You got it? Anyway, I thought I was supposed to be the book worm."

Petros chuckled.

"You are a book worm and you are my very own worm, Stauvro *mou,*" he said, trying to articulate a joke in English. It didn't work.

"And I suppose you are the bloody crow," I said, taking mercy on him trying to resurrect the flow of his tangled joke.

"Don't laugh at crows. They are very intelligent birds."

"Yeah, well, like all of us, they shit too."

Petros projected mock shock. "Good retort," he said, "… for a worm."

2

I continued to cover the trial of the British soldiers that the British papers called 'squaddies', their nickname for army privates, although one of the accused was a corporal. The Cypriot government wanted to get it over and done with, so the case was given priority. The soldiers belonged to the Royal Green Jackets and were on their first tour of duty on the island.

In Cyprus, as already mentioned, the justice system is broadly based on English common law and is presided over by the Supreme Court. There are seven courts, but criminal cases such as this are tried in the assize courts where three judges listen to all the evidence, confer and pass judgement. There are no jury trials.

The assize courts are vested with unlimited power to try all criminal offences and to pronounce the punishment provided by the law. Other than for three exceptional cases in the early 1960s, when acting president Glafcos Clerides declined to grant clemency, Archbishop Makarios, the first president of the republic, had refused to apply the death sentence after independence, even last year for the crime of treason.

The soldiers were tried in the Assize Court of Larnaca and Famagusta Districts Court, which became amalgamated after the invasion. From what the court heard, they were all from working-class backgrounds. Two were from the worst slums of Birmingham, one from the East End of London and the last from Wales. As always, there was a leader, the corporal, who led them down the path of their murdering enterprise. He was a short, mean-looking young man of twenty-two. Apparently, he was blooded in Northern Ireland. He seemed totally unaffected by the whole procedure. They pleaded not guilty. The evidence against them was overwhelming. Their lawyer told the court that they enlisted in the army to escape their economic disadvantages as if that was a real extenuating circumstance for murder. They all got life in prison.

3

Two days later, I finally rang the number that I got from Father Sosima. A woman answered. I introduced myself in Greek. I said that I was hoping to arrange a meeting with *Kyrios* Delphinidis. The woman asked me what it was about. I said that Father Sosimas thought that I may benefit from meeting *ton Daskalos*. The mention of Father Sosimas seemed to clinch it.

"Come tomorrow at eight in the morning," she said. "He will see you for half an hour. He has a meeting in the *stoa* at eight-thirty. He may invite you to attend."

The next day I left the apartment at seven and stopped to have a coffee before I drove to Tseri. The village is about two miles south from Nicosia and was named after *tseri*, the beeswax that is produced for church candles.

In the end, as always in Cyprus, where there are rarely street names in villages, I had to ask a local where Delphinidis' house was.

I must admit that I was still very sceptical about Delphinidis, the Master, the Magus of Tseri, or simply, *o Daskalos*. But I had decided to go through with it and here I was. There was no going back now.

I was shown into a simple, lime whitewashed room. When I was whitewashing my grandparent's house in Mpalloura, I found out that the lime is used to disinfect a house and it was used once as a way to fight cholera and the plague. Later, it was discovered that whitewashed houses were cooler in the summer as the white reflected the sunlight – and also the heat.

The windows in the room were shuttered against the cold outside. Their ultramarine colour contrasted starkly against the white plaster of the walls. There was a small, high table with several icons and a lit lamp, and my senses became so focused that I could smell not only the incense but also the burning wick. I could also smell the burning wood in the fireplace, crackling and flickering its blazing light and warming the room. Above the fireplace was a shelf with a small carved wooden statue of the three wise monkeys: one with his mouth covered, another with his eyes covered and a third with his ears covered. Like Mahatma Gandhi, who rejected all possessions, Delphinidis also kept among his meagre possessions a small sculpture of the three apes of the Japanese pictorial maxim "See no evil, hear no evil, speak no evil".

A tall man, slightly taller but heavier in bulk than me, entered the room. He had a pasty face with a mop of unruly black hair. He wore an open white shirt, casual faun slacks and black slip-on slippers. I introduced myself. We shook hands and he asked me in a gentle and quiet voice to sit down.

A woman who I assumed was the same I talked to on the phone came in with conserves and water on a tray which she placed on the table. She went to the fire, threw another log on it and left as quietly as she entered.

"*O Kyrios* … Stauvros? Yes?" he said, reassuring himself that he picked up my name correctly.

I nodded.

"So, *Kyrie* Stauvro. You know Father Sosimas?"

I nodded.

"I haven't seen Father Sosima since the coup. He saved my life from EOKA B who were going to shoot me because one of our villagers told them that I was a communist … God forgive them. You see, everyone who is not right-wing is seen as a communist here. Even centrists. Father Sosima is a good man and a devout priest. He tries to improve himself every day and because of it he is a wise man."

"Yes, he is that," I said.

He paused a moment, articulating his mind.

"Your Greek is newly learned, I think, and your accent … is it Canadian or is it Australian?"

"I was born in New Zealand," I said, somewhat defensively.

"Ah! New Zealand. A beautiful country … my cousin, who is a seaman, has told me this. He said that there are twenty-four sheep there for every New Zealander. He said the hills are covered with sheep. Is that true?"

"Probably. It depends on where one is."

Delphinidis nodded his head in understanding. "You are a long way from home?"

"Cyprus is my home," I said, my tone a little too sharp maybe. Probably, as I didn't really know how true that was.

He sensed my reluctance to start. I honestly didn't know how to. All my questions disappeared into thin air.

"Why don't I tell you what I see, *Kyrie* Stauvro?" he said, taking the lead.

I didn't say anything and he took that to be an assent.

"First, *Kyrie* Stauvro, if you are so kind as to join me in a short prayer, please." He bowed his head and murmured the *Pater imon* – Lord's prayer – in Greek.

He looked up. His blue eyes seemed to darken and locked on mine. He then closed them and, taking a deep breath, opened them.

Then his voice, acquiring a sweet tonality, changed to English.

"With the help of the Holy Spirit, I see that you have travelled and suffered much, *Kyrie* Stauvro," he said. "I see a bruised aura that I have seen before in men who have been to faraway wars." He crossed himself. "Thank God, I have not had the misfortune to have that experience …well, other than that affair last year," he muttered, crossing himself. He steepled his elegant open hands together as if in prayer and continued. "This bruising is the same bruising that I see on Joshua Emanuel the Christ, our Lord, after the crucifixion. That is how I see him on my regressions through time ... You have a gift for writing, and you pursue the truth as you see it. You have many

116

questions, as you should do, and you are currently caught in a fog-laden place you are trying to find your way out of. There is a mass of tangled negative energy, maybe a secret that you have buried deep within you … you may have forgotten that it is there. It has to do with a woman. She was someone who you thought you loved, and she betrayed that love … I also see next to you a vividly defined white angel. She's a thin, tall young woman …"

My blood suddenly ran cold.

"Yes … I think she is ... she is your guardian angel."

I could feel my mouth drying up.

"She is sad but determined in her mission to look after you. I also see other white angels that you have helped in some way. They, too, are positive towards you. But there are other angels. Yes, other angels ... who are dark … they are Satan's servants. I see one in particular who is living … he has a darkness that is almost palpable, and he holds a deep enmity against you. The others are maybe people that you have hurt in some way. They are caught in a sort of limbo, and I am able to tell you that you can finally release them by forgiving yourself. Until you have done that, I do not think that you are ready to seek the way of the spirit. You must unclutter your life, *Kyrie* Stauvro."

I said nothing.

"Have you any questions for me?" he asked gently.

"No." I mouthed, instead of *yes*, as I struggled for something to say. I was still stunned.

"Please, finish your *glyko*, *Kyrie* Stauvro. It's orange peel and is made by a friend. She uses oranges from her very own grove."

I picked up the little glass plate and bit into the preserved rolled orange peel. As always it was sweet, but this had a bitter edge to it.

"What do you think? It is nice?"

"Yes, it is. A little bitter, perhaps. But nice."

"Yes. My sister added some lime. That is the sour taste. Life gives us nice things for a purpose, *Kyrie* Stauvro. It makes it bearable, even if there is a touch of bitterness to it."

I looked at the man and tried to sum him up. He was very ordinary, other than his height and his strong presence. He was a little overweight, but he carried it without any problem. His gentle blue eyes indicated a deep intelligence and I suspected that metaphor was a tool that he used widely in his discussions. He may have been cold-reading me, but what he said about Elizabeth was something that he could have never have known.

However, despite the shock of the revelations, I was still compos mentis enough to realise that an opportunity may have presented itself here. You never know when someone else can help to give a different perspective on a story that has been eluding you. I knew that I was probably pushing my luck, but I decided to bounce a few things off him to see what his take was on what was going on around me.

"Actually, thinking about it, I do have a question, *Kyrie* Delphinidi."

Delphinidis cocked his head and nodded, encouraging me.

"Going back to the dark angels. You see, I am a writer. I have been working on an essay – excuse me for saying this – on sex tourism. I am sorry … it's something that I observed and wanted to understand. And I want to write something serious about it. I know prostitution has been around for thousands of years. But this, I think, is slightly different."

I briefly told him what happened to Mikis in Agia Napa, leaving out the grisly details of the murder and the investigation. "Rather than poor women or children, we now have poor countries prostituting their citizens to rich countries. That story, though, has suddenly taken a turn and may have instead become an article on modern terrorism. So maybe that is the dark angels that you see." I hoped that I didn't sound condescending. "You see, *Kyrie* Delphinidi, ever since last year with the coup, I have been trying to get a handle on why people are driven to do the things they do for an idea."

I stopped and put the now empty conserve plate down on the tray.

"Please be a little patient with me if I ramble too much, *Kyrie* Delphinidi," I explained. "Sometimes, I need to talk to clarify my thoughts."

"I do the same," concurred Delphinidis.

"You see, I don't have anyone to bounce ideas off … so I hope you will excuse my presumption."

"Go on," urged Delphinidis with a nod and a smile.

"I can see clearly how people rebelled against colonialism … as the imperial power that occupied them had no inclination to give them their independence because its prosperity and material wellbeing depended on its subjects' misery.

"I know that it is a strange irony, given what the Americans are now doing in Greece and Cyprus and elsewhere, you wouldn't know that once they were a colony and fought for their own independence from Britain. As you know, after the Second World War, many other colonies struggled either by peaceful or military means to get their independence ... the Indians under the leadership of Ghandi or the Mau Mau in Kenya. All that is easy to see. However, what I cannot understand is what happened after, although there is some logic to it.

"In the sixties the children of my generation were cutting their parental apron strings and looking critically at the world around them. In New Zealand, we were lucky because a social contract enacted by progressive governments allowed people to become educated, enjoy the necessities of life and the right to choose what government we wanted. Not that we didn't have our ups and downs.

"In the sixties, we wanted the freedom to experiment with finding our own path into the future. Some of us opted out of society and followed alternative lifestyles. As in America, young people were influenced through films and books ... They set up communes and wore their hair long and were proud to be called hippies and experimented with sex and drugs. Others became actively involved in urban subcultures, which led to direct action against what they perceived to be a corrupt and inflexible ruling class. In New Zealand, it was anarchist and libertarian socialist groups influenced by different branches of Marxism. It was a general rebellion against the established upper-middle class that initially got us into the wars in Korea and then Vietnam. In Europe, in West Germany, for example, their youth movement grew out of a sense of disenfranchisement as an oligarchy made of ex-Nazis was reappointed by America and Britain, who said that they were trying to stabilise what to them was a front against a new threat posed, the Soviet Union.

"In West Germany, student groups began to be radicalised and, encouraged by their leaders, took direct action against the state. Some sought military training from other groups that are still fighting liberation wars, like the PLO ... the Palestinian Liberation Front.

"Returning to their own countries, they set up urban terrorist groups with successful communication lines that cut each member off from knowing too much or too many of the movement. Some of their leaders were and are highly intelligent but, in some cases, psychopathic. One does not know if that is due to their new life-style or if they were always like this. Many now are charismatic and determined. Although revolutionary pamphlets told them how to go about organising their urban revolt, like in most revolutions, they don't have a clear idea of what the end game looks like.

"First of all, they robbed banks to buy arms and set up safe houses. Then they hit selected targets, killing and maiming enemies or supporters or members of their ruling class. Like in Cyprus with EOKA B, they agitated themselves into a frenzy, and eventually they took their first fatal step and killed someone. The brutal overreaction of the state spurred them on to kill many more. In Germany, Italy and Spain there may be no so-called 'overt war', but there is a war of sorts. A secret, underground war that only surfaces here and there, and as always those not directly affected ignore it.

"In Germany, the Baader Meinhof Gang is probably the most famous example. Like Joseph Stalin and his gang who robbed banks to finance the Bolshevik revolution, the Baader Meinhof Gang robbed banks to support their political activities. Because they are fighting a post-Nazi establishment made up of actual ex-Nazis, the German people turn a blind eye to them and in some cases, even support them.

"So … what I don't get, *Kyrie* Delphenidi, is how those groups go on and on until they self-destruct."

4

The Teacher looked at me throughout my monologue with some puzzlement, which he finally reappraised into a gentle smile.

"You obviously studied the subject well, *Kyrie* Stauvro." Giving himself time to gather his thoughts, Delphinidis took a drink of water.

"Have you heard of *Erysichthon ton Thassalo*?" he began.

"No, I do not think that I have."

"In English, he's called Erysichthon the earth eater," he said, his voice gaining the urgency of one who enjoys meaningful discussions. Maybe he is another *sympanista*, like my friend Old Xenis.

"No, I am sorry, but I don't think I have heard of him."

"Well, Erysichthon was the son of Triopas, king of Thessaly. Do you know where Thessaly is?"

"I think so … Central Greece, yes?"

"Yes. Have you heard of Demeter?"

"The goddess of harvest and agriculture?"

"Yes. Well, Erysichthon got on the wrong side of Demeter. You see, he had ordered that all the trees in her sacred grove be chopped down. On one tree were the votive wreaths hung by the devout for every request Demeter had granted in their prayers … much like the tree covered with kerchiefs and scarves tied to twigs as offerings to the Virgin Mary at the *Skamni tis Panagias* – the seat of the Virgin Mary. They can be found on that desolate promontory in Kykkos where the Virgin Mary was deemed to have rested during her travels through Cyprus, or at the catacombs of *Agia* Solomoni, the first woman believer in Christianity in Kato Paphos."

I made a note to add *Agia* Solomoni's name to the three other female saints' names I had collected: *Agia* Eirini, the daughter of *Agios* Spirithon, *Agia* Maria, the sister of *Agios* Pauvlos, and *Agia* Toulla from Rizokarpaso. Four female saints compared with approximately sixty Cypriot male saints. It seemed that equal opportunity between the sexes did not apply to the saintly vocation in Cyprus.

"Erysichthon's workmen had refused to chop it down and so he grabbed one of the axes and chopped it down himself. Inside the tree, like in all trees of the time, there was a tree nymph and she died with the tree. However, before she expired, unlike the others, she managed to cast a curse on Erysichthon that Demeter, who was infuriated by his action, used as an inspiration to cast her own punishment on the arrogant king. She begged a favour from Limos, the spirit of unrelenting and insatiable hunger, to place himself in the stomach of Erysichthon. When Erysichthon ate, food acted like benzine does to fire: the more he ate the more he wanted to eat. Erysichthon consumed all his riches and estates to satisfy his insatiable hunger and even sold his daughter into slavery. In the end, to escape his fate, he ate himself."

Delphinidis took another sip of water.

"On the funerary text on the tomb of the pharaoh Tutankhamen ... you've heard of him, haven't you?"

"Yes."

"Well, a strange symbol makes its first appearance. It is a snake or dragon eating its own tail. It surrounds an image of Ra and Osiris, unified in the underworld after their death. The symbol is a manifestation of their protective deity Mehen, and to the ancient Egyptians, he represented the beginning and end of time. This became an alchemical text symbol and was used in the second-century text *Chrysopoeia of Cleopatra*, where an *autosarcophagous* snake – *autosarcophagous* means self-eating – is wrapped around the words *en to pan,* that means, one is the all. It was then adopted by Gnosticism and Hermeticism and you can see it in the fifteenth-century text by alchemist Theodoros Pelecanos. It's a red dragon with a green belly eating its own tail."

Delphinidis coughed and took another sip of water from the glass in front of him.

"A contemporary of Pelecanos equated the symbol to what became known as an *ouroboros*, the cyclical nature of the year. In the earliest version of the symbol the top half is rendered as black and the bottom half as white. Strangely, it's an echo of the prehistoric Taoist yin and yang symbol: two foetus-like fat commas enclosed in a circle, beginning to devour each other's tails only to give birth to itself. You must have seen that symbol in your travels through Asia."

I nodded, noting that I had not mentioned Asia to him. Come to think about it, I had said very little about myself.

124

"This is a form of *placentophagy* – the eating of the placenta – which is proposed by some as a way of averting postnatal depression and as a source of energy for the mother after she gives birth, giving her the ability to improve lactation. One can argue that it is a form of self-cannibalism. Interestingly, in China, in traditional medicine, the placenta is dried and given to people to treat impotence and infertility. As you probably know, a large amount of self-cannibalism occurs unwittingly. We are, *Kyrie* Stauvro, the subconscious inheritors of Erysichthon … we consume our cheek and tongue cells without any regard to what is actually happening. And, of course, there is the unconscionable inhumanity of men to other men … such as reports of indigenous people in South America being forced to eat their own testicles by the Spanish Conquistadors and Elizabeth Báthory, the infamous Hungarian serial murderess in the late sixteenth century who forced her victims to eat each other's faces and limbs.

"I can, I think, propose that the rebel or revolutionary progresses to a stage where he transmogrifies into the ouroboros, a self-eating snake … just as a pupa turns to a cocoon and then a butterfly … and then after it lays its eggs, to beget other butterflies, it dies.

"So, it's the way that life ensures that those individuals self-destruct, like someone who sets fire to themselves. We saw this in South Vietnam when the Buddhist monks objected to the way their co-religionists were treated by the Vietnamese Catholic ruling class and decided to die for their cause. They set themselves alight. A young man, Kostas Georgakis, who was twenty-two at the time, did the same in a public square in Genoa in protest against the Greek junta in 1970. He doused himself with benzine and set himself alight and then ran around shouting, 'Long live Greece', 'Down with the tyrants', 'Down with the fascist colonels' and finally, 'I did it for my Greece.' You see, he thought, like the Buddhist monks, that he was espousing a noble cause. They

125

all suicided really, as they were engulfed and killed by the flames. Their thinking was, I suppose that their ideas would catch fire in others and they would be reborn like a phoenix from the ashes of its own fire. In our Christian tradition they became martyrs, just like those unfortunate Christians who on Nero's orders were nailed to the cross and burnt alive as torches to light the arena of the Coliseum."

Delphinidis crossed himself, to avert the evil that image conjured up, leaned over, took his glass of water and finished it. He wiped his tongue across his lips and continued.

"*Cupio dissolvi* is an interesting phrase, *Kyrie* Stauvro. It came into Latin from the Greek when Saint Jerome translated Paul's epistle to the Philippians. The phrase literately means 'I wish to self-dissolve.' Freud called it *todestrieb,* the death drive. It is the opposite of the will to live, which is manifested in the sex drive ... All those negative things like, fantasy, delusion, intellectualisation, passivity, psychotic denial, aggression, etcetera, are encompassed by the death drive. Of course, on the other side we have the positives like humour, altruism, sublimation, hope and so on.

"This self-destruction can be seen in human actions of physical adventurism or intellectual expansionism or in political movements and in the rise and fall of nations. Look at EOKA. As you said, they started off as revolutionaries, EOKA A rebelling against the imperialism of Britain, part of the anti-colonialism wave that you described. Many of them suicided for their cause, despite taking a religious oath in a religion that forbids suicide when they were inducted into EOKA. As you may know, in our faith, if someone commits suicide, they cannot be given a church service or be buried in a church cemetery."

126

Delphinidis was right. I remembered that when Vasili's wife committed suicide back in Mpalloura because she could not stand the pain and other effects of what, the autopsy showed, was a large brain tumour, many villagers implored Father Ouranios not to give her a church service nor to allow her to be buried in the village cemetery. It was a testament to Father Ouranios' strength of character that he ignored them.

"You have heard of Grigoris Afxentiou and Kyriakos Matsis?"

I nodded.

"Well, they suicided instead of falling into the hands of the British Army. But this did not happen in the counter-revolutionary EOKA B ... they had become middle class and had something to lose and although they pushed their boundaries and even carried out foolhardy operations against Archbishop Makarios that could be equated to suicide, they decided not to go to our Maker in the exaltation felt by the early Christians. However, in their act of trying to overthrow Archbishop Makarios, the elected first leader of our republic, they partook in an act of self-destruction. When they pushed the boundaries of their own behaviours and they, like Erysichthon, became the snake who ate its own tail ... they ate the body of our own republic, the legitimate government elected by all Cypriots, which many fought for and sacrificed their lives for after many millennia of subjugation. Did you know, *Kyrie* Stauvros, that only once during its history has Cyprus been a master of its own destiny? That was under King Evagoras, a descendant of Teucer, but eventually, he also became a vassal of the Persians. Some would say that we were free under Alexander the Great because they see him as a fellow Greek. Well, we weren't, as was demonstrated when he died and we became a hand-me-down to his general Ptolemy and then to Ptolemy's progeny in Egypt until the Romans.

"We now have the rebirth of this cruel blood-curdling aberration we call terrorism before us, and who is going to stop it, *Kyrie* Stauvro? No one can see the yin and yang of this situation that we find ourselves in … which they should. You see, *Kyrie* Stauvro, we will never understand why people do those things, and I hate to say this, but I think it is true, we can never know what other people plan and think. In a democracy, one relies on the law to deal with such aberrations. My view is that trying to fathom other people's actions is not helpful. The only person we can understand and control is ourselves, *Kyrie* Stauvro. That is why I said unclutter your life, unburden yourself."

He stopped and looked at me, and I could see that his eyes were welling up.

Then suddenly, something occurred to me. "What colour is the hair of the young woman that you see, *Kyrie* Delphinidi?"

"She is clear and vivid to me. Her hair is blonde and she has blue eyes. I think she suffered greatly, but you are not to blame …" Delphinidis' voice dropped an octave, "… for her suicide."

At that moment I felt the hair stand up on the back of my neck. Elizabeth had been blue-eyed and had long blonde hair …

"Her name is Elizabeth. The poor soul lost her way. She is making up for it by looking after you. She does not want you to also lose your way."

… And she suicided.

My reaction must have shown on my face because he reached over and took my hand.

"I am sorry, Stauvro *mou*, have I said something that I maybe shouldn't?" He had dropped the formal epithet and included a possessive.

"No, it is fine, *Kyrie* Delphinidi." I managed to say. "Thank you. I mustn't hold you up any longer." I got up, but he indicated by waving his hand for me to sit again.

"Before you go, Stauvro, I need to make something absolutely clear. We humans are not as resilient as we think. We find some sort of equilibrium after our turbulent teenage years, where we form the beliefs and values that make up our personality. That sustains us for quite a while, but then things happen … sometimes bad things, like the death of a loved one or a revolution or even a war. Those things can throw us overnight into turmoil … our balance is compromised, and we question our previous equilibrium, so we face a quandary of either changing our behaviours or our values or finding something outside us that helps us to rationalise this to give us peace. There is a danger here that sometimes we begin to blame other people. One of my favourite sayings is that of Friedrich Nietzsche – He who has a *why* to live for can bear almost any *how*. I think it is a good observation. He says basically that if we have a reason to live for, we gain a purpose, which in turn gives us hope and leads us to face any adversity. Find something to live for, Stauvro *mou*."

Delphinidis was not finished yet.

"A friend who went to a university in America told me about a behavioural psychologist who carried out a series of experiments with rats and mice in the fifties and sixties. This scientist placed six pregnant females in a pen. The rats were supplied with food, water and everything else they needed except space. He calculated the pen could house 5,000 rats. To his surprise, the population stabilised at 150 and never exceeded 200. Within a period of two years, the society the rats had established began to collapse and rapidly headed for extinction. Among a wide range of abhorrent behaviours, some rats started to withdraw, wither and die. They were not suffering from any physical trauma or disease … in fact, to the eye they were quite healthy. Something happened and they just died. It was quite an elaborate experiment, and I am not entirely sure that I have grasped its real significance other than the slimmest possibility in that experiment that we glimpsed in us a mechanism for self-destruction.

"You see, over the years, I also learned about how human societies have self-regulated mechanisms for self-control. They are used when extraordinary situations arise. When someone was thought to be a threat to the state or a potential tyrant and a danger to their society, the ancients Athenians ostracised them – banished them by sending them into exile for ten years. Other societies have similar mechanisms to deal with deviant and dangerous behaviours. There, instead of exile, they cast a curse on them and unbelievably, those individuals wither and die. It happens in Australian Aboriginal societies where they call it the pointing of the bone, or in Haiti they call it voodoo death, but the same occurs in many other societies. You see, Stauvro *mou*, there is in us humans a flaw. This flaw allows an outside entity to enter what I can only so far describe as a portal. This portal allows others to access our psyche and convince us, for example, that we are cursed and because of it we will die. It can also be self-induced, like when someone becomes sick to avoid something that they want to avoid."

What Delphinidis was saying reminded me of my brother Peter, who had the ability to announce to me the night before that he was not going to school and the next morning had a temperature and a fever that convinced our parents that he had a serious illness. Once we all left the house, he told me, he'd lie in bed reading comics all day.

130

"It's a trick, sort of autosuggestion, but it is deadly and people can actually die from it. I call it *autothesia*. The one thing, though, that protects a person from a curse is if they are not from the same cultural grouping. For example, a curse put on one by a Cypriot does not necessarily work on one who is from Brazil or South Africa, although those cultures have something similar as well. What I am saying is that a spell or curse only works in the cultural context that it is cast in. So when the wish to die and a suggestion to the subconscious through a curse unite, they become a ravenous worm that drills itself into the engine room of the body and then it switches off each part like a caretaker who switches off the lights to a stadium. This mechanism, this sort of switch, I call the kill switch.

"I have learned, Stauvro *mou*, that a talisman like a cross can help in those situations. By focusing on the talisman, bringing up positive thoughts or pictures and relaxing, you are closing the door of this portal. It is not some superhuman ability but an action that we can use to defend ourselves from those who wish us harm."

Delphinidis reached up and unhooked the small wooden cross from around his neck and handed it to me. Inset in the middle of the cross was a blue glass eye-stone.

"See this as a small gift … have you seen this glass eye before?"

"Yes. It's an *amatopetra.*"

"Yes, as you say, it's an eye-stone. It's there to avert the evil eye. We believe that the evil eye can even be put on someone without them being aware of it. I don't know how true that is. However, the belief in the evil eye has been around for thousands of years. Right back to the ancient Greeks. I happen to think, though, that it actually goes right back to the ancient

131

Egyptians as their Eye of Horus is also a protective amulet. The Egyptians held that Seth and Horus fought – very much the same way that Cain and Abel did, ending with Abel's death – and Seth plucked his brother Horus' eye out. To the Egyptians, the story was a fight between good and evil. You see, Seth is the precursor of the devil.

"Even the Prophet Mohammed believed in it and it is recorded in the Hadith that he warned that 'the influence of the evil eye is a fact,' and suggested prayers to avert it. This cross, like those prayers, is a prophylactic and may help you when you are fighting those black angels … Good and evil angels are within all of us, Stauvro *mou*, and until we recognise that we do not make much progress and understand the evil acts of humans."

He paused and wetted his lips again. I was sure that for some reason the man was trying his best to articulate his thoughts in order to help me, even if some part of me still questioned his logic. "You see, Stauvro *mou*, when I see the aura of a child, it is saffron coloured, like the robes of a Buddhist monk … in adults, the saffron is shaded to black, which I recognise as evil, and tinted to white, which I recognise as good. To me, you are white with patches of black. You see, Stauvro, we are all capable of committing evil acts, atrocities, when we give ourselves up to darkness … evil. So we have to fight. It's a fight that goes on within us all the time. This cross may help you regain your balance. You see, equilibrium is a very natural state of being, but sometimes we lose our balance and fall off its tightrope. We humans need this balance and we will do anything to regain it, but sometimes we create an illusion of it, we delude ourselves. It's then, as I said that we blame other people for what has befallen us … or we blame this system or that system …

"Systems are man-made, Stauvro *mou*, and because of that, fallible … although there are some systems that, for a time, are better than others. One such system was *isonomia* ... from the Greek *isos*, equal, and *nomos*, law, and is referred to by ancient Greek writers such as Herodotus and Thucydides. Although often translated as 'equality of law', *isonomia* was, in fact, something else. 'The rule of the people' probably defines it best ... as you see, all the people determine who holds office, and power is held accountable as all deliberations are conducted in public. The word essentially denoted a state of no-rule in which there was no distinction between rulers and ruled. I would argue that the Greek *polis* was therefore conceived not as a democracy but as an *isonomy*.

"But in the end, when you think of it, what all systems are, Stauvro *mou*, is forms of behaviour, contracts that we make between each other that enhance the whole of society ... Unfortunately, in no society is there real equality ... even in *isonomia,* Athens depended on the work of slaves, and women had no rights ... so really, there is no system that gives its people equality of either power or wealth ... I think we will only ever be truly equal, Stauvro *mou,* when we appear before God on Judgement Day. And as for economics ... I think that we humans should be able to engage with others in settings that are not ruled by economic considerations. The goal of all systems should be to enhance the life of all its people. So instead of seeing ourselves as a cog in a giant man-made machine ... we should be able, if we are brave enough to step back, to look at ourselves in the mirror honestly and take responsibility for our actions and make the changes within ourselves that will give us peace. We make those changes slowly, one day at a time ... engaging in things that we are really interested in, and by doing so we give our life meaning. When our life has meaning, we find peace because we are finally content. I say this to you because the only person who can really help you in the end, Stauvro, is yourself. That is all I have to offer."

He looked at me with welling eyes and stood up.

"Thank you, *Kyrie* Delphinidi, for seeing me," I said, also rising. "I think what you said is interesting."

"Interesting?"

"Useful. Food for thought."

"I am glad," he said and walked me to the door.

"Again, thank you … And thank you for the gift … the cross."

He opened the front door.

"Go with the grace of God, Stauvro *mou*, and may all your ills pass and may you live a fruitful and fulfilling life," he said, and then he shut the door gently after me.

There was no way that this man could have known that I had been in another war and in Asia. I never even mentioned that to Father Sosima. Nor had I mentioned to him or anyone else Elizabeth's name. His description of her hair and eye colour and the fact that she suicided totally dumbfounded me.

In fact, I was in a kind of shell shock.

I drove back to Nicosia as if I was in a dream.

Later, I found out that he was thirty-six years older than me and was born in the same month. He worked in the government printing office for many years but also spent some years in Africa and China. He set up a spiritual group called "The Truth Seekers" and lectured and healed people, wrote books, loved the arts and travelled the world preaching. As Father Sosima told me, he faced excommunication from the Greek Orthodox Church who initially saw him as a magus, but they were finally convinced that he was a harmless, pious man and they left him to lead his life and do good in what is a world that needs a lot of healing.

5

I said nothing to Petros about my visit to see Delphinidis as I needed to think through all the things he said and digest them. Obviously, my Cyprus experience was delivering more than I bargained for. The mystical aspect, which I was sceptical about although it seemed it was buried somewhat deep within me, had been recognised by Father Ouranios and Father Sosimas and now Delphinidis. If I was going to resolve my problems, I realised that I had to analyse the different currents that tore around in the dark and turbulent waters that I found myself in and make some sort of decision.

*

It was the day before my last dispatch on the story I was working on about Tracy Baxter and the squaddies when I received a letter from my Māori mate Frank, postmarked London. He wrote that he was owed some leave and would be dropping into Cyprus for a break. He said that he'd be arriving on the Thursday and apologised for giving me such short notice. He also said not to worry about accommodation as he had booked to stay at the Castelli, a small, multi-storeyed traditional hotel in Nicosia and that included being picked up from the new airport in Larnaca.

I had first met Frank in Vietnam. The helicopter flight I was on had developed mechanical problems and was diverted to the New Zealand base they shared under the Australians' command. It wasn't long before he and I became quite close. It was an unusual friendship as SAS soldiers usually kept to themselves. Although he followed the corps' code of silence, he and his tightly knit unit were totally committed to the team but had the capacity and training for independent thought and action. He was sent back home with the rest of the New Zealand army contingent before I was wounded.

He wrote that he was tied up with the High Commission in London. He had been in Paris during the Vietnam peace talks. Probably getting up to whatever SAS blokes get up to when they are reassigned. He didn't mention his wife, Hine, who I knew – from a Christmas card that eventually caught up with me through Reuters – had also been in London. But as there was no mention of her, I assumed he was coming alone.

Frank was a conundrum. There's no doubt that he was a trained killer, but if one simply looked at him, he looked very ordinary. I had no doubt that in Vietnam, he killed his share of Vietcong when the need arose as the SAS was mostly sent out on surveillance and intelligence-gathering operations. Despite that, the Vietcong had ascribed them a nickname, white ghosts, and put a price on their heads.

Once when we both found ourselves in a reflective mood I leaned over and quietly asked him: "Frank, how the hell do you cope with all this ... you know, the killing ... when you are in the field and back home?"

Frank looked at me carefully. He chewed on his fingernail, squinted and averted his eyes.

"Well fella, when we Māori go to war, we are sent off with prayers and blessings from our family and tribe. It's the Māori way. When we return, they do the same. Except this time the prayers ... how shall I put it ... are a sort of ...

136

a sort of exorcism which wipes us clean of the spirits of the men we have done harm to. I don't know the psychobabble about how it works ... but for me it works. It's like you peel off your warrior skin and put on your civilian one and go back to who you were. That said, I know some fellas who came back and they weren't able to deal with what they had done, including some of our Māori fellas.

Frank's IQ, like most of the SAS guys, was very high, and he had the exceptional ability to suck up facts as if they were pasta letters in a spoon of alphabet soup and have instant recall of them. I rarely saw Frank throw his weight around, and if he did it was to separate warring drunk Australians, who seemed to take a particular liking to fighting Kiwis at every opportunity when on leave.

Frank's pending arrival cheered me up and gave me something to look forward to. I spent the next two days shopping and tidying up the apartment.

6

On the Wednesday, the day before Frank's arrival, I thought I'd do some of my own digging into the Agia Napa double murder. The *Cyprus Mail* published the second scene-of-crime photograph of the woman with a brief, unassuming report on the murders. It's amazing how gory forensic crime scene pictures are allowed in the Cypriot press, something that does not happen in New Zealand. I rang up Petros and asked him if he saw a problem with me ferreting around. He reported to me that Interpol were dragging their feet and told me to "go for it" but to let him know if I came up with anything.

Armed with photocopies of the *Cyprus Mail* passport and ID pictures, I drove to the seaside resort. I was already intrigued by this case. Not because of my peripheral involvement but because I was now even more convinced that with what had happened to Mikis there might be a lead story that I could possibly latch onto ... terrorism ... something that owed its origins to the Latin verb *terrere* – to terrify – which around 1375 was borrowed from Old French *terreur* to become the Middle English term *terrour* – intense fear – and then in 1794 took a blood-tinged hue during the Jacobin Reign of Terror, becoming the French *terrible* – extremely serious ... When the French philosopher François-Noël Babeuf denounced Maximilien Robespierre's Jacobin regime as a dictatorship and as *terroriste*, meaning "terrorist", the word was then fully realised. The French Revolution and its terror sparked by the enlightenment and the disassembling of the doctrine of Divine Right – under which the monarchy through the Church ruled France – eventually came through to the present, influencing a new age of terrorism.

Now, this new direction would be easily concealed by my initial track of inquiry on the emerging sex tourism industry in Cyprus. After all it wasn't the first time that Cyprus was widely renowned for its sex tourism. Women of the ancient world would travel to Cyprus and then to Paphos to be devirginised or, according to Herodotus, "to sit in the temple of Aphrodite and have intercourse with some stranger once in her life ..."

So, armed with the perfect cover, I drove south and then east.

When I arrived in Agia Napa, I decided to get a general view of the place. I drove around for about twenty minutes before parking.

The most prominent feature was a limestone brick Venetian-style monastery in the middle of the fishing town, halfway up the hill to the left, off the main road. Unusually, its stand-alone bell tower was built high above on an adjacent terrace next to the church. I entered the enclosure wall and walked towards the entrance. After a few minutes in one of its peaceful cloisters, I came across a fountain spouting from a stone boar's head at the end of a Roman aqueduct. The water was supplied by a spring that has apparently been running since Hellenistic times. Then someone in the sixteenth century declared the water as favourable to curing certain diseases and, because of that, the fountain, the two 600-year-old sycamore-fig trees and the monastery managed to survive to modern times.

The temperature was dropping as a fresh wind was coming off the sea, so I went back to the car and got a jersey.

I found and had a quick look at the Helenis Hotel and it seemed a waste of time showing the photo to the receptionist. She'd probably either refer me to the police or simply confirm that it was the woman killed there. So I decided, as it was late in the afternoon, to start canvassing the nearby shops before they closed. The Greek Cypriot papers had not published the picture, but all the locals knew that there was a double murder at the Helenis Hotel. Just in case, I still concocted a cover story about a young woman who I didn't know, nor where exactly she lived, but who I hoped could help me find my niece who had come to Cyprus to stay with her. I added to the story that my niece's parents had had an accident in which they died, and it was important that she be told as soon as possible so that she could make the funeral in London.

So Carpenter the devious and lying prick, comes into play like a snake reclaiming its shed skin. On this occasion, it was a rueful endearment rather than an outright condemnation.

No one bothered to ask me for any more details. Finally, one of the three tavern proprietors that I showed the woman's photograph to remembered a tourist woman who looked like her and said that she was hanging around with a local boy and that they had eaten at his establishment many times.

I canvassed all the shops and *kafenía*, but it wasn't until eight o'clock that I came across an elderly, warmly dressed man who roasted and sold chestnuts. He was set up with a little charcoal-heated brazier stand outside a *kafenio* and a small general store in a two-storey building. I bought a handful of hot roasted chestnuts wrapped in a newspaper cone. When I showed him the photograph, he said that a woman, like the one in the photo, used to visit a building opposite. She'd stay a while and then would leave before he'd shut down at ten o'clock. I thanked him and went over to the building. It looked like a typical boxed two-storey concrete Cypriot house of no architectural merit. There was no sign on it, and it was on the same main road as the Helenis Hotel, which was three blocks away.

I suppose that I was really stupid doing what I did next. I crossed the street and I started calling out, "Toulla! Toulla! Are you inside?" and banged on the front door.

The chestnut seller looked at me in bewilderment as I kept knocking and shouting the name. Thankfully, someone came out of the nearby *kafenio* to buy some chestnuts and the chestnut seller turned his attention to his customer.

Finally, a woman opened the shutters of the downstairs apartment to see what was going on.

"I am looking for my niece Toulla," I said to the befuddled woman who was dressed in a nightgown ready for bed.

"There's no Toulla living here," she said. "*To diamerisma* – the apartment – upstairs is rented to a man. He is away on business."

I looked at the piece of paper that I held in my hand, raised my shoulders in dismay, looked around as if I was lost, apologised and walked off.

I walked back to the Helenis Hotel and looked at the facade. It was nothing extraordinary. Compared with the Hilton in Nicosia, it was a couple of stars down. Maybe it was special for Agia Napa, though.

I decided there and then to go inside. I went to the reception desk, rang the little bell and waited for the receptionist to come.

When she arrived she was young and good-looking, dressed in a tightly fitting, vermilion-taped beige uniform.

"I am looking for somewhere much quieter to stay," I said in English. "My hotel is too noisy and if you have a room at the back of the hotel, away from the main road, I'll move over tomorrow."

The receptionist seemed happy that she was getting another customer and gave me the rates for the room and information on what facilities were available.

If a murder had happened in the hotel, no one could tell the difference. It was cosmopolitan, smart, and seemed clean and hospitable. The candlelit decor in the restaurant that I could see through the nearby door was very tasteful, and there were already many well-dressed patrons.

I asked about how far the beach was and for anything of interest that I might visit. I left loaded with pamphlets.

I went to the Morris and decided to drive to the beach, which was five minutes away, and there I rediscovered one of the taverns that I had already visited. It was small but it was right by the sea. I went in, sat down, ordered fried squid, chips, a village salad and a Carlsberg beer. Cypriot potatoes cooked in olive oil make wonderful chips.

On the way back to Nicosia around eight, I was stopped by a police Land Rover. I was sure that I wasn't speeding, so I wasn't surprised that after the police took my details, they let me go on my way. Later, on reflection, it did occur to me that it was a bit strange, but at the time, after my running around in what became an unusually busy afternoon, I was too tired to think anything more about it.

7

About eight o'clock the next morning, there was a knock on the downstairs door. If I weren't already awake from one of my awful dreams, I probably wouldn't have heard it.

I got up, pulled on my jeans and went downstairs barefooted. The knocking persisted.

I knew that it wouldn't be Frank because his flight wasn't arriving until noon. As the hotel shuttle service was picking him up, I had left a note at his hotel's front desk the previous night, saying that I'd see him at seven in the evening.

I opened the front door and there was Petros, holding two paper bags of something.

"*Kalimera*, cousin," I said. "Come on up."

He followed me up the stairs, and while I finished getting dressed and had a shave, he busied himself, making us coffee.

When I got back to the lounge, he already had the steaming olive and onion bread broken up roughly into four pieces on the table with two spinach and halloumi pies. The smell was mouthwatering. Although he was busy sorting out the food, I realised that something was wrong. It was the silence. It hung like a mouldy muslin sack of strained yoghurt: heavy and limp.

"What's up?" I asked.

"I suppose I am to blame," he offered.

"Blame for what?"

"You poking around in Agia Napa."

"For Christ's sake, what are you blathering on about?"

"Going to Agia Napa."

"But you said it was okay."

"That's what I mean … It's my fault."

"Why? What happened?"

"Well … this morning … I was woken up by Karageorgis. Apparently, someone from our Special Branch rang him up and said that they saw you poking around the hotel."

"So?"

He stopped and lifted the *briki* so the coffee wouldn't boil over while he gave me one of his looks.

Then the penny dropped.

"Oh … I see. They are keeping an eye on —"

"My cousin is not so stupid, after all."

"So, they are keeping the Helenis under observation. So what?"

"Well, I have been told to tell you to stay away."

"Why?"

"I asked them the same. They said someone else is taking over."

"Well … I am a fully accredited journalist, and as far as I can see, I am not breaking any laws."

"Listen, *vre patiha* – you watermelon – there is something serious about this double murder thing. Interpol won't answer my calls and the French ambassador has already complained to the boss about not having access to the woman's possessions. Did anyone stop you last night?"

"Yes, a traffic patrol."

"It wasn't a traffic patrol. They stopped your car to confirm who you were. Lucky for you, Karageorgis was talking with a friend of his in Special Branch when the report came through, and he phoned me just before the boss rang me this morning."

I sat there looking at Petros as he put the coffee cups on the table and poured the coffee. Then he sat down, took a piece of the spinach pie and started gobbling it down.

"Do Special Branch get involved with the sex trade?"

"Who said anything about the sex trade? And to answer your question, no, that's CID's responsibility. Special Branch looks after internal security, just like their British counterparts do. This isn't just about some Greek boy poking a German woman. Don't you get it? … There's more and they won't tell me."

"Well, do you think it does have something to do with hijackers or terrorists or something?"

"Fucked if I know … But I am going to find out. And you keep digging, but please try and be careful. I don't want you stumbling into a bloody *sphēkes* – wasps' – nest, eh?"

"Okay," I said and tore apart another chunk of olive bread. The steam again rose in a small saliva-inducing cloud.

"You like it? Fresh from Bambis. The traditional village fare, not that crap that we get in the city." He finished his spinach pie and sipped more coffee.

"I like it," I muttered through a full mouth.

"What are you doing today?"

"I was planning to go to the British Council reading rooms to catch up with the British newspapers, and then I've got an appointment to see a criminal lawyer about the British soldiers' case as I am trying to wrap it up.

After, I am meeting my friend Frank. I told you … we met in Vietnam … he is coming over from Britain for a break."

"You mean the *Neo Zillandos lokatzis* guy."

"Yup, him. He is a good man and you'll like him. Maybe you and Eleni can come out with us one night?"

"I thought you said he was sent back to New Zealand."

"Yeah, he was, but they gave him some post in London at the New Zealand High Commission, and he has got some leave owed to him, so he's coming over to see me."

"Let me talk to Eleni. It will probably be better if you bring him over to the house. I'll cook a *souvla* and we'll show him some real Cypriot hospitality."

"He'll love that," I said, not knowing what was really waiting for Frank.

8

At seven on the dot that evening, I went around to the Castelli Hotel near the Paphos Gate, where Frank was staying. I gave my name to the receptionist, and she rang up to let him know that I was downstairs. Within five minutes Frank appeared from the lift.

"Steve! …" he exclaimed. "Great to see you, fella!"

"Frank," I said, shocked to see how grey-peppered his hair was. He wore jeans, a white T-shirt under a V-neck jersey, and sandshoes. His hair was medium length and it suited him.

We clasped arms and half hugged.

"You seem to have survived their fuckin' war, okay," he said, looking at me at arm's length.

"Yeah … I'll tell you all about it … Listen, there's a quaint little tavern five minutes away. Why don't we go there, have a couple of beers and then order something to eat?"

He handed his key in to the receptionist and we walked out side by side as if it was yesterday that we last saw each other in Auckland, after my initial time there recovering from my shrapnel wound.

On our way, we passed a line of excited cinema-goers lining up to see Bruce Lee's *Fist of Fury*. They were virtually all males and some of the younger ones were throwing roundhouse kicks at each other. I suppose if you lose a war you can't help but embrace the fantasy offered, where it takes twenty minutes of choreographed kung fu fighting before you down your opponent and finally good triumphs over evil.

As we walked to the car, I blathered on to Frank, telling him about the city walls. Driving through the Paphos Gate, a cutting put into the city's walls during modern times, I showed him where on the roundabout the Russian-made T-34/85 tank, driven by men of EOKA B, had parked during the coup d'état when it blasted its shells into the Paphos Gate Police Station, perched on the city walls. I noticed that they had already repaired most of the police station.

I pointed out to Frank the low old city gate built into the wall under the police station and explained that it was made small so that it could be closed quickly against raiders and that it was one of three gates that led through the walls of the city. The second gate was the grander of the three, Ammochostos or Famagusta Gate to the east, through which horses, camels and carts entered the city, and the third, the one to the north, led to Kyrenia. I described the eleven pentagonal bastions that were dotted around the three-mile-long walls. I pointed to the moat that used to surround the city and told him how the Pithkias River was diverted from going through the town to fill the defensive moat around the outside wall of the city.

After we managed to find a park, I pointed out a couple of other things of interest.

The tavern was small and very traditional. As always, Frank headed for the back corner of the room next to the exit door and sat down, facing the front door. It was something that I also learned to do in Vietnam and still do it so I can spot trouble and make a quick getaway if need be.

I sat diagonally next to Frank. I ordered two beers after explaining to Frank what food was available. He decided to leave it up to me to order.

After I had ordered, we sat there sipping our beers and taking each other in.

"You look like shit," he said. "You're still your scrawny self, though."

"And what about you … peroxiding your hair nowadays?"

"It's my distinguished and wise look. How's your leg?"

"Fine. I'll never make the Olympics now," I joked. "It aches at the beginning of winter. I was left with some nerve damage, but I have full mobility and get around without much trouble."

"Good to hear, fella."

"Yeah, well, to old friends" I said, and we raised and touched our glasses.

I had ordered mezes and the hors d'oeuvre appetisers started arriving one small dish at a time. Frank obviously had little to eat on the plane and got stuck in, and we spent the next two hours telling each other what had happened in the period between our last meeting. Frank said that his wife, Hine, was fine but couldn't stomach London, so she took their youngest, Tane, and went back to Auckland. She enjoyed looking after their grandchildren now while their older two girls and their husbands worked. He told me about Prime Minister Norman Kirk's death. Kirk was the charismatic left-wing prime minister who finally managed to regain power for the Labour Party, which had been in the political wilderness since 1960. Frank's encyclopaedic mind rattled off dates and figures like a machine. It came as no surprise that Wellington, the electorate that I was born in and where many Greeks lived, continued to elect a National MP.

"I took Hine down to Christchurch to watch the Commonwealth Games when I was home for Christmas. Dick Tayler won a gold for the 10,000 metres. All together we got nine golds. It was fantastic to watch, Steve. Everyone got into it." Then he told me that there was talk of a second TV channel. I think he saw that as a possible new journalistic opportunity for me.

He didn't say anything more about what he was doing in London except that it had to do with the High Commission's security, something that he had already implied in his letter to me.

"When I finish with this, I am going back to buy a piece of land and grow kumara."

"Christ, Frank! What do you know about kumara?" I asked. Kumara was a sweet potato that was thought to have been brought by early Māori from the South Pacific and had originated in South America.

"Nothing, but I can learn. It can't be that hard. Our people use to grow them in South Auckland for years for you whiteys. There's no sweeter a potato than the kumara."

"If you notice, this Cypriot is as brown as you, you Ngāti Porou racist ... and wait until you taste the Cypriot potatoes," I said.

After we covered most bases quickly, I proposed that I become his guide for the next week.

"If you want time to yourself just tell me to piss off," I added.

It was about one o'clock when I dropped Frank back at his hotel. We agreed to meet at ten the next morning to give him a chance to sleep off the weariness from the journey.

9

For the next three days, I drove Frank around the island, sometimes taking him to places that I had already visited, like the Monastery of *Agios* Neophytos and the western city of Paphos, but also other places that I had never visited before. We were favoured by moderate weather and cloudless days. After we visited the Baths of Aphrodite, a cave-like grotto with a pool where it is said eternal youth is endowed to those who bathe in it, we stayed a night in a hotel next to the sea near Latchi in Akamas, the furthermost northwest tip of Cyprus, and on the way back we spent another night in Paphos. The third night we stayed in Platres, the Cypriots' favourite summer retreat, where George Seferis wrote his famous line "The nightingales do not let you sleep in Platres." Then the sanguine question posed "Platres, where is Platres? ..." Yes, where was Platres, really ... if you are in Saigon or Wellington?

When I got home on the Monday, after I dropped Frank at his hotel to have a shower and a bit of a kip before we met for dinner, I found a note on my table from Petros. He had dropped in to feed Scipio while I was away, and the note invited us to go around on Tuesday night.

After early dinner at a small restaurant inside the city walls, I took Frank around to my *kafenio,* and as it was still too cold to sit outside, we sat inside next to the kerosene heater that *Kyrios* Louizos had lit for his customers. I started showing Frank how to play backgammon. We drank our beers and ate the roasted peanuts and chickpeas brought with them.

About nine o'clock one of the waiters came over to tell me that I had a phone call.

I excused myself and told the waiter to take two more beers to our table and picked up the phone.

"Yes?"

"Stauvro?"

"Petro! What's up, cousin? I got your note."

"Good ... actually, that's not why I am calling you. Why I rang is that we heard from Interpol at long last. A real turn up for the books. The French woman's name was a false one. Madame Auguste is not Madame Auguste."

"What do you mean?"

"The passport and her papers are forgeries. Very good, top-grade forgeries."

"So, who is she?"

"They don't know ... or so they say."

"You still think that something fishy is going on?"

"More than ever. Hopefully, I'll have something more by tomorrow night."

"Good ... I think Frank is dying to meet some genuine Cypriot peasants."

Frank laughed. "Okay. Just for him I'll sharpen my sickle and wear my *vraka*." A *vraka* was an eleven-yard length of black material that was wound around a man to form breeches – before trousers became fashionable. It was an Ottoman choice of breeches attire and now is still the national costume for

Cypriot men, albeit the elderly, and ironically, it is the national costume for the young flag bearers on national days.

I chuckled too. "Look, I got to go. Frank is sitting waiting for me. I am teaching him how to play backgammon."

"What, YOU are teaching him backgammon? God protect us …"

I put the phone down on him, laughing.

I was still smiling when I went back to our table.

"What's up fella?" asked Frank.

"I told Petros that I am teaching you backgammon and he nearly choked. He thinks I am the worst backgammon player he ever met."

I told him about the invite. We played until eleven and then I walked Frank back to his hotel. We agreed to visit the Cyprus Museum on the following day and that I'd pick him from his hotel at midday.

10

When I went around to Frank's hotel the next day, the receptionist told me that he had gone out very early, but he had said to her if a friend of his turned up to tell him that he would be there for our meeting. I sat down and read for half an hour before he eventually strolled in carrying a bag of purchases.

"I thought I'd buy some souvenirs for the girls and the grandchildren," he announced. "I'll take them up and I'll be back in a jiffy."

When he came back, I asked him if he'd had breakfast and he said that he hadn't.

So I took him to a small kiosk and bought him a *halloumopita*. He chose a Coke and I had a coffee.

While we were sitting there, I decided to see what he knew about passport forgeries.

Then I explained to him about the bodies that were found in Agia Napa and the latest developments.

I had his full attention.

"Petros said that those passports are very good forgeries, Frank. What does that mean?"

Frank finished his mouthful of *halloumopita* and wiped his mouth with the serviette. "Well, Steve, from what I have picked up in London, it seems that there are low-grade crooks who take stolen passports and change them to fit a client. There are also some like the Israelis who have experts producing almost the real thing and it takes someone with a good eye to pick them from the genuine thing. The Russians just get the East Germans, Hungarians and Czechoslovakians to issue real passports with false identities for their agents and spies. Since Forsyth's *The Day of the Jackal* came out, and now the film which has made it worse, it's become common knowledge how to get a dead person's passport – a quick trip to the cemetery to find someone who would be the same age but died when they were young. Passport security is one of our High Commission's major headaches because there's a big demand for New Zealand passports. Lots of kids on their OE run out of money and sell them and then get a new one. They can go for as much as $500 New Zealand depending on who is paying for it. Drug traffickers like them because it can get them into the UK and through there to many other countries."

"So, if there was a woman with a forged passport, you are saying that she could be a drug trafficker?"

"Well, that or a terrorist. The PLO use them to pass airport security and get onto planes that they hijack, especially if they are on someone's wanted list."

"So how does one get one?"

"I don't really know. You would have to ask around, I suppose."

"Well, if you wanted to get one, how would you go about it?"

Frank thought.

"I s'pose I'd try and sell my own passport, using it as bait to make contact and then say that I want a new identity and I am willing to pay."

"Where would you go, though?"

"Start with photographers' studios. The grottier, the better. It would need patience, but eventually, you'd hit pay dirt."

"When do you leave?"

"Next Monday."

I leaned over. "How do you feel, mate, about being my bodyguard as I try my luck tomorrow?" I said it as a joke, but I was half-serious.

Frank looked at me with his SAS look. Stern, black-onyx eyes unwaveringly focused, oblivious of friendship or any kinship, if there was any.

"Steve, this is not something that you should not be doing, mate. Some of those fellas are dangerous … in fact, deadly. Why do you want to do this?"

"Well, I thought that this was a story about the tourist sex trade. But it looks like it may be something else. Like Petros, I don't know what. But if I could find someone who deals with stolen passports, there may be a great story in it."

Frank kept his eyes on mine, still deadly serious. Then his face cracked up and he laughed.

"I think you are an idiot, Steve … and I am not going to help you get yourself killed."

"So what you are saying is that you are a useless bodyguard."

"Fuck you, Steve … Come on, let's go to the museum. Hopefully, there'll be some skeletons there to show you what happens to nosy parkers."

"Yeah, whose mates are useless bodyguards," I said, laughing.

"Yeah, you are right about that, fella." He chuckled and patted my back.

We didn't make it to the museum as on the way we came across so many sights of interest and spent so much time browsing through the Moufflon bookshop, one of my two favourite bibliophile haunts, that when we finally got there the museum was closed.

That evening I stopped at a *zaharoplastion* and bought a cake dessert for our dinner. I could guarantee that Eleni would have made something for dessert, but I wasn't by myself and I think Frank liked the fact that we were taking something. Māori have a *koha* tradition where goods or money are gifted to the host to ensure that a meeting, feast or funeral has enough food to provide for everyone that may come, which can include thousands of people from all over New Zealand and sometimes Australia.

Eleni opened the door and I introduced Frank. She was dressed in a black skirt and colourful blouse patterned with a series of entwining red roses. Like Petros, Eleni speaks reasonable English, so Frank was not going to need me as an interpreter.

Petros was in the back yard checking the earthen oven. He came in, taking off a black apron from around his waist. He was dressed in an open white shirt, grey dress slacks and brown shoes. No *vraka* or sickle in sight.

I introduced Frank to him and they shook hands.

"I decided to put on a *kleftiko* for you Frank," said Petros after shaking hands. "*Kleftiko* means stolen. In olden times shepherds who looked after other people's herds would steal each other's sheep and roast them in a closed oven so no one could smell it while it was cooking. Then they'd invite the shepherd, whose herd it was from, to share in the feast. My father said that they used to take turns in doing this and the victim never knew when they would strike so he could plead ignorance. We usually stoke the oven with wood and after the base of river stones gets very hot, we put in the meat, potatoes, onions and anything else. I have been preparing this since lunchtime.

I have not had a chance to cook this for Stauvros, but I know he has had it before at our daughter Maria's wedding."

"It's sort of like a *hangi*," I explained to Frank. The Kiwi boys had put down a couple of *hangi* in Vietnam to which I was invited.

"Bloody hell … that's brilliant, fella. Thanks, mate," Frank said to Petros, who beamed.

We sat down and Eleni brought us a walnut conserve and water. Frank was obviously enjoying the hospitality that was offered to him by my friends.

"I am sorry to hear about what you people went through last year," said Frank. "I read about it, but from what Steve, I mean Stauvros, has told me over the last few days it was more serious than I thought."

"Well, what can one do, Frank?" said Petros. "The world is full of idiots and sometimes, as happens with idiots, their brains fill up with air and then you have a disaster. We, thank God, are lucky – when you consider that there are almost 200,000 of our people and about 20,000 Turks displaced, many still living in camps. We are blessed that God also brought our daughter Maria's husband Leonidas back to us safe. As Stauvros may have told you, Leonidas was captured and held in Adana in southern Turkey. However, there are several thousand soldiers and civilians still missing. The only good thing that's happened is that local crime is down and every one, according to my daughter Maria, is writing poetry, if you can believe it. It's as if a boil burst and all the pus came out … but still, things happen. Did Stauvros tell you what happened in Agia Napa?"

Petros gave me the opening and before Frank could answer, I jumped in.

"Yes, cousin, I told him," I said. "I know it's probably not the right time, but I may as well say it now, so there's no misunderstanding. Like with you, I trust Frank with my life, Petro."

Petros looked at me, the humour disappearing from his eyes. What I said may been ill-prepared and hackneyed, but it was important to get the record straight as I didn't want anything to come between my cousin and me. He looked at Frank then back at me.

Eleni had just walked out with a tray of shot glasses of brandy and a mixture of peanuts, almonds and roasted chickpeas.

Petros picked up the nearest small glass.

Very formally, he looked at Frank and Frank looked back at him. He lifted his shot glass.

"Frank, you are warmly welcomed to our humble house as a friend, and like Stauvros, you are now part of our family."

We picked our shot glasses up.

"To family," proclaimed Petros and clinked our glasses.

I had never seen before on Frank's face the emotion he showed that night.

Not to be outdone, like all Māori in a formal setting, but unlike apparently on a marae, he was short and to the point.

"Petro, I am honoured by you and your kind wife and both of you can consider yourself as part of my family … to you and Eleni," he said, raising his glass once more to Petros, then Eleni and then downing his drink.

"Right, let's eat this *kouthela* – mutton," suggested Petros and picking up a hammer he went outside and started knocking off the caked mud that sealed the oven door. The smell that poured out wafted into the house and was mouthwatering and the taste of the cooked meat could only be described as divine.

12

We all sat around the kitchen table and the food was passed around. Eleni had done us proud. As well as Petros' superbly cooked mutton and the roasted vegetables, there were salads, fresh bread and even pickled capers and braised hare.

We ate and drank a red wine Petros said was from a vineyard in the Troodos Mountains. Then Petros began telling us how he caught this particular hare that we were eating, which led to Frank talking about pig and deer hunting with his father and uncles as a child.

"I don't know if Stauvros has told you, but my family is from the East Coast of New Zealand from a tribe called Ngāti Porou. Think of Ancient Greece and the city states of Sparta, Athens and Corinth. Māori tribes in New Zealand are like those city states. They look after their own affairs and customs, and in days gone by, they used to go to war against each other, like the Spartans and the Athenians. My mother is related to another tribe called Tūhoe. That is how we were allowed to hunt wild pigs in the Ureweras. We were among her people ... they are called the Children of the Mist because they live in the misty valleys and peaks of the mountain range. From what I have seen so far of Cyprus, it strikes me that we have the same *aroha* ... that is love ... for our land. I regret not being able to bring my wife here, Eleni. It's a pity that she went back to New Zealand, thinking that Europe is London and

160

never experiencing what I am experiencing now. You see, my father fought in Greece and Crete. He always had a lot of respect for the Greeks, and I know of several Māori families whose men went back to Crete and married Cretan women. I could never understand what he meant about us having the same heart. Now I think I understand."

It was Eleni's and Petros' turn to be moved. It hit me that night that what Old Xenis had told me back in our village Mpalloura, what seemed an aeon ago, about family, friendship and honour, was bearing fruit. That night I considered myself a very lucky man. I silently offered a toast to the old man and hoped that he had put the memories of the war and the refugee camp behind him now that he was settled in his son-in-law's village in Larnaca district. He deserved a longer life to pass on his profound wisdom to his grandchildren and others.

13

After dessert, Eleni suggested we go into the sitting room while she cleaned up and washed the dishes.

Petros offered us a whisky, and cigarettes to Frank.

Frank accepted the whisky but turned a cigarette down.

"You haven't got a liking, like Stauvros, for those foul things that he smokes?" joked Petros.

Frank laughed.

"No, actually I've stopped smoking, Petros. It was interesting really … when I got back home from Vietnam, I just quit. I think I realised that I really didn't like it and only smoked because they were so cheap and all the other boys smoked. Don't miss it. But this is a nice whisky."

"Yes, it is. It was brought back from London by this disreputable character, that we both know, who calls himself a journalist. Did he tell you about the story he wrote with someone about stolen cars?"

Frank looked at me and shook his head.

"Well, this man is a *kolokasi*, what do you call it in English? A pumpkin," he said warmly, looking at me.

"No, it's called taro," I corrected. "In English *kolokasi* is called taro."

"Whatever … you know what I mean, Frank …"

Frank looked confused for a second.

"Taro is …" I tried.

"Yes, my cousin, who informs us that he is called a taro in English but *kolokasi* in Greek … This taro or *kolokasi*, drove a Jaguar across Europe to Cyprus and broke up a carjacking ring. Only a *kolokasi* would do that, eh?"

"Sorry, Petro. You fellas lost me. How do you fellas know about taro?"

"What do we know about it? It's grown here. To the south in what we call the Red Villages, in southern Cyprus. There's plenty of water there and rich soils."

"Really?"

162

"Yes, ever since Romans times, apparently. The Romans also used to grow it in Egypt and take it to Rome. It was to them what potatoes are to us today."

"Wow! How about that … I didn't know that. Back home, taro is grown in the Pacific and imported … although some Pacific Islanders now grow it in their gardens in South Auckland. I never knew that it existed here."

"Yes, it does. It's a very dense vegetable. That's why I used it to describe Stauvros. Sometimes he gets an idea in his head and won't let go." Petros laughed.

Frank finally caught up with my cousin's humour. "You are telling me!"

"Yes, he is a *kolokasi*. Albeit a New Zealand *kolokasi*."

Frank laughed.

"Did he tell you about his latest scheme?" asked Frank, getting into the spirit of putting Marangos *à la* Carpenter down night.

"What scheme is that?"

Obviously, Frank thought he had an ally in Petros and was going to spill the beans to stop me doing what I had suggested to him the previous night.

"He is going to investigate passport forgeries and wants to infiltrate the underworld to see how you get one."

"What! Why?" Petros asked, looking at me.

"I told Frank about the murders in Agia Napa and the development that it may be something to do with terrorists. Then we were talking about how one gets what you had called a high-quality forgery."

163

"*Christo kai Panagia*! – Jesus and Holy Mary – are you mad?" reprimanded Petros, mixing his Greek and English.

"Well, you didn't think I was mad last year when I was running around with you, chasing for those murderers while that bloodbath was going on."

"That was different, it was war."

"What's the difference. This is a sort of war. Jesus, haven't you read what is happening in the outside world – the Red Brigade, ETA, Black September, the PLO – how do you think they are moving around the place?"

"And you, Mr Superman, are going to put a stop to all of those terrorists?" said Petros with an edge of sarcasm in his voice.

"No … Like a good journalist, I am going to write about it."

Stop pushing it, Stevo.

"Well, you could end up dead," said Petros.

"That's what I said to him," said Frank.

"Two against one," said Petros. "You are outvoted. Forget about it."

The benevolent feeling I felt earlier in the evening for my two friends disappeared. Then I reluctantly realised that this is what families or friends are all about. They look after each other.

I finally managed a laugh. "Okay. You bastards. You win, but if I go broke, you pay my rent and food."

"We'll get you toothpicks, too," added Petros.

Chapter 4

1

By the time Frank and I arrived the next day outside Paralimni, in the southeast, the sun was going down and casting its last rays of white gold. Going past the hundreds of rusted windmills, rotating or broken down, that dotted the lush green landscape, drawing water from underground aquifers, we arrived at the top of an old river terrace that looked across to the occupied city of Varosi, about six miles away.

I explained to Frank how the Turkish army had driven everyone out using tanks and fighter planes and occupied the city before they laid mines and fenced it off. "It is totally deserted now. They also use it as a buffer zone between the Greeks and the old city of Famagusta, that was the Turkish enclave before the war."

"So, where are the mines planted?" asked Frank.

"Somewhere down there. Both the Greeks and Turks have put them in now. Even if there aren't any, the farmers still refuse to go there to work their orchards or fields. Everything is going wild."

"It looks so peaceful," said Frank.

"Yeah. As peaceful as that strip of overgrown wasteland next to your Biên Hòa camp in Vietnam," I reminded him. Frank had told me that sometimes the Vietcong would drive an old ox onto the minefield and follow it with a surprise attack if it didn't get blown up. If it did, they would still let off a few shots to remind the New Zealanders and Australians that it was their land they were camped on.

I realised with all the catching up we had done I hadn't asked Frank how the peace talks were going in Paris, so I asked.

"We lost," said Frank bluntly. "The Yanks are trying to save face really, but when it's said and done, it's over. I pity the local Vietnamese people we dragged onto our side. No one knows what will happen to them."

I remembered the people who worked for Reuters, especially Lu Vin, our South Vietnamese office manager. I hoped that Reuters did the right thing and got him and his family out. I made a mental note to ask Terry Ogilvy what happened to him.

"Look, it's late, why don't we go down to Agia Napa to have something to eat and then drive back home. We can eat fresh fish there."

"Lead on, Macduff," said Frank uttering the famous Shakespearian phrase. I cracked a wry smile at the quote. Our English lecturer at university pointed out that the actual quote from Macbeth was "Lay on, Macduff, and damn'd be him who first cries 'Hold! enough!'" The misquote suggests that Macbeth wants Macduff to begin preparations for the fight, but the actual quote makes it a direct order to start fighting. I didn't know then that Frank's misquoted utterance would be somewhat almost prophetic.

*

I drove southeast to Cape Greco and we walked to the edge of the cave-riddled cliffs of stratified limestone that fell off into the azure Mediterranean. This was a place that had had a visceral impact on me when I first visited nearly two years before. The same feeling that I felt when I first visited Milford Sound in Fiordland National Park, one of southwest New Zealand's most untamed regions. Sheer rock faces rising out of the black waters of the fiord to near 4,000 feet, surrounded by lush primordial forests and hundreds of waterfalls, some flowing upwards – a miracle that needs to be seen to be believed.

Frank and I stood there, breathing in the fresh sea air and watching the sunset.

"Takes your breath away," said Frank, finally.

When we got to Agia Napa, I drove to the monastery. There were spotlights on, and I parked the car and we walked around its cloisters while I told Frank all about it.

Then we sort of drifted to the Helenis Hotel where the double murders of Mikis and the woman with the Madame Auguste nom de plume had happened.

Afterwards, Frank and I walked up the street until we came across the chestnut seller. The old man recognised me and asked me if I found my niece. I said that I hadn't. After buying some of the roasted chestnuts, we walked a little bit while I explained to Frank about the niece thing. I showed Frank the apartment where the old chestnut seller said he saw the French/German woman Claudine Auguste going in. We walked slowly, pulling the hot chestnuts apart, blowing on them to cool them down before eating them, and then made our way down an alleyway to a narrow street that ran behind the apartments. There was a gate and one could see that the apartment underneath was occupied as there was a light on, but the large Judas window to the right, which presumably led to a dark corridor and a staircase that went up to the first floor, was dark.

"She was probably banging two fellas at the same time," said Frank.

"Could be. The woman in the apartment below did say that a man rented it," I said.

"Did you tell Petros about this place?"

"No … Shit! I forgot …" I felt that I needed to explain why. "You know, with his boss sending him to tell me off for poking around … I forgot … I told you. I'll ring him as soon as we get back."

We walked back to the Morris.

I drove us to the same seaside taverna that I had visited about a week before. The proprietor recommended the barracuda, which had been caught that afternoon. I asked what size it was. My father always said that large barracuda can be dangerous to eat because of some toxins they carry … especially in countries with reefs and there are plenty of reefs in Cyprus. The proprietor brought the small fish to show us. The fillets were cooked just right and tasted good. With the chips fried in olive oil and *horiatiki* – village – salad, we drank our beers without a worry in the world.

Except the devil must been having a slow night. I thought again of the French/German woman's apartment.

"Hey, Frank," I said. "Up for some fun?" This was the reckless Steve talking.

Up till then, Frank was the soul of the party, but suddenly he became wary. He knew reckless Steve from Vietnam and always tried avoiding him and his ideas.

"What sort of fun?"

"Some breaking and entering."

168

"What! ... What the fuck are you talking about, Steve?"

"Well, that apartment I showed you ... did you see the entrance at the back?"

"No!"

"Yes, you did. You see everything. But you know me, Frank ... I am a nice, pampered middle-class softy who wouldn't know how to break into a paper bag. But you, on the other hand ..."

"No," said Frank.

"Look ... all you'll do is pick the lock. You go back to the car, and after I have a quick look around, we'll go home."

"Are you shitting me, fella?"

"It'll be easy."

"Jesus! Are you fuckin' crazy? Have you forgotten I am here on holiday? Imagine what London will say if we are caught." Then searching for any flimsy excuse, "I don't have diplomatic immunity here, you know."

"C'mon Frank ... If we get caught, we'll say we were drunk and I was to blame."

"What do you think your mate Petros would have to say about it?"

"We won't tell him unless I find something. Look, he is chafing at the bit to get his teeth into this thing but someone is moving the chess pieces all over the stage, in fact, knocking them right offstage. That kid Mikis didn't deserve what happened to him ... he was only seventeen and a half, you know ... and a fucking killer, a professional, snuffed him out. Just like that." I added

169

clicking my fingers. "No, I beg your pardon." I put my hand up formed a pistol with my fingers. "Pop. Pop, Just like that."

"Not my business, Steve."

"Jesus, you've turned into a wuss …"

Frank's eyes darkened. He didn't need to say anything.

"He was only seventeen, Frank."

Silence.

"How old is Tane, your youngest, Frank?"

"Keep Tane out of this."

"He's about the same age, isn't he? How would you feel if Tane was killed like Mikis, Frank?"

Silence.

"Don't you think that Mikis deserved to grow up and have a life?"

Silence.

"Seventeen, for Christ's sake."

Silence.

"Seventeen …"

Again silence.

"Okay. Forget about it. It doesn't matter. I'll come back tomorrow and find a way to get in."

More silence.

"You finished, or do you want a coffee?" I asked.

Frank let out a long breath.

"Jesus, fella! You are a real shit. I forgot what a fuckin' pain you can be. Okay. You win. Petros is right. You *are* a fuckin' taro. And I don't mean dense ... I mean *thick*. And Tane is sixteen. He's in the fifth form."

I breathed out a sigh of relief.

"Well, let's go – you pay," said Frank. "I am driving. Then I am gonna take you back to Nicosia and tuck you up in bed. I think you've caught more than a bit of that Cypriot war madness that's been going around."

2

I think the things that I said about Mikis and Tane must have got to Frank because when we got into the car, he put his hand on the wheel and sat there for several minutes.

"If we are going to do this, we do it right," he said finally.

Then he sat there thinking for almost five minutes before he outlined what he called the "infiltration and exit plan."

"If anything goes wrong," I said, "go and ring Petros. He'll be pissed off, but he'll arse over here as soon as. Here's his phone number."

I wrote it on a page from my notebook and then ripped it off and handed it to him.

I drove up the hill and parked the Morris on the left, two shops down from where the old chestnut seller was stationed the previous time. Frank would have a clear sight of the house and the alley beyond.

"Okay," said Frank. "As I said, if you hear one beep of the horn, it means someone is approaching to enter the building, two means it's the police. As soon as you hear it, get out the back door. After, I'll wait for you down at the restaurant where we ate … that's if I miss picking you up. God, you had to have this fuckin' old bomb. It sticks out like a sore thumb."

"Don't talk like that about my car," I complained.

"This is not a fuckin' car, Steve," he said.

"It suits me and it's a great car."

"A Falcon or a Holden are cars, fella."

"This is Cyprus, you drongo. It's not a nine-hour Auckland to Wellington run. Four hours and you go from end to end of this place … well, at least you could before the war."

"Yeah. Well, it's a woman's car." I think Frank was just mouthing to release his anger over me sucking him into my foolish enterprise.

"What's goodbye and goodnight in Greek?" Frank asked.

I told him. He practised it several times.

"Have you got a torch?"

"A penlight. In the boot."

"Get it."

I got out and walked to the back of the Morris, took out the torch and shut the boot quietly.

"Now, let's go … and when you go in, close the curtains. The shutter louvres are open … and don't switch on any fuckin' lights. Use the penlight."

When we got to the back of the building, Frank took out an all-purpose pocketknife he carried. Whatever was on it did the trick. We heard the clink of the key hitting the tiles. He left me to it.

*

I entered, easing the back door open, and as I assumed, it led to a corridor that met the front door. I picked up the key and reinserted it into the lock.

There was enough indirect light coming in through the narrow frosted judas window of the front door to see that the plastered interior was painted white. The staircase with its wrought-iron balustrade was to my left, rising up to a landing above the back door. The door of the downstairs apartment was halfway between the staircase and the front door. Against the apartment door was a small hall table with a vase on it. I gently tried the doorknob, but it was locked. Looking under the table, I noticed that there was a thin film of dust at the foot of the door, confirming that the downstairs apartment must have another entrance from the outside. Maybe another back door. It was an easy way to subdivide the upstairs apartment. I could hear loud canned television laughter coming through the heftily built door. My rubber-soled shoes hardly made a sound on the marble-tiled floor and I was glad that I wasn't wearing anything with leather soles. I carefully climbed up the stairs, holding on to the handrail of the balustrade. For a second I panicked, thinking that the upper part may have another front door, but on the mezzanine landing, the staircase

173

turned once back on itself to the right and I faced a larger landing at the top of another flight of stairs.

On reaching the top landing, I saw three doors and I let out a sigh of relief. One, down a short corridor to the left, one further along and one almost opposite me. This was obviously once a whole household and now it was subdivided into two apartments. *The demands of tourism,* I thought. The door to my far left was partly open. I approached the far door quietly. I held my breath listening. I didn't want to walk in on someone sleeping. I stood where I was for two minutes, but I could hear nothing else other than the canned laughter from the TV downstairs. I switched my penlight torch on and pushing the door fully open I scanned the room quickly. It was the lounge. I looked to the left and saw that it led to an open plan kitchen and dining room. Next to the kitchen to the right was another door. I quietly opened it and saw that it led to a bathroom and beyond to another partially opened door, the toilet. I suddenly felt this urgent need to have a piss. I ignored it. I then surmised that the first two doors that I went past were the bedrooms. I walked out of the lounge slowly and carefully walked to the first bedroom door to my left. I opened it and looked in.

There was a double bed made up with a colourful quilt. The next door led to a smaller bedroom with a single bed made up with a similarly colourful quilt. I scanned it carefully with the penlight. I caught myself from shining the beam on the window as I realised that the curtains weren't drawn. Moving around the bed, I drew the curtains. I opened the small stand-alone wardrobe, but there was nothing in it. I went back to the main bedroom, switched the torch off, drew the curtains and opened the wardrobe that was built into the wall. Switching the penlight on, I saw there were some women's and men's jeans and tan and grey trousers, shirts, T-shirts and several pairs of shoes and sandals. Two stylish Armani suits, one black and the other grey, were also

174

hanging up. The sizes for the man were large and for the woman what I assumed to be medium.

I went back into the lounge. I switched the penlight off again and pulled the curtains shut. I listened for any movement outside and switched the torch on. The table had a lot of papers on it and glossy tourist pamphlets on Cyprus, Lebanon and Syria. There was a portable Olivetti typewriter, a later model than the one that I use.

I opened all the drawers to a cheap drawing cabinet but other than office supplies, there was nothing. Then I hit pay dirt. On top of the glass china cabinet that had no china but a couple of bottles of spirits, there were two tickets propped up in a ceramic serviette stand. I used the torch to pinch the tickets against my thumbnail and lifting them up, I laid them on the table. With considerable care, I opened them.

The first ticket was for an Urlich Fererer, leaving Limassol for Beirut. The second was for a Madelaine Sorver. Also for Beirut. They were dated for departure two days after the German woman was killed with Mikis. Was Madelaine Sorver the new name used by the German woman? Or was it for someone else? Who was Urlich Fererer?

I put the tickets back where I found them and then went back into the kitchen and looked around. The cupboards were full of tinned beans, meat, soups and other things that one would take camping. There was a jar of coffee and a packet of tea. I opened the refrigerator and it started purring. There was a carton of milk that I smelled. It had gone off. There also was cheese, a loaf of local bread that had just started going mouldy, and there were a couple of large bottles of Carlsberg beer and white wine.

At the top right inside the refrigerator there was a small icebox. That was when I started sweating because when I opened its blue plastic door, on top of the ice cubes was a German Luger semi-automatic pistol. Next to it was a silencer. I reached to pick it up, but … Beep! The Morris' car horn. One beep. I quietly closed the refrigerator and dashed out of the door, along the corridor and down the stairs two at a time, switching the torch off as the front door opened.

Next thing I knew, there was the phut! phut! of a silencer echoing in the concrete hallway and bullets flying around me. The percussion of the rounds, despite the silencer, still knocked my ears out. I opened the back door and threw myself outside, hitting the concrete path with a thud as I missed the step, and picking myself up, I found myself running for my life. Luckily, I slammed the door behind me, and because of it, the bullets made huge clanging noises as they smashed into the steel of the door. One bullet, though, smashed through the small Judas window and slammed into the wall beyond the wrought iron fence.

I ran out the gate and turned right, trying to follow my nose down the back road to the restaurant where Frank arranged for us to meet. Although my ears were ringing, I heard running feet behind me. The streetlight bulbs were small. They hardly lit the street. The shooter took a couple more shots, and I felt the bullets whizz past me. I cut left and then right. I banged into something and it nearly took my legs from under me. The shooter was now catching up but obviously couldn't get a clear shot. Then I heard a thump behind me, and the suddenness of the sound made me turn briefly to see Frank's stocky silhouette, about twenty feet back. I froze. A man was lying in the shadow in front of him.

"This way," Frank hissed. "There's another keeping watch. He could be here any minute." I could barely hear him.

I backtracked and looked down at the guy he had knocked out. Using a handkerchief, Frank picked up the man's semi-automatic pistol with its fat silencer, dropped the magazine and threw the pistol with the attached silencer over the wall. He put the magazine in his pocket. He then searched the man's pockets, coming up with a wallet, some keys and a passport. He put those in his pocket and then indicated the direction of the Morris.

It was parked down a one-way alley, but luckily there was no one about.

We got to the car.

I was out of breath, but Frank was calm and collected. "When I saw them," he said, "I knew you were up shit creek. There were two. They arrived by car and went into the building opposite. Before they went in, they were looking at the apartment we broke into. Then after a couple of minutes, they came running out and headed for the apartment. They must have seen the penlight beam … or something. Even I saw it, fella. Didn't I tell you to close the curtains?

"So I made that I was just leaving, yelling out *yia sas* and *kalinikta* and tooting on the horn. As I made a U-turn, I saw one picking the lock and going in and another standing outside. They must have been scoping the place," said Frank. "I stopped halfway down and came around, hoping that you followed my instructions."

Frank was driving as he spoke and the Morris responded to the urgency he required from it.

"For an old bomb, it's not bad," he grudgingly conceded.

177

"Listen," I said. A siren had started up somewhere towards the harbour. "I am sure the police will block off the road to Larnaca as soon as someone rings through. Petros said that Special Branch are keeping an eye on the hotel. But I don't think the shooters were Special Branch. They would have surrounded the place. Our best bet is to take some of the back roads parallel to the main road. I know some from last year. The problem is we have to be careful that we don't end up in the Turkish sector."

At Xylophagou, we turned north to avoid the British base, then we headed towards Pyla, the only bi-communal village left after the war, and at a T-junction turned left again, away from the village.

"From here, we pretend we were heading home and we got lost," I said to Frank. "Stop and let me drive, and if we come to a checkpoint, just pretend that you are sleeping."

I was shaking and light-headed, but Frank was steady as a rock.

Frank stopped the Morris and turned the engine and lights off. Frogs or crickets were going at full bore. The night was black as pitch. We both got out and had a pee before we got back in. I could hear sirens in the far distance, but it could have been my imagination.

"Give me your penlight," said Frank.

I pulled it out of my left pocket and brushed something warm and sticky.

"Fuck, I've been hit," I said to Frank.

Frank turned the penlight on to the thigh of my left leg and saw where the bullet went through my jeans.

"I thought I smelled blood … It looks like a flesh wound," said Frank. "Can you drive, or do you want me to?"

"No, I am fine," I said as Frank poked the front of my thigh to see, I suppose, where the bullet came out.

Well, that was the last thing I remember.

3

When I came to, we were entering the outskirts of Nicosia.

"It's just the shock," said Frank. "I'll take you home … you'll have to tell me where to go. There is no way I can find my way through that rabbit warren on my own."

"Yeah, easy to get lost. Like in Saigon. We'll have to take one of the entrances into the old city," I said and gave him instructions on how to enter from Solomon Square and then which turns to take until we found the car park building.

We got out and I found, to my relief, that I could still walk, although the leg throbbed.

Mister-cool-as-a-cucumber still insisted that he support my arm. With Frank, everything he did with the superb army training was instinctive. I was happy to let him take some of my weight.

We got to my front door, and after I opened it, he flicked the switch on. I shut the door carefully so as not to alert the neighbours and we climbed the stairs.

Scipio came rushing up to me, but when he saw Frank, he hesitated and ran away.

"Shit, a fuckin' rat," yelped Frank."

"It's just my fuckin' cat, you Ngāti Porou wuss," I said.

"I hate cats," said Frank.

"Well, you and Petros makes two," I said. "But now he comes around simply to see him."

"C'mon, Scipio …" I called out. "Come and meet my wuss of a mate, Frank."

Scipio appeared, still wary, at the bedroom door.

"Scipio, meet Frank. I know you don't see Māori around here much, but they are the same as everyone else. He does have his faults, but he's okay."

Frank scoffed and moved to the table. He took the keys, wallet, passport and the pistol magazine wrapped in the handkerchief out of his pocket and lay them in front of him. He looked at them briefly, then came back and made me sit down.

"Take your jeans off," he said.

I dropped my jeans and found that a white cotton bandage was tied around my thigh. I looked at Frank and I saw the bottom of his T-shirt was missing. He saw me looking at it.

"You owe me a T-shirt," he said.

The bullet had grazed me, but it had still gouged a nasty trench all the way to the front. It looked more like a cut and the edges were swallowing up. If it had hit a bone or moved to the right and hit the femoral artery, I would have been history. I would have gone down, and even if the shooter hadn't finished me off, I'd have been dead before Frank got to me. As it was, the achy pain was what I had to deal with. It felt as if I had been hit by a cricket bat.

I told him where my first aid kit was in the bathroom and he cleaned the wound with hydrogen peroxide, and after he liberally spread the antibiotic cream, he bandaged it tightly and simply said, "You'll live ..." and went back to the table.

Despite my leg throbbing, I hobbled to the sink and made us Turkish coffees and brought them over with a small platter of *koulouria* that Eleni had given me. I also placed two glasses of water on the table and sat down opposite him.

For the first time, Frank had a look around the apartment.

"Nice place," he said laconically and went back to looking at what was before him.

"Well, fella," Frank said. "We are in deep shit."

"What do you mean?"

He indicated with his finger as he took a sip of his coffee. "First, the passport is Swiss. It's probably a forgery. From the photo, this fella here could be anyone. Secondly ... see this," he said. He pointed at the black magazine clip.

"'Yeah. It's a gun magazine."

"Yeah, a gun magazine ... but not just any magazine. It's a two-tiered *zic zac* 9 mm fifteen shot magazine."

"What the fuck does that mean?"

"It's the two-tiered cartridge magazine for a Hi-Power Browning. It takes five more bullets then the normal ten. Fifteen shots. Fourteen shots in the magazine, one up the spout. And those are Parabellum cartridges in it."

"Parabellum?"

"From the Latin, *Si vis pacem, para bellum*, 'If you want peace, prepare for war.' Those cartridges were originally invented for the Luger pistol. NATO decided to make a custom over-pressured round variant and created a standard load for it. You are lucky that the bullet only scraped your thigh."

"So, I should be grateful?"

"Yup. This is serious shit, Steve. Those are hollow points. Dumdum bullets. If it got you square on, there'd be a big hole on the other side. Those fuckin' things mushroom. They are designed to kill, not maim."

I knew what Frank was trying to tell me.

I was lucky.

"The Brownings were initially made by the Belgians for the French military. You see, the Frenchies wanted a compact sidearm that could hold at least ten rounds, a magazine disconnect device, an external hammer, positive safety, and also wanted something robust – simple to disassemble and assemble and capable of killing a man at 150 feet. It can do all this with a 9 mm or larger bullet and it only weighs just under a couple of pounds – or a kilogram as we call it back home now. I thought that was what it was when I picked it up, but this confirms it. Remember that fat thing on the gun barrel? It was a silencer ... probably custom-made from a car filter or something. The Browning is still made by the Belgians and is used by NATO forces ... however, and this is where we could be in the shit, it's also used by the new Israeli counter-terrorist units."

"What, do you mean that the arsehole who shot at me was an Israeli?"

"Could be."

"So, the woman was an Israeli agent?"

"I don't know. But they could be involved, and I don't like it, especially because now I'm caught on a piddly little island, and effectively, we are on the run."

"What are you talking about. Did the guy see you?"

"I don't think so."

"Well, all he saw of me was my silhouette ..."

"I hate to tell you this, Steve, but I think we have to tell Petros."

"He's going to go ballistic."

"I know, but as I said, this is serious shit, Steve. That guy was shooting to kill. You are just lucky you had me there to alert you."

Then, suddenly the seriousness of our situation finally hit me. "God! ... Shit, Frank ... Shit! Shit! Shit! ... Jesus, I am sorry, mate. Sometimes I get carried away. Fuck! ... I am really sorry, Frank. Jesus! What a fuck up. That's ...

"That's why I like working alone, mate … because if I fuck up, no one else is affected."

"Listen, don't worry about it. What is done is done. Can I crash here on your sofa? I'd kick you off your bed, but you'll need that scratch to heal."

"Scratch? You call this a scratch?" patting my thigh, only to get a sharp pain. I flinched.

"Have you got anything strong to drink?"

"What about brandy?"

"Fine. Let's have a brandy, and we'll hit the sack and ring Petros tomorrow. But you'll tell him after I leave and I am well on my way to London. It's been great, but I need to get out of this place. It gives me the creeps now."

"What? The big Māori fella is scared."

"Always have an exit strategy … and the only way to get off this rock is to swim. How you survived that Turkish shit, fucked if I know."

'Okay," I conceded. It made sense to me, although Petros would be furious.

4

The next morning, Frank and I got up, took turns with the bathroom and then dressed. Until then, I walked around in my underpants. I gave Frank one of my T-shirts and then I took three Aspros to kill the pain as my leg was throbbing. I sat down, took the bandage off and cleaned the wound, putting new gauze on it and tying it tight by running the tape of medical plaster right around the thigh. I put on a clean pair of jeans and put the bloodied jeans to soak in a bucket of cold saltwater, a trick I learned in Vietnam. While Frank was shaving with my brush and razor, I made a coffee. Then we went over his exit plan.

It all depended on whether he could get a flight out of Cyprus. If not, we came up with a plan B, which was, for Frank, to take a ferry from Limassol across to Haifa in Israel, or to Rhodes, one of the Greek islands. Then he'd fly from either place to London. We went down to *Kyriou* Louizou's *kafenio* and asked if Frank could use the phone. The one outside had been vandalised since we were last there.

Frank rang Cyprus Airways and talked himself into a seat to London, leaving at one-thirty in the afternoon.

"What did you say?"

"I told them my wife was in the hospital after an accident and I needed to get to London ASAP."

"That simple. I never heard of Cyprus Airways bending backwards to help someone in an emergency."

"The fact that I upgraded by paying the full one-way fare must have helped."

"I thought so. Money speaks, eh?"

"How long will it take for us to drive to the airport from here?"

"About an hour."

"Fine. I need to make another call, though. It has to be a bit private. You know, work."

"We can go to the Telephone Exchange near the museum. Just watch what you say over the phone. Petros says that their Special Branch listens in. After, we can kill a bit of time at the museum if you like. It is worthwhile seeing."

"I need to get back to the hotel, pack my stuff and pay. Why don't we do that first and after leave my stuff in your car boot?"

"Sounds good."

I paid for our coffees and then we walked to the car park. My leg hurt, but it bore up to the weight put on it.

At the hotel, I parked right outside and we went inside. Frank headed for his room. I sat down to wait for him. After about a couple of minutes, I got up and told the concierge that I was going to go down the road to pick up a paper and come back.

I hobbled down to the nearest kiosk. I bought the *Cyprus Mail* and *Phileleftheros*. While waiting, I looked at the headlines and tried to see if there was anything about the shooting.

Frank came down and paid for his room. He carried the big duffel bag to the car boot, put it in and I locked the car. He put a small cabin travel bag under his legs. We both got in and I was about to take off when I decided that maybe there was news of the shooting on the radio.

"It won't take a minute, mate. Want to catch the news," I said.

I took out my transistor from the glove box and tried several stations. On the nine o'clock morning news, there was a small item saying that there was some shooting in Agia Napa and that the police were investigating. I translated for Frank what I heard. I had thought that maybe the silencer would not have been loud enough to alert someone, but then I remembered the slamming of the back door and the bullets smashing into it.

I drove Frank to the Telephone Exchange.

"Don't forget about what Petros said, eh?" I reminded him.

He had to wait in line before he was designated a phone booth and connected to whomever he was ringing.

After about half an hour, he walked out and came to the car.

I drove until I found a park next to the Moufflon bookshop, waving to my Armenian friend, the owner, who was leaning against the wall, smoking. I pointed at the car, indicating if he would keep an eye on it. He raised his thumb, confirming that he'd do it. It seemed that he didn't hold it against me if he had heard that I was now mostly patronising Ari's bookshop, which was much closer to my apartment.

We walked to the museum. When we got there, it was closed again. The guard couldn't give us any specifics about why it was closed.

"Fuckin' public servants," I vented, "the bane of this country. Plan B, Frank. Why don't we go to Larnaca and visit the museum there? It's not as good, but it will only be half an hour or even less to the airport from there."

We arrived at the Larnaca Museum in good time without any problems. To my relief, it was open, and we paid to go in. We walked around, looking at the display cases. I don't know if either of us was concentrating. Then Frank stopped and became quite animated.

"Jesus! Look, Steve."

I went over and looked, but all I could see was an earthen pot with spirals.

"Look," he said, "It's a double koru, fella."

"It's a spiral," I said matter of factly.

"No, fella! It's not just a spiral ... it's a positive and negative spiral, what we call a double *koru*. To us Māori it represents two lives growing together."

Then two minutes later, he stopped before a huge basalt sculpture. It was Bes, the big-headed thickset man standing in a front-on squat pose I had seen on my previous visit.

"I can't believe it. Christ, Steve! This is a *tiki*. It's almost the same as the figures you see in our marae meeting houses."

I wasn't into Māori art forms then as I had only visited a marae for tourists as a kid when my parents took us to Rotorua, in the centre of the North Island, during our summer holidays, so I didn't really know what he was talking about. On reflection, now I remember that there is such a meeting house at the Dominion Museum on Mount Cook in Wellington, but as kids, we generally ignored it and headed to the diorama displays of stuffed exotic animals.

Then he read the label. "Who the hell was Bes?"

"Bes? He was a pagan god." I looked at the menacing figure whose acquaintance I had made on two previous visits. "I read he was Egyptian. But he was important to Amathus, the Phoenicians' main city in Cyprus – that's just east of Limassol. Next time you visit, I'll take you there. He was really important. If I remember right, he was the god of war and defender of good." It was then that I realised that I hadn't seen a statue of Bes in the Museum of Cyprus in Nicosia. I wondered if there was some sort of subtle Hellenising agenda going on to emphasise the Greek rather than the Phoenician culture. The struggle for *enosis* with Greece would have encouraged that. It was not impossible; when the Ottomans withdrew from Greece the philhellenic Bavarians, who sponsored the Greek revolt, destroyed all the Islamic architecture leaving what was primarily that of the ancient Greeks, and around them they built a new Greek identity complete with *foustanella* – a kilt like Albanian garb – instead of the *vraka* – breeches – that both the Cretans and the Cypriots kept as their national costume. They also implemented a purge of the Greek language, purifying it of foreign words with the *Katharevousa,* that ironically, ordinary people couldn't fully understand.

"Look, he has a broad nose like us Māori."

"Lots of people have broad noses, Frank."

"No! Look at him, Steve, he looks like a bloody Māori fella," said Frank in childlike wonder.

"He is just a short, fat man standing in a squat …"

189

Frank, abruptly dropped to a haka squat, a Māori fighting stance. He held it for a while, slowly raising himself to stand upright, muttering something under his breath. I took it to be some sort of salute.

"Bloody hell. Well, fella, this has made my day."

"Why?"

"Well, it never occurred to me that I'd see something like this so far from home. Bes, eh? Never heard of him. You learn something every day, eh?"

Frank stood there in real awe. With everything I had forgotten what an eidetic mind he had. European museums must be a mine of treasures for him. I decided this was not a time for a smart-alecky retort.

6

We decided to wait and have lunch at the airport. A few minutes after midday, I was parking the Morris. I helped Frank with his hand luggage and he took the suitcase. The leg was sore, but I suppose it was some macho shit that made me want to help, especially since what happened to me was my own fault.

I had used the new international airport at Larnaca several times. It was very basic as it was set up in two old British army hangars that were converted to house the departure and arrival lounges. The British had used it on and off as an airport since the 1930s. It didn't even come anywhere near to the stunning, modernistic Nicosia Airport that now lay unused in the demilitarised zone under UN command.

We entered the terminal and looked for the Cyprus Airways counter.

Then I froze.

Petros was smoking a dangling cigarette, with his hands in his suit pockets while leaning against the edge of the nearest airline counter, smiling at us. He looked like a hardened detective in a Mickey Spillane novel.

"Hello, boys," he said, steel behind his eyes.

Frank stopped, totally wary of everything around him. I just looked at Petros.

"*Yiassou*, Petro," I said, maybe too casually. "Are you going somewhere?"

"Are you going somewhere?" parried Petros.

"No, I am just seeing Frank off."

Petros looked at us both.

"Is that all?"

I knew immediately that somehow the cunning bastard knew what we were up to the previous night.

When I was a kid, I wisened up quickly that the punishment from my father would not be as severe if I owned up quickly to whatever I had done.

"You got me," I said. "Fair and square."

Petros looked at Frank. At that moment, Frank looked like that god Bes.

"No goodbye, Frank?"

"Frank had nothing to do with it. Let's get him on the plane and I'll tell you all about it."

Petros weighed what I said. Like all policemen, he liked to create silences, but Frank said nothing. I didn't know if he had any inkling what the New Zealand SAS went through from their own side before they qualified to join the corps, but if he didn't, he got some idea from Frank's blank look.

Petros though, didn't get where he was without knowing how to handle tricky situations.

"Why don't we all go and sit down," suggested Petros. "What would you like, Frank?"

Frank relaxed a bit, but his eyes remained alert, darting all over the place.

"Lemonade, please," he said quietly.

"And you, cousin?" Petros asked, the *cousin* grating.

"I'll have the same."

"Right, you find a table and I'll get them."

We found a table at the back of the cafe and sat down. Not long after, Petros came carrying the drinks on a tray with a Coca Cola for himself.

Petros sat down and lit a cigarette. "Let me start, boys ..." his voice dropping a register. "I told you, Stauvro, this is a small island and we usually solve cases quickly. But I give it to you, both of you nearly made a clean getaway ... So, after what happened at Agia Napa, Karageorgis brought me over the travel lists for today. We just check them after something like that to see if anyone is in a hurry to get out ... we look for something that sticks out.

192

Well, Frank, I am afraid your name stuck out, especially the fact that you changed your flight from four days hence to today. The only one with a New Zealand passport too. So, I thought I'd come over and say goodbye. I suspected my friend and cousin, Stauvros, might be with you, so I thought I'd kill two Kiwis with one stone," he said, chuckling at his own joke. "Figuratively speaking, of course. Why would I want to kill two of my friends, eh?"

I looked at Frank, my eyes asking the question. Frank finally nodded.

"All right," I said, putting my hands up in surrender. "First and most important is that we both agreed that once Frank was on his flight to London, I was going to ring you and ask you to meet me at my apartment so that I could pass on to you what we got, right?"

Frank nodded.

Then taking a long breath, I told him about the previous night. I left out the bit about Frank picking the lock.

When I finished, Petros sat back and thought about all of it.

"So, your leg is okay?"

"Yeah, it's fine. It just throbs. I'll have to go and see a doctor and have a penicillin injection."

"What do you think about the man that you knocked out, Frank?" asked Petros.

"I got him totally by surprise, but he was wiry and, I'd say, someone's Special Forces or ex-army. I think you'll find that his papers and passport will be forged. If I was him, I would have got out last night."

"It's not that easy."

"You are telling me, fella!"

"Any idea what nationality?"

"Not a clue. The passport is Swiss. But that means nothing. I put him down, so he stayed down. He'll be sore, but he'll live."

Petros looked at me. I held his gaze. He then turned to Frank. He lit another cigarette.

"So, Frank … Are you going to tell Stauvros about Limassol, or should I?"

Frank froze. I looked at Petros than at Frank. Frank took on the god Bes pose again. But it was a sitting Bes.

"Oh, I see. So it's me again, eh?" said Petros, his tone, again, grating. "Well, Stauvro, Frank has not been candid with either you or me. It wasn't until this morning, back at the office, that I put it all together. Two weeks ago, we were told by Special Branch not to interfere in Limassol if there were any, how do you say … firecrackers going up. Apparently, there was an operation by the British to locate some gunrunners who had been supplying the IRA with weapons using Limassol as the transfer point from Lebanon and Libya …"

I was stunned. I floundered around, taking it in.

I put my hand up to stop Petros going on. I turned on Frank, leaning over the edge of the table, fuming. "You bastard," I hissed. "You were on the job? What, you're back in the service or … Jesus! Who the fuck *are* you working for now, Frank … the Brits?"

194

I stared at Frank, willing him to answer, but his face was set hard. Then suddenly he nodded twice. The SAS are actually trained to resist interrogation. But, as Frank told me many times, everyone can be broken over a prolonged period. The trick is to take your time and disassemble the truth to an approximation that satisfies your interrogators. He must have calculated that the best way forward was to be candid, own up to what Petros knew and hope that the brownie points he had built with our friend were enough to get him out of Cyprus.

"Not the British but for NATO intelligence," Petros continued. "Frank was already here. His visit to see you was his cover. The British thought they could pull the wool over our eyes. You see, after last year, our republic does not have a good relationship with NATO. He did his thing in Limassol, ferreted out the Irishmen at the bars they visited and then located the ship. He left it to the British navy afterwards to board the ship and to arrest the gunrunners when the boat crossed the British base territorial limits. Apparently, they caught some big fish and lots of guns and explosives. As the British helped us so much during the invasion, our side just observed and recorded what was going on. Then they approached the British and managed to get an apology from them, ignoring the NATO part. I've been told from up high that Frank is not to be touched. At first, I thought it might have something to do with what happened in Agia Napa last night. But now I know different."

Then, as if he had said nothing, "You sure you don't want to stay until your holiday ends, Frank?" No irony. A genuine Zimaras question.

Frank cracked a smile.

"No, Petros, I would rather be on my way. I don't want to outstay my welcome."

"If what Stauvros says about last night is true, then I don't see that happening."

"It's all true. All the same, I'd rather get back to London. Maybe next time."

"Well, as far as I am concerned, I hope there will be a next time, eh?"

Frank's smile broadened.

"How did you manage to stumble across this *kolokasi*?" asked Petros.

"It's a long story," said Frank.

Obviously, Petros had made his peace with Frank, but I knew that I had more coming.

We finished our drinks and Petros and I walked Frank towards the departure lounge.

At the gate, Petros turned to Frank.

"Frank, as I said, my house is your house. Please come back soon, eh? I may need to ring you about this business … is that all right?"

"No problem. Steve knows how to get in touch with me," said Frank.

Petros shook Frank's hand and half hugged him.

Then Frank did the same to me.

"So how did you get the postcard dated just before you came?"

"Pre-planning. Left it to be sent when I phoned them."

"So how long you are staying with the Poms?" I asked, still pissed off with him.

"It's just a training programme that's taken a weird turn. It's as Petros said, NATO shit. They thought I'd blend in better. The world is changing, Steve, and our lot want to be ready for it."

"Well, I am still pissed off with you."

"Look after yourself, bro," he said.

"You too … you, you Ngāti Porou bastard," I said, my eyes welling. I realised, once again, that the disparaging parting remark marked true friendship between two Kiwi mates.

7

Petros and I drove separately into Nicosia. He led me to the Nicosia Central Hospital, where he waved his credentials and got me instant medical attention. While I was injected and re-bandaged, he went and got us a sandwich each and a soft drink. We went and picked up penicillin pills from the hospital pharmacy. Then I followed him until we both parked in my parking building and walked to the apartment. Once inside, I took another two Aspros and started making a Turkish coffee while he went to the table.

He sat down and looked at the shooter's papers, the passport and the Browning magazine lying on the table. He sat there looking at each of the items without touching them until I brought him his coffee.

'Have you got a clean tea towel," he asked.

"Will a serviette do?"

Petros nodded.

I went and got him a pile of serviettes from a drawer and handed them over. He used one to open the passport and he sipped his coffee while looking at the photograph.

"Julian Aebischer. Yes, from the look of him, he could be anything," he said.

"That's what Frank said … well, he said he could be from any European country, although the passport is Swiss."

"You say he had a silencer?"

"Yeah, it was fat … as big as a baked beans tin. Never saw anything like it. Frank said it could be something they made here from a car oil filter. He said they taught them how to make them if they ever needed one. The guns are already threaded."

Petros picked up the kerchief-wrapped magazine and weighed it in his hand. "Half full, I'd say," he said.

"Yeah. Oh!" I quickly added, "We forgot to tell you … Frank threw the pistol over a wall."

"What! Why didn't he keep it?"

"I s'pose he didn't want us to be caught with it."

Then I told Petros what Frank told me about the Browning and the Parabellum cartridges.

"So, this bastard wanted to cause you serious harm?"

"He wasn't just trying to frighten me, although I was petrified. There's nothing like someone shooting at you and all you can do is run."

"Well, what we have to find out is was he shooting at you because you were trespassing on his turf, or was he keeping an eye for someone to come back?"

"Why keep an eye on the apartment if they've killed the woman?"

"Maybe she was part of a cell or something."

"You mean, what, like a terrorist cell?"

"Why not … As you said, they are everywhere nowadays."

"And if it was his turf?"

"It means he is planning something."

"Wouldn't that be blown now?"

"Could be. But those guys always have a plan B. You are lucky that Frank was there to help you."

"Don't I know it? Thanks for letting him go. It was my fault he got involved. Poor bugger, he didn't even finish his holiday … well, after the Limassol thing …"

"Stop feeling sorry for him. Frank knew what he was doing. It would have been nice if he had tied the guy and left him."

"He saw them arrive and he knew the guy had backup. So he decided that the best thing to do was to get us out of there."

"Yeah," said Petros. "Imagine trying to explain a gunfight to the commissioner if you were killed. It's still worrying. I'll take those and see if any fingerprints can be lifted. Do you think Frank touched them?"

"He touched them, but he used a handkerchief."

"What about you?"

"No. Frank laid them out last night, and I left them there as you see them."

"Right. I am going to go home. I'll ring Karageorgis to get someone to seal the apartment in Agia Napa.'

"Frank said that the shooter and one other person came out of the building opposite."

"I'll get him to seal that place as well. I think your gun-toting friends would have left it by now. You said you heard sirens?"

"Well, I can't see how the neighbours wouldn't have been alerted, even if the shots were with a silencer. Again, you know how apathetic people can be."

"I'll pick you up at eight tomorrow. We'll go to Agia Napa, and I want you to show me where you think Frank threw the pistol over the wall. If we can find the pistol, we may be able to match the bullets to our two victims. The problem is to explain how I got those items and keep Frank out of it."

He packed everything separately and then wrapped them with newspaper and put them under his arm.

"Sorry, Petro," I said. "I seem to be getting you in all sorts of trouble lately."

"Don't worry about it, cousin. As I said, I told you to poke around. And you did just that and nearly got bitten by a *koufi* – an adder."

8

Just before eight in the morning, I was on the corner of Rigenis and Ledras Streets waiting for Petros. You could feel that winter was waning. The temperature had risen a couple of degrees and there was the smell of spring in the air despite the heavy odour of burnt diesel and benzine. He pulled the Alfa Romeo right up to the narrow kerb and I jumped in.

I had passed another uneasy night with all those Vietnam dreams. This time the streets of Agia Napa morphed into the jungles of the eighteenth parallel. Elizabeth made an appearance. Petros mentioning snakes meant there were plenty of them too. Among the many different smells of war and death that assaulted me was a subtle, tenuous, but still indefinable smell that unnerved me. They say you aren't supposed to smell when you are asleep. The strangest thing also happened. At some stage in the dream, Auntie Loulou made an appearance. Auntie Loulou was our babysitter, and as always in my dreams, she appeared totally and utterly naked. I hadn't dreamed of her since I was a kid.

"You look a wreck," commented Petros.

"Didn't get much sleep. A close death experience has a lot to commend itself for."

"Like what?"

"It dredges all of your previous demons. It is, I suppose, a humbling experience."

"You, humble? Give me a break."

"Well, that's how I see it. It stops me from becoming too full of myself. All my experiences must count for something."

"What?"

"I don't know. Maybe they eventually accumulate to some form of wisdom."

"You have a long time to go before you get to that, *mikre*."

"Go on, pull that seniority shit again. I wish you'd stop doing that … Once over twenty, the age difference means nothing …"

"Nothing? There's a difference … and you'll never catch up."

"Yeah, right. Speaks the philosopher."

I decided that this was leading us nowhere.

"So, did you get in touch with Karageorgis?"

"He rang me this morning to say the team he sent found the apartment spotless. He said there was an apartment opposite that was only rented out two weeks ago. Nothing there. Cleaned from top to bottom. I'd say that is a strong indicator the apartment was used as a base. Special Branch are pissed off they didn't find it before you stumbled on it."

"What about the owners? They must have heard the shots."

"They say they had the TV on loud and they heard nothing."

"Apathy strikes again."

"Well, that's what they say."

"Could they be being paid off by the shooters?"

"Possibly."

"Well, when I searched it, I found fuck all. I told you all there was there was brochures of Syria and the ferry tickets. Oh, yeah … I forgot to tell you, there was a Luger in the freezer compartment."

"Yeah. They found it. It's actually a Ruger. So, whoever cleaned the apartment out could not have known that the pistol was there. It's used as a target pistol. It simply looks like a Luger. It's a .22. Someone upgraded its use by adding a real silencer. How did you forget to tell me?"

"Sorry, cousin. With everything else going on, I just forgot."

"Well, don't worry about it. It's being analysed as we speak."

"So, what else? Any ideas?"

"Well, maybe it was a safe house," suggested Petros.

"You mean where someone holes up?"

"Could be … you wouldn't want too much in a place like that."

"So, there may be another base on the island?"

"That's what I am thinking."

"Well, if I was that guy, I would have scarpered out of here by now."

"Yes … Probably by boat. A yacht, maybe, waiting off the coast, pretending to be fishing. Those guys don't do airports and ships unless they have to. The ticket that the woman was going to use means to me that she was here without too much support. The question is what was she hoping to achieve … and who wanted to stop her achieving it."

By then, we had made the Larnaca to Dhekelia turn-off.

"Let's grab a coffee," said Petros, and pulled in outside a small *kafenio*.

There was a newspaper kiosk next door and I went and looked at the headlines.

On the front page of several of the papers was the photograph of the guy in the passport.

I bought the *Cyprus Mail*, the *Phileleftheros* and Sampson's *Mahi*, which was still being published. Sampson had been the acting president, appointed by the Greek junta the previous year. His presidency lasted five days. He was now in jail.

I showed Petros the picture before I sat down.

"How did this happen?"

"*Us ston Diavolo,*" swore Petros under his breath. "Sorry, cousin, I forgot to tell you. I changed my mind … I went back to the station and sent the photograph to all the newspapers before I went home last night. If you had brought it to me the first night, we would have had a twenty-four-hour lead on it, but now we are running behind. The boss didn't ask too many questions, pleased that we have a lead. I'll have to tell him the truth, but that can wait because I still need you before he throws you to the wolves." He laughed.

"What … what do you think he'll do?"

"Probably stick you in jail for obstructing our investigation." Then, seeing the impact, his comment had on me, "Don't worry, New Zealander … Mother Cyprus makes exceptions sometimes. Especially for the progeny of immigrant Cypriots who take a bullet for her. He'll make a lot of noise, but he knows that without you, we had shit to go on."

"Oh, that is very comforting," I groaned.

9

Agia Napa was quiet, even around lunchtime.

Petros had told me as we went past the Helenis Hotel that Sergeant Karageorgis thought that whoever killed Mikis and the German woman must have gained access to the room by picking the door lock. "The other possibility, he said, was that the killer had entered when the room service girl was changing the sheets and tidying up the room. Then he hid under the bed or in the wardrobe and waited."

"That's a long time to wait, Petro."

"Well, not if he was on a mission."

I remembered what Frank said about lying in the Vietnam jungle for days and just waiting, like a spider, for the Vietcong to go by. If he or his squad needed to *go,* they would roll on their side and do it in a plastic bag that they took with them. No trace of them was ever left behind.

"I suppose you are right."

*

When we got to the apartment, we found both buildings surrounded by police and also, surprisingly, members of the Army's Special Forces, the *Lokatzides*. I couldn't make out which branch they were. They were armed to the teeth, and I could make out their Czechoslovakian semi-automatic rifles. Petros parked the car and we got out. He, as usual, lead us to the front entrance, waving his warrant card to anyone who challenged us. To our right were a man and a woman who I assumed were the owners of the building.

"First things first," said Petros.

He walked through the front door and the downstairs corridor to the back.

However, I had stopped and looked at the open door of the downstairs apartment. There was a young policeman guarding the entrance.

Petros came back and looked at the door. There was a key in the inside of the lock. Probably provided by the owners. He closed and then reopened it and examined the dust on the threshold and the cobwebs around the frame. He looked at the small hall table. In daylight one could see it had been moved.

He called one of the forensics team and pointed to a partial shoe print.

"Photograph that shoe print and lift it. Someone came through here. It may be the landlord. Go and ask next door if and when he or his wife came through. Take all their shoes."

At the back entrance, there was another young policeman. Petros looked at the door where the two bullets impacted and the mushroomed lead projectiles that were still stuck on it.

"You, come with us," commanded Petros.

He approached the high wall opposite the door and looked for bullet holes.

"Where do you think, Stauvro?" he asked.

I looked at the wall. It was made of a variety of bare polytherm bricks, which are made in Cyprus from local clay and for Cyprus conditions. While I was looking, Petros went to the house next door and prised some crumbling white plaster from the wall.

When I found the first bullet hole, he marked it with a big, white circle. Then he also marked the next one.

He turned to the young constable. "Go back and tell whoever is heading the forensics team to send someone to dig those bullets out after they are photographed. Then I want you to catch up with us because there's more." Saying that he turned towards the right and looked down the alley.

"This way?" he asked.

I nodded.

We walked briskly down the alleyway. I started limping as the leg began throbbing but kept up. The first bend we came to, Petros started looking again. There was a soldier posted there, keeping anyone from going back up the alley. Petros waved his warrant card. This time the bullet hole was higher as the concrete pavement was sloping towards the sea. That was why the guy missed. That and the fat silencer compromised his aim. We walked about twenty feet and there was another slight deviation to the alley where it met a cross alley. On the corner was another bullet hole at thigh level. The bullet that grazed me. Again, Petros marked it. By then the young policeman had caught up and assured us that he saw the previous circle marking the bullet hole.

"Well, here is another," said Petros. "How many more, Stauvro?"

"Maybe another somewhere down there."

As we walked, we all looked at the walls around us. We then came to the narrow intersection where Frank ambushed the guy.

"This is where Frank was waiting. He came down from the main road that runs parallel … down there," I said, pointing west.

"Which way did he throw the pistol?"

There were three possible walls.

"I think it was that one," I said, pointing to the one on the left corner from where we came.

"Up you go," commanded Petros to his young constable.

He joined his hands so that the young man could use them to climb and reach the top of the high wall.

When he was standing on the top of the wall, the young constable walked along, looking down at the other side.

"I can see it, *Kyrie* Zimara."

"Good boy. Jump down and stay there and I'll send the photographer and the forensics team to record and collect it."

As we left, we heard a door open and an old woman started berating the young constable. We could still hear his protestations and her curses when we reached the forensics team.

"We left the boy guarding a pistol at the end of the block," said Petros to the nearest team member.

"Photograph it and bag it. Then bring it to the apartment."

We continued up the alleyway until we came to the back entrance of the apartment. It was about three yards in from a wrought iron fence.

When we went in, Petros asked the first policeman we came to if they checked the rubbish bins at the back.

"We were getting to them, *Kyrie*," said one, a plain-clothes policeman.

"Good, there could be something useful there. Sorry, what is your name, please?"

"Sergeant Barnavas, *Kyrie*,"

"Well, Sergeant, I am Inspector Zimaras. We are going upstairs now."

I think the plain-clothes policeman was a little annoyed that someone from Nicosia had taken over his patch and had already found something more that was linked to the crime scene – if that was what it was, there was nothing else left.

Petros and I climbed the stairs. He followed the sequence that I used to search the apartment. When we got back to the lounge, he looked at the mantelpiece.

"The tickets were here?"

"Yes, and the brochures were there," I said, pointing to the table.

We both looked around and I realised that the apartment looked bigger in daylight.

"Whoever your gun-toting friends were, they cleaned up everything. No clothes, no drinks, everything cleaned quickly but efficiently."

Petros went to the toilet.

"Look, they ripped it up and tried to flush something down the toilet. Not Cypriots obviously, otherwise they'd know that we don't have the water pressure to do it the European way. It's bad enough with toilet paper, never mind glossy, coated paper." He was right. In the cities, despite the finest Italian porcelain, people had to wipe their behinds after their number twos and deposit the toilet paper in a container always kept next to the toilet. The paper was either burnt or sent to the tip. For that reason, some upmarket houses had bidets.

I looked into the bowl.

"It's the brochure," I said, recognising parts of the colour design.

"Well, we are making progress. The boss is going to very pleased with us and hopefully will feel less aggrieved about you, New Zealander. Let's have a cigarette to celebrate."

We went down the stairs. Petros ordered Barnavas to retrieve the brochure from the toilet.

"Be careful, there may be something else further down too. If the water does not run easily, get someone to open the sewer to the pit drop at the bottom."

Down at street level, Petros skipped the cigarette idea. He crossed the street to the apartment opposite. We climbed the narrow staircase. This apartment was only a one-bedroom affair with conveniences, a small kitchen and a lounge. The window looked out into the street and one could see the house and apartments opposite without any obstruction. The policemen who had photographed and examined the place were packing up.

"Found anything?" asked Petros of the nearest policeman.

"Nothing."

Petros thanked him, and we again went downstairs and exited on to the street.

Once outside, Petros crossed the street for some shade. Some of the other policemen looked at us as if we were spacemen.

He took out two cigarettes and lit them.

"Here," he said. "You still look like shit. Draw some nicotine in and it will help relax you."

"I hate the stuff," I said, taking the cigarette.

"Well, what do you think?"

"We only found those things because we already knew where they were. The problem is figuring where their other safe house or base is. Any ideas?"

"Whoever that guy was, I am sure he's already gone."

"I s'pose losing his passport had blown his cover. Thank God for Frank."

"What you wouldn't give to be able to do that?"

"What?'

"That Frank stuff."

"You are kidding me," I said. "I know I did karate, but that guy would have had me for breakfast."

"Well, my friend, you must be careful. Although he is gone, he may have left belligerent friends behind, and they don't know you are one of the good guys."

I didn't want to believe it, but I think I already knew that.

Chapter 5

1

When I got home, I fed Scipio then I watered the geraniums and the basil on the back balcony and then on the front veranda. I made a coffee and lit half of an Il Moro and after switching the transistor to the RIK's Third Programme went back outside to sit on the front veranda. They were broadcasting Eric Satie's *Gymnopédies* pieces of music that, for some reason, I found convivial to my mood that evening. As I positioned the chair to my liking, I stepped on something which felt strange. I lifted my foot and looked down. It was a jagged piece of stainless steel, cut and twisted in the most counter-intuitive way.

I put my coffee down on the small table against the wall and bent and picked it up. It was about the size of my hand. I was surprised how sharp it was and cut myself without meaning to. I licked the cut on my finger and holding the piece of metal gingerly, I put it on the table. I sat down staring at it, and it was only then that I realised that it was a piece of shrapnel. I think it probably took me so long to come to the realisation because it was in the most unlikely place and it was pristine and undamaged, if that means anything when contemplating shrapnel. Suddenly an unease hit me as it also occurred to me that it might be some sort of threat. Did someone throw it up from the street to intimidate me in some way? My blood went cold, and I swear I started shaking. There's nothing like a threat where you have no idea where it's coming from to put the willies up you. I prefer threats spouted in my face. At least with those you have a choice of how to deal with them. Attack or run. Then I started looking around me, and finally, to my relief, I saw an indentation about three-quarters up in the wall and realised that it must have been lodged there, probably from a nearby explosion the previous summer.

*

I was wounded by shrapnel from a mortar shell in Vietnam, but I never saw the piece that shredded my Achilles tendon. I just took the paramedic's word for it that it was from a mortar shell. The doctor who stitched the tendon and bolted the bones together said I would be lucky if I ever walked again. I had seen the sort of devastating damage that shrapnel did to other humans, but I never got to pick up and hold a piece until this day.

I sat there thinking what Lieutenant Henry Shrapnel of the British Royal Artillery would think of my discovery. He was the one who invented this more economical way to kill or maim people and to help outnumbered soldiers win battles. When I was learning about Lieutenant Shrapnel, I also learned that shrapnel was first delivered by cannonball in 1804 against Dutch settlers on the northern coast of South America. The settlers surrendered after the second barrage.

However, the shrapnel that Lieutenant Shrapnel invented was nothing like what was before me. His were spherical musket balls made of lead – probably as deadly, but they looked less menacing. His later innovation of the shrapnel shell, where the casing became part of the killing projectile, was superseded in the 1950s by the high-explosive fragmentation shell, in which the shell casing was filled with an explosive that fragmented into hundreds of deadly pieces upon detonation. This is what was before me. I knew from my walks that there were bombs dropped by the Turkish Air Force jets in this part of Nicosia because when I first arrived, I came across many damaged buildings and houses. Many still lay in ruin along the Green Line, just down the road, a memorial of man's inhumanity to man. Some of those bombs were percussion bombs, which basically create a sonic boom, like percussion grenades. They deafen and disorientate people but leave building structures relatively undamaged. I experienced one of those explosions when I was driving back to Mpalloura just before we had to evacuate from it. I was quite some distance from it, but I did see the roof of a house fly straight up and then settle back down to where it was.

In Vietnam, there were primitive anti-personnel bombs used by the Vietcong that were filled with nails, and thinking about it, I also had seen what vicious damage those caused.

I put the shrapnel on the table and sat there staring at it, sipping my coffee and finishing my cigar. Scipio decided that the veranda was a good place to curl up and go to sleep. He made sure that he was touching my foot. I didn't know if he wanted reassurance or felt the tension coming off me and was extending reassurance to me.

2

The following day, a Wednesday, I had gone to the United States embassy to find out when their next press conference was going to be. I talked to a pretty public relations woman who gave me a couple of press releases from the speech of the American Secretary of State, Henry Kissinger.

When I got home, I found Scipio agitated. It didn't take long to work out why.

The lounge had been ransacked. There were papers all over the place and the bedroom had been tossed. One flap of the back French doors was partially open as I always left it for Scipio to go to his dirt box outside or lie in the sun and dream of catching the sparrows that flitted around him. I was going to clean up but decided to check any damage to the front door and go and ring Petros to let him know. I was sure that I had locked the door before I left. Considering the drop from the back veranda, I dismissed the French doors as the entry point. Whoever broke in must have picked the front door lock. It seemed that not just Frank had lock-picking skills.

I went down to the *kafenio* to use the phone. Petros had not got back to the police station yet, so I asked to speak to Sergeant Karageorgis and told him what happened and asked him to pass it to Petros. He said that he'd find him and pass on the message, and if not, he'd drive over as soon as he was able.

I went back to the apartment and started picking up all the scattered papers, then I decided to check on my passport. It was where I had left it, as was a jar of change that I had next to my bed. Although my wallet had been moved, it was also still there. So, this was not a robbery.

I went downstairs and found the haberdasher sitting in a wicker chair outside his shop. I had met him on the day that I found the apartment as he was the one who kept the key for the owner and we always exchanged greetings.

"*Yiassou, Kyrie* Prokopi," I called out.

"*Kali sou mera, Kyrie* Marange," he replied.

"Can you please tell me … did you see anyone going up to my apartment?" I enquired, keeping the alarm out of my voice.

"Actually, I did," he answered immediately. "A woman. She came over and asked where your apartment was as she's been trying to find you. She said it was urgent."

"Did she?"

"Yes. A pretty woman in jeans. She spoke in English."

"And?"

"I pointed it out to her as I thought she may be a girlfriend," he said, giving me a lecherous smirk and a wink.

"Oh, yeah," I said. "I mean, no. I don't have a girlfriend. What did she look like?"

"Maybe twenty-six or so. She had blonde hair and was heavily made up. For some reason, I thought she wore a wig."

"A wig?"

"You know, some women can wear them and you can't tell the difference, but with her, there was something wrong. I think it was the shade of her eyebrows."

"So, what colour do you think her real hair was."

"Dark brown, like her eyes."

"And her height?"

"She was short, about five foot six."

"Anything else?"

The haberdasher shook his head.

"Wait a minute … She wore a nice perfume," he said, that lecherous smirk coming back.

'Thank you, *Kyrie* Prokopi," I said matter of factly, and unwilling to get into the male tit for tat on the merits of perfume or its wearers, I went to the public phone booths at the top of Onasagorou.

I rang the police station and they said Petros was still out. They couldn't find Karageorgis either. I left a message again that I had been burgled. On the way back to the apartment I thought I'd clean up as best as I could and instead of waiting, I'd go and see Petros at the police station and give him my statement.

3

I suppose Scipio saved my life. When I opened the door of the apartment, he had scuttled past me down the stairs. I turned to see where he was going when … Phut! A bullet went past my face and hit the wall. That turning action saved my life. I threw myself scrambling down the stairs where Scipio was waiting. I opened the door and Scipio shot outside with me at his heels.

Another phut! and another bullet missed me by inches. I was on Onasagorou Street and saw Scipio frozen and looking around, having never been at street level before. I was suddenly starkly confronted by my vulnerability because the shooter would have a clear field if I ran either way. Instead, I ran across the street to the haberdasher's shop. I charged in and shut and locked the front door. *Kyrios* Prokopis was bringing out a tray with a coffee cup and a glass of water. He looked up at me in surprise.

"Have you got a telephone?" I managed to stammer.

"No, I use the ones up the road," he said.

I heard a loud bang outside. No silencer. Then it was followed by another. I turned and leaning against the wall I peeked carefully into the street. Then the shooter, a tall man, ran past holding his side, limping towards the north. He turned and fired a shot behind him. He had a conventional silencer on his automatic. I saw Petros diving into the next doorway, taking careful aim with his revolver. He fired another shot. The shot echoed around the narrow street. Then there was a pause. I opened the store's door and called out.

"Petro! Here!"

It wasn't long before Petros reached the doorway and crashed inside. He peeked out down the street, his revolver at his side.

"The bastard got away. Are you all right?"

"Yeah. He was waiting for me. You've hit him – he was holding his side. If it wasn't for Scipio, he would have shot me … as I entered the apartment."

"Did you see him?"

"No, Scipio drew my attention and I turned towards him … then when the shot came, I just took off down the stairs. He must have come up the wall from outside because I locked the front door when I came back and remember reopening it."

"Who do you think it is?"

"Fucked, if I know," I said in exasperation.

Petros looked carefully outside and, holding the gun up, stepped into the street looking towards the south. I followed him.

A policeman ran down the street towards us.

"He went that way," instructed Petros, pointing north.

I quickly told him about the woman and the description the haberdasher gave me.

By then more policemen came from different directions, plus several soldiers.

Petros gathered them around him and gave them instructions. He ordered two to run back up to the top of Onasagorou and keep an eye out for anyone holding his side and limping. He told one to ring through to the Paphos Gate Police Station to put up a cordon on the exit of the Paphos Gate and to send several officers in a car to close all the other entry points of the old city walls.

"He may be with someone else on a motorbike," he cautioned. "He is definitely wounded and may be bleeding. Look for a blood trail." Then as an afterthought, "Don't forget Kolokasis," – the open-air car park behind the public library in the moat.

"Sorry, Stauvro. I stopped to get some cigarettes," said Petros, by way of an explanation and an apology for his lateness.

"Don't worry about it. I am glad you were late because if we were together, he could have definitely shot at least one of us."

"Yeah!" said Petros.

Suddenly my legs went like jelly, and I sat down on the chair next to the entrance of the haberdashery.

I felt Scipio slide under the chair and rub himself on me. I leaned down and picked him up.

"Is that cat yours?" asked the haberdasher.

"Yeah," I said, hugging my cat. "He saved my life!" I didn't bother explaining further. I just kept taking deep breaths and stroking Scipio, waiting for the adrenaline to ebb.

Petros came and stood in front of me. He took out his packet of cigarettes and took two out, lit one for me and put it in my mouth and then lit his own.

"We have to do something about those *pezevenkides,* cousin," he said.

"Do you think he could have got away into the Turkish side?"

"No, the Green Line is covered, not only by us but also by the Turks. They'd be on the alert having heard the shots. The Green Line will soon be bristling with soldiers." As an afterthought, he ordered one of the soldiers to ring the UN and tell them what happened so the Turks wouldn't think they were being attacked. "The last thing we want is another war," he muttered.

"Why have those pricks decided to take me out?" I asked in English.

"You tell me, Stauvro. Maybe they think you know something."

"But I know nothing more than you guys."

"I have already got a description of the woman out, so if she tries to leave by plane or ship, we'll nab her."

"Well, you hit the bastard who shot at me."

221

"I was too busy firing at him to size him up. I saw him waving his gun around, looking for you. I suppose. Did you get a good look at him?"

"I have a feeling he wasn't the same one who shot at me in Agia Napa. Maybe his mate or something? He was about five-ten with black hair. He was looking behind him, away from me, as he went past here, so I didn't get a good look at him. He was wearing a dark brown leather jacket and a jersey over a black shirt. He looked pretty wiry. I think the jersey was dark grey. He wore jeans and sneakers. I'd say he was late twenties but could have been older."

"When Karageorgis comes, give him a statement, eh. Why don't you take your cat upstairs and I'll bring him up when he arrives?"

I nodded my head.

"Panagioti," he called to a nearby policeman who was holding a Czechoslovakian automatic rifle. "Go with Kyrios Marangos and wait. No one gets through other than us. Use your rifle if you have to."

I got up and made my way to my apartment's entrance and then climbed up the stairs. When I got up to the top, although the constable entered downstairs first, I peered around the apartment's door frame to make sure there wasn't anyone inside. I let the constable go in first and followed soon after. I shut the door and put Scipio down on the floor. Scipio scuttled towards the bedroom where he always hid if I had any strange guests. I walked towards the sink and poured myself a glass of water. I pointed at the glass to the constable and he shook his head. For good measure, I had a second one. I went into the bedroom and had a look to see if anything had changed. I then went back into the lounge and over to the table and sat down. I suddenly got up. I realised that the guy had moved the chair that I was sitting on to have a clear view from outside the back veranda when I arrived. I left the chairs as they were and went and sat down on the settee. Just then, there was a knock on the door.

"It's me, Stauvro," called out Petros.

The constable, who was beyond the French doors looking down the wall of the back veranda, came back in and unlocked and then opened the door.

Petros came in, followed by Sergeant Karageorgis. The constable shut the door. Then Karageorgis came over shook my hand and made sure I was all right. Petros lit another cigarette. I explained that the chair was moved but other than that, things were in the same mess that I had left. Karageorgis looked at the table and told me that he'd get someone to fingerprint it.

"He was just here to do the job," said Petros, matter of factly. "We won't find anything. Those guys are too good."

"I need some fresh air," I said and moved towards the front veranda, changed my mind and moved towards the back French doors, opening them wide. I went outside and stood there, taking long, deep breaths.

"Here," said Petros, bringing me my packet of Il Moro cigars that were on the bureau. I took one out and put it in my mouth. My hands were shaking. He lit it with his lighter.

He looked over the edge.

"Yeah, he probably climbed on the *fournos* – the oven – and then up the wall."

I said nothing.

"Well, let's recap," said Petros. "You got those bastards' *arkithia* – balls – in a tangle when you broke into their apartment in Agia Napa. I think the woman, Auguste, or whatever her name is, was a scout for some operation that was being planned. The shooter that shot at you first was either someone after her accomplices or whoever shot Auguste. But the problem is, we don't know if the blonde woman who broke into your apartment was part of their team or part of the team that took the woman out. There could be two teams. Also, we don't know if the guy who just had a go at you is tied to the Auguste woman or even the blonde woman who broke into your apartment. Because of the mess she left behind, it's more likely that she was sent to find out what you knew … you must have seen something that she thought compromised their operation. Think. Did you see or take anything from there that may have made them think this?"

"No, all the things that Frank picked up I passed on to you …" Then I stopped and turned towards the door. "Hold on a minute," I said.

I walked back into the apartment and then to the bedroom. I looked at my pile of books. They were strewn around the bed and on the floor, and I quickly gathered and piled them up. I looked down the spines, having to turn the odd one, scanning the titles. It took me a while to realise that Joseph Conrad's *The Secret Agent* was missing, as was *Guerilla Warfare and EOKA's struggle; a politico-military study*. It was written by Georgios Grivas and had been translated from Greek by A A Pallis and published by Longman, Green in 1964. I had found a second-hand copy at Ari's bookshop and had bought it because someone had told me that the Vietcong had used some of the tactics suggested by Grivas. I had just started reading it but, as I usually have a pile of books on the go, I wasn't making much headway.

I went outside and told Petros what I had discovered.

"I never heard of either book," said Petros. "What are they about?"

I gave him a rundown on what the Grivas book was about and then described the plot of *The Secret Agent*.

"I can't see why anyone would want either book," I said, perplexed. "They are both second-hand books and I bought them from Ari's, the Armenian book shop, you know, Le Mouton Enragé ... in the old city ... just down the road. They are both out of print. I think the Conrad book was published at the beginning of the century ... it's a great story ... it involves the bombing of the Greenwich Observatory in London by the leader of an anarchist group who works as a secret agent for a foreign power. Conrad based his novel on an actual event, where an anarchist accidentally blows himself up not far from the Greenwich Observatory. It's basically about an incompetent spy who owns a shop in Soho, the red-light district of London, and among other things he sells pornographic magazines and prophylactics.

"Eventually, his handler coerces him to prove his worth as an asset. He persuades his feeble-minded brother-in-law to blow up the observatory, but the brother-in-law stumbles and blows himself up. The police find the young man's coat with his name on it and trace it to the spy. Then things get progressively worse. It's a tragedy really, worthy of Sophocles, but wonderfully written. It's a grim story, but I can't see why someone would steal it when they can buy a copy from a bookshop. It's still pretty popular."

"Why did you buy it?"

"Well, I have made a point since leaving Vietnam of reading some of the classics, and this is one of them. It's also a first edition. I suppose, like others, I hope one day to have my own house and I would like to set up my own library of classic novels and other books."

"Can you see anything parallel or the same between this writer's book and the events that we are caught up in?"

"Well, other than perhaps we are dealing with spies or terrorists … not really."

"What about the Grivas book?"

"Well, I have been working on another book on Vietnam and I thought it would be good to compare Grivas' methods and strategies with those of the Vietcong. I don't know how true it is, but as I said, I heard from someone that their military strategists had studied his book."

"So, what have those books got to do with what's happening."

"Well, other than that Grivas was an expert on guerrilla warfare, nothing really. It is well known that the Palestinian Liberation Front is offering free training to European terrorists who want to take on their respective governments, and I can't see what this book has in it that would be of relevance now. It could be a solidarity thing … between terrorists, I suppose."

"What a sort of *ifisi* – detente?"

"Could be. They do happen, you know, sometimes even between enemies."

"What, *my enemy's enemy is my friend* sort of thing?"

"Yeah … like EOKA's collaboration with the IRA."

"What? Did they?"

"Yeah, well, it's not widely advertised. Ask Terry Ogilvy next time he comes over … Similar to that IRA thing that Frank was involved in, but it happened a long time ago."

"What. The 1950s?"

"Yeah, the 1950s."

Then Petros stopped and clicked his fingers. "Cousin … do you remember the story I told you about the goat I shot when we were stationed on the Pentadactylos on coast watch?"

"Which led to you meeting Eleni?"

"That's right. Maybe it was an Irish boat we were looking out for?"

"It could have been … but I think it was later, Petro. Charles Foley says in his book that at the beginning, a lot of guns were imported from Greece."

"Yeah, the St George caique incident. But that was in Paphos." Petros was right. The British intercepted the fishing boat in 1955, carrying arms and explosives.

"Well, Terry says that the EOKA–IRA connection is a fact. He has written about it. He told me that after the British started hanging young EOKA fighters, the other prisoners rioted. After quelling the riot, the British flew the ringleaders to serve their time in Britain, where they met imprisoned IRA members. They had a common cause and became brothers in arms. That was when they started cooperating. No one has denied it so far, as he keeps telling me, so it's a fact."

"It's a bloody wasps' nest, that's what it is, God protect us," said Petros and sat down and lit another cigarette.

4

The next day, the Thursday, Petros and I met at the Hilton for coffee. The waiter must have recognised me from the previous year.

"It's been a long time since we last saw you, Mr Carpenter," he said.

"You people managed to sort out all the damage from the war?" I inquired, mostly out of politeness.

"Yes. We have redecorated. The war is behind us and the tourists are coming back. It is going to be a busy season."

"That is good to hear," I said, taking out my Il Moro cigars. The waiter rushed over to another table and brought me an ashtray.

Just then, Petros arrived and we shook hands. I ordered a coffee for him and sandwiches for both of us.

We both lit up and I sat there waiting for him to start.

"I've had a hell of a morning," he said. "The head of KYP ordered me to get to the Presidential Palace, and then when I got there, he proceeded to give me a bollocking."

"The head of KYP? What the hell has he got to do with it all?"

" 'I'll send you back to chasing poachers!' he screamed. 'How dare you do this, how dare you do that …!' He said, I should be shot for letting Frank go … he was shouting so loudly that Archbishop Makarios came out of his office to calm him down."

"What, the president?"

"Yes."

"You met the president?"

"Well, if you can call it that, although I kissed his hand, and he asked me where I was working now as he said he heard about the case we solved last year. He seemed amused by the whole shouting thing, and I think the KYP guy got even angrier because of it."

"I am sorry," I offered. "It was just a matter of time before Frank's presence was leaked out."

"Well, I am on notice now. He, the KYP *mangas* – hipster – said that you and I will be in great trouble if I don't get a result. What he means by that, fucked if I know, although those secret service *manges* can make life difficult for one."

The coffee and the sandwiches arrived and we both extinguished our cigarettes and got stuck in.

When we finished, Petros lit up another cigarette.

"Well, I managed to get some information from the KYP prick, even if he was raging most of the time. It seems that they had been following a hit team that arrived by boat on the island and had lost them. They think they may be terrorists and laughed when I suggested that they may be Mossad. 'They aren't Mossad,' said the prick 'If they were, we would know.' "

"How would they know that?" I asked.

"Because of their military service, they can't help but look like soldiers. We tend to let our agents gain some fat, so they blend in … or so the word that is out, says."

"So you think the guy who shot me was Mossad? Frank did say that the magazine is from a Browning and that the Israelis also use them."

"I really don't know, Stauvro. It could be. Maybe he and the woman were working together sort of undercover, using the Agia Napa apartment for something, or maybe she was his target."

"Do you think they may be connected with what Frank was doing here?"

"I can't see it really. That had to do with the IRA and guns. Oh, I forgot! We finally got the report back from the lab. The Browning magazine and silencer had no fingerprints on them and neither did the bullets. The Ruger that was in the apartment and the bullets match the gun that killed the Auguste woman and the boy, though. They found fingerprints on it, but they are smudged."

"What? I don't get it. A professional wouldn't leave any fingerprints, would they?"

"Maybe he was careless. We know the gun was used and then returned to the apartment by someone. The smudged fingerprints may be those of a previous user. Maybe an accomplice. Or maybe they are trying to frame someone."

"Well, I can't see Mossad killing her and leaving the gun behind, Petro. In fact, why would someone return and leave the gun in the icebox of the refrigerator? They could have kept it or thrown it into the sea."

"There are a lot of questions we don't have the answers to, Stauvro."

"Well, I have to go now," I said, getting up. "I am doing another story on the British base at Akrotiri for Reuters. They need it as background for something someone is brewing. I am going home to feed Scipio, and then I may go to the American embassy and see what they have to say about things at the moment."

"Thanks for the coffee," said Petros. I left some money for the waiter, more than I should have, but he did remember me. We both got up, shook hands, patted each other on the shoulder and parted.

5

I had spent Friday afternoon at the American Information Centre in Nicosia, looking for anything that I could find on terrorism and the CIA. I also looked up KYP but could find very little information. I had asked Petros to tell me where their offices were, but the place he told me was so discreet that initially I thought he had just told me any old address so I would shut up. It was an indistinguishable concrete building in Agios Andreas, just northwest of the Cyprus Museum.

It was while I was in the American Information Centre's reading room, thinking about what Petros had said, that it occurred to me that maybe it was KYP that had leaked where I lived and that they may be collaborating with one of the groups that were stalking me. I suppose what sprang the thought was the conversation I had with my cousin about my enemy's enemy thing. I was almost absolutely sure that no one would have seen me well enough to identify me when Frank and I broke into the apartment in Agia Napa. It was dark, despite the small street lamps, and we were both careful. I made a list of all the people who knew that I was in Agia Napa. There was Petros, Sergeant Karageorgis, maybe Inspector Phantis, Petros' boss and the commissioner. It was the report from Special Branch, telling the police that I had been in Agia Napa, that Karageorgis had intercepted. So I included them. There's no doubt that Special Branch would have discussed the case and maybe passed my name on to KYP. Petros was hauled over the coals by the head of KYP about letting Frank go. One of those two must have leaked my apartment address in Nicosia for the woman to come around. She might be an agent or a bona fide accredited diplomat. Or she might simply work at an embassy. It's not unknown for tea ladies, gardeners and journalists to infiltrate and act on behalf of another country's intelligence services, as I was aware from reading Cold War newspaper revelations. Both the CIA and MI6 used them for what were called soft operations. Mainly to gain unclassified information. The problem was whether the KYP leaker was a subversive or was following a presidential directive.

6

The next day, Petros suggested that we meet up as Karageorgis had managed to get some information from someone he knew in KYP.

"It's something that Karageorgis and I can lose our job over, Stauvro," he cautioned. "So it does not go anywhere ... it stays between us. Ground rules, triple."

"That's fine," I said.

We decided to meet at a *kafenio* outside the city walls on Makarios III Avenue, which, with its Italian and French high fashion boutiques, was the trendy place to have a coffee nowadays.

"Well, apparently Karageorgis' friend," began Petros, "has been keeping an eye on one of his officers who has strayed and is bedding a woman who is the cultural affairs officer at the West German embassy. I don't know if you know, but Germany was the first country to recognise our republic in 1960. The man's name is Pyros Patroklou … he is an army officer who was drafted into KYP after the war last year. I can't remember if I mentioned it before, but KYP is mainly made up of ex-police officers and ex-army men from different ranks but of Greek Cypriot descent."

"No. I must have missed it if you did."

"Well, they are chosen by the president personally, and he tries to ensure that he has their loyalty, although we know after what happened last year with the coup that it's bullshit. Anyway, Patroklos – his father-in-law is Matsoukas, the construction magnate – is seeing this woman who is attached to the German embassy. Karageorgis' friend suspects she works for West German intelligence. So, like all embassy staff, she has diplomatic immunity. So if we can prove that she broke into your apartment, we can only throw her out of the country. Karageorgis' KYP friend thinks that there may be a link between her and Mikis' girlfriend Madame Auguste's death. I think the link is tenuous as it's really only because they are both German. The man who lived in the apartment could be another German, but so far, all we are hitting is false names and ambiguous descriptions. KYP are keeping it quiet, but Karageorgis' friend said he had to tell him because the woman is now connected to our case and he wants us to ensure we don't give the game away. So, what do you think?

"You won't believe it, cousin, but it actually did occur to me yesterday that maybe the leak was from KYP and there might be an embassy connection. So … This is how she found my address … through this Patroklos guy?"

"Sometimes, some men should swallow their own cock, eh Stauvro *mou*?"

"Is that a wise Cypriot saying, cousin?"

"No. I just made it up."

7

I parked the car in Hippocratous Street and entered Ari's Le Mouton Enragé bookshop. I still thought that *The Angry Sheep* was a great name for a bookshop. I also found it amusing, what with the Moufflon bookshop also named after a sheep. *Moufflon* are the wild sheep of Cyprus that roam the Troodos Mountains on the Paphos side and they are protected. The Moufflon bookshop was also set up by an Armenian, the father of the current owner. He escaped the Armenian genocide as a teenager, and instead of going through to Alexandria decided to stop here, raised a family and wrote the first travel guide on Cyprus. It was his son that waved to me several days ago when Frank and I parked outside his shop. Ari's family, though, apparently had lived for generations in Cyprus as in AD 578 more than 10,000 Armenian prisoners were captured by the Byzantine general Maurice the Cappadocian when fighting the Persians and 3350 of those were exiled to Cyprus.

It seemed as if those two representatives of one of Cyprus' influential minority had some sort of a competitive branding war going on between their bookshops. I kept reminding myself to ask Ari if that was the case, but I knew that, as always, his ebullience would take over and I'd forget.

Although Ari was with a customer, his black eyes, as always, lit up and he gave me a brief wave acknowledging my presence. I loved looking around bookshops and since my arrival in Cyprus, would often do the rounds to supplement my reading with books that I could not get from the UN library bus. Usually, I used the Moufflon bookshop. I only discovered Ari's bookshop after I moved into the old city walls of Nicosia because it was tucked in a dark, little side street. I was amazed at how many tiny, discreet shops existed within the city walls, mainly artisan shops. Per head of population, Cyprus probably had the highest number of shoe cobblers in the world.

The customer, satisfied with the suggested book, paid and left. Ari's bulk moved on me like a great battleship. He grabbed and shook my hand and gave me a half hug. His white shirt was pushed to its limits by his large stomach, which for some reason, made him look strong rather than fat. His builder-like arms probably completed that impression. He was clean-shaven, bar the short goatee and moustache, and wore round, gold-rimmed glasses. His shiny black hair was held down with some sort of cream. Whenever I saw Ari, I was always reminded of the Nazi stereotype of the hook-nosed Jew. When I was in France and Italy, I saw many men with large hooters that they'd refer to as Roman noses. Ari was a large-nosed Armenian. There may have been many hooked nosed Ashkenazi Jews in Europe because of interbreeding, but from personal experience a large nose was also to be found throughout the Middle East including Iran and Iraq, and it was not necessarily an indication of one's ethnic background, despite what Goebbels and his Nazi minions claimed. In fact, there were many Cypriots with such long but graceful proboscis.

"Steve, good to see you, my friend," he beamed. "How is the Fourth Estate treating you?"

"I am still scraping a living, Ari," I said. "How are you?"

"I am great. Coffee? Lemonade? What? You name it." He hadn't changed much since I last saw him, and I quickly realised that like everyone, he, too, had lost weight. But not enough to diminish his substantial bulk.

"A chamomile tea, if it's possible."

"Of course, no problem. I'll put the kettle on."

"Come and sit down," he said, pushing a chair my way as he moved to the little table where he had a kettle on a small Primus.

"I've managed to get my darkroom going," he said, as he arranged the loose chamomile leaves into a little dipper that he unscrewed and then lay out a cup from a rack on the wall. "I've been doing a great series of photos on our cemetery next to the Ledra Palace. You know … photographing the tombstones … so our history in Cyprus is not obliterated. When I saw the damage that the Turkish bombs had done after the war around the Ledra Palace, I realised how easily our presence can be erased from here as well."

"You should have an exhibition," I suggested.

Once the water boiled, he poured it in the cup and hung the dipper in it. He brought it over with a plate of *kourampiedes,* an almond-filled shortbread, that magically appeared from somewhere.

"No one would come," he continued, as he lay everything before me on another chair. "Here in Cyprus, no one appreciates photography. When George Seferis visited the bookshop, he said it was the same in Greece. Did you know he was an excellent photographer?"

"You met Seferis? No, I know him only by his poetry."

"Yeah, when he visited with his friend Diamantis, the artist, they would sit down and we'd have a coffee together." Adamantios Diamantis, who I had met when I did an ephemeral story on Cypriot artists, is a modernist and, like many Cypriot artists, a former Lyceum art teacher. I still saw him occasionally on the way to and from the apartment and he would wave to me.

"Seferis had a Leica like mine," continued Ari, "He used photography as a memory aid and was great at capturing a parallel, more complex essence of our modern world with all its tragic overtones. I think it helped his poetic voice by calming and focusing his visual eye."

Then he went back to the rack and picked another cup for himself. "Listen to me, rabbiting on … Now, what can I do for you, my friend?"

I thought that the best way was to be direct.

"Ari, do you remember that Conrad first edition that I bought off you?"

"Yes, of course."

"And also that Grivas guerrilla warfare book that you got for me?"

"Yes."

"They were both second-hand, yes?"

"Yes, they were.

"Can you tell me where you got them? There's no problem, but something has come up and it will help if you can tell me whatever you can about them."

Ari closed his eyes and rubbed his face. "Strangely, they both came from Neoptolemos Papageorgiou's collection," he said. "Very rich. From one of the Cypriot oligarchies. You probably don't know, but he was a close collaborator of the British administration, but some say he was a double agent and spied for EOKA and later, with independence, that was why he was a friend of

Georghadjis. Papageorgiou was murdered during the coup. No one has worked out the why, yet. From what people tell me, he worked in KYP and was trusted by Georghadjis as a courier. There are rumours that he was the one who took the explosives in the diplomatic pouch to Greece for Panagoulis' attempt on Papadopoulos' life." Alekos Panagoulis was a Greek anarchist who tried to assassinate the leader of the Greek junta, Papadopoulos, but fumbled the attempt by entangling the detonation wire, and because of it, he had to shorten it and was caught as he didn't have enough time to escape after he blew the culvert up. Also he blew up the wrong car.

"Probably he was shot by someone who was pro-Makarios and who was biding his time … although, from what I hear, the guy was of the right, but he wasn't pro-junta. His widow came around and asked me to value his books because she was selling up to go to Athens, where she originally came from. I went around, looked at the books and made an offer that I thought she wouldn't accept, but she did. A surprise, really. Anyway, there were a lot of gems among them, several biographies of Grivas, one or two signed by Grivas himself. Papageorgiou was also an avid collector of poetry pamphlets that used to be sold at bazaars and fairs." Digression was something that I was used to with Ari. "I don't know if you've come across any, but when I was a kid there used to be balladeers who would write up current events, especially murders, then print them and chant them in the bazaar, selling them for a few pennies. I remember being totally captivated by them and wanting to be one, but I didn't have the talent for putting words together like they did."

A customer entered, and recognising him, Ari went and got a parcel from the back of the room.

"Girlie magazines from London," he said, coming back after the customer left. "There is a great demand for them … you'd be surprised who

238

orders them. Anyway, where were we? ... There were many first editions, and I already had a pristine copy of *The Secret Agent* and because your copy was so marked, I put it on the shelf for sale."

"Yeah, I remember, there were passages underlined in it. I may as well tell you, Ari, that both that and the Grivas book were stolen from my apartment the other day. Is there anything else you remember?"

"Sorry to hear that, Steve. Well, the Grivas one was also marked. I think it's a travesty when people fold pages or write on books. Except that the Grivas book had comments written all over in pencil. I am sure it was Papageorgiou disputing things that Grivas had written. They seemed to me to be ravings prompted by some sort of jealousy."

"Unfortunately, I had just started reading it, but I know what you mean."

"I had to laugh really," said Ari, chuckling as he poured the hot water into his cup and allowed the chamomile to infuse. "Did you see the portrait in the Grivas book where he is posed like a saint, except he was anything but. It is a great example of how the power of photography can be misused ... it's pure propaganda. Grivas knew the power of photography to mythologise a movement, as I suppose did Goebbels, Castro and Che Guevara and even old Gandhi. Did you know that Grivas was a Metaxas fascist before the war and at the end of the war, set up X, an anti-communist extermination squad?" Metaxas was a fellow fascist of Hitler and Mussolini, but Mussolini damaged the relationship by invading Greece.

"Yeah, many here don't know it and all the others who do ignore it."

"If he'd called it quits in 1959, he'd still be seen as a hero by everyone. He is our own Marshal Philippe Pétain, the Lion of Verdun in the First World

War, who twenty years later collaborated with the Nazis by leading the French Vichy government. Grivas collaborated with the junta."

"A journalist friend told me that Makarios was pro-fascist before the war as well."

"Well, it's the nationalist's conundrum really," said Ari, folding his big arms across his chest. "You take the boundary away between the State and the Church, you brainwash the youth using different catch-cries, demonise your perceived enemy and then they are ready to do anything you want them to. Mussolini and Metaxas did the same. That was when Makarios, as a young theology trainee, was in Athens, during Metaxas' reign. Remember, the Church has always been on the side of the rich and powerful. Metaxas set up a fascist youth movement like Hitler. Just like the British have done it with the Boy Scouts. Except Metaxas became a hero because he refused to surrender Greece to the Italians. That *OXI* – NO – made him an icon of resistance. Although EOKA was a revolutionary movement against British Imperialism, and when you build a guerrilla army, you ensure, as Grivas said, that you have cells that restrict knowledge of the whole, so if anyone is captured, the whole can regroup and replace the severed part. I had a Greek uncle who helped EOKA, and he told me the terrible torture that some of those EOKA boys were put through. And most were boys. Unfortunately, there were innocent boys who would be caught up as well. As you know, some paid for it with their lives for no more than possessing a gun."

"Yeah, I read Charles Foley. But what you are saying, Ari makes sense, and it will help me clarify some ideas I am working on, about an article on terrorism." A white lie, but necessary to get the conversation to where I wanted it to go. "You see, I am working on an article on what is happening in Europe with the Baader Meinhof Gang, you know, the Red Army Faction."

Ari gesticulated his assent with his thick arms. "In those bastards, you have EOKA B in a nutshell. Like them, they attacked police stations in West Germany, trying to destabilise the country. Although, EOKA B didn't rob banks to buy its arms because it got its money from the Greek junta and, some say, the CIA."

"I am also interested in the women."

"Phut! Women!" exclaimed Ari. "Harpies! They can be worse than men, my friend. The real brains behind Andreas Baader and Ulrike Meinhof is Mader's girlfriend, Gudrun Ensslin. She is the one who has articulated the dark anarchic impulse that drives Baader. She's the real brains of the organisation. Well, that's what I think. People underestimate the power of women in revolutions ..." He reached into his pocket, took out a large handkerchief and blew his nose.

"Have you heard of the Milicianas?" he continued.

I shook my head.

"It was a women's brigade in the Spanish Civil War ... the seamstresses and the washerwomen who became soldiers, equal to men ... they even led brigades into battle. *La Pasionaria*, Dolores Ibárruri, who uttered the famous catch cry 'Better to die on your feet than live forever on your knees' and her deeds as a fighting warrior made her famous. Christ! It was the same with Bouboulina, in the Greek War of Independence of 1821." Laskarina, with the onomatopoeic surname Bouboulina, took command of her husband's battleships after he was killed in action against Algerian pirates and led them in the 1821 Greek war of independence.

"Even EOKA of the 1950s had a women's branch. I came across some of them when I was a boy at anti-British demonstrations, and they could be maniacal, screaming like harpies."

I knew I had to advance carefully from here.

"What about Jewish women?"

"Well, when I was young, I went and worked on a kibbutz for couple of months in Israel, and there the women are seen as equal to men … in everything: medicine, fighting, science, politics … They even had Golda Meir as prime minister, until last year, and she was not only instrumental in the setting up of the state of Israel but was also the one who ordered Mossad to assassinate all the leaders of Black September and the PLO who were responsible for the Munich Olympics massacre. She wasn't called the 'Iron Lady' of Israeli politics for nothing. A woman with balls of iron."

The next question was going to be trickier. "So do you think that Mossad operates in Cyprus, Ari?"

But Ari did not hesitate. "Of course they do. That Fatah chap who was rumoured to have been the PLO liaison officer with the KGB … He was blown up in his hotel in '73 … That was Mossad … But they do keep a low profile …I am sure that KYP keeps them in its sights. Beirut is the spy capital of the Middle East, but Nicosia is a close second. If you go to any diplomatic function, most of those who are there are spies trying to find leverage over someone or get a line on something. I get invited to those things because they come to my bookshop."

"Maybe they invite you because they think you may know something of those Armenian terrorists that just started up," I said provocatively.

"Maybe. But come on … for Christ's sake, Steve," said Ari, sidestepping my comment, "the Armenian Secret Army for the Liberation of Armenia? Give me a break," Ari scoffed. "What a convoluted fuckin' acronym, eh? Only an Armenian could come up with that. Those boys are living in la-la land. Turkey will never recognise the Armenian genocide, let alone pay reparation like Germany did to the Jews. As for recognising a historical homeland and returning it to the Armenians, well, that too is a pipe dream. They are too powerful and will remain so with the help of America. I cannot see Turkey becoming so weak that they will give up a part of what is now their own territory. Maybe in the future, when there is – and I am sure will be – a counter-reaction to Kemalism when the secular state becomes corrupt. But until then, I don't even think of them."

"Of course, if you did belong to them, that is what you'd say, Ari," I said, smiling.

"True, but those rotten animals who planned and guided the genocide like Talat Pasha, who by the way, according to a Turkish customer, was a Freemason, got their comeuppance, and I'd have gladly joined Operation Nemesis that assassinated him in Paris. The fuckin' Freemasons. They have their dirty fingers in everything."

Ari was slowly straying into his conspiracy paranoia about Freemasonry, and I didn't want to go down that way. I had spent one afternoon listening to him expound how the British consolidated their imperialism by using Freemasonry to select and then pluck out the young and up and coming leaders of their colonies and convert them to their brotherhood. He went on and on about how one sees it in South Africa where two secret societies, the Afrikaner Broederbond, which until then I had never heard of, and the English dominated Freemasons, are fighting it out for the hearts and minds of the white republic, and according to him, the blacks were the meat in the sandwich … caught right in the middle. From my viewpoint, the Afrikaans, who lost the Boer War, were now running South Africa, and technically they may have lost that battle but in the end finally won the war.

According to Ari, that was how the British denied any revolutionary movements that rose up against them the intelligentsia needed to lead them. "They start young with the Boy Scouts," he had explained to me. "Then they pick the best and make them Freemasons." I remembered then that of the few things my father denied my brother and me, joining the Boy Scouts was one. "NO!" My father had thundered and that was that.

On that occasion, I remember I said to Ari something like "they missed Gandhi, Kenyatta and even Makarios …" but there was some logic in Ari's madness. If I were an imperial power, I would do everything I could to undermine my subjects' dreams of freedom. I knew from Terrence Ogilvy that the Freemason fraternity, based symbolically on the stonemason guilds of the late fifteenth century, was invented by the British, and it was and is a powerful establishment institution that was and is led through the monarchy. According to Terry, British prime minister William Pitt made sure there was no plot to depose King George III as the king of France was deposed during the French Revolution. Many of those revolutionaries were Freemasons. Pitt stirred the *Unlawful Societies Act 1799* through the British Parliament, an act that compelled all secret societies set up by the seditious Irish, but including the British Freemasons, to table their membership to parliament annually under the threat of transportation if they did not obey the directive. King George III's brother Prince Edward, the Duke of York and Albany, was already inducted as a Freemason. The Duke, in turn, sponsored the Prince of Wales, who was eventually crowned George IV, to be inducted into the brotherhood, becoming Grand Master of the Lodge of England 1792–1812. From then on, a tradition was established that the Grand Master should be from the elite of the British monarchy.

I knew nothing other than what Ari had told me about Freemasonry in Cyprus and the fact that the Church of Cyprus, like the Catholic Church, was against its parishioners becoming Freemasons and passed aggressive edicts prohibiting membership of the brotherhood. This made me reluctant to give his claims any credence as far as Cyprus was concerned. There may indeed be Freemasons here after all. Even in New Zealand, every town seemed to have a Masonic Lodge. According to my father, my godfather, an owner of a milk-bar and a fellow Greek Cypriot, was one.

"So, don't you think it odd that anyone would want to steal those books, Ari?"

Ari thought for a second or two. "Not really, Steve. But knowing what we know about Papageorgiou, they could be used to decipher codes."

"What do you mean?"

"One of the tricks used by spies is to designate a popular book and use pages and lines to set a code. Having the book helps you decipher the code."

"Really. Are you sure?"

"Well ... Yes, for the Joseph Conrad book because you can get it almost everywhere in Europe, although it would need to be the same edition."

"Isn't it too obvious? *The Secret Agent* ... For Christ's sake ..."

"Yes, maybe ... but the Grivas book, I am not so sure. It was written in Greek and translated into English. The notations were in English. Cypriots, like Papageorgiou, those who know English, scribble in English in them to

245

confuse any nosy parkers like their wives from reading their entries. They do the same in their diaries."

It was then that Ari mentioned Terry had written that he was coming to Cyprus that week and to let me know as he didn't have my new address. I wrote my address out for Ari to pass on when Terry made an appearance.

Ari knew my friend Terry because he'd helped him locate several people he interviewed in Cyprus who had survived the Armenian genocide during and after the First World War. It was for an article he wrote and published in the British press on last year's anniversary of the slaughter.

As a general practise, journalists and historians, much like grocers, round things off – 24 April 1915 was officially assigned for the Armenian Genocide and 25 April for the landings of the British, Indian, Australian and New Zealand forces at Gallipoli. In the article, Terry pointed out that

... because of the different time zones, it is a quirky but also cruel irony of history that on the dawning of the 25th of April in the Southern hemisphere, unknowingly, the citizens of Australia and New Zealand actually commemorate the start of the Armenian genocide which was unleashed on the 24th of April at 00.00 Gallipoli time. The landings in Gallipoli began at 4.00 hours Gallipoli time on the next day, the 25th. In Australia and New Zealand, the commemorations ever since that day begin six or eight hours late at 4.00 local time but 12.00 hours Gallipoli. By that time, the survivors of the battle and their mates would have already marched past, stiffly saluting their cenotaphs. After they'd gather at their RSAs and raise their beer glasses to the memory of their fallen comrades before falling into the stupor of drunken oblivion offered by the goddess Lethe, a moment of welcomed respite from the horrors they

246

had inflicted or seen. At no stage would it have occurred to them that the British and their allies' naval bombardments of the Dardanelles throughout March may have provoked more suspicion and ill-will against the new Turkish republic's minorities, and that their landings added fuel to the paranoia that lit the hatred that eventually wiped out nearly two million of Turkey's Armenian citizens …

That conjunction of circumstance was something that Terry and I worked out after we attended an ANZAC Day commemoration in Vietnam.

What did Father Sosimas say? "Never provoke the beast in man."

And Terry Ogilvy? "Sometimes, unexpected and tragic consequences arise from the firestorm and madness of war."

*

When I first visited Dunedin, in the South Island of New Zealand, as a student, I took a few minutes to contemplate the trickle of water named the Water of Leith that flows through the university quarter of the city. On that day the Leith, with its steep, concrete channel walls, looked more like an open sewer than a stream. However, I quickly learned otherwise as without warning and out of nowhere it suddenly turned into a manic, roaring torrent, pushing all before it into the sheltered waters of Otago Harbour.

At first, I had thought that it was named after one of the five rivers that flowed in Hades, the Lethe. Then a passing, somewhat drunk but dapperly dressed Australian lecturer of English pointed out that it was named after the river Leith in Edinburgh, Scotland. Years later, I came across a rather interesting proposition: that it may indeed be named after the Lethe as it's from Brythonic (old "Welsh"), which means either "grey" or "flowing" and also may imply forgetfulness, and is related to the name of the Leithen, which flows down to Innerleithen on the Scottish borders. Also, as Edinburgh's nickname is "the Athens of the North" and the Leith certainly sounds a bit like the "Lethe" and it rhymed better ... the matter, in my mind at least, was settled.

So I didn't get my Leith and my Lethe mixed up, but because the piece was in some way conceived in Dunedin, "New Zealand's Athens of the South", I consciously decided to go with the Scottish version.

The poem though, was born in Cyprus. Its godfather was Terry Ogilvy, who invoked the Lethe to pluck the Scottish Leith from the depths of my subconscious. And maybe some sort of despair.

Oh, what a timorous but twisted life ...

No, mate ... Just, poetic licence.

The Leith

Quiet flows the Leith ...

        quiet the sound

that muted

    sound

      that

        guttural

growl

    that sound

      from

rolling boulders

        its incisors

           its teeth

              as quiet

as quiet

    as quite

        flows the Leith ...

Quiet flows the Leith ...

           quiet the flutter

quiet the flutter

        that flutter

that flutter

    of flight

        that flutter

           of fantail flight

that flitter

    that flitter

      of light

that flitter

    of black light

        meandering

the shift

    to meet

the cheat

        beneath the sheath

of the beast.

Who'll flay the priest

        for the feast?

The sound of water

        descends rapidly

                to the sea ...

From the mountain

        to the sea

quiet flows the Leith

        quiet the gnash of teeth

and

    the prophet's prophecy

        his odyssey

is in its infancy

      and

        the Leith

this autumn

    is

      dammed

pent-up

     with

the venom

     of jealousy ...

The coming winter

     will wipe

the leprosy ...

... the cure has no permanency

     the draftee has no sanity

gone is his purity

     maggot-ridden his liberty

amputated his honesty

     false his majesty

futile his barbarity

     wasted

his charity.

On the banks of the Leith

     the leach will preach

     they'll

impeach the odyssey

     condemn the tyranny

     reveal the piracy

plead

    for amnesty.

Whilst the teeth …

       the teeth will gnash

the teeth will gnash

      as quiet flows the Leith.

  .

8

It was great to see Terry.

He arrived three days after my visit to Ari's bookshop.

Ari had already told me that Terry was on his way to Jordan. He was to interview King Hussein. Afterwards, he was also going to Lebanon because a right-wing group called the Christian Phalange had murdered two dozen Palestinians and three Lebanese Christians in a bus ambush. Terry thought that something important was brewing there as for a long time Lebanon had enjoyed relative peace, and Beirut was not only the pleasure capital but, as Ari also emphasised, the spy capital of the Middle East. He wrote to Ari that he hoped that the massacre was not the harbinger of a civil war.

As per usual, Terry brought a bottle of alcohol with him and a ready smile. He had put on some weight but still looked like the matinee idol that I shared a hotel room with in Saigon. His blonde hair and rugged good looks gave him his choice of girls among the American nurses there.

He held up the whisky and announced in a put-on broad Scottish accent, "Mr Glenfiddich, may I present Stauvros Marangos, alias Steve bloody Carpenter, fellow hack and intrepid adventurer. Mr Carpenter may I present me old chum, Mr Glenfiddich, a twelve-year-old, single malt whisky."

Scipio, who was sleeping on the settee, scurried to the bedroom.

"Hello to you too, Ogilvy."

"Hellooo, *charaid* ... I bring ye greetings and felicitations from bonnie Scotland."

"But I thought you flew from London."

"Yes, but I flew to there from Glasgow."

I laughed.

"And single malt ... what the hell is that?"

"You may well ask, old sport. It is unique. It is different ... much more refined than the usual mass-produced hotchpotch. It is, even if I say so myself, me old sport, a product of genius and, because of it, a sensory delight."

"Then you are wasting it on me, mate," I said as I picked up the bottle and looked at the label. "Not only don't I know anything about whisky but I also never heard of this." Then I found two small tumblers and poured some of the amber liquid, filling them.

"Well, old sport, how else are you going to be educated about the finest frigging firewater made by men?" Then lapsing into his cultivated Etonian twang, which he swore opened establishment doors for him in London, informed me that single malt whisky was made in one distillery, usually from malted barley.

This form of unfurling trivia was our way of reacquainting ourselves.

One of the things that I learned early on about Terry was that his Etonian facade was totally put on. He, like a lot of other Brits, simply went to a state grammar school, and although he gained first-class honours in history and politics at Cambridge University, every so often the facade would drop and the Scottish brogue, loaded with swear words, would come through. Back in New Zealand, when I worked during the university holidays in the woolstore, I got used to swearing like a trooper. Every second word was a swear word and the more foul, the more of an indicator it was that you were worth listening to and one of the boys. People would say that swearing is a sign that one is uneducated or of lower intelligence. Well, that is a lot of bullshit. Some of those guys at the woolstore were some of the best-read people that I have ever met. The swearing was a tribal signature of the working class, and the same men who would profusely throw profanities at each other at work would, chameleon-like, adapt their speech when others of the middle or upper-middle class were present.

Similarly, Terry found a way to still hark back to his working-class roots, but his *frigging* for fucking, *darn* for damn, *nincompoops* instead of arseholes, *butter* for bugger, *bullspit* for bullshit, *cobblers* for crap or balls, and *son of a pup* instead of son of a bitch still colourfully embellished his speech. When I asked him about it, he said that working for all the posh newspapers, it became a minefield if you dropped a swear word in the conversation. "It simply was not done, old sport. However, get a few beers in you at a Fleet Street pub and everything is fuck this and fuck that."

254

Taking a sip, "It is nice," I conceded. "I never understand why you Scots dilute it."

"It's a refinement that you uncivilised Cypriots and Antipodeans are incapable of," he retorted. Then he told me that there was more to drinking whisky than just downing it. Apparently, the water helps to release a different, more subtle flavour. "Also, back in the Highlands, there's whisky that is usually sixty per cent proof. By watering it down, one removes the burning sensation."

"Oh, silly me. I thought the purpose of drinking alcohol was to get drunk as soon as possible."

"Yeah, well, that can happen too. It's like that *zivana* thing that you drink here."

I laughed. "Well, the last bottle I got of that was when I last drove up to Troodos. The old guy who made it insisted that I have a drink with him. He was taking it straight from the still, and I was pissed before I knew it. I had to stop and have a sleep so I wouldn't drive into a ravine. People have their own stills up there to make it. I am sure it was ninety per cent proof. Petros puts it in the deep freeze in the summer. Boy, does it take off the edge! They also use it here to help get rid a cold. They use it for 'cupping'."

"Cupping? What the devil is that?"

So I contributed some more of my trivia to the conversation.

"I saw Eleni use it on Petros once when he had a chill. She used a fork with a cloth tied around the prongs, then dipped it in methylated spirits and lit it. Then she ran the flame on the inside of the glass cups and put them on his back. The cup is made of tensile glass. The skin is drawn into the cup by

255

creating a vacuum, drawing the skin to form a haematoma, and then when it cools down it releases. It's a form of deep massage. You must have come across it?"

Terry recalled coming across the treatment in Taipei. "Yes, I think they call it *ba guan zi* if I remember right, which means *right fire* or something. I had sprained my back and the acupuncturist used it … to loosen the muscles. He said that it had been used in China for many thousands of years, but I am sure I read somewhere that it dates right back to the ancients, the Egyptians."

"Well, here, when you get a cold or the flu, they cup you, and after that they rub you with *zivana*, and then you go to bed. Eleni, Petros' wife, swears by it."

"That's good to know … going back to the whisky, though, old sport," said Terry grinning. "Like you, I rarely use water or ice."

"You bastard," I chortled. "After all that palaver. You were having me on, right?"

"Not me, old sport. You see, the use of ice really suppresses the flavour and it cools the mouth, but one does it to cheap whiskies. Nice, eh?" taking another sip.

"Yeah."

"I told you, you need educating."

"A waste of time. Anyway … how are you?"

"Actually, really good, Steve." Then he stopped and looking at me seriously, he gave me a coy smile. "I am getting married," he announced.

I was shocked because the last person that I thought would marry was Terry.

"Congratulations," I managed to say. "Who is she? Where did you meet?"

"She's fantastic! We met in Berlin. She's half Scots and half German."

"Well, that is a mixture worthy of the Enlightenment," I said, smiling. It was Terry who first told me that Scotland and Germany used to be the beacons of Western civilisation up to the scramble for Africa in the eighteenth century. The Germans were seen as the most enlightened and educated of all the Europeans, but when they decided to set up their own empire, that reputation was blackened by the British and French, who resented the competition they offered in the scramble to colonise the African continent.

"What's her name?"

"Alexis."

'Well, here is to Alexis and to the future Mr and Mrs Ogilvy," I said, raising my glass and really meaning it.

9

I had put out some bread, salami, pickled cucumber, tomatoes, olives and halloumi as *mezes*, and we spent the next few hours catching up. The usual stuff. His trips around the world, friends and enemies. Terry had many enemies. The real thing. Mind you, I seemed to be collecting them too.

"So what's your take on all those terrorist groups?" I finally asked. "Ari said that you were digging into those Armenian ones. He showed me your article."

If there was anything that I had missed, I knew that Terry would be the one to tell me.

His post Second World War terrorist take was generally the same as mine, although he was able to add a couple of other groups and in-depth detail that I knew very little about.

He filled his glass with a good measure of whisky, took a sip, and helping himself to some bread and halloumi, he began. "Like Friedrich Nietzsche, Steve, I believe that we humans first use our will to gain power over ourselves and then over the world around us, so that we can exist in some sort of equilibrium with all those who are also driven by the same purpose."

"Yeah, that was something that someone told me recently ... about equilibrium, that is."

" So, I don't believe old Friedrich envisaged or promoted domination of other humans or saw it in Darwinian terms. Although, there is something to be said about us inheriting a violent streak from our ancestral relatives, the apes. Have you ever seen a chimpanzee barney in a zoo, Steve? No prisoners taken there over territory or contestable females. You see, old sport, like our ape cousins, we are mainly motivated by our needs: a safe territory to find food in, a safe shelter, and most importantly, we are motivated by our desires. So keep that in mind when I prattle on with my litany on terrorism.

"Let's get the overall viewpoint out of the way." He sipped his whisky. "Ever since the fall or the neutering of monarchies, freedom and rights for

258

ordinary people haven't been granted, they have been taken. They have been won through acts of violence or revolution. The Magna Carta arose from the mayhem of the Battle of Hastings, which really resulted in the destruction of the English nobility.

"As you know, the French Revolution triggered the global decline of absolute monarchies, replacing them with republics and liberal democracies. It became the springboard for the development of all modern political ideologies, leading to the spread of liberalism, radicalism, nationalism and secularism. For the first time, it gave the French citizenry universal suffrage guaranteed by statute … the Declaration of the Rights of Man. Soon after, many subjugated nations fought for their independence from their imperialist masters: Haiti from France, and Mexico, Chile, Bolivia, etcetera from Spain, and of course, Greece from the Ottomans. So violence or revolution is not new.

"Do you remember back in Saigon, Steve, when I tried to discuss 'just war theory' with that son of a pup US colonel?"

"The one that took a swing at you at the Five O'Clock Follies briefing?" The Five O'Clock Follies was the US Army's daily briefing to the press.

"That's the prig. Remember that I tried to explain to him how it was as unethical for the Vietcong to hide among the civilian population as it was for the US Air Force to carpet-bomb North Vietnam?"

"You were pissed."

"Correct. I was."

"Yeah, and he had us both thrown out."

"You got it. Well, you can't discuss terrorism without revisiting just war theory. What do you remember about just war theory, Steve?"

"Oh … only that it's split into to two parts: *jus … ad bellum* … the moral right to go to war, and *jus in bello* … the moral conduct in war … and that it says something about war, under some instances, being acceptable … That's it."

"In what instances?"

"Come on, mate!" I raised my glass to indicate the whisky's effect. "Pass."

"As in a sovereign country's responsibilities. As in defence pacts ... undesirable outcomes ... being bombed first ... or preventable atrocities. All those may justify war. That's why the Yanks in Vietnam went to so much trouble creating a false flag in the Gulf of Tonkin, so they could justify their carpet bombing of North Vietnam. A real bugger of a thing to do, but to the Yanks necessary.

"The Indian Hindu epic, the *Mahabharata*, offers one of the first written discussions of what is a righteous war, Steve. It establishes rules like 'just conduct'; 'proportionality'... for example, chariots can only attack chariots, and cavalry can only attack cavalry; 'just means' such as no barbed or poisoned arrows; and 'just cause', no revenge killings, and humane treatment of the wounded and prisoners. It is surprising that even the Romans, although they were a bloodthirsty lot, also had to justify going to war – an unjustified war was forbidden and the penalty for such a transgression was death.

"Well, to be honest, just war and terrorism do not fit. Unlike governments, terrorists do not have legal standing or moral authority. They use violence outside the rule of law with political, theological, or philosophical purposes in mind. Their purpose is, among other things, to terrorise the public and change government policy. I cannot think of one terrorist group that has an ethical 'right intention' and does not deliberately targets civilian targets, even if, as you say, the Baader Meinhof Gang may have a good reason."

"What about 'one person's terrorist is another's freedom fighter'?"

"Well, Steve, that is about the ethics of war ... how war is fought. The debate, in that case, is not about strategic claims but instead about tactics. So the answer is NO. True freedom fighters abide by the laws of armed conflict, even if they are insurgents or guerrillas. For instance, legitimate freedom fighters wear a patch demonstrating their identity as an organised combatant organisation. They make clear, public, political demands that correlate with justice, order and peace. In just war terms, they accept the Geneva Conventions and they submit to some form of organised authority. One can fight an asymmetrical or unconventional war, Steve, against a superior foe by attacking government employs and property without attempting to terrorise members of the public."

"You mean like Castro in Cuba?"

"A good example, but a better one is George Washington, who operated under a civilian political authority, the Continental Congress. He insisted that his troops remain disciplined and he forbade and punished theft, rape and abuse of civilians. Terrorism, as an operational strategy, Steve, violates the principles of ethical combat and, wittingly or unwittingly, draws civilians into the battlefield. When civilians are killed because terrorists have gone underground among them, as the Vietcong did, the moral responsibility for those deaths is placed, at least in part, on the terrorist. When a war is justified through a false flag event like, as I said, when the US carpet-bombed North Vietnam in '64 by arguing that their attack was justified because the USS Maddox and USS Turner Joy were attacked by Vietnamese gunboats … one can see it a mile off as CIA bollocks … but I also have that from a very good source, someone who was there."

Terry reached for more of the morsels I had provided and sipped his whisky again.

Then he continued his expanding exposition on terrorism with the Weather Underground, an organisation he had done an in-depth article on. Because of that article, I knew that they were a Michigan University-based, left-wing military group, nicknamed the Weathermen. They were inspired from a line from Bob Dylan's *Subterranean Homesick Blues*, "You don't need a weatherman to know which way the wind blows."

"They really did want to overthrow the American government," said Terry. "They declared war and started a campaign of bombings. You see, they actually had a cogent agenda. They were against the Vietnam War and promoted the rights of American blacks through Black Power."

Then Terry reminded me of the jailbreak by the Weathermen of one of the '60s hippy icons, Timothy Leary. Leary was a Harvard psychology professor who advocated the use of lysergic acid diethylamide, better known as LSD, and the naturally occurring psychedelic product compound found in the psilocybin mushroom to treat psychiatric disorders. He had been jailed many times for his views. He also promoted the use of LSD to expand the mind, both physically and spiritually.

I had come across American soldiers in Vietnam who adhered to Leary's views and were experimenting with drugs, not only to counter the fatigue of war but also to avoid their own shitty reality.

"That's why Carlos Castaneda's books were so popular." Terry was right. Castaneda books were the rage among the American troops in Vietnam. You would find Castaneda paperbacks in every camp and hospital. According to Castenada it was Don Juan, his spiritual guide, who instructed him in the use of tequila and peyote to reach higher states of consciousness.

"It was all about an alternative way of developing the spirit," continued Terry. This hit a nerve as it reminded me of what Father Sosimas had said about the *Daskalos of Tseri*. Another seeker of the truth, another mystical outsider.

"Leary travelled around America giving lectures and building support to the degree that Richard Nixon called him 'the most dangerous man in America'. He visited John and Ono in Montreal in 1969, and Lennon wrote a campaign song, *Come Together*, for Leary in 1969 based on his campaign slogan when he ran for Governor of California against Ronald Reagan. In 1970 the Weathermen, for a price, broke Leary out of prison and managed to get him and his girlfriend to Algeria. From there, he went to Afghanistan, which has no extradition treaty with the US. However, the US found a way and got him extradited and he ended in prison … one stint, in a cell right next to Charles Manson. He is still in prison. The Weathermen also organised the Chicago riots against the 1968 Democratic National Convention in protest at Lyndon Johnson's bombing of Vietnam. Their goal or desire was to create a more democratic society in which everyone had a stake. In all their attacks they made sure that no one was hurt. No mean feat, really. They would give the authorities plenty of warnings. The only casualties of their actions were when a bomb went off in their Greenwich apartment in New York, killing three of their very own.

Greenwich ... Greenwich observatory, Greenwich Village, accidental self-destruction ... fiction from fact ... fact becomes myth ...

Terry helped himself to some bread and olives. He munched on them and again sipped his whisky. Giving a slight chortle, he cleared his throat and continued.

"You'll love this, Steve ... One hilarious incident of this American counter-culture revolution fiasco was when the Chicago Seven were charged by the US federal government with conspiracy, inciting to riot and a string of other charges having to do with anti-Vietnam protests." The Chicago Seven's arrest – actually, originally they were eight – also arose out of demonstrations against the 1968 Democratic National Convention. "One of them was called Hoffman, Abbie Hoffman. The judge of the case was also called Hoffman. The Weatherman's Hoffman provocatively kept baiting Hoffman the judge from the dock to declare before the court that he, Abbie Hoffman, was not his son. The judge finally reluctantly agreed and confirmed that the accused was not his son. Then Abbie, quick as a flash, interjected with his now-famous verbal jibe, 'Dad, Dad, have you forsaken me'."

We both laughed at this.

"The Weathermen, as I said, confined themselves to blowing up buildings and banks, and gave the authorities lots of warning. They practised 'just conduct'. Those chaps pushed the state as far as they could by insulting the whole apparatus of the courts. With the Vietnamese peace accord now in Paris, all those American terrorist groups are unravelling into the abyss of historical amnesia."

Terry leaned over, took a cigar out of the packet that I had put on the table and lit it. Then, as was usual with him, he went off on a tangent. "You know, Steve, one of the things that really freaked me out when I was young was when I read Marco Polo. Have you read his book *The Travels of Marco Polo*?"

"Yeah. But only the Classics Illustrated comic version," I added sheepishly.

"No shame in that, old sport. There was nothing wrong with the Classics comics. Like Everyman's Library and Penguin books, they brought history and literature to the masses. Anyway, do you remember the Old Man of the Mountain whose command was unquestionably obeyed by his followers even if he asked them to throw themselves off the parapets of his fortress? I can't comprehend ever doing such a thing, for anyone."

"Yeah, it put the willies up me too. But weren't they doped up or something?"

"Yes, they were. You see, the Old Man of the Mountain was actually a religious leader. He led the Assassins – the equivalent to the Muslims of what the Templars and Knights Hospitaller military orders were to the Christians … 'assassin' in Arabic means 'eaters of hashish'. As Polo said, the Old Man would drug his young followers with hashish and then, when they were asleep, would move them to a special garden that he constructed, which was a carbon copy of the paradise promised by the Prophet Mohammed, but this one was on earth. They woke up from their drug-induced stupor to find the proverbial 'land of milk and honey' full of beautiful maidens who would meet their every need. When he had a mission for them, he would drug them again with hashish and promise them that when they completed their mission alive or dead they would go back to this paradise … and so, because of that promise, they were fully committed to his cause and willing to carry out his every order, even if he asked them to kill themselves. Yes, they were drugged … they were on a hashish high – the same as some hippies on acid who think that they can fly. It seems us humans don't take too much convincing to self-destruct, eh?"

It was here that I told Terry about what Delphinidis had told me about *cupio dissolvi* – I wish to self-dissolve – and about Freud's *todestrieb*. I was pleased to be able to add something to what really had become a Terry monologue.

"Yes, *Herr* Sigmund Freud was bang on, old sport … Imagine, eh, what rational Germans must have thought after they went through the whole Hitler debacle. Aimé Césaire, though, summed it up brilliantly in the fifties when writing on the colonial origins of the Jewish Holocaust. He said that 'the Nazis applied to Europe what, until then, was only applied to the Arabs of Algeria, the coolies of India, and the blacks of Africa.' He missed the Aborigines of Tasmania, though. Anyway, there were many other precedents including the genocide by the Young Turks of the Armenians.

"However, most Germans, Steve, must have asked themselves how they let it happen. I came across an old forties *Life Magazine* last year that reported waves of suicides in the last days of the Nazi regime – people who couldn't reconcile defeat or their consciences for what they had done and decided on *selbstmord*, self-murder."

"What, killed themselves?"

"Yes, they did. In one case, a thousand together in one hit in a town called Demmin in northwest Germany."

"You mean like those women in Souli who threw themselves off a cliff so that they wouldn't fall into the hands of the Ottomans?" The siege and fall of Souli was a story that I grew up with. Sixty trapped women and their children committed mass suicide by jumping into a ravine from Mount Zalongo. They formed a dance circle and at the end of each refrain, they would dispatch themselves into the abyss below.

"No, what happened at Souli was slightly different. That was altruistic suicide for the honour of their kin, much like the Jews who killed themselves in Masada so that they would not fall into the hands of the Romans. They valued freedom and honour above their lives …"

"What then, like Afxentiou and Matsis during the revolt here?" Grigoris Afxentiou and Kyriakos Matsis were Greek Cypriot leaders of EOKA who chose to die by their own hand rather than surrender to the British.

"You've got it now, old sport."

Terry took another sip, finishing his whisky. So I poured him another.

"The Germans' suicide was caused by unadulterated, mortifying and humiliating shame. Their ego and self-worth were blown apart, really.

"Anyway, back to what I was saying … And then there's the SLA. Have you heard of them?"

"S … what? No, I don't think so."

"The SLA, the Symbionese Liberation Army. They were into robbing banks like the Red Army faction."

"Never heard of them. Who were they?"

"Who *are* they? They are still going. It's those chaps who kidnapped Patty Hearst. You must have heard of her?"

"Oh. Patty Hearst, yeah … There was an article in *The Times* … she was a newspaper heiress or something?"

"Yes, she's the daughter of William Hearst, the American press tycoon."

"Symbionese? What's that? An American Indian tribe or something?" I tried speculating

"No. They aren't named after anyone … it's a word derived from symbiosis. Those chaps and chapesses see themselves as in a symbiotic relationship with other left-wing groups, like the Black Panthers, fighting racism and for equality between men and women and different generations. Their goal or desire, ironically, is for people to live together peacefully. Their symbol – all terrorist groups have a logo sort of thing – is the seven-headed cobra."

"Really? How the hell did they come up with that and aren't cobras only endemic to India and Africa?"

"It is from India, or maybe Ceylon – Sri Lanka – or maybe from both. Anyway, it's a symbol for the seven principles of *Kwanzaa*." He raised his hand and counted them off. "Unity, self-determination, collective work and responsibility, cooperative economics, purpose, creativity and faith. I learned all this when I wrote an article about them, but again *The Times* turned me down. They said it wasn't of interest to their readers. Sometimes they can be one-eyed, just like the Yanks. They just want tame articles like the one that I'll be doing about King Hussein."

"And what about those … Symbiosis army characters?" The whisky was getting to me.

"Symbionese … Well, like most of those terrorist groups, they eventually ended up killing someone. Last year one of them used a twelve-gauge shotgun to kill a mother of four when they robbed a bank in California. Patricia – Patty, Mr Hearst's daughter – was the getaway driver." Then Terry raised and waved his glass at me in anger. "And you wait, Steve … when she's caught, and she will be caught, her family will buy her out of the mess she got into. They'll get the best and most expensive lawyers in the US who'll, in turn, hire the most expensive psychiatrist there is, and she'll get away with it … plead some diminished responsibility bollocks. Sometimes, Steve, I think we are all psychos waiting to happen."

I was tempted to tell him about what I was going through but decided against it. Instead, I told him what I was working on and the close call I had in Agia Napa with Frank.

He was genuinely interested in what happened and asked me questions about it. He was also pleased to hear about Frank, and when I mentioned what happened with the IRA in Limassol, it was then that he mentioned that Reuters wanted him to go to Northern Ireland, but he had turned it down.

"It's a frigging mess, old sport, and with crazies like that Protestant bastard Paisley, they are going from one disaster to another. A man of the bloody cloth," he scoffed. "Give me a break … A man of the frigging butcher's apron more likely. Ireland is one of those civil wars that will go on bleeding until there's fuck all blood left, Steve, and then everyone will drag themselves to the negotiating table to find some sort of a solution. Religious wars stoked by fanatical priests, and in this case a civil war to boot … I'd say, 'God help them', but they are both the domain of the same god and I think God, if he exists, has really given up on them."

I told Terry about the Jewish zealot Artemion and what happened in Salamina. Terry listened intently. Any new information was, as it was for Frank, not only of interest to him but something to file away for later use.

"Never heard of him. I must chase it up. But he fits the bill. But going back to what I was saying about Ireland." His face became farrowed and desolate. "I pity the poor kids, Steve. The adults are too damaged to do anything with."

"What do you mean?"

"Remember how in Vietnam people got used to the violence? … It was normal. Not one of the locals for generations knew what peace was … Now they have it at last, and I hope they are too exhausted to go into another war. One hundred thousand South Vietnamese soldiers surrendered. Their fat cat officers abandoned them and scrambled on the helicopters that eventually got them on to the aircraft carriers that took them to the US. That was a week ago, first of April. But here's a turn up for the book, though."

"What?"

"Remember our office chap at the Reuters office in Saigon?"

"Lu Vin. Yeah. I was only thinking about him the other day."

"That's him. Remember his mate Pham Xuan An who was the head of desk for *Time* magazine?"

"Yeah."

"Well, you won't believe it, but now the war is finished, I got it from a very hush-hush source that he was a blooming Vietcong intelligence officer. That's how our Lu Vin used to get us out of harm's way when there was a Vietcong attack. Pham Xuan An looked after Lu Vin and, through him, us."

"So was Lu Vin a Vietcong too?

"No. I think it was more a strange, collegial sort of thing bound by the fact that they both were Vietnamese working for the Western media. Pham Xuan An and his Vietcong mates worked out very quickly that we were really – unwarily – helping them in their cause by fuelling the anti-war movement in the US with our reports. So they protected our office and us … You remember that other chap …?" Terry was moving on to something else and I quickly guided him back.

"Hey, Terry … hold on a minute, mate. Going back to Patty Hearst … Why do you think a well-educated, rich and good-looking bird like her would join a group like that?"

"She was kidnapped, Steve, and they say she was brainwashed ... a relatively new word coined from the Chinese *xinao* – which means, wash brain. A disreputable, fellow journalist of ours and suspected agent provocateur for the CIA, called Edward Hunter first used it in an anti-communist article he wrote for a Miami newspaper in 1950. But to answer your question more accurately with one word: sex. I am absolutely sure it's a big component in all this revolutionary stuff. It's like becoming an artist or photographer – so you get to lay lots more women who are prepared to take their clothes off for you. It's the same with pop singers. Look at the Beatles and the Rolling Stones. Women just throw themselves at them."

"C'mon, Terry, if she was kidnapped, wouldn't she have gone through that Stockholm syndrome thing?" I tried cautiously. Stockholm syndrome was a new phrase that was coined by criminologist Nils Bejerot and psychiatrist Frank Ochberg about two years previously. It explained the perplexing phenomenon of what happens between kidnappers and hostages to help the police to manage such situations. It was recognised after a bank robbery in Stockholm in 1973 when, to the surprise of the police, the bank employees became emotionally attached to the robbers to the degree that, at one stage, they rejected help from the police and even defended their captors after they were freed. "Like those Swedes, the victim saw their captives' good treatment of them as something to be grateful for."

"Well, I don't think so sport. She's like all of those urban guerrillas, or the hallelujah brigades like the Charles Manson family ... they are rich kids who have been spoiled by their upbringing and are probably bored to paralysis," said Terry scathingly, "who want to be part of the action and just want to feel alive. And with Patty blooming Hearst, those guys come along and kidnap her, and before you know it, they turn her on like a wound-up toy and then ... she's buzzing, she has a purpose ... her life has meaning. All those dick-heads are mostly middle class, bored with their existence and wanting to strike out at someone." Terry's theory, ever since I met him in Saigon, has been that all revolutions are started by a bored or discontented middle class. The Black Panthers Party, Terry said, were probably the exception as they come from poor urban black working-class backgrounds.

10

It was now up to me to keep the momentum going.

"But surely Terry, some have a good reason to rebel. It can't be easy as I said for the young generation in Germany to see the very people that led them to a disaster still ruling the roost."

"Well, that's only because of the Cold War."

"The Cold War ... how's that?"

"The Cold War, old sport ... You know, the Soviets versus the rest ... Aptly named, really, by Mr Blair."

"Yes, yes, yes. Who the hell is Mr Blair?"

"Eric Arthur Blair. You know him as George Orwell. Georgie boy, my democratic socialist hero."

"Oh yeah. That Blair. But I thought you were a bloody anarchist!"

"With age, we mature, old sport ... like a butterfly, we escape the cocoon of youth."

"Never heard of a better turncoat metaphor."

"Well, that's why I am a journalist of great repute and you are a hack of low repute," said Terry with some relish, but I knew that he was joking.

"Anyway, Mr Blair coined the Cold War term."

"I don't know how many times I have used the phrase, but I don't think I knew this. When?"

"In '45. He used the term in something he wrote for the *Tribune*."

"Why did he say that?"

"His view was that the Russians deliberately moved the confrontation into a state of "cold war" rather than a "hot war".

"You mean a stalemate instead of fighting?"

"Yes. A stalemate with a lot of belligerent shadow-boxing."

"So the Russians were all set to take on the West?"

"No, the reverse. The Russians looked at American capitalism as moving into an aggressive imperialist phase. You must remember that the Russians lost twenty million people, and at the end of 1945, they were just about bankrupt. They couldn't afford to fight another war. The country was a total mess. It was the Americans who were all geared up to take them on … Remember, the Russians were their former allies. Their Second World War alliance with them was like that tripartite alliance between those erect salamis Octavian Caesar, Mark Antony and Marcus Aemilius Lepidus … an alliance of convenience. Those three Roman salamis hated each other, but they put their enmity aside and got together against Cicero and the republic that Cicero was trying to resurrect. Except in the Americans' case, the alliance of convenience with Russia was against Hitler."

I couldn't believe how Terry was keeping it all together because by then we had nearly finished the last quarter of the whisky.

"Well, Steve, the Americans realised that they needed to retain the Nazi bureaucracy to restore order in Germany. I think they were all geared up to take on the Russians, pushing their weight around in Germany, taking over from Britain in Greece to support the monarchy after the Greek civil war and they only pulled their head in when the Russians managed to get their atom bomb secrets. The world owes a lot to Klaus Fuchs and the other scientists who leaked the secrets of the atom bomb to Russia. They were scientists with a conscience, and maybe one day they will be honoured for what they have done. Erect salamis like Patton and MacArthur were all primed to march on to Moscow, and if not, the Brits and the Yanks planted underground right-wing cells all over Europe in case Russia invaded." Terry took a small sip of his whisky. "I don't think the Yanks ever forgot or forgave the humiliation, Steve, of the US army having to retreat after their march to Moscow in the 1920s."

"What? What march to Moscow? What the hell are you talking about, Terry?" Terry was straying into Ari's delusional landscape.

"The Americans ... they frigging went into Russia with the Brits, the Canadians, the Australians, the Japs, the Czechoslovakians, the French, the Italians, the Chinese ... and even the blooming Greeks went. They went to help the White Russians against the Bolsheviks."

"Bullshit! You are rambling, Terry. Never heard of it."

"Well, not many have old sport. It just doesn't feature in our history. Just like in Vietnam, there was a civil war in Russia. Everyone outside Russia scrambled in, siding with the White Russians who were representing the old order, the monarchy. Those countries didn't like the idea of the version of communism that was evolving there. The Americans suffered a heavy defeat in Romanovka when the Red Russians, the Bolsheviks or communists, surprised them. They ran for their lives, abandoning their allies.

"You see, old sport, I think the US army has its own institutional memory, and when they see an opportunity for revenge, they get a hard-on and go for it. I am sure that if the Russians didn't have the bomb, the Yanks would have nuked them. All for what? They reckon the Russians wanted to take over the world. Well, as I said, the Russians hadn't recovered from the Second

275

World War yet, never mind start another. What was happening was the world's poor were looking for alternatives to the Yanks' way of seeing things. Instead of spending millions feeding and clothing people after the war, the Yanks spent the money on armaments and attacked anyone who raised their head against them, pulverising them. What we now have in America, Steve, is what Eisenhower warned us about, 'a military-industrial complex'. Try telling that to the bloody London papers, but they won't listen."

"Yeah, but the domino theory is true, isn't it?" I interjected. "Didn't the Soviets start to export their Marxist ideology to other countries ..."

"Wrong! It's the other way around. Marxism was exported to Russia from Britain, Steve. Remember, Marx, during his own life, led an obscure existence and was derided as the *ein buttergolem bärtig Kraut* – the chubby bearded cabbage – from Trier in Germany. He wrote the whole frigging *Das Kapital* closeted in the library of the British Museum.

"Marx basically came up with a description of what happens when the motivating force of capitalism is the appropriation of the surplus-value that is left over from the exploitation of low wage labour.

"His analysis, all three volumes of it, was a polemic narrative and its intention was to stir readers out of their 'rut of inertia', to quote Winston Churchill, and into action to transform society. What Marx and Engels were unable to foresee, though, was the consequence of their prescriptive solution. Like the New Testament, their work attracted disciples and believers who, in many cases, hijacked it to gain power for their own advantage and by doing so, inflict a terrible cost on the world. Look at what Theodosious I, the last Roman Emperor, did in Thessaloniki, in the fourth century ... He invited his Greek subjects to the hippodrome for a special Roman circus treat where his Albanian mercenaries shut the gates and butchered over 7,000 for refusing to follow his prescribed new religion, Christianity. Probably double that number considering the biased sources. So, one cannot blame Marx, old sport, for what Stalin and Mao did, just as one cannot blame Jesus Christ for what the Church has done over the millennia since its establishment ... And that includes declaring Theodosious a saint.

"Anyway ... It was British capitalism that Marx was writing an antidote to. But to some degree, you are right, Steve. Those Third World countries had no industrial base, and they had to do something about their colonial masters and for their poor. They also wanted their independence ... To stand on their own two feet and take their place as equals in the world. All Western capitalism wanted to do was turn them into serfs, modern slaves, and instead of , as I said, going in and helping those countries to recreate the infrastructure that had been bombed to smithereens and their tattered educational and health systems, they basically created ruling elites that kept the majority of the people in servitude. In reality, the threat of communism helped enlighten thoughtful people to propose alternatives, and for those to be accepted, albeit reluctantly, such as the welfare state, which New Zealand was at the forefront of. Ho Chi Minh was a nationalist first and a communist second, even if he was trained in Moscow. It was the same with Aris Velouchiotis, the communist resistance leader in the Greek civil war. That's why, eventually, even in a little place like this, there was an armed struggle for independence. Back in London, they'd look at Cyprus and say, 'By gosh, would you believe it, old chap. Those wogs have the gall to complain. How dare they? We civilised them. And what do they do? They bite the hand that feeds them, that's what they are doing. What, those wogs govern themselves? ... Give me a break! Without us, they are nothing.' We British have a superiority complex, Steve, as bad as the Nazis had with their Aryan bullspit. And it is chauvinistic ... no, racist! We see ourselves as God's chosen in many ways and that our civilisation is the best there is. We proselytise our language, our religion, our mores, our prejudice, our psychosis. In fact, we were responsible for many ways of dehumanising black people so we could sell them like cattle to cotton and sugar plantation farmers in America and the West Indies.

"And what do those oppressed poor do? They fall for our bullspit, and if not, they find it hard to divorce themselves from it. Go to India. If you are an Indian and don't speak English, you cannot get a high paying job. It's a status symbol. And when the so-called wogs start fighting each other, we forget that Britain has a long history of civil wars – and don't forget the War of Independence in America was effectively a civil war among British people. You trample over people, Steve, eventually they will find a way to strike back … read Camus' *The Rebel*".

Terry poured himself another whisky. He sat for a few moments staring into the distance.

"Thinking about it, though, Steve … as for here, I think Makarios should have been more conciliatory to the Turks after independence – given them heaps so they would think twice before they listened to their nationalists. I know that you chaps hate the Turks for that old bollocks that happened in 1821, but it wasn't just one-sided, the massacres then, although the Greeks say that. The Greeks were just as vicious. No one has a monopoly on viciousness."

"Yeah, an old priest friend of mine said the same thing."

"We Brits are vicious too, although our polite veneer allows us to escape the consequences. It is a black velvet glove, and it is worn by the dark monster that feeds on the British Empire, and this is a unique monster, and it is not in Loch Ness, Steve … it is in London.

"What I think was really interesting about Lord Byron – his *foustanella* aside – was that for 200 years after the Ottomans took over Greece, the Greeks loved it because they were given the right to own land, speak and write their own language and practise their religion, which the Venetians denied them. It was only when the Ottomans started overtaxing them and pushing them back to serfdom that they eventually found a way to be successful in their rebellion. The same happened in France before the revolution: taxes, famine, drought … like your Cypriot chaps who rebelled. What they did was undertake a revolt against my compatriots, and it *was* a revolution and not a bloody *emergency* as the Foreign Office called it. We British have a devious and quaint way of understating other people's misdemeanours, Steve. It is a form of deprecation, don't you think?

"After independence in 1959, some Greek Cypriots still wanted to fight the 1821 revolution and all they managed to do was to provoke the Turkish Cypriots to have their very own uprising. I know it's more complex than that, but really, as I have told you before, one must appease the middle class, give them – within reason – what they want, and then you don't have revolutions by whomever they are – Greeks, Vietnamese or Turks. Except, of course, now, in the second half of the twentieth century, trying to subjugate them as part of your empire ... As you know, Ireland was the first British colony to rebel against British rule … and that is still going on. And the Russians are no better … look at what happened in Hungary, and it will keep happening because they have also changed their modus operandi and see their vassal states in imperialist terms. They missed the fact that it's a post-colonial world, Steve."

Terry poured and sipped another measure of whisky. Then amazingly, still in full flight, "Now to the final motivation for those terrorists, other than sex, Steve, it is revenge. *Brennendes Verlangen* – the burning desire for revenge. In India quite a few years ago, I came across, a very interesting woman. She introduced herself as Savitri Devi Mukherji. It was one of those diplomatic do's held in New Delhi. Her real name is Maximiani Julia Portas and she is of Greek descent ... actually, her father was only half Greek, the other half was Italian, and her mother was French. She was a mongrel like all of us. She studied philosophy and chemistry, earning two master's degrees and a PhD in philosophy from the University of Lyon.

"But as you know, old sport, neither a degree nor a PhD denotes moral character or creditable intelligence. She latched onto the Greek quarter of her identity because after she visited the Athens museum and saw Heinrich Schliemann's Troy treasures with their swastikas, she became convinced the Greeks were Aryan. When a million Greeks were thrown out of Asia Minor by the Turks in 1922 during the Greco-Turkish war, she developed a deep hatred of the British and French, whom she blamed for the sacking and burning of Smyrna and the suffering of thousands of refugees trying to eke out an existence in Greece. She became a fervent Greek nationalist and, like many late converts, a real zealot and applauded Metaxas' fascist party. To cut a long story short, she embraced National Socialism and, through it, Nazism ... She loved animals, especially cats, but like a lot of German animal lovers she had no problem promoting the extermination of the Jews, and she saw herself as a spiritual equal to Hitler ... who, as you know was a practising vegetarian and supposedly loved his dog. It's that warped mystical spiritualism that drove her to India. There she changed her name, married a Hindu, who she saw as one of the original Aryans, and joined the Hindu nationalist movement, and because of her anti-British sentiments and pro-Nazi bias, she spied for the Japanese. She still lives in India and lectures a form of Hindustani Nazi nationalism, and she's got away with it because of the influence that she has gathered there. A rabid hater of the English and French forged by a poignant formative experience.

"And here's another example … When I first came to Cyprus in 1965, I came across a very interesting Turkish woman. At that stage, she was running the propaganda wing of the Turkish Cypriot nationalists promoting *Taksim,* union of Turkish Cypriots with Turkey. I asked her quite bluntly what happened to turn her against the Greeks – she used to be the chief nurse in the hospital in Nicosia. She had spent the whole evening up till then very cleverly and subtly promoting her view of things and illustrating how devious the Greeks were and how they couldn't be trusted. She finally told me, when I pressed her, that in 1963 during a major Turkish-Greek Cypriot conflict, the hospital in Nicosia was full of wounded. As the head nurse, she was coordinating the treatment of all the wounded. That night, she heard that Greek Cypriots were going to come into the hospital and arrest or kill all the Turkish Cypriot wounded. She bundled two of them and took them home, which was an apartment in the middle of the hospital compound. Then, after she settled them in, she received a telephone call to go back and see her boss at the hospital. When she returned, she found both young men had been murdered. Her name was … wait, it will come back to me," finally the whisky was getting to Terry. "… No … Well, someone told me her father was the man responsible for eradicating malaria from Cyprus. So she was from an educated, privileged background in terms of Cyprus because her father was a colonial government employee. Aesha! ... Aesha Ozan ... that's her name ... She was trained as a nurse and sent to study to become a head nurse in London. She was given a Colonial Office scholarship. This was just before the Second World War started. I remember she said that after her training it took nine months for the Brits to get her back to Cyprus. She had to travel down the coast of West Africa and up the other side by ship and then fly to Cyprus from

Egypt. She loved the English. A true and devoted Anglophile. It is possible that her feelings against the Greeks had been developing for years but the straw that broke the camel's back was that one singular event in her apartment, in the grounds of Nicosia hospital ... that one, personal, very poignant experience turned her into a rabid anti-Greek.

Terry stood up stretched and then sat back down. "To finish off, Steve ... A few years back, I read a book by an Israeli journalist who wrote about a group of about fifty Holocaust survivors who called themselves the Avengers. They had planned to kill six million Germans in revenge for what the Nazis did to them. Imagine that ... six million, among them women and children. They, the Avengers, planned to poison the drinking water of four German cities. They failed because the poison got intercepted by the British, but apparently, they had a backup plan ... instead, they poisoned some 2,000 imprisoned SS soldiers with arsenic-laced bread. The SS soldiers ended up sick as dogs in hospital emergency, but none died. Revenge, Steve ... probably a greater motivator than sex ..."

"Don't get me wrong though, old sport. I think that most terrorists never achieve their goals, but some, like that right-wing Zionist Irgun group who bombed the King David Hotel, their acts of terror did help the Jews to eventually win the war and their very own state. That's how modern Israel has come about. But what goes around comes around ... because, old sport that's what has led to the emergence of the PLO."

Delphinidis' Ouroboros. The dragon that eats its own tail?

We kept talking like this until the early hours of the morning. In Vietnam, although we shared a room, it was on rare occasions that we were together, and those evenings were spent by doing the same thing. Unloading and vocalising our thoughts. Or, I suppose, as far as Terry was concerned, when he wasn't chasing nurses.

It was great to see Terry. He was someone that I could always rely on to get my brain out of a rut. I didn't agree with everything he said, but he got me thinking outside the square.

"So, are you going to keep doing this foreign correspondent thing?" I asked.

"I talked it over with Alexis. We agreed that I'll do it for another year, and then I'll get a desk job either at Reuters or one of the London newspapers, or I may even try television."

"I can't see you behind a desk, Terry. What about politics?"

"I hate politicians, so I suppose I also hate politics."

"Yeah, I can't see you as a politician."

By now, the whisky had taken the rise out of the man and he became introspective.

"Well, old sport, to tell you the truth, I think I've had enough. I thought I'd make a difference. You know. But wherever you go, there are fuck-ups or fuck-ups waiting to happen. Let someone else have a go, I say. You should do the same. Find some bird and settle down. Do something different."

"More easily said than done."

"This is a nice place. Things seemed settled. Open a *kafenio* or something."

"They want me to do National Service."

"Well, go to Greece then or to London or back to New Zealand. Life is short, Steve, and shorter if you are a journalist nowadays. Look at all those people we lost in Vietnam. Philippa and François ... what a waste." He meant Philippa Schuyler and François Sully. Both got killed in helicopter crashes. "Did I tell you I was head over heels in love with Philippa? I had just arrived in Vietnam. She was gorgeous, absolutely gorgeous, and a brilliant concert pianist. What a frigging waste."

"Why did she do it?... Give the concert thing up, I mean."

"It had something to do with her parents. I think she did it to spite them."

"But why Vietnam?"

Why do we all do it? It's the rush, old sport. There's nothing like it. Survive your first skirmish and you become invincible ... and that rush is addictive."

Thinking about it. I had to admit that Terry was right. In the last couple of days, I had had no headaches or voices in my head and I slept like a log. If I remember right, before I passed out when I was with Frank in the Morris, I was almost euphoric. I was walking the edge ... or so I called it. Of course, I ignored the fact that even a blunt edge with enough force can do a lot of damage – even cut one in half.

11

Terry got up early and took off for the day, chasing someone or something to do with his interview in Jordan. Like a good traveller he folded the sheets and blankets on the couch where he slept. After I got up, I went to the *kafenio*. I had just got into reading the *Phileleftheros* when Petros came into the *kafenio* looking really pleased with himself.

"We've tracked down the German woman."

"The dead one?"

"No, the blonde. The one that broke into your apartment. She's West German … she works at the German embassy."

"And?"

"Her name is Kessler. Bridgette Kessler. One of my men, Vasilis, who is following her, said that she looks as if butter wouldn't melt in her mouth. She's got blonde hair but, as your neighbour said, it's probably a wig. From what Karageorgis said, she's attached to the embassy and she's supposed to be a cultural affairs officer but could just as easily be an intelligence officer. Like all the Germans there, she has diplomatic immunity. I traced her car and found where she lived and had Louka keep an eye on her. Sure enough, Patroklos paid her a visit for a quickie and then left. Then Vasilis followed him to his home in Agios Demetios and surprise, surprise … Patroklos is married with three children."

"So she may have latched on to him for the information that he'd give her?"

"Could be …"

"On Saturday when she left Nicosia, Vasilis followed her. She went to Agia Napa where she has a small apartment. He said she spent the day at the beach. Topless. Vasilis was really impressed by her tits. He couldn't stop talking about them. He said it was cold, but for those Germans, our winter is like summer. Vasilis took a photo of her, cropped it to head and shoulders and showed it to your neighbour the haberdasher downstairs, and he confirmed that it was her that asked him where you live."

"So, what you going to do about it?"

"At the moment, nothing. We sit and wait."

"Why?"

"As I said, she has diplomatic immunity, and all we'll achieve is her leaving without us having any answers to what she was doing in your apartment. It's better to keep her under observation. KYP won't like it, but we'll also keep an eye on Patroklos. Some of those secret service guys think they are James Bond or something. The real James Bonds, you never know who they are. They are very ordinary, like she is, except for her tits.

"One interesting thing that came out of this, Patroklos has two friends that he hangs around with. One is from KYP, the other from Special Branch. The KYP guy is Savas Spitha and the Special Branch one is Nikólas Politis … they call him Koli for short. The whole intelligence thing is pretty incestuous when you think about it. But we are a small place. Those two are also *manges* and all three go out quite a lot together. Coffee bars, restaurants, tavernas, etcetera. If KYP knew about the arrival of the hit team, it must have been making the rounds and could have alerted the Americans and the other embassies and consulates. Or if they are Palestinians, they are giving them a free pass."

Just then, a plain-clothes policeman appeared. He made a beeline for Petros. Petros did not introduce us.

"*Kyrie* Zimara. You are wanted back at the station."

286

"Fine Vasili. I'll be with you in a minute. Turn the car around, eh?"

He took out a cigarette and lit it.

"By the way, was there anything else missing?"

"At the moment … just my brain. I can't make head nor tail of this."

He got up.

"In England, the Lancashire police have a motto, cousin. 'Softly, softly catchee monkey'. It's my motto as well. So patience and persistence … we'll sort it out."

12

There are coincidences in life that sometimes one cannot but see as weird. I mean, if someone said to me that this would happen the next day, let alone that the woman would have almost the same name as Terry's fiancée, I would have said that you are crazy. But it did happen, and in more than one way, it knocked my world off its axis.

I had driven Terry to Larnaca Airport to catch his flight to Amman. On the return trip, I decided to stop and have a coffee at a roadside shack. There, I saw a woman having a row with the proprietor, a hard-looking Greek Cypriot, thickset and unshaven. She had raven black hair tied in a ponytail and was dressed in smart, tight white trousers cut below the knee like French women wear, a loose white blouse and white high heel sandals. The exchange was in Greek.

"I gave you a five-pound note," she shouted at him, eyes flaring.

"You gave me a pound."

"This is not the right change. You owe me four pounds something."

"*Na pas na gamithis* – go and fuck yourself," shouted back the man.

"Well, thanks for your advice, but I am not in urgent need of that right now. What I need is for you to give me my money, or I will call the police and then we'll see who will be fucked."

I just stood leaning on the Morris enjoying this when the proprietor finally threw a five-pound note at her. The woman bent over, picked it up, spat "*Euharisto yia tipota* – thanks for nothing!" and walked towards me.

"Keeping the locals honest," I said in Greek.

She fixed her olive-black eyes on me.

"They sense a tourist and their inner vulture comes out."

"But you speak Greek?"

"Well, like an idiot, I ordered in English."

"So, you are Greek?"

She changed to English. "Born here but raised in London."

I don't know why I did it; maybe it was the fire in her eyes.

"I am Steve," I said.

"Stathis?"

"Stauvros."

"Alexandra," she said suddenly, her eyes focusing directly on mine, and I could swear they dilated.

"Where are you heading?"

"Nicosia." She threw her head back to get rid of a strand of hair that dislodged itself. "Well, I was. I am waiting for a taxi to go by. So far, they are all full. The car that I hired broke down about a quarter of a mile back." I vaguely remembered a car parked on the shoulder of the main road.

"I started walking and then I thought I'd get something to eat and a coffee."

"I'm going to Nicosia. I could give you a lift."

She gave me a long look and made her mind up.

"We'll have to go back and get my suitcases."

"No problem. Jump in." I said, forgoing the coffee.

It is hard to explain what really happened because it wasn't anything we did or said.

"You're on holiday?"

"No. I am working."

"Here?"

"In Nicosia."

I didn't ask the question.

"I'm a doctor. A surgeon actually. I've been brought over for two weeks to do plastic surgery on some soldiers who were burnt up by napalm in the war."

"Why haven't they got any plastic surgeons here?"

"No, they have. It's just that I need the practice and, as always, there's nothing like a war to give us a range of challenges. It will help reduce the backlog."

"What, you are doing it for free?"

"Not really. Someone that I know in London has bankrolled the project. He pushed all the guilt buttons."

"Your boyfriend?"

"No, just a friend. I get a small fee, but nothing like what I normally earn. One needs to live, you know."

"To buy coffee?" I said, cheeky Steve making an appearance. *Where have you been, mate?* I didn't think I had flirted since my Auckland days.

She looked at me sharply and then laughed. After that laugh from those red lips around pearly teeth, I was putty in her hands.

"I gave that crook five pounds and he gave me change for a pound." She felt she needed to explain. Then the lips went all serious. "My father died four years after we got to London and our mother brought us up in a little hole in Fulham. We were always short of money. Not all London Cypriot Greeks are rich, you know."

I didn't say anything.

"Well, then I married my husband, who turned out to be a gambler and a womanising bastard of the first order. Bad choice. When I objected to the womanising he raised his hand to me, saying that his father told him that 'there are three things that should be beaten: an olive tree, a dog and a woman.' One of those fuckin' old Cypriot sayings … He was full of them … You know, 'A beating comes from Paradise' etcetera, etcetera," she said sarcastically. "Then I caught him in our bed with my second cousin. For the first time in our marriage I fought back, threw the whole wedding crockery collection at him, and the next day I packed my bags. Now, I have managed to get a lovely apartment in Chelsea and my mother lives downstairs. My brother has made something of himself … he's a journalist … but there is no money in that."

"You are telling me," I said, laughing. "I, too, am an impoverished but devoted representative of the Fourth Estate."

She looked at me, squinting. "You don't look like a journalist."

"What do journalists look like?"

"Long hair, moustache, unshaven … needing a bath."

"Are you describing your brother?"

There it was again, that laughter and the eyes sparkling.

"Yes, actually, I am."

"Well, they broke the mould when they manufactured me," I said, cheeky Steve still in play.

"So, where do you work?"

"Well, hard to tell, really. I freelance and work for Reuters whenever there's a war in Cyprus and try to make ends meet in between."

"There's only been one war if you don't count the Sampson fiasco."

"That's what I mean ... I actually do try very hard to persuade them to have one every second year, so that I'll be gainfully employed, but neither the Turks nor the Greeks will oblige."

"Now, I know you are pulling my leg."

I shrugged, "Well, it helps pass the time."

"I suppose it does," she said, smiling and sat back but kept glancing at me.

When we got to Nicosia, she told me to drop her off at the Hilton Hotel.

"I don't live far from here," I said, as casually as I could. "What about something to eat tonight?"

"Where?"

"There's a nice restaurant around the corner, just outside the city walls. It serves great *souvláki*."

"I love *souvláki*."

"Well, what about eight o'clock?"

"Sounds good, but I can't stay late because I have got to go to the hospital early tomorrow. They've got the first batch of patients all lined up for me."

We arranged that I'd pick her up from the hotel at eight.

*

We got to the restaurant and just eased into each other's company.

We ate the *souvláki.* I had a beer and she a 7 Up. She said that she never drank alcohol the night before the operating theatre. At eleven, she asked if we could leave. I didn't mind as I knew that something was happening and that things could be taken slow. Then I remembered what happened between Melani and me … maybe taking it slow was a bad idea. But, as usual, I didn't listen to my inner editor, and I let the cautionary thought go.

When we drove back to the Hilton, I walked her through the front door, and at the foyer, we stood looking at each other. She reached over and squeezed my arm before leaving.

"What about tomorrow night?" I asked.

She looked at me with a real, serious look.

Then after a pause: "Fine. Same time."

I nodded.

"*Kallinikta,* Stauvro." Her long black eyelashes dropped as she gave me a last shy look.

"*Kallinikta,* Alexandra. *Kalon ipnon* – sleep well," I managed to add.

The next morning, Petros stormed into my *kafenio*, raised his hand in greeting to *Kyrio* Louizou and ordered a coffee. I was reading a Greek newspaper and took the last gulp to finish my coffee. He sat down and said nothing, taking out his packet of cigarettes and lighting up.

"What's wrong with you?" I cautiously ventured.

My cousin was on the warpath. Fuming.

"*Ase me* – leave me – Stauvro. Because I may, for the first time in my life, commit murder."

"What the hell's happened?"

He dragged on his cigarette and held the smoke before exhaling it.

"*Gamo ton kapile tou* – It's that fat bastard – Patroklos," he finally said. "Would you believe it, he bailed me up outside the courtrooms and pulled a gun on me."

"What?"

"I was there to give evidence on a case that we were presenting to the court and went outside to have a smoke. The little turd pulled a gun on me, threatening to shoot me as a traitor. He said that one of his men saw him being followed, and he, in turn, followed the man – he meant Vasilis – back to the Central Police Station. How dare I have him followed, he screamed … I was blowing his cover, etcetera, etcetera. Then he started telling me that he'd fuck my mother and my sister, and to cut a long story short … I lost it. I took his toy gun off him and whacked him with it. One of the judges – Alecos Stilli, a friend from my army days – was going past and intervened, stopping me from shooting him. Shit, I tell you, cousin, I was really tempted. Then the security guards rushed outside and pointed their guns at me. Even showing them my warrant card didn't stop them from arresting me. Jesus, what a fuck up."

Kyrios Louizos brought Petros his coffee and water and withdrew, alarmed by the state that my cousin had worked himself into.

"So then what happened?"

"Well, my boss came down to the courts and so did Patroklos' boss. By then, the bastard was bleeding like a slaughtered pig, but he had come to his senses. My boss insisted that the matter had to be dealt with there and then because it was very serious. They cleaned him up, wrapped a bandage around his head and then they put both of us in an empty courtroom with Alecos adjudicating, and we all had it out.

"I went first and I let them have it. I said that our investigation had tied the Kessler woman, the German cultural attaché, to the German woman shot in Agia Napa and that one of my men found out that he, Patroklos, was screwing her. From our point of view, he had compromised himself and may have put your life at risk by passing your address on to her ... so I said he was a person of interest, given all the shit that was getting spread around ... and I said he should surrender himself to me for questioning.

"Well, then both the KYP boss and Patroklos started quoting the Official Secrets Act ... They said that Patroklos was on an undercover assignment ... Yeah, more like under the bedsheets, I retorted, and this went on for a while. Then out of nowhere, he tried to whack me one, but I was so wound up that I managed to fend him off and throw him into the wall. Finally, his boss grabbed him and pulled him outside, and all I heard was how he was going to kill me and make me eat *ta archidia mou* – my testicles.

"Then my boss took me back to the office and he tried to calm me down. As I wouldn't settle down, he sent me home. So here I am, with egg on my face … waiting for you to tell me what an idiot I was and what to do next."

I ordered another coffee for myself and sat there, waiting for Petros to calm down. The coffee arrived and I took a sip of water first.

"This case is really getting to you, eh, cousin?"

Petros didn't reply. He lit a cigarette and drew on it.

"Yeah. You are right," he finally conceded.

"Well, I can't see any harm done," I said tentatively. "If Patroklos has strayed out of the KYP patch, that is exactly what I'd expect him to do … rather than withdraw and keep a low profile, he chose to attack … you know the old saying, 'the best form of defence is attack'." It was not a Cypriot saying but my rough paraphrase from a war manual by the Chinese General Sun Tsu, who lived about the time the ancient Greek civilisation was at its peak. "The problem is we don't know what role Patroklos is really playing. Has KYP infiltrated the terrorist or the reverse?

"I wouldn't worry about it," I continued. "At least it's in the open now, and if he does try something, he'll be the first one that everyone will be suspicious of. Enjoy your coffee, cousin. Now, I have another theory for you. I forgot to tell you. On the way to the airport Terry said he had been thinking about what is happening with the Agia Napa thing and thought to mention the possibility that what all this is about is a kidnapping. He reminded me of what happened to J Paul Getty's grandson in Calabria three years ago … Do you remember it?"

"Yes. I remember it well because there were rumours that he may have been brought to Cyprus."

"You are joking?"

"No, but it was an idiotic suggestion … Why bring him here when they could have taken him to Sicily or Sardinia? He was kidnapped in Rome, right? By the Mafia?"

"Yeah, according to Terry, he was taken to Calabria. They demanded a $17 million ransom for him and at one stage they sent a lock of hair and one of his ears as proof that they had him. To cut a long story short, eventually the kidnappers were paid $2.9 million, but the police arrested them all, although only two were ever convicted. Terry wonders if those idiots here were planning something similar. He also mentioned Patty Hearst and her kidnapping while he was here. There was a ransom demand for her, as well. It would give them a lot of cash."

"I don't think so, cousin. Our rich are not that rich. I can't remember a real kidnapping for money for a long time here … Even during EOKA days, kidnappings were only carried out against British army personnel. It's more likely to be something that the PLO are cooking up, although generally, they have kept away from Cyprus because they use it as a transit point. Also, our government has kept the Arabs on-side by its non-aligned stance."

"What, some peculiar form of Cypriot neutrality?"

"Maybe, cousin," said Petros.

"Maybe?

"It's a catfight between the Jews and Arabs, Stauvro. And like all catfights it won't end well."

*

What we didn't know at the time was that Sergeant Karageorgis was having lunch with his wife in a cafe on Makarios III Avenue. They were seated inside but next to an open window, and he heard an argument going on outside between two men. One called the other Sava and the Sava guy called him Stelio. They were quite animated, unaware that others may be listening in on their conversation. The one called Sava was telling Stelio how they should make sure that the New Zealander and his cousin were taken care of because they were drawing too much attention to their 'business'. "Follow them and take Taki," he said. "If they get close, you know what to do."

Karageorgis pricked up his ears when he heard the New Zealand reference and indicated to his wife to keep talking while he tried to see what the two guys looked like. As he was only a few feet from them and turning his head would draw their attention, he indicated to his wife that he would go to the toilet. By the time he came back, he saw the two men were stubbing out their cigarettes, dropping some money on the table and leaving. He asked the waiter if he knew who those men were.

"He's a regular. His name is Spithas. Savas Spithas. I've seen the other guy with him before, but I don't know his name." Karageorgis walked his wife to their car and asked her to drop him off at the Paphos Gate Police Station. Asking around, he discovered that Spitha used to work with them but now was with KYP. Armed with this information, Karageorgis went looking for Petros.

Chapter 6

1

Early the next morning, I was awakened by the church bells of *Panagia Phaneromenis* church, and because of it, I still held on to the tail end of a dream.

An idea then sprung from it.

I had been jotting down ideas for short stories in my diary but on this occasion, it was more than an idea. The narrative unravelled as I sat typing next to my desk lamp with Scipio lying on my knee.

I was starting to become aware of a stillness that would come over me just before I had a creative outburst, and I felt that maybe something was gestating that would allow me to move away from journalism. It seemed that it was something that, as Delphinidis suggested, would give meaning to my life.

This was not to be confused with the mood swings that used to threaten to engulf me like crashing surf on a beach. Those moods were dark and foreboding. This was different. Energising.

Recently, I had heard from Petros of cases where people were taking the law into their own hands to exact restitution for what happened to them during the war. Petros told me of one incident where a Greek officer was shot by his Greek Cypriot sergeant for leading them into a trap during the war. In Vietnam, the killing was called *fragging,* because it was done with a grenade. There were also civil disputes that did not end well for parties as rough justice was served, and in most cases, a sort of *omertà,* as the Italians call it, a code of

299

silence existed where the police did nothing as no one would testify or offer evidence. The dream gave me the idea whereby I could imagine myself being caught in such a situation where, as a witness, I found it hard to reconcile going to the police. So I decided to set up a conflict situation in the steam baths that I visited in the old town. A sort of a moral dilemma. At the same time, I wanted to explore the sort of ideas about a sense of place that gives colour to the works of fiction writers. Maybe I was running before I could walk, but I couldn't see myself being a journalist forever, and I felt I had to give this opportunity of being in relative isolation, even if it was to a small degree, a go.

I became aware that my subconscious was gathering information, and when I was writing, I was assembling bits and pieces from all over the place, from my own and others' pasts and even projecting into the future. I did wonder if I was laying down my own moral code and testing myself to see where the breaking point was. It was, of course, hypothetical, but nonetheless, I was becoming aware that in such a terrain may lurk the possibilities of compelling storytelling. Since I had completed *The Wheat Field*, which I sent back to New Zealand and was published in a literary magazine, I had written the skeleton of half a dozen other short stories and several dozen poems. I found it hard to finish them. Maybe I was waiting for some sort of inspiration. Perhaps that was what Alexandra, by her mere presence, had inadvertently offered me, and perhaps even that was why I was up so early.

I have heard of artists having muses who inspired them to paint great works, and I knew that that was replicated in the literary arts. John Keats was inspired by his great love for Fanny Brawne, Scott Fitzgerald was inspired by his wife Zelda and even unrequited love like that of Jane Austen for Tom Lefroy and W B Yeats for Maude Gonne had the same consequences. I had not felt anything like that emerging from my affection for Melani, *Giagia*

300

Androutsou's niece, and maybe that was the real reason she intuitively did not trust my marriage proposal. The story is called *The Public Baths.*

The Public Baths

The public baths or *hamam* were found in the heart of the old city, one street over from where the prostitutes plied their trade. Built at the same time as the city walls by the Catholics who had conquered the local Orthodox Christians, they were dedicated to Saint Mary. After they were partly destroyed by cannon fire, they were rebuilt and converted to a mosque by the Ottoman general who finally captured the city from the Catholics. He dedicated it to the prophet Omar, who it was said rested there during a brief visit.

Later, a new and more splendorous mosque was built, but the Ottomans eventually left, and it was turned into public baths. The public baths had, over the years, served the needs of the city's dwellers. There Muslim and Christian men – no women were allowed – would undertake their weekly ablutions and relax after a hard-working week. Women had their own bathhouse. An imported massage technique, where a masseur massages with his feet by walking on his client, was available for an extra price to all those who felt the need.

The baths were built from blocks of limestone mined from a quarry in the nearby sparsely cypress-planted mountains to the north and plastered with gypsum mined from the plain. The walls were whitewashed every year, a form of disinfectant. The roof comprised three concentric domes arranged as a classic Islamic motif. Large, rough, square white marble tiles met the visitor at the door where he was expected to leave his shoes. The smell of eucalyptus would start working on the visitor as soon as he opened the solid wooden door. Before he knew it, his breathing would ease and the fine desert dust from across the water that clogged his lungs would release itself in thick phlegm that he'd deliver in spittoons appropriately placed around the corridors and the swimming pool, where he cooled himself off before a dip in cold water and showering for a massage or a shave.

The proprietor of the baths was a fat but jolly Anatolian, and although his features spoke of some northern nomadic pedigree, one could distinguish a telling thick foreign accent as he welcomed his customers, dispensing a large white towel, soap and a waterproof pouch for the clients to keep their wallet and watch in.

His nickname was the Spaniard, one supposed because, at some stage, he spent time in Spain. He would answer to that name; however, loudly or softly it was uttered.

On this day, a tall but thin and sinewy young man entered the baths. He was casually dressed in khaki slacks, a white shirt and well-designed sandals. The Spaniard limped over to the young man, dragging his left foot behind him.

"Good day to you, sir. Please come with me," he instructed. And seeing the young man's eyes moving towards his foot, he said by way of explanation, "A present from Franco." Then picking up one of each of the needed items – placed on a high bench as if they were the most precious things in the world – he led the way.

The young man followed him without uttering a word. At the door of the changing rooms, the Spaniard put the items on a small table and then turning to the young man he said, "If you please, sir, take the locker key with you. Will sir need to be reminded of the time?"

The young man shook his head, which the Spaniard took as a dismissal.

The young man hung the strung key around his neck, entered

the changing room, stripped and wrapping the towel around himself, opened the heavy cedar door and entered the steam room. He heard the creaking of the spring and then the snap as the door closed behind him. It took a while for his eyes to get used to the darkness, which he soon saw was diffused by the light coming from the small wood-stocked ceramic stove on which were placed a pile of river stones. Someone, whose features the young man could not distinguish as his face was in shadow, was using a long-handled ladle to pour water with eucalyptus oil onto the stone, which immediately hissed steam in an ominous fashion, reminding the young man of the hiss of a snake. The man who raised the steam was fat, with an enormous belly, and he coughed, as did the young man. The young man then saw the silhouette of the man move back to the far corner.

As well as the key, a gold crucifix hung around the young man's neck from a long, thin, rounded leather. The young man touched the crucifix to assure himself or for something for his hands to do, and then he took a seat at the nearby bench. He sat there, looking towards the fire and the man beyond. In turn, the man from across the room looked at the young man briefly and went back to dozing.

The young man sat very still, breathing in the eucalyptus, feeling the phlegm draining down his nose. He pushed on one of his nostrils, and getting up, he moved towards the fire, blowing out through his open nostril and clearing it on to the white-hot stones. The sound of hissing filled the room. Then he performed the same action on the other nostril. More hissing. He coughed, and any phlegm that came up he accurately spat onto the stones. Once again, he was rewarded with more hissing. Then the young man stoked the fire with more kindling and went back to where he was sitting. He sat upright, one leg in front of the other, like some athlete ready to spring out of his marks at the beginning of a 100-metre dash.

"It is hot," said the fat man with a somewhat effeminate, high-pitched voice, breaking the silence.

"Yes, it is," replied the young man.

"Yes, it's hot," said the fat man again.

The young man didn't feel that he had anything further to add to this and stayed silent.

Ten or fifteen minutes went by.

Another man entered the room. The door snapped shut behind him. His body was in silhouette, but the young man could see that he was short and stocky with a white towel wrapped around his middle. He somehow exuded power and, with it, a ruthless, electric energy. It may have been the way he held himself together or walked. The young man could not see his facial features, which he imagined to be even more menacing. The stocky man went through the coughing and spitting ritual and then flopped down on the side opposite the door, between the young man and the other man opposite. The young man could hear the stocky man's heavy breathing. Then there was a prolonged coughing spree. The stocky man lifted himself, muttering below his breath, and moving towards the fire, he spat on stones. He grabbed the ladle and threw a dash of water at the same spot. Steam rose as the hissing once again filled the room.

All three men sat soaking up the heat, sweat pouring off them.

The door opened and the proprietor called out, "Ari, your hour is up." The fat man from the far side of the room eventually got up and moved towards the door. As he walked past, one of the stocky man's hands darted out and a knife flashed in the dim light … there was a cracking sort of slapping sound, and the stocky man flopped over.

"Not a word, *múle*," hissed the stocky man as he held the knife at the man's throat.

The fat man whimpered.

"You fuckin' touch my little girl again and next time, I'll slit your throat." The stocky man rose and threw something onto the fire. There was a hiss and the smell of burning flesh. The stocky man turned towards the young man. "Don't follow for ten minutes. You saw nothing," he growled. Then he opened the door and disappeared. The young man looked towards the fat man, who writhed whimpering on the floor, passing out as a pool of blood formed around him.

The young man was conflicted. Had he heard correctly? Hadn't the stocky man said that the fat man had molested his daughter? He looked at the writhing creature who had managed to come to and had begun a deep whining, "I did nothing … I did nothing …" Picking up the towel, the young man bundled it together and put it into the man's crotch. Then after what he thought was enough time for the stocky man to have left, he got up and followed into the light. He went straight to the front counter, where he saw the Spaniard unconscious on the floor, and he brought him to by slapping his face. He then helped him sit up.

"What happened?" asked the Spaniard, shaking his head.

"You have been knocked out. Did you see who did it?"

The Spaniard shook his head. "He came up from behind."

"Your customer is lying in a pool of blood. The man who came in after me did a terrible … a nasty thing to him."

"No, Christ and Virgin Mary … Ari," cried out the Spaniard, and getting up, he stumbled towards the steam room. The masseuse and a man from the pool rushed out at his calls.

"Go outside and raise the alarm. Ask them to bring the police," he yelled at the young man over his shoulder.

The young man, still half-naked, did as he was asked. He managed to stop and convince a passer-by to go and find a policeman. He then went back, hurriedly dried and dressed and went out to the foyer.

The Spaniard was talking to the people who had gathered, answering their questions, swearing and gesticulating his despair.

"I cannot understand it," complained the Spaniard. "He is like a five-year-old. Who would want to do that to him?"

Two policemen arrived in winter uniform and began interviewing the witnesses.

"He won't miss it," scoffed one of the policemen after the young man told him what happened.

However, they did take some notes. The young man added a vague description of the man who did the deed. But he was conflicted: in all conscience, he couldn't defend a child molester by giving a more accurate description of the attacker.

"I never saw the man before. There's no way the boy would do something like that," explained the Spaniard. "His father ... God forgive him ... when he was young ... he fixed him ... that's why he is so fat ... all I can think of is that someone else blamed him for something that they did."

"That doesn't happen, does it?" asked the young man.

"Everything happens here, my boy," said the Spaniard. "God, how am I going to tell his parents?" he asked in despair. Then he explained that the young man was the son of his sister and he agreed to him coming to the baths every day so that the boy's parents could work – and also to keep him out of harm's way. "I was looking after him. This is a travesty," moaned the Spaniard.

'Well, I better go," said the young man and wished him all the very best.

A week later, the young man came across a young lawyer that he knew.

"Guess what I saw today?"

"What?"

"I still don't believe it."

"What, for Christ's sake?"

"I was walking along the city wall over the moat, and I saw a crowd gathered around, yelling in excitement at someone who was kicking a football. Except it wasn't a football … this ball didn't move. It stayed in place and the man kept kicking it. I went closer and saw that the man was kicking someone's head. It was a man buried into the dry floor of the moat and just his head was sticking out. The man kept circling and kicking the head and screaming. You could see the buried man, however, was unconscious as the head lolled from side to side, wherever the kick would take it. Eventually, the police arrived and they arrested the man."

"Did they find out why he did it?"

"I asked some of the bystanders who were there from the beginning, and they said he kept yelling that the man molested his little girl."

"What?"

"Yeah, that's what he said. Well, a colleague of mine who was in court when he was indicted said that the man has no girl child. He lost her and his wife in the war. He went mad. They keep him in the asylum outside the city, but every so often he escapes. A symptom

307

of his condition is that he blames whomever his madness latches on to, much like a cocklebur seed that catches a ride on a mangy dog. But his lawyer said this was the first time he physically hurt someone."

"No, it isn't," said the young man. "He emasculated someone in the Turkish baths."

"What! That was him?"

"Yes, it was him. He said he did it because the guy had abused his little girl."

"And?"

"He obviously lost his mind. Another casualty of the war, I suppose."

"I must go ... I need to report it to the police."

"Too late for that."

"Why?"

"Well, the guy was stabbed outside the court by a cripple. The police were taking him to the Central Prison."

"So no, 'and'?"

"Yeah. No, 'and'."

2

The devil must been having another slow day again that Thursday, or maybe it was the buoyancy that I felt with having discovered someone that I thought I could live with for the rest of my life. It never occurred to me for a second that there was a risk and that the rest of my life might not last long if things went pear-shaped with what I had got myself into.

I parked the Morris down a side road and approached the West German embassy with the determination of someone who had urgent business and knew who he was going to see.

That morning I had pressed my grey flannel slacks so that the creases were sharp and put on a clean white shirt and a dark brown corduroy sports coat. I even polished my tan Oxford shoes.

There was a pillbox at the gate. I flashed my passport at the Greek policeman who was part of the diplomatic protection contingent. He noted my name and my passport's origin and number. He waved me through. I drew my shoulders back and walked between the roses and thick, dark green lawn that was superbly maintained by a gardener who was obviously oblivious to the shortage of water. I walked up the steps and was immediately confronted by an armed guard. I showed my passport and the business card stating my name and profession that I had printed for such occasions. Also included underneath in capital letters was REUTERS – London. The guard waved me through, pointing to the woman behind the receptionist's desk. I headed towards her.

Opposite on several benches were people lined up, possibly waiting for entry visas. The young woman behind the desk, a Greek Cypriot, asked me what she could do for me.

"I am looking for your cultural affairs officer. I think her name is Kessler," I replied in English.

"Have you got an appointment, sir?"

"No, but tell her that I am here for the Joseph Conrad lecture that she is organising."

The receptionist looked blankly at me, but she nonetheless picked up the phone and dialled someone. She spoke in German to the person at the other end of the conversation, but all I made out was my name and that of Joseph Conrad. There was a question. The receptionist looked at me. She dropped her voice and said something again, in German. Then whatever the person at the other end said, the receptionist moved the phone away from her ear as if someone had spat in it. She then promptly put the phone down and asked me if I would kindly take a seat further down the corridor.

Not a minute went by before a tall, impeccably dressed blonde man of around forty approached me. His greyish suit was casual but well-cut, and his light blue shirt was offset by a yellow patterned tie.

"Hello, Mr Carpenter, I am Herman Gunter," he said in good English. "Miss Kessler is not available. Maybe I can help you. I am her colleague."

"No, I prefer to see Miss Kessler," I said. "It's a private matter."

"If you give me some indication of what this is about, I may be able to get her out of what she is doing."

"I don't think your English is any good, mate," I said. "I told you, it's a private matter. Maybe that concept has not reached Germany yet."

Herr Gunter did not like being challenged and his blue eyes contracted as he gave me the death stare. I was sure this boy was a tough cookie, but I stared back, confident that with so many people around he wasn't going to action the implied threat. He may be a colleague of Kessler, and therefore also an intelligence officer, but he wasn't up to dealing with the obtuse Kiwi prick that woke up that day in Nicosia searching for a windmill to beat the shit out of.

What's your problem with this being a private matter, Gunter?" I asked in French, just to up the ante.

He suddenly turned and walked back down the corridor and up the stairs.

Within three minutes, a petite brunette in a black mini skirt and white blouse showed up. She wore black high heels and no wig. Her face was lightly made up with a cherry tomato gloss lipstick setting off healthy white teeth. She fitted the description that *Kyrios* Prokopis had given.

She stood looking at me, trying to work out how to start, but I didn't give her a chance.

"Steve Carpenter. I work for Reuters," I said in English, trying to mimic Terry's Etonian accent and feeling that, in this instance, Patroklos' operating maxim that the best defence is attack was the best way to go. Two could play this game.

"I don't think we have met before," she tried.

"No, we haven't. But you did visit and ransack my apartment in Onasagorou Street in the old city. I have come to pick up my books," I continued, keeping my eyes riveted on hers.

She was shocked by my bluntness. Also, by then, she must have placed me in her scheme of things and was thinking about how to play me.

"Ah, that Mr Carpenter. You look different. Can you please come with me where we can talk?" she suggested.

"No, I have said to you what I came to say," I replied, standing my ground and plunging in the metaphorical knife. "I imagine that you don't have them here, so I would be grateful if you returned the two books you took by

311

tomorrow's post. Then, as far as I am concerned, that is the end of the matter. You know where I live."

The woman stood looking at me now, starting to bristle. "I think we should talk about it," she tried again, aware that our conversation was drawing the receptionist's attention.

"I don't think Patroklos would like that," I said, giving the same metaphorical knife a twist.

Her dark brown eyes flared.

"Fine, if that's how you want it," she said.

"Yes, that's exactly how, I want it, *Fräulein* Kessler," I growled, and turning, I walked out of the embassy.

When I was outside of the perimeter of the embassy, I let out a long breath. I was trembling. Then as I walked down the street, I saw Vasilis, Petros' man, parked in an old Mazda. If he was dozing, he was now fully awake.

Well, that should get the wasps' nest going. Hopefully, into a fuckin' frenzy because the woman now knew that at least someone had her number. She'd be wondering who else I had told and whether her position in Cyprus was tenable. I didn't give a shit.

3

I had a great weekend with Alexandra. She worked half of Saturday but after she finished, we took off together for Limassol. We walked along the promenade and ate ice cream and talked. She must have had a shower at the hospital because she smelled of Lux soap. She wore no makeup.

We sat down at a small taverna and ordered coffees. I excused myself to get a paper. When I came back, Alexandra was sitting down while two young men in their late teens stood above her chatting with her, or so it seemed at the time. Both men were stylishly dressed in fawn sports coats and open blue shirts and their trousers, one in leaf green and the other blue, were flared. As I neared, I heard one of the men say to her in English, "Come on. We have a good time. My friend is a taxi driver and he'll take us anywhere you want."

Alexandra was not amused, and I could see that she was giving them enough rope to hang themselves. I walked up and stood behind Alexandra.

"*Yiassas pethia. Then ehete tipota alo na ganete*? – Hello boys. Don't you have anything else to do?" I asked in a grating tone.

"These two gentlemen have assured me that they would give me a good time, Stauvro *mou*," said Alexandra, fixing both men with a look that could only be replicated with two stethoscope heads.

Terry was right. We are nothing more than upright monkeys. For no real reason I was bristling and ready to knock the shit out of those two guys. Obviously, they were soldiers on leave and on the prowl.

The second young man turned red and said sorry. They both took off with their tails between their legs.

"So my *cavaliero* has returned," said Alexandra.

"Yes. Indeed he has." I snapped, still flushed by that almost primordial feeling that swamped me.

313

That night we returned to Nicosia. I bought us both *souvláki* and a couple of beers and we had them at my apartment. Alexandra loved Scipio, and I think I began to love her because of that. After a tea and more talking, around one o'clock, I drove her to the Hilton.

Then on Sunday, we went to Khirokitia, where they had unearthed a 9,000-year-old Neolithic village. We had a picnic next to a running brook that used to supply water to the people who had built their beehive-shaped houses on a hill that was protected by sheer cliffs on three sides. They buried their dead under the houses. Alexandra brought some sandwiches that were prepared for her by the hotel. She also had a thermos of coffee and a small basket of fruit. After, we went to Tenta, where another Neolithic village was discovered in 1947. They were gearing up to start excavations the following year. Nothing much to see. Only the low hillock where Agia Eleni – Constantine the Great's mother – had her tent erected during her brief stay in Cyprus. It was on a road that linked the Troodos Mountains with the southern coast.

Alexandra had an early night because she was to be back at the hospital the following morning. I became aware that our time together was slowly disappearing, and that I had to do something if anything was going to happen between us.

4

That Monday, no parcel arrived for me from the cultural affairs officer Bridgette Kessler.

*

I said nothing about my visit to the West German embassy to Petros as he was in a sullen mood. We were heading to his place for lunch when he suddenly did a U-turn and headed back into town. Fifteen minutes later, we parked in a side street in the suburb of *Agios* Andreas.

"Isn't this the street you said KYP was in?"

"Come on, cousin, we are going to see someone."

"Who?"

"You'll see."

After we identified ourselves, he asked the guard at the door where Savas Spithas' office was.

It seemed that my cousin had decided on the same strategy that I had tried on Bridgette Kessler the Thursday before: surprise and confront.

The guard said that I was not allowed to go with my cousin, but I could wait in the lobby. So Petros went up to see if Savas was in his office.

I had been looking out of the window while I lit a half Il Moro, admiring the small garden outside the KYP building. It was one of the discreet buildings that I had passed when I initially tried to see where KYP were housed. Yellow sandstone blocks and white painted windows with leaf green sills and shutters.

I caught movement in my left peripheral vision and turned to see a man going up the stairs. He took the stairs two at the time. I didn't know at the time who he was. However, halfway up the stairs, he stopped. Just then, my cousin came down around the turn of the stairs and stood hovering above him. He tried to get around him but Petros blocked him. It must be Savas!

At first glance, there was nothing unusual about this Savas guy. He was smartly dressed in a well-cut dark suit and black brogues and he wore a bold striped blue tie. He had very angular features and was fit. He sported a Clark Gable moustache.

"Down! Now!" Commanded Petros.

Savas turned to see if anyone was watching and saw me. I saw the flicker of recognition in his eyes. The guard was busy reading the newspaper. By then, I had thrown what was left of the Il Moro into the sand tray. Savas paused for a second, taking me in. Then he descended the staircase to the bottom, and turning, he shook his shoulders to resettle his jacket and waited until Petros was on the same level as him. My cousin was bristling and Savas wasn't sure what to do.

"What do you want?" he finally asked.

"What is going on?" asked Petros.

"What is going on where?"

"You recognised Stauvro! He is the New Zealander you don't like," he said, nodding in my direction. "Why are you and your friends trying to kill him?"

Savas was taken aback by the blunt accusation and tried assuming an expression and posture that showed that he didn't have a clue what was going on and was obviously facing a madman.

"I don't know what you are talking about."

"You don't know what I am talking about?"

"No, I don't."

"Well, get this and plant it deep in your fuckin' brain," hissed Petros. If Frank could pull off a death stare, that day, Petros pulled a double. "And pass it on to your crazy mates. If something happens to my cousin, I am coming for you first. And no one is going to stop me from finding you one dark night and beating your fuckin' head to pulp and then burying you somewhere in the Pithkia where the eels will fatten on your fuckin' carcass. And then I'll work through your scumbag mates, one at a time. So you've been warned."

Savas cracked a crooked sneer and said nothing.

Then he corrected his cuffs, straightened his shoulders, walked around Petros and went up the stairs. But this time, he took the stairs one at the time.

Petros watched him until he was out of view.

"Come on, Stauvro … I need a coffee to get the taste of that scumbag out of my mouth."

While we drank our coffees, Petros told me what Karageorgis had overheard at the cafe.

5

Late on Tuesday afternoon, Petros met me at the same cafe on Makarios Avenue. I had rung him from the public library and he invited me to dinner. I explained that I had a rendezvous at the Hilton at seven, and he said he'd give me a lift after a coffee. My cousin was in high spirits because he had got a bit of a break with the case.

Apparently, there was a row at a petrol station at Astromeritis, eighteen miles west of Nicosia, and there was also a shooting. The village has a population of about a thousand people and is in what is left of the Morphou District since the invasion. A man died and the petrol attendant was now in a serious condition in Nicosia Hospital. From what was first reported to Petros – unusually – the petrol attendant attended to all the cars stopping for benzine by washing the windscreen and the back window. According to a man who sat on the other side of the road selling fresh string beans from his stall, the driver of the car told him not to do it and the petrol attendant, being slow-witted, ignored him and continued completing his set work routine. He had already put the nozzle in the car and made sure it was working before he started on the windscreen. On the way back to wash the back window, he saw a man slumped down in the back seat of the car, leaning against a fourth man. He said to the driver, "*Re koumpare*, your friend needs a hospital," and as he had seen them coming from Nicosia, he added, "You are going the wrong way. The hospital is in Nicosia … back that way." He pointed east. The next thing, the mechanic and owner of the petrol station, who heard the conversation and was working in the oil pit, said he heard shouting, a bit of a scuffle and a shot. The string-bean seller explained that it seemed to him that the petrol attendant, realising that the customer was going to shoot him, grabbed the gun and there was a struggle. The two men fell, both holding onto the gun and then the gun went off, killing the driver. Then a second man in the car got out and shot the petrol attendant. After picking up the discarded gun, the second shooter got back into the front of the car and drove away. The mechanic came out of the pit and found his brother bleeding on the forecourt. The car left behind the dead gunman and the nozzle and hose were torn from the pump. Petrol began gushing from the petrol pump, and the mechanic rushed to turn it off, afraid that a stray spark would set it on fire, so he didn't get the car's number. The string-bean seller said the car was a dark blue Volvo, but he was so shocked he, too, never thought of looking at the registration number.

After he related to me what had happened, Petros told me that the dead man left behind was a local hood called Modestos Kali. "He has a long record but mainly for fencing stolen goods. He also has a reputation as a bit of a fixer. One of the local policemen said that he'd seen him drive past and thought he might be from Kalopanayiotis, although his licence gave a Nicosia address."

By then, we were driving to the Hilton, which was not very far.

Suddenly Petros pulled the car over.

He turned and looked straight at me. "What's wrong?" he asked.

"What?"

"There's something wrong."

"No. I am fine."

"But you look so … light. Usually, you look as if you are carrying the world on your shoulders."

"No. Nothing's wrong."

"You are sure?"

"Yes, I am fine."

"I don't believe you, cousin. Remember, I am a policeman and I know when people lie."

I gave up because I knew he wouldn't stop. "It's just that I think I may have met someone," I said in an even voice.

"A woman?"

"No, a blooming donkey. Yes, cousin. A woman."

"What else? Who is she?"

"I am not saying anything until I have something to say."

"You cannot do this to me, cousin. As your cousin, I have the right to know …"

"You are only my third cousin. Third cousins don't count."

"Yes, they do, and I have a right to inspect her."

"Christ, Petros. She's not a camel!"

"No, she is not. But I think, as family, Eleni and I have a say."

"Well, if it goes anywhere, I'll bring her around to meet you. Now tell me more about the shooter."

"Stop changing the subject."

I remained staunch and silent.

Giving up, Petros said, "I bet anything you like that the scum bag in the back was the guy that I shot outside your apartment."

"It seems to me those guys are not amateurs, although this Kali guy may be. Maybe he was their Cyprus connection taking them from A to B."

"I don't know, but the petrol attendant saw someone wounded and … well … we'll eventually find out. Fancy a trip up to Kalopanayioti?"

"Why?"

"I told you. Kalis is from Kalopanayioti."

"When?"

"Tomorrow."

"Do you think they'll go there?"

"Well, possibly. We need to check it out. We could leave it to the Morphou District Police, but we can't stop in mid-chase ... we don't want to let those guys plan an escape."

"They probably have an exit plan because they have him on the move. If they are what Frank said they are, they'd be working three moves ahead of us."

"Yeah, but things have not exactly been going their way, and if they make a mistake twice, they can make more. If you don't want to come, that's fine."

"No, that's not a problem. What will your boss say?"

"If he asks, I'll tell him that I am taking you to Kykkos monastery to light a candle as a thank you to the Virgin Mary for protecting your life and to ask her to help us."

"So the Cyprus Police allows its finest to go, on a whim, on pilgrimages of thanksgiving and asking for divine intervention?"

"Well, the way that things have been unfolding the last few years, cousin, we need all the help we can get."

6

My mind was full of Alexandra the following day, and Petros was preoccupied with an accident he had had not long after we parted the previous day. He started venting as soon as I got in the car. My cousin had arrived driving a fairly new Opel. Apparently, a mindless teenager smashed his motorbike into his Alfa Romeo. "The stupid little bastard nearly got killed. He went straight through a red light. What he was thinking off, fucked if I know. Never mind … cars and motorbikes can be fixed … I nearly had the soul of the little turd on my conscience. When will we learn to drive carefully in this fuckin' country?" It was a rhetorical question. For Petros, the high road death toll was something that he had to contend with as a policeman. He would take his turn to go around and break the bad news to the deceased's family.

He lit a cigarette with the car's lighter. "This Opel is not bad," he finally conceded. "The boss's. He uses it, but he's loaned it to me until I can get my Alfa Romeo back."

When we were out of the Nicosia suburbs, he said, "Eh, Stauvro. I hate to tell you this. There's a car following us. Ever since I left the station, he's been on my tail. Don't turn around."

I stiffened, waiting to see what Petros was planning on. I was tempted to turn around.

"Who do you think it is?"

"It's a BMW ... Two men in the front," said Petros, sneaking looks into the rear vision mirrors.

He kept up his reports for twenty or so minutes. We stopped at the Astromeritis *Petrolina* benzine station to look at the scene of where Modestos Kalis and the petrol attendant were killed. We could still see the bloodstains from the two men and there were flies on the bloodied ground, despite someone throwing several shovels full of earth on the stains. We could see that the place was locked up. We got out and Petros slowly reconnoitred the scene that he had described to me the previous day.

He then walked around to the back of the petrol station, pretending he was going to have a pee, but he was looking to see if the BMW was anywhere near.

"Nothing more here," he said as he pretended to button up his trousers, and we got back into the Opel. "They have turned around and are parked and waiting for us to go back to Nicosia," he said under his breath. "Let's see what they will do when we keep going. You still up to going to Kalopanayiotis?"

"Are you armed?"

"Loaded and ready to go," said Petros patting his sports coat, under which was his holster.

When we came to the Troodos turnoff about half a mile later, Petros took a left.

I just sat back and enjoyed the view because I decided that Petros was just being paranoid about being followed. After about four miles, I could feel the Opel starting to rise off the plain onto the foothills.

We continued and tall trees like poplars, eucalyptus, pines, citrus trees and a variety of shrubs began to close in with the encroaching hills. Petros had lit another cigarette and was driving with one hand when he nudged me.

"They still there."

We continued driving for about ten miles. At a turn off the main road, Petros took a right that led northwest and would take us to Kalopanayioti. The road was similarly asphalted but much narrower. The car behind was still keeping up with us. After about five minutes, Petros saw a chance, and he pulled over on the road next to a man selling a range of farm produce. When he stopped the car, he got out. He waited until the BMW sped past and then noted the number plate. Petros waved at the disappointed man who thought he had a sale and got back in.

"It's a civilian car,' he said, reciting the number. "I think it's stolen because the registration number is older than the car."

"How do you know that?"

"It's one of those things that I keep track of."

"Did you recognise them?"

"No, too fast and they wore hats."

He had already put the car in a lower gear and moved after the car. He took his revolver from his shoulder holster and put it under his thigh, pointing towards the door.

"Just in case."

I looked to see if there was a radio to call for help. The car had no radio.

Seeing my searching eyes, "Yeah, the boss hasn't any need for one. We are on our own."

There was a sort of a crossroads and we continued going straight ahead. The village of Linou was on our left. We continued for another five miles, but we couldn't see the BMW.

"Where have they gone?" asked Petros.

Just as he said that something punched the back window of the car and a hole appeared on our windscreen. I turned around and saw, through the webbed hole in the rear window, the BMW emerging on the right from an acute side road that I later found out used to go to Lefka, which is now on the Turkish side. The bastards were waiting for us.

"Jesus, Petro, the fucks are shooting at us," I hissed, as if my cousin was too dense to realise what was happening.

"Hold on," said Petros and he dropped the Opel back into third. The Opel surged forward and seemed to be gaining momentum – even if we *were* going up a continuous slope. I looked behind and saw the BMW follow. It was catching up. I glanced back again. Although two-way, the road was still narrow, but the BMW was trying to position itself so that the man with a gun on the passenger's side could have a better angle to take us out. Petros moved the Opel into the middle of the road, only giving a clear overtake at the corners where he couldn't see what was coming the other way. It had rained and the road was slippery.

Really, we were going too fast for the road conditions, and I thought he might take us over the edge down the drop on to the side. I tried not to think about it. Taller trees, some showing new leaves, again were leaning over the road, but being in front of the other car, Petros must have seen something coming down the acute left turn further up the road, so he went right. The bus that emerged instinctively went to his own right as well. We just missed the bus. The BMW, caught in the left lane, didn't have time to avoid it and hit a glancing blow on the front bumper of the bus and then veered off the road into a concrete culvert to our right. On a steep rocky ledge next to the culvert was a small religious shrine and the BMW's front was buried in it.

Petros screeched the Opel to a halt at an angle.

"Out," he shouted, and as I hit the asphalt, he followed right behind me. He stood up and took a position behind the front bonnet and with his revolver pointing forward, he peeked to where the wrecked BMW was.

I heard people screaming.

"Stay out of sight until I deal with these bastards," commanded Petros in a booming voice.

He moved cautiously down the road, holding his revolver with both hands. By then, several people who were on the bus were scrambling out, crossing themselves and yelling to each other and at Petros. When they saw the gun, they shut up and froze, giving Petros some respite as he moved towards the BMW.

"Get behind the bus!" he yelled at the passengers. He advanced towards the BMW's front passenger door. When he was sure that there was no immediate danger from the car, he holstered his gun. He opened the passenger door and leaned into the BMW. He first attended to the passenger, then to the driver. He stood upright and took a deep breath and then leaned into the BMW and rifled the bodies for ID or wallets.

Withdrawing, he turned and looked at me, shook his head and gestured to me to go forward.

Whomever the saint of that the shrine was dedicated to, he did not protect the passengers of the BMW in their hour of need. As it should be really.

"Nothing," said Petros. He met me halfway. He said that the driver of the BMW was thrown backwards and his neck was broken when he recoiled, bouncing off the steering wheel. The passenger who was the shooter was halfway through the front windscreen. Both were dead.

Petros went to the bus driver, who was suffering from shock and head injuries.

A car approached from the direction of Troodos and Petros waved for it to stop. He showed his warrant card to the driver and then explained that he needed him to drive back to Linou village.

"Find a telephone and report the incident to the police. Tell them that Inspector Petros Zimaras needs help, immediate help. Describe what's happened and then tell them we are about two miles after the Lefka turn-off."

Then he moved up and down, calming the passengers who had emerged from behind the bus or finally climbed out. They had been on a religious pilgrimage to Makhairas monastery and they were returning to Nicosia.

It took an hour before reinforcements arrived. It took an hour before reinforcements arrived. Petros' enigmatic boss also came out this time. He went over to the BMW and looked at the two bodies. Retreating, he scowled over the damage done to the Opel. He gave me a dirty look before taking Petros for a walk up the road. He was dressed in what looked like a dark

Italian suit, but was probably made by a highly skilled Cypriot tailor, and wore expensive shoes. I could hear him shouting and swearing, and after about ten minutes, the boss stormed past me, got into a teal green Audi and drove back to Nicosia.

"Come on, I am taking one of the Land Rovers and we are going up to the village. You'd think he'd be pleased that we are fine," he said, looking over his shoulder. "But instead, he is worried about the fuckin' car. They're going to tow the bloody thing back to Nicosia."

"Shouldn't we go back too?"

"No, those *pezevenkides* mean business, cousin and they didn't want us to go up there, so there must be something there. And by the way, one of the dead men," he said, indicating towards the car, "is a KYP officer. The boss knows him. He said he's called Stelios Tsangaris."

"And the other?"

"No one knows him so far. It could be that Taki that Karageorgis overheard of."

"Why would they not carry their IDs, Petro?"

"A better question is, why were they trying to kill us, Stauvro?" asked Petros.

"They had nothing else to do," I said flippantly and soon regretted it.

"I think we are getting close. They were trying to stop us from going somewhere, cousin … maybe *ston Kalopanayioti.*"

7

Petros and I drove further up the road to Troodos. The Land Rover was not as comfortable as the Opel. It also was very noisy. You could see new bright green leaves and colourful wildflowers emerging from the abundant plant life around us, heralding a late spring. Petros was right. It renewed your energy just watching this unfurling green and multi-hued wonder.

We weren't entirely sure that Modestos Kali was actually from Kalopanayioti. As Petros said, that was the word from people interviewed by the police, including police members of the Morphou prefecture. But villagers, once they latch on to someone, work away until they place them in the scheme of things. It seemed more likely that like a lot of people who live and work in Nicosia, Modestos was at least born in Kalopanayioti. I never visited the village before, or so I thought until we passed its dammed lake and entered its quaint stone-paved streets. I then vaguely remembered getting lost somewhere up there on a trip. Going through it, I remembered the stone terraces and the lush green valley that it was draped down.

"Let's go and find the *muktar*," said Petros.

"Where?" I asked.

"He could be anywhere up here. Those people eke out an existence, and although there's plenty of water, it is still tough work. When in doubt, head for a *kafenio*."

It didn't take long before we found a *kafenio* with, as usual, its elderly clientele, all men, sitting outside in the afternoon sun.

"I'll go and ask. You wait here. I won't take a minute."

I watched Petros go over, and it wasn't long before he was given instructions on where the *muktar* was.

When we found him, he was in the middle of a field propping up some grapevines. His name was Marios Poulos and he looked like he was in his late fifties. He spoke English well and told us that he learned it when he lived in New York, driving cabs. He returned, unlike many others, built himself a house and was spending his days ministering to the civic needs of the village and tending his small estate, where he produced wine.

It wasn't long before we were sitting at his home, tasting his latest vintage and chewing on almonds and dry figs, which, he assured us, were some of the produce that brought him a modest income.

"So, tell us about Modestos Kali, *Kyrie* Poule," suggested Petros.

"Well, he is … I mean, was … a bit of a rough diamond … a real *mangas*. He was one of the boys that the army didn't help. He mixed with the wrong crowd and got into trouble in *Lefkosia*. I don't exactly know what happened, but he came back up here and kept his nose clean for a while. His parents died in a car accident a few years back. That didn't help either. Sometimes he and his friends used to drive up here, but they always stayed up at his house. The whole village was shocked to hear what happened to him. But I don't think there was anyone who was surprised."

"Has he got any siblings?"

"Only a sister, Eleni, *Kyrie* Zimara, but she's married in Agros. Her husband owns a hotel." Agros was a small mountain village popular with tourists north of Limassol. "Her husband didn't get on with Modestos. It happens, I suppose, but I think Modestos did something to make it worse. I

330

heard on the grapevine that he had sent some foreigners to stay at the hotel without telling his brother-in-law and something happened."

"So, you never saw any of those characters?"

"No, as I told you, they kept to themselves and avoided coming down to the *kafenia*. I am sure if you ask the brother-in-law, he'll probably tell you."

"Do you know the brother-in-law's name?"

"He is called Marios. His surname is … I think it's *Kampouris* … no *Kambouridis*. Yes, Marios *Kampouridis*."

"So how do we get to the house?" asked Petros.

"Go back up, Markou Drakou Road," he said, pointing behind us, "and then take the fork to your left and follow it around until you see the bridge that leads to the Monastery of *Agios* Gianni Lampadistis. Go past, with the monastery to your right, and follow the road up the hill. The house is on the corner overlooking the Setrachos, the river below. It's got a lovely view and you can hear the waters rapids below. I would come with you, but I want to finish the grapevines as I think tomorrow we may have rain."

We said our goodbyes and headed the way that the *muktar* instructed us to go. It was amazing to see the houses of this village still intact, nestled in the steep-sided mountain valley. They all had tiled roofs, and despite many houses looking empty, there seemed to be enough people still living here to make it viable, staving off the temptations of modernity – although there were a few TV aerials scattered about.

We found the house built out of stones without any problem, and the cicadas were as loud here as they were at the *muktar's* plot. Even with the din

331

that the newly hatched cicadas were making, we could still hear the gurgling sound of the river rapids below. Well, a river in Cyprus, but just a gurgling mountain stream in New Zealand. Cicadas usually spend the majority of their life underground and hatch when the temperature reaches 64°F or 18°C. When you hear them, you know that summer is on the way. Most of the 3,000 or so species live about a month and spend all that time having sex. *Way to go really.*

"This is a lovely spot," said Petros. "In the summer, this place fills up with people who work and live in *Lefkosia* most of the year. They escape the heat of the plain. I wish we could afford to have a little place to come to every so often."

"Looking at this place, you wouldn't think there was a war on, eh?" I said.

"No, the war hasn't touched places like this. That is why the refugees are starting to resent the way they are being treated by people they see as not having suffered at all from the little misadventure we put ourselves through. Many of the extreme right-wingers live up here in the mountains."

"I thought that Makarios came from up here."

"Yes, but he was born further west and his power base is in Panagia village in Paphos district. It's about ten miles southwest from here. The roads are terrible and can take you hours. Even I get lost up here. There are, as always, left-wingers up here, as well as people who worked in the mines and found some protection and solidarity in belonging to communist-led unions. Through the unions, they became educated and politicised. There were a lot of strikes for better conditions of work against the British and American companies who exploited them. Did you know that the communist party of Cyprus is the largest per capita in the world?"

"Really?"

"Yes. But they are different from other communists. They hold *Das Kapital* with their left hand and the Bible with their right. Let's be honest, cousin, if Jesus was alive today, wouldn't he be a communist?"

"I think it's a little more complex than that Petro. Marx saw religion as an opiate used by the Church to control the peasants. Then by controlling the Church, the capitalist-state controlled the people."

"Well, that is what I think," he said, quickly calling an impasse. "Anyway, from the earliest times, there was everything you can imagine up here – gold, copper, silver, pyrites, asbestos, you name it. Some of the mines still operate. I'll drive you past Amiantos so you can see what they now look like." *Amiandos* is the Greek name for asbestos and gave its name to the famous opencast mine. He took out his packet of cigarettes, knocked it on the steering wheel and took one with his mouth. Then he lit it with a cheap lighter he found in the side pocket of the driver's door. "From ancient times, Cyprus had all those minerals that every conquering power that came to our doorstep wanted. In the Bronze Age, Cyprus provided all the copper for bronze. They say tin – which is mixed with the copper to make bronze – was valued as much as gold and was brought all the way from Afghanistan and the Taurus mountains of Turkey. Of course, there was also Cyprus' strategic position, especially after the Suez Canal was built … Anyway, enough of a history lesson. Let's go and have a look to see if it was worth coming up here, eh?"

He got out, threw his cigarette on the ground and stomped on it. I got out as well. The air was fresh; the temperature was warming up even more, which explained the cicadas.

We walked down the side of the house until we saw a courtyard. There was a chicken-wire fence held up by wooden poles and a wooden gate. Petros opened the gate and headed for the front door. I followed close behind him. The front garden was full of wildflowers and I could smell their sweet fragrance in the air.

Petros knocked, but there was no response. A flight of pigeons perching on the roof flew off. He went over to the right, and as the shutters were closed, he pried upwards the louvres of one window. He cupped his hands to stop any reflection while he peered inside the house.

I heard the hiss. It was an intake of breath; then, "*Asiktir* – fuckin' hell!" Petros had sworn in Turkish.

I waited for him to explain, but instead, he tore the shutters open and leaned over and picked up an empty earthenware pot and smashed the windowpane. A few flies sitting on the windowpane flew out. He reached in and opened the window.

Standing back, he lit a cigarette. "We'll wait a minute or two for the room to clear a little."

He finished his cigarette. "Come on, climb in, but breathe through your mouth," he instructed, and I followed his command, by now fully realising that something very unpalatable awaited me inside. Sure enough, I wasn't long in the room when I saw the dead body of a woman, face down, her hands tied behind her back. I resisted the temptation to make a beeline towards her and headed back towards the front door to let Petros in. He came in slowly, but the smell of the dead body hit him, and gagging, he dashed outside.

"God, she stinks something terrible," he managed to say.

By then, I was also gagging, but I still went around opening windows and flicking flies out of my way.

Despite that, after only a few minutes of walking around the body, we both had to go outside for a while. Petros lit a cigarette and gave it to me before lighting another for himself.

When we finally went back inside, he looked down at the woman. She wore a stylish red miniskirt and a green blouse. One of her white sandals was discarded to the side while the other hung limply off her foot. Even from the side, we could see that her face was pummelled to torn flesh and broken bone. Worse than the British girl in Dhekelia. There was a large cavernous hole in the cranium and brain tissue was leaking out. Clusters of newly laid fly eggs and fattened, wriggling maggots were in the open wounds, although many prepupae maggots could also be seen. Next to the body was a discarded ancient clothes iron, the sort that is heated by being filled with lit coal or wood cinders.

"God, cousin, I never get used to it," said Petros with a deep sigh, and he crossed himself.

He walked behind a fallen chair, leaned over and picked up the blonde wig. "Looks like she's the woman who rifled through your apartment, Stauvro. Bridgette Kessler," he said, looking at me.

It explained why I never received the books from her.

8

On the way back to the village, I finally told Petros about my encounter with *Fräulein* Kessler at the German embassy.

"Now, why would you do this, Stauvro?" asked Petros, more calmly than I expected.

"I am sick and tired of running from shadows too, Petro," I explained.

"Well, cousin, someone did not like what she did, but it is hard to work out why that is. So I need to tell you to remember what happened the last time you stirred a fuckin' viper's nest."

"What happened to the wasps?"

"Wasps' stings are nothing, cousin. With a viper, one bite and you are history."

*

When we arrived at the village square, Petros used the public telephone to ring Nicosia, asking them to send a team up to Kalopanayioti. The Land Rover radio had no reception. We went to the *kafenio*, ordered coffees and sat down waiting for them. One of the villagers indicated to the *kafetzis* that he was shouting us, and the old men gathered their seats in a circle facing us. Petros indicated with his finger touching his lips to let me know that he didn't want us discussing the matter.

It was about an hour and a half later that the first police Land Rover arrived. After the second arrived the villagers started stirring like agitated bees, and their agitation got more frenzied when Petros told the *kafetzis*, whose name was also Marios, to go and find the *muktar* and tell him that a body was found up at the Kali's house.

Another Marios. How many fuckin' Marioss were there up here?

By the time we got back to the house, a crowd had started gathering, mainly old men and women, and one of the constables had to raise his voice to get them to move back.

Petros walked into the house and the team followed him. I stayed outside. I didn't need to see the carnage again. She must have pissed someone off a lot for her to be pummelled to death. It was clearly an ugly form of execution. Considering that some of the adult flies probably came in through the chimney I estimated that she was probably dead for at least five days. The room was warm and some of the larvae had gone through over half of their life cycle: from egg to hatching and then the prepupae stage, when they stopped eating and left the corpse. *Maybe the same day or the day after I visited her.* Depending on the temperature, in ten to fifteen days hence, the fully developed flies will emerge.

I started trying to work out where Bridgette Kessler fitted in. If she was part of the group that was running to Kalopanayioti, then who killed her? … and why. Did the whole group know about her or just Modestos, whose house it was? Or maybe Patroklos … after all, he was the one screwing her. Five days is a long time for someone to lie dead, even in Cyprus. Was she checking the place out and she came across someone who didn't like her snooping? Or was she meeting someone? Did the shooter at my apartment kill Kessler? Was she an accomplice? Again, could she have been killed by another group? The whole business was getting even murkier, and it was hard to see clearly what was what.

After Petros was sure that everything was covered at the murder scene, he left Karageorgis in charge and we set off in the Land Rover, hoping to make Agros by late afternoon. After taking a wrong turn, we finally arrived at the village named after the monastery, *Megalos Agros*.

Agros is another picturesque village in the Pitsilia district of Cyprus. It is built like an amphitheatre and faces south at about 3500 feet above sea level. The houses are of ornamental stone with red tiles. It took us about half an hour to get there from where the murder happened. Petros approached the village from the north, from the top of Troodos.

Agros was established by migratory monks from Kizikos in Asia Minor who sought refuge in Cyprus' Church, which was *autocephalous* – self-ruling – and thus not under the jurisdiction of the Byzantine emperor during the *Eikonomachia* – war on icons – era. The First Iconoclasm, as it is sometimes called, lasted between about 726 and 787. The Second Iconoclasm was between 814 and 842. It was accompanied by widespread destruction of icons and mosaics, and persecution of all the supporters who venerated images. The surviving sources accuse Constantine V of being the most vicious: moving against monasteries, having relics thrown into the sea, and stopping the invocation of saints. Monks were forced to parade in the Hippodrome, each hand-in-hand with a woman, in violation of their vows. In 765 Saint Stephen the Younger was killed and was later considered a martyr to the Iconophile cause. A number of large monasteries in Constantinople were secularised, and many monks fled to areas beyond effective imperial control on the fringes of the empire. One such group of monks was the one that came to Agros. They built a monastery to house the icon of Mary, the Holy Mother of Jesus Christ. In 1692 a pandemic hit the island, killing about two-thirds of the population.

The villagers that survived moved closer to the monastery and established and built the new church, the *Panagia* of Agros. Petros drove past to show me the church and then on to give me a glimpse of the magnificent view over the southern coast as far as the eye could see.

Petros then drove back and found out where Modestos' brother-in-law's hotel was and parked. The white, newly painted, multi-storied hotel hugged the steep slope of the amphitheatre. On the way there, Petros had related to me that Agros was the headquarters of Grigoris Afxentiou during the uprising against the British. As I had been repeatedly told, he became a martyr to the enosis cause as he was incinerated in his hideout near the Macheras monastery on the other side of the mountains. Petrol was poured into the bunker and journalists were offered seats to watch the spectacle when the bunker was torched. To my shame, it gave the word *vulture* a new meaning and potency when describing a journalist … but again, thinking about it, it wasn't too different from what we saw the US army tunnel rats doing to the Vietcong's underground tunnels in South Vietnam. "If he had lived, maybe the whole mess against the left-wingers wouldn't have happened," added Petros.

It had occurred to me more than once that if I had grown up in Cyprus, I wouldn't have been accepted into EOKA because my father leaned to the left, and despite my mother being a devout churchgoer, he saw the Church as an anachronism.

"Afxentiou had military training in Greece and was commissioned as a second lieutenant in the Greek army serving on the Bulgarian border before he returned to Cyprus in '53. He was an intelligent military strategist and a popular commander. He had a lot of compassion for people. Maybe this was to his detriment because he was betrayed by someone that he knew," continued Petros.

"Well, not for the British," I said, somewhat spitefully.

"True," said Petros calmly. "But they were our enemy and we theirs."

We both knew that was another of those circular arguments which end nowhere, so we lapsed into silence.

Our approach had been noticed. A woman came towards us from the veranda above and met us at the top of the stairs.

"*Kalosorisate* – welcome," she said, thinking that we were guests.

"*Yia*," said Petros, taking his credentials out and introducing himself.

"Can I speak to *Kyria* Eleni?" he asked.

"That is I. What can I do for you?" said the woman, her intelligent brown eyes taking both of us in.

She was dressed in a plain green smock, a uniform, and her hair was wrapped in a thin, colourful scarf.

"You are the sister of Modestos Kali?"

"Yes."

"*Kyria* Eleni," said Petros, coughing, no doubt feeling uncomfortable in giving the bad news. "I regret to tell you that I have some bad news concerning your brother ..." That was enough for the woman to start crying and keening ... She obviously knew that one day someone was going to come with some bad news concerning Modestos.

A man came rushing out of the hotel entrance and ran up to her. "*Ti ehis kori* – what is wrong, girl?" he asked anxiously. "What the hell have you said to her?" he shouted, his accusing black eyes darting between us.

"They are police, Mario," she managed to say. "It's about Modestos."

"What has that useless fool done now?"

"I am afraid he has had an accident," said Petros, understating the situation until he managed to get them off the street. "Can we please go inside?"

The man relented, and as we followed him into the hotel, he introduced himself and said that he was Marios, the woman's husband. Some of the employees who heard the keening came out to see what was going on, and half a dozen women gathered around their employer, trying to ease her grief. It was a while before Petros managed to persuade them to go back to their work, telling them that he wanted to talk to their employers privately.

When they left, he then related to the couple what had happened and what Modestos had been up to. Then he told them how he died. His tone was considerate and empathetic. Then, to give them time to take it all in, he asked if he could smoke.

He offered a cigarette to the husband, who accepted.

"I know it must be a bit of a shock, but are you able to tell us what you know about Modestos' movements in the last three weeks?"

"We haven't seen him since I threw those friends of his out of our hotel."

"What friends?"

341

"Some foreigners. He brought them here, and although they were very quiet, they got me worried. They seemed up to no good, and I asked them to all pack up and leave."

"Just like that?"

"Well, not really." Then reluctantly, "One of the maids told me that when she was tidying their room one morning, she saw that one of them had a pistol."

"Really?"

"That was enough for me. He has always been in trouble since the army and I have had enough, although Eleni defends him. I don't blame her, though … he is her only brother … I mean, was her brother … her only relative alive." If he realised the new contradiction, he let it go.

"What do you remember about his friends?"

"As I said, foreigners. They spoke good English, but they never told us anything. I have their details from their passports if you want them."

"Thank you," said Petros, "that would be very helpful." We spent the next twenty minutes getting descriptions of the three men Modestos had been looking after. The description of one fitted the man that Petros shot outside my apartment in Nicosia.

"Did you know if one was a KYP officer?"

"Yes, or so I thought. A Cypriot. He came up here a couple of times with Modestos. He actually said he was a policeman. I suspected he was something more by his scowl and the way he ordered Modestos around. Modestos made a big thing about it as if he was finally getting somewhere in life. Now we know all he was getting was closer to his death."

"Well, that is all, *Kyrie* Mario," said Petros. "Can I please have your ID details and we will contact you when the body is released. As it's a serious criminal investigation, it may be a couple more days."

The man nodded. He took out his wallet and passed his ID to Petros, who noted down the details in his notebook. Marios sent his wife to get the hotel's register with the other men's details.

Harbingers of death, for some reason, are not offered coffee or water. I wondered why? So I got Petro to stop at one of the village's *kafenios* for us to recharge our caffeine batteries.

10

Socrates, in Plato's *Republic,* argues that justice is not owned by the rich and powerful because it is a virtue, and because of that, justice is equal to the other cardinal virtues such as courage, moderation and prudence. He urges the individual that it is in his interest to be just rather than unjust. His antagonist in the dialogue, Thrasymachus, on the other hand, saw justice as a tool to be used by the strongest citizens of Athens. Obviously, Thrasymachus, if he wasn't a figment of Plato's imagination, had Darwinian sensibilities 2,000 years before Darwin or his theory were even conceived. I tended to go with Socrates on this.

So I kept an open mind about Savas Spithas after Karageorgis informed Petros that his father and mother were killed in the Turkish invasion and his daughter has cerebral palsy. The fact that he still looked after his daughter at home gave me pause in passing judgement on him.

Petros, as usual, was not as accommodating in his report to me.

"Blame it on the vagaries of command," he said. "A fish rots from the head down, cousin." It was hard not to agree with him as Cyprus had many examples of this.

I knew that I had to be careful. There had to be some fallout from the KYP officer's death because KYP and Patroklos had something going that probably was not in my interest. It may even include my elimination by whatever means.

So when two National Guard military policemen, burly and thuggish, came to see me, I wasn't entirely surprised. I was on my way to Louizos' *kafenio* when they intercepted me. I had just closed the front door, and they asked if they could come inside. I reluctantly opened the door but made sure that I waved to *Kyriou* Prokopis, who was watching what was going on and was a witness to their presence before I led them upstairs.

They introduced themselves and asked to see my entry visa. Thankfully, I had renewed it after my R & R trip to Greece the previous November. Petros did warn me that this could happen. These boys had been sent on a fishing expedition. An expired visa was one way they could press-gang me into the army. Once in there, anything could happen to me, including a small accident.

I stayed calm and spoke in English, putting them at a disadvantage because their English was not the best. I explained that I was a New Zealand citizen and worked for Reuters, a British news agency.

They said that my name was Stauvros Marangos and I was from Mpalloura. I said that was not correct as my name was Steve Carpenter and I was born in Wellington, New Zealand, as it said on my passport. When I showed them the front of my passport, they said that it was a forgery. They threatened me using their overbearing presence and then said because my father is Cypriot that I had to go into the army in the next intake, and if I was reluctant to do so I would be thrown in a cell for three months in a military prison and they'd feed me "onions, water and bread". If I kept refusing, I would do another three months and so it would continue until I agreed to serve.

Calmly I responded that I was not a Cypriot citizen and that I had a valid visa until the end of April and I did not think that their government would be happy if the London newspapers got hold of the story of my arrest and incarceration. I assured them that my employer and my government would make a hell of a fuss. I didn't know if that was true, but it sounded good. The two thugs both looked at each other and finally they left. Scipio, who was following all this from the bedroom door, came out and jumped on me.

"So Scipio. Who, of all my local friends, has sent those two goons?" I asked.

Scipio had no idea.

11

Alexandra and I went to dinner that night, and after dropping her off at the Hilton I went home. I found an envelope taped to my front door. The fold was sellotaped shut. I went upstairs and after feeding Scipio, I tore it apart and read it. It was written in English.

It would be good if we met. We have a proposition for you and your policeman friend. Come alone, though. We will be watching you. There is a miniature chapel next to the road outside the village of Amiantos as you come from Nicosia. It is an accident shrine. Be there tomorrow at twelve noon. There will be a note under a jar telling you where to go next.

I re-read the note and put it down.

The question that occurred to me immediately was not surprising: Who wrote the letter and why?

I changed and went downstairs to go back to the car. I thought better of it and went to my *kafenio* and rang Petros.

"Who is it, and why does he want a meeting?" asked Petros.

"The same thought occurred to me. Do you think it's the guy that you shot?"

"I suppose it could be. I still haven't worked out for sure how they found out where you lived in the first place."

"Well, I think Patroklos or Savas possibly mentioned it to the Kessler woman."

"And she's dead. And he?"

"Fucked if I know, Petro. You are the policeman," I said, losing my patience with his cool composure. "Do you think I am safe?"

"Well, if they want to talk to us, it must mean that for the moment at least they aren't interested in killing you."

346

"That's fuckin' reassuring."

"Well, that is what I think. Come on, I'll pick you up and we'll go and see what Eleni has cooked."

12

On my way home from Petros and Eleni's, I dropped by a kiosk that was closing for the night to buy a paper. I walked past a stray dog that ignored me as he was busy spraying other dogs' scent, trying to reclaim his territory and, I suppose, his honour, and I turned into the top of my street. I then saw someone walking suspiciously down the road and noticed that he would stop every so often and turn towards the walls to the left, which were in shadow.

I was so strung up that it took me a while to decide whether to intervene or not.

Then I realised that he was painting graffiti.

I followed him until he stopped to paint on the wall of my building. I then quickened my pace, and before he knew it, I was next to him.

He jumped out of his skin, if that is possible, and dropped a small bucket and brush. The paint spilled on to the road.

"How the devil did you get here?" asked the young man.

"I followed you."

"How far did you follow me?"

"From where you started painting the graffiti."

347

He looked at me closely, and I could see that he was working out whether he could down me and make a run for it.

"Why are you painting swastikas on my wall?"

"Why do you care? Are you an *Evraios*?" he spat the *Jew* out as if it was the dirtiest word in his vocabulary.

"Actually, I am not. Wait a minute. Don't I know you?"

"No! So, you like Jews?"

"No. I neither like them nor dislike them."

"Well, I hate them."

"Is that why you paint swastikas on other people's walls?"

"Because of this symbol, they will burn in hell."

"Are you serious?"

"Of course, I am."

Although exasperated, I still tried to have a rational discussion with him using what Father Sosimas had said to me. "This, my friend, is a very ancient and potent symbol. Before the ancient Greeks. It's all over our early pottery. It means peace."

"Bullshit. It means war!"

"Look it up." I was losing my patience. "That's why we have libraries. For idiots like you. Go on … go to the library and look it up."

"You are a Jew?"

"No."

"You are a Jew. You have a large nose."

"I am not."

"Ah, you are a *Chiliastis*?" he asked, trying to find a straw to grab on to.

"No, I am not a *Chiliastis* either!"

The Greeks called Jehovah's Witness members *Chiliastes*, which means millenarians. I remembered the Jehovah's Witnesses who used to knock on our door in Wellington and how they tried to give my father or mother their *Watchtower* magazine. My father, although very polite towards them, used to call them "the deluded, lost tribe", but I subsequently learned that that was not very accurate. Like all Christian sects, over the years they have evolved a complicated dogma. Jehovah's Witnesses reject the Holy Trinity, the inherent immortality of the soul and hellfire. They consider all three to be unscriptural doctrines. They do not observe Easter, Christmas and birthdays. To adopt the latter, they must have read the second-century Alexandrian Christian theologian Origenis Adamantios' edict against birthdays. Jehovah adherents commonly refer to their body of beliefs as "the truth" and consider themselves to be "in the truth". My girlfriend Elizabeth's parents were Jehovah's Witnesses, and when they left, they suffered disfellowshipping, the sect's term for a formal Jehovah Congregational expulsion: they were shunned. Baptised individuals who formally leave are considered disassociated and are also shunned. Disfellowshipped and disassociated individuals may eventually be reinstated if deemed repentant. Jehovah's Witnesses also reject the secular power of the state and lead their lives as separate from others as they can. Elizabeth's parents eventually split up. Her father did not return to the sect, but her mother did. I often wondered if it had any bearing on Elizabeth's suicide.

"And what do Jehovah's Witness have to do with the Jews?"

"They are the same, as the Freemasons … well, not the same … they collaborate to overthrow religion."

"Whose religion?"

"Our religion … Greek Orthodoxy … the Church of Jesus Christ."

"You assume that because I am Greek, I am Greek Orthodox," I said, goading him.

"What! What are you then? An atheist … a communist?"

"That is also a question that I will not answer. But I will tell you this for nothing … You are full of shit and like all those anti-Semite dumb mates of yours, you have a bag of useless wares that you peddle to justify your shitty existence. I should drag you down to the police station."

"They will not arrest me because they are with us."

"Who is with you?"

"The police. They are patriots. We are patriots."

"Yes? What? EOKA B?"

"No. We are patriots … We want to protect our country and our religion."

"By inciting violence against Jews and *Chiliastes*? … anyway, you idiot, there are fuck all Jews in Cyprus."

"They are the Christ-killers! They are impure!"

"The Romans killed Christ, you dumb shit. He was killed under Roman law."

As is the usual thing with such nutters, there's no way to convince them otherwise. They have the innate ability to slip the handcuffs of logic.

Suddenly, I remembered where I had seen him before. He was at Louizos' *kafenio* the day Mikis and Antónis searched me out there. After they left, he came up and tried to sell me some religious book he was hocking.

"Wait a minute," I said, the thought that had been quickly gestating suddenly came to the surface. Maybe I was beginning to think in a similar irrational way, trying to make sense of him. "You don't think that a Cypriot lad screwing a foreigner is a threat to the Greek Orthodoxy?" I asked, not wanting to hear the answer because if he answered in the affirmative, Petros and I would have been chasing our tails. Also, it would be a startling new tangent.

"Yes, he is impure. He defiles our race."

"So you killed him?"

He looked blankly at me.

"The impure boy … in the hotel room … with the German woman?"

"What, boy? What German woman?"

"The ones in the hotel in Agia Napa."

351

"I have never been to Agia Napa," he retorted defensively. "Agia Napa is like Sodom and Gomorrah. It will be destroyed by God with brimstone and fire."

I had finally had enough of this character's deluded nonsense. I grabbed him and spun him around. I then pulled his jacket down, trapping his arms. He tried to kick out at me. I reached in and sought his wallet. It was in his left coat pocket. I let him go and moved to a lamp post. Keeping an eye on him, I opened the wallet and searched through for his ID. It said Manolis Karapanos. He lived in an apartment on Pythagorou Street in Strovolos, a suburb of Nicosia. I threw his wallet one way and his ID the other, and as he untangled himself from his sports coat, he lunged to retrieve them in the dark alley.

"I know your name, fuck head, and where you live," I said to him. "And do me a favour, eh … Go and piss against your parent's wall. And also – stay away from Father Sosimas' church."

13

The next day, in the Morris, I eventually approached the village of Chandria from upper Amiantos

*

I had told Petros about the graffiti painter, Manolis Karapanos, because after my encounter with him it seemed that he fitted the profile of someone who could kill the German woman and Mikis for some convoluted, deluded religious cause. After all, he knew both Mikis and Antónis and had a perverse hatred for anyone who did not see things the same way as him. However, how did he get to Agia Napa and to the apartment to pick up and then return the Ruger? And how did he fit into all the terrorism aspects of the case?

Petros wrote Karapanos' name down and passed it on to Sergeant Karageorgis. "You never know, cousin," said Petros, "from breadcrumbs, one can make soup."

*

Petros had shown me Lower Amiantos, the actual mining village, after we found the body in Kalopanayioti. We had driven through Kyperounta and he had pointed out Chandria on the way back from Agros that day ... so I thought I'd find it easily.

My cousin said he'd give me a head start because the road might be watched. I found the miniature chapel. It was a replica of a Byzantine church and a *kandili* – a glass filled with water and oil with a floating lit wick – was lit in it behind a small paned door that sheltered the flame from the wind. Next to the *kandili* was a *kappnistiri*. It confirmed to me, as the letter hinted, it was a memorial to someone who was killed in a car accident at that very spot. Under the door was a tin draw. In it were two small glass jars. One had boxes of matches in it and the other liturgical incense wrapped in silver foil. As well, there was a handful of loose dried olive-leaves. Under the jar was a note.

> Go to the gate of the Chandria Primary School at 1 pm. Look
> under the stone on the V where the road forks.

There was a little map drawn with the road, the school on the right, and a small circle with a cross on the bottom of the V where the road forked.

Chandria is on the border of the Limassol side of the Nicosia district and is to the east of the Amiantos mine. It's also draped up a western scarp of the western slopes of Madari mountain, another Troodos peak. It also belongs to the Pitsilia group of villages famous for their wines, especially a port-like aperitif *Commandaria*. Originally known as *Nama*, the wine was later renamed *Commandaria* after "La Grande Commanderie", the headquarters of the Knights of Saint John and the Knights Templars in Kolossi. They had bought Cyprus from Richard the Lionheart, who had apparently toasted his wife with a goblet of the sweet wine at their wedding on the island. He liked the wine so much he took vines with him back to Britain. Chandria is the second highest village in Cyprus at just over 4,000 feet. Villagers work in small orchards in the surrounding valleys, tending walnut, apple, pear, peach and other fruit-bearing trees. Vines and almond trees are cultivated on the steep slopes of the rocky mountain.

Once I entered the village, I asked for directions from an old woman who was sitting in the sun outside her house. She was dressed in black from head to toe. Unusually, her directions were spot on. Often, a villager would point somewhere and say, "It's not far," and you'd find it, if you were lucky, a couple of miles later. The primary school was a new building. Looking around, the house I was invited to could be any one of a half a dozen. There were no street signs and no numbers on the houses. As I looked at the houses up the hill, I couldn't see any sign of life in them. Most seemed empty, although people would be about, maybe climbing the nearby steep, hilly paths to tend their grapevines. I parked next to the school and I could hear the chatter of the kids inside, but there was no one outside. Some pigeons were sitting on a wire cooing, watching me from their perch. I saw the rock. I walked over and turned it over. There was another note. It was another rough map showing me where to go. I walked up the left fork, which rose quite steeply, looking for any sign of someone watching me from the surrounding houses. At the top where the road narrowed, I saw the house to my right, marked on the map with an X. It was just an old, weathered whitewashed bungalow. Nothing special, except the front door was open. I walked up and knocked on the doorframe.

"Enter."

I must say, despite the fact that I knew that someone was waiting for me, I was still surprised. Maybe it was the assured, accented voice.

I closed my eyes and entered the dark room. When I opened my eyes, it still took me a while to adjust to the gloom. There he was, a Caucasian man, smoking and holding onto a mug of something.

"Thank you for coming." A touch of facetiousness. In English but he wasn't English.

"Thank you for inviting me." A touch of facetiousness back.

The man coughed and then flinched. He was in pain.

"Well, the bodies have been piling up, and I thought we should have a talk." He put his cup down and looked at me with a wisp of a smile. "Your policeman friend has had a small accident."

He must have seen my immediate concern. "No, nothing serious. Just a couple of blown-out tyres. You'll find him on your way back."

"You have been following me?"

"No, just waiting. I had a friend keep an eye out for you and he spotted your friend. It's a wonder what a sniper rifle can do."

"So what do you want?" I asked, not entirely sure that I had anything to give.

"Clear passage out of this shithole. I am wounded, thanks to your friend, and I need to get to a hospital."

"Where?"

"Overseas."

"Overseas? What are you? Mossad?"

"That's not important. What is important is that we don't want anyone else to be hurt."

"Well, mate, that's a bit of an understatement," I said, starting to feel my temper rising. "You mean you don't want to kill any more people?"

"The man at the petrol station was an eye for an eye. He was not innocent."

"Your man shot him."

"Well, he killed our friend."

"I hear that there was a fight and your friend's gun went off. The guy was just defending himself."

"Is he still alive?"

"Yes. Just."

"Good."

"Is that all you have to say?"

The guy was getting pissed off. "What else do you want me to say?"

"What about sorry?"

"We don't do sorry," he said drily.

"Yeah, well that's why I am up here. If he was dead, the police would be dealing with you. They would have surrounded the whole village and …"

"We are not amateurs."

"You could have fooled me," I said.

"Shit happens."

I gave up.

"So, what do you want from me?"

"Tell your inspector friend that we want to surrender, but only to him. Also, we want for him to arrange a fishing boat that we will board in Agia Napa."

"What …Where are you going?"

"Well, you have several choices. Where we are going is not part of the negotiations. All you need to know is that we are going home."

"What's going to stop him just putting you in jail and throwing away the key?"

"You."

"Me? How?"

"You'll be our guarantee that nothing will happen to us."

"How do you figure that out?"

"Well, you'll come with us up to your country's territorial limits."

"My country? Cyprus is not my country, mate. I was born in New Zealand. It's my parents who were born here."

"You know what I mean. Anyway, I am not here to discuss your citizenship, just as you are not here to discuss mine."

"And then what happens?"

"We'll leave you in a rubber dinghy, and your friend and whoever will be following us can pick you up. And as a bonus, I'll also tell you what happened at the Helenis in Agia Napa."

"And if I don't do that?"

"Well, a bomb that we have placed in a very inconvenient place will explode."

I paused, thinking. That was their insurance.

"How do I know that you are not bluffing?"

"Well, by now, a small device would have exploded next to RIK."

"What! Why would you want to place a bomb next to a radio station?"

"It's not very powerful, all it is … is … what you call it? A taster … Letting you know that we are capable of doing it."

"And how do we know that you will let us know where the larger bomb is?"

"I'll tell you before we put you in the dinghy."

"Why should I trust you?"

"Because we do not have a quarrel with you or your country … um, sorry … I mean," he chuckled, raising his hand in apology, "your parents' country. As well, you'll have a scoop … you can write about what happened. You see, I know now you are a journalist. And if you don't know our country of origin, you can't write about it."

"I could guess."

"You won't be the reporter that apparently you are. So what do you say?"

I ignored the compliment.

"Well, I don't really know what my friend Inspector Zimaras will say. He's a policeman. You know how policemen can be. Then there's his country's Special Branch and KYP. They want you badly."

"KYP. Yes … He just doesn't tell them."

"Are you crazy? This is not a banana republic, you know. KYP is well known in this part of the world, and if your country is Israel … you know your eye for an eye bullshit … Mossad knows what happens when they mix it up with them."

The man said nothing.

"Did you think that KYP didn't know it was you guys that blew up that Palestinian in '73 at the Olympic Hotel? You know, don't you, that your little vendetta chasing Palestinians all over Europe and the Middle East, leaving tens of innocent civilians dead, has not given you any strategic advantage. In fact, it probably helped you miss all the signs of the start of the Yom Kippur war."

"I am not Israeli. It does not concern me."

Again, I gave up.

"Okay, so how do we do this?"

"You will go back the way you came. You will explain to your friend what I said. I will be gone if he decides to come up here. I am going to give you a field radio, and the frequencies and the times that I'll call are on this piece of paper." He moved the piece of paper across the table. I noticed he wore gloves. Then he reached to his left and pulled a radio out and put it on the table next to the paper.

"I will make the first call in two hours. The others will follow the schedule that is written down. If my proposal is acceptable, I will wait for you at the Larnaca Agia Napa turn-off. If all goes well, another two men will join us. We will have someone observing our surrender. The bomb can be remotely detonated if need be. We have another observer at Agia Napa. We will signal to him that we are safe and on the way out. The money will be left at a place that I will reveal to you – to cover the cost of the fishing boat as it will be scuttled."

"You aren't Russian … are you?" I guessed. Scuttling brought up the idea of a submarine.

"You have a vivid imagination. I told you, it does not matter who we are."

"Okay," I said. "I got it."

"Right. Leave and walk to where you are parked. I can see a long way from the veranda outside. I want you to stop the car on that ridge, across the gulley, opposite … that's the road that looks back towards this village. Ten minutes will do. By the time you get to the Troodos to Nicosia road and meet up with your friend, I will be gone. Thank you for coming."

I moved towards him and picked up the radio. It was only then that I saw the automatic pistol which was lying in front of him on the table. It was a Hi-Power Browning. It looked exactly the same as the one Frank threw over the wall in Agia Napa. If he *was* an Israeli, Frank would have been right. Closer, I could see that he had a strong, furrowed face, the sort of square-jawed, rough warrior type that women find attractive. His hair was greying, although he looked no more than perhaps thirty. His eyes, though, did not fit his kindly features. The irises were a cold blue. Eyes that you don't forget. I turned around and walked towards the door.

Then I stopped and turned. "Oh, by the way, did you see the woman who broke into my apartment before you let rip at me the other day?"

"What, woman?"

"The West German woman."

"What West German woman?"

"Bridgette Kessler."

The name meant something to him because he went really quiet. He straightened up and sat absolutely still. His eyes were aflame, if blue can actually catch fire.

"By the way, she's dead," I added bluntly.

It was obviously a shock to him because the colour drained from his face. Then he brought his hands up and dry-wiped his face. He looked down and then up, straight at me. The thought did cross my mind that he might just kill me and forget about his escape plan from the island of Aphrodite. But instead, he let out a long sigh.

"When?" he asked.

"We found her yesterday at Modestos Kalis' house in Kalopanayioti. The pathologist reckons about a week ago. Last Thursday or Friday."

"How?"

"She was beaten to death. Very personal, if you ask me."

"What you mean?"

"She was virtually unrecognisable. Whoever killed her beat her face in with one of those old charcoal clothes-irons."

The man took it in but said nothing.

"It had nothing to do with us," he finally said. "She was just meant to check you out."

"If a West German embassy official was checking me out, then are you West German intelligence?"

"No. One of our sources runs her."

"Someone runs her. What from KYP? You mean, Patroklos?"

No response.

"I don't know much about this spy game thing, mate, but isn't it more likely that she was running him?"

Again, no response.

"Look," I said. "Someone killed her. The Cyprus police think it's you guys. Why did she have to die? I don't get it. We know that Patroklos was screwing her. If Patroklos killed her, why do it in Kalopanayioti? There are lots of places to do it around Nicosia. Was Modestos screwing her as well? It's his house. So did he do it?"

"No. I don't think so," he said pensively, "because he was driving us up there before we stopped at the gas station. Then he got killed. He would not have driven us up there if he did it. He would have brought us here. No, it was not Modestos."

"So it's Patroklos?"

There must be loyalty between fellow spies or something because he didn't answer.

"Look, mate," I said. "Inspector Zimaras, the guy who shot you, is less likely to let you go if this isn't cleared up."

Finally, "It's not this guy you call Patroklos," he said firmly, and I believed him. "That's all you are getting, so ... meeting's over."

"You're not working for the Yanks, are you?" It was my last attempt. "You said *gas* station."

He cracked a smile. "God, you are a pain."

"Yeah, you are not the first to tell me that, mate." And I turned to leave.

As I walked out, I couldn't help but mutter under my exhaling breath, "See you later, alligator."

Yep, the man was a predator, but I wasn't sure if alligator was an apt descriptor for him. He was certainly cold-blooded, but it was more likely he was a predator of the deep, a white shark.

*

After the ten-minute wait, I headed towards Amiantos and took the road that led to Nicosia.

I found Petros, leaning against his car and smoking.

"You won't guess what happened to me!"

"Someone shot out your tyres."

"How did you know?"

"The Delphic Oracle told me."

14

As I said, I cannot exactly explain it. But I think Petros put his finger on it. He said that I looked light to him. I definitely felt lighter. As if a huge weight had been lifted off my shoulders.

I did, in some way, still, blame myself for Elizabeth's death. I also think that when I caught the M14 thrown at me by that US sergeant as he screamed "C'mon boyos, we are fighting for our lives here," something happened. When I blindly shot into the sulphurous and cordite-loaded smoke that surrounded us, I knew that I must have killed someone that day. They say that, just like Julius Caesar, everyone has their Rubicon. That day I crossed mine and didn't even know it. Now I realised that, like Father Sosima, I had gone across a line that I could not go back on. And all I could do, like the old priest, was search for some sort of redemption. Maybe in writing this and other books that is what I am trying to do.

After the battle that day, when the smoke had lifted, there were hundreds of dead North Vietnamese among the shredded foliage down the side of the hill, as far as the eye could see. They were layered on top of each other, two or three deep in places. There was blood, guts and torn limbs everywhere. The smell of body parts, excrement and different spent munitions was a potent mix. Their odds were virtually nil, and it was then that it hit me that the Americans had lost the war. When people fought with such tenacity, "like Spartans", as Frank once told me when we met on R & R in Singapore, then you knew you had met your match. Not that the Spartans were totally invincible, as I learned later when I read Thucydides' *The Peloponnesian Wars*. Other than Thermopylae there were two other occasions when they were defeated. However, the most famous occasion was when the best of the best, the elite, the so-called *Spartiates* were forced to a humiliating surrender at the island of Sphacteria by a lightly armed superior number of Athenian infantry led by Demosthenes and Cleon. Their surrender was something that up till then had been unheard of and it shook the ancient Greek world.

Americans, in terms of armaments, had everything, but like Frank said, they didn't believe in what they were doing.

Yet here in Cyprus, I came across people who did believe in what they were doing and were prepared to die and kill for it as well. Many had just jumped on that bandwagon. The EOKA B were men who were not agitating for civil rights, although some of them said they were as they accused Makarios of being a dictator who was depriving them of their deeper wish for union with the motherland, Greece ... and really, who could accuse them of simply being fascists? They saw themselves as participating in an enticing nationalist metaphor: Cyprus playing the part of the raped daughter, stolen from the patriarchal home, who wants to go back and be clutched and consoled by her mother. Except we all know that mothers are not, in reality, forgiving, at least not in this part of the world. Nor are fathers. A daughter raped is a daughter lost: to be expelled, banished and forgotten. I heard horror stories of how young women, if they were spared an honour death, were left with no other alternative when they lost their honour than to marry an older man, preferably a returning rich immigrant, or go and work in a whorehouse. In almost all of such cases it was women whose father was old and unable to protect them or dead. The fact that my grandparents did not throw my mother out and my father still married her after she was raped was the exception, and now I am very proud of him for doing that.

Don't get me wrong. From my short experience in Cyprus, I came across very strong women like my Mpalloura neighbour *Giagia* Androutsou. Women who not only helped their menfolk in the fields but also worked hard

366

at home feeding, dressing their entire family with their handcraft and caring for their home. Many ruled the roost, but you wouldn't see that unless you were privy to their inner lives. You would see the men in public more because they would spend some of their spare time at the *kafenio*. But they also worked hard, battling moneylenders, drought, locusts, floods, and sometimes fires set off by lightning. But it was only the men that you saw strutting around like a rooster in the street. However, at church, despite men and women being separated between the two halves of the congregation, or at weddings, which were affairs for the whole village, you could evaluate and judge both sexes' character and status within the village by their attire and grooming, which attested to their wealth, as is seen in many countries. Cars also revealed the status of families and the more cars they had, despite the very high import taxes, the more affluent the family was. To some degree, the war put an end to that.

But Alexandra was obviously a strong woman. Intelligent, educated, easy on the eye and there was empathy between us that was hard to ignore. She was a woman with a cause, and I also saw journalism as such, really, despite all the misgivings and self-doubts. I thought that we had a lot going for us. I had not rushed things, but I knew I was running out of time.

15

Petros wanted to head to Chandria and go to the house, but I managed to talk him out of it.

I repeated what the man asked for after I passed on the portable radio. Then I described him. Petros asked me if I could identify the accent. I said that

367

the accented English sounded eastern European with an American twang, but if he was Israeli, he could be anything because there were a lot of Russian Jews who immigrated to Israel. "And like Russian diplomats, they speak English with an American accent."

"Do you think he was the one that shot at you at Agia Napa?" he asked.

"We didn't discuss it, but from what he said he was definitely the one that you shot outside my apartment. He is the leader. He must be in bad shape to be negotiating all this."

"Yes, if he was Mossad, he and his comrades would have stolen a boat and got picked up by one of their fast boats or a submarine."

"Yeah. There's something about all this that makes no sense," I said.

"Well, Spithas has disappeared."

"Really, when?"

"Fucked if I know, but the boys have been searching for him."

"Do you think he was behind those KYP shooters?"

"Absolutely. As I told you, Karageorgis heard him discussing taking care of you at the cafe. Stelios Tsangaris' mate, the driver, was a Special Branch freelancer, his name is Takis Prokopi."

16

One of the pleasures of living in Cyprus is the variety of landscape that can be found on such a small island. Cyprus is the same size as Lebanon or Jamaica. Not that everyone would take the opportunity to explore it, though. There

368

were several villagers in my parents' village, Mpalloura, who had never even been to the sea. Every so often since my arrival, I would drop everything and go on a trip to the Troodos Mountains where I'd find a gurgling stream and just lie down and have a sleep. Those sleeps were the best I have had in my life. On the way back, next to the main road, I'd stop at vegetable kiosks and buy some fruit or vegetables. On a lucky occasion, I might come across a local at a *kafenio* and spent the time talking about the surrounding area, picking up stories, some of them far-fetched but entertaining. The monasteries were always interesting to visit, and I was amazed by the number of religious relics and body parts of different saints that would be kept in well-designed, museum-like display cabinets. Usually, they would be encased in gold or silver. On several occasions I came across the odd person that I had met in Nicosia, but usually they were with their family having a traditional Cypriot *souvla* – meat on a spit – at a restaurant, so I was reluctant to approach them as Cypriots tend to draw you into whatever they are doing, especially if food is involved.

The exception was when I met the director of one of the main philanthropic foundations that I had done an article on. The foundation was set up by a rich South African Greek who tried to emulate the structure of the Rockefeller Foundation.

The director was there with his wife, to whom he introduced me after we exchanged pleasantries. She was a good-looking woman, but as her husband was a handsome man, I did not resent him of her. They invited me to join them. The taverna was busy and window shutters were put up for winter. A big fireplace was stoked with wood that every so often exploded, spitting sparks.

The man was called Lycurgus and his wife was called Sophia. I remember when I first met him saying something about Lycurgus, the Spartan lawgiver having inspired Marx. My comment went down like a lead balloon. From that meeting, I already knew that he was born in Kokkinotrimithia, attended secondary school in Morphou but studied in London, where he met his wife, another student, who he said was from Deneia. He added that they were lucky because during the war they missed being included in the Turkish sector – they lived between their two villages on the Nicosia to Morphou road, south of the new border.

They talked of their children, one of whom studied in Athens and the other in Paris. They seemed like a solid upper middle-class couple, content with their lot in life. Of course, they quizzed me, and I reciprocated with a short history of myself. They were impressed that I was a journalist working for Reuters. They asked me for the title of my first book and then asked me to write it down for them. We spent an hour talking about films, travel and, surprisingly, fishing. Before we knew it, we had finished our main meal and were eating dessert.

One of the things that I do when I meet people in Cyprus is I try to guess where they stand on the political spectrum. I guessed by their liberal attitudes that they were possibly of the centre-left. Maybe they belonged to Lyssarides' Socialist party. How wrong could I have been? What gave them away was when Lycurgus said that one of the things they felt sorry about was how Nikos Sampson was made the scapegoat for what happened the previous summer.

"You know, when he was appointed president, he received thousands of telegrams congratulating him. Now he's been cast aside like a leper." They talked about him as someone who was erudite, courageous, well-read and a devout Christian. Lycurgus also said that he was honoured to have served with

Sampson during the 1963 inter-ethnic riots. I could have challenged them with what I knew about Sampson, who I considered a psychopath. But I didn't. I already knew that one man's psychopath could be another man's hero. On this occasion, I was fascinated to meet people of the right on a friendly basis, so the critic in me withdrew and went for a wander down a path in the dense cedar forest.

The food was pleasant, I had a couple of glasses of wine, and if anything, despite their political beliefs, Lycurgus and his wife were very erudite with their views. So I started to ask them questions about Cypriot religion, which led to Cypriot politics.

"So, what do you think Makarios is going to do now?" I asked.

"What do you mean?" said Lycurgus.

"I mean, is he going to be president for life or pass the baton to someone else?"

"Oh, no," said Sophia. "He'll be in for life now. We won't get rid of him until he is dead."

"So you don't think he has a succession plan?"

"No," said Lycurgus. "There is no one of his stature to take over. He might pass the presidency to one of his loyal followers though, if he is sick or something."

"Who do you think that might be?"

"Oh, Kyprianou."

"The foreign minister?"

"Or he might pass it on to Glafcos Clerides. After all, he stood in for him after the coupists' fall."

"So what do you think Makarios' legacy will be?" I asked.

They both looked at each other as if they were about to let rip but contained their vehemence and tried very hard to be balanced. "Well, he was the political leader during the EOKA years, he introduced a sort of welfare system to Cyprus, free education in secondary schools, free health care and …"

"And sired half a dozen little bastards that are now being brought up by nuns and monks in the monasteries," interrupted his wife.

"*Ate, Sophia … kopse to* – C'mon, Sophia, cut it out."

"Well, the truth must be told, Lycurgus," said his wife primly, and she crossed her arms over her chest.

"Isn't he supposed to be celibate?" I asked, feigning ignorance. "I thought he came up through the monk tradition of the Church."

"He did," said Lycurgus, "but there have been rumours that he had affairs with nuns. I think *ine paramythia* – they are fairy tales – but Sophia thinks they are true.

"I personally don't think that is his problem, really. His problem is that he gave up our quest for *enosis* with Mother Greece. Also, he has done us great harm by making Cyprus part of the non-aligned movement. He has pitted himself, and therefore us, against America and Britain and makes friendly overtures to the Russians, who are atheists. He is playing a dangerous game and last year was the result of all this posturing. Where did it get him?

One would need to be blind not to see that we the *ethnikofrones* – patriots – are now again in control: he pardoned all the coupists and the government employees of our side are running his government." I don't think Lycurgus was boasting. He was very matter of fact about it. "We have made some small concessions to the left to neutralise them. Even they didn't mind the Greek junta. The only one who did was Lyssarides, and he is now in the political wilderness. He doesn't think he is, but take my word for it, he is out of it. That's why I said that Sampson was the scapegoat. Every one of the coupists, except the ones who died, have got away with it."

"So, what was Makarios' relationship with Greece?"

Lycurgus took another sip of his wine, speared a piece of roasted lamb and placed it in his mouth.

"Well, he studied theology in Greece. So he has a strong connection with the motherland and even more when he led the cause for *enosis*. At first, he reconciled himself with the junta, even inviting Colonel Papadopoulos, who became president here, and giving him a great welcome. Remember, the junta was popular with the rural sector – all the farmers – in Greece because the junta forgave them all their debts. Their only resistance came from the left that dominated in the cities. Georghadjis organised an assassination against Papadopoulos and his agent stuffed it up. Whether Makarios knew about it or not, it is so far unknown. Two friends of mine were involved in the whole thing, but one was killed in the war and another is in jail."

"What for?"

"He was found guilty of manslaughter … you know, a fight that went wrong."

373

"Loukas is a devout man, but it was a silly thing to do," interrupted Sophia.

Finally, my patience and critical non-engagement had seemed to have paid off.

"Well, that's where he is now. A waste of a brilliant mind. Hatzimichaelis is a real patriot."

"Loukas Hatzimichaelis?" I asked to confirm the name.

"Yes. A real patriot."

Like a good journalist, I collected patriots. I filed the name away to be added later to my concertina file.

"Would you like some coffee," I asked.

"No, thanks."

"Well, I have to go. Thank you for the company and the stimulating conversation." I raised my hand to the waiter for the bill.

"No, *Kyrie* Stauvro," said Lycurgus. "The meal is on us. You are our guest."

I made all the appropriate departure noises and got up, and after shaking their hands, I left. That was the first time I heard of Hatzimichaelis.

Chapter 7

1

It was Karageorgis who gave us the full low-down on Loukas Hatzimichaelis, a friend of Neoptolemou Papageorgiou, the man whose book collection Ari purchased from his widow.

"He is in the Central Prison for manslaughter," said Karageorgis. "But he knew Papageorgiou. They were thick as thieves with Georghadjis, but then they fell out. He should be able to fill you in if you can get him to talk. I had come across him a couple of times when he was working at the Ministry. He was rather full of himself. Word is he has become very religious. He goes to every Sunday service held at the prison chapel."

"Anything else, Karageorgi?"

"Well, his file has been destroyed during the coup along with those of many others who were imprisoned. That opportunity only comes, though, during a war. As I said, he was convicted on the charge of manslaughter and is now in prison. It was something to do with his politics."

"That's it?"

"Well, he was Patroklos' father-in-law. From Patroklos' first wife."

"Really! Where did you get that from?"

"My friend in KYP told me. Some of those KYP lads have minds of their own and don't suffer fools. But sometimes political cronies get appointed and they have to deal with them with kid gloves ... And by the way, Patroklos has a brother called Ektaros who runs a bit of an import–export business. He has been on our radar for smuggling leather goods from Syria. And before the war, there was talk that he was facilitating the export of marijuana to Britain. During the war, he was one of those brave ones who "chose" to stay behind and guard their village during that invasion." He said this with grating sarcasm. "He was EOKA B only for where it helped his pocket. Now he plays the innocent and has joined Clerides' party and marches in support of Makarios."

"Well, get someone to check him out and see if he has anything to do with all this."

2

I had been interned for a night in Nicosia Central Prison during the coup, and I felt that one visit was enough. This time, when Petros and I drove through the prison gate, I saw it in a different light. It wasn't as disorderly and did not have the same pervading stench of failed sanitation as on that day. The colonial limestone walls that surrounded the courtyard were quite restful in contrast to the greystone prison styled in the British fashion that was Mount Eden prison in Auckland, back in New Zealand.

Petros held a rolled-up file in one hand and a cigarette in the other. We were met by a prison guard wearing his dark blue uniform and a peaked hat. He saluted Petros, who dropped the cigarette and stomped on it, and the guard led us inside.

Mopping the floors was a stooped old man that I thought I knew. As we walked past him, I stopped and took a closer look.

He looked up and recognised me straight away.

376

"*Kyrie* Marange, *Kalimera. Pos apo tho* – how did you come by here?"

Then he looked at Petros. "*Kai o Kyrios* Zimaras."

Petros nodded.

"We are visiting someone," I managed to say. Despite still abhorring what the man did, I somehow found the grace to be polite. "How are you doing, *Kyrie* Pauvlo?"

"*Kala*, thanks to God. How is your family?"

"*Kala*. Yours?"

"They are good. They visit me every week, which is probably more than I deserve. Before God," and he crossed himself, "and on the grave of my parents, I don't know what madness took control of me to do what I have done. I am glad that you both put a stop to it. Yes, I am thankful to both of you for that, and as well I am sorry for Pitas and also Giangos ... even he did not deserve it."

Both Petros and I didn't know what else to say.

"Well, we have to go," said Petros, and we both turned and left the former *muktar* of Mpalloura to his chores.

"*Pigenetai sto kalo* – go to the good," intoned the old man.

As we moved away, Petros asked the prison guard, "How is the old *muktar* doing?"

"He is fine. I think he is genuinely remorseful for what he did. He gives us no trouble at all. I wish many more were like him. He is a testament to why the death penalty is not carried out nowadays. Of course, as always, it does not bring any peace to the families of victims."

"And what about Hatzimichaeli?" asked Petros.

"We haven't been able to get anything out of him," said the prison guard. "He's a hard nut to crack."

We followed him down a long corridor to an office and he showed us to two chairs. It didn't take too long before the prisoner we were there for was shown in. He was gaunt and grey haired and looked nothing like the photograph that Petros showed me. He wore a jersey over a white shirt and had on a pair of well-worn khaki cotton slacks.

As always, when interviewing or interrogating people, Petros was respectful and polite.

"*Kyrie* Hatzimichaeli. Thank you for seeing us. Please sit down."

The prisoner sat down opposite us behind the desk. His back almost touched the yellow sandstone wall.

Petros had rearranged the seating while we were waiting. "It will make him feel more secure," he explained. Whether that was true or not, I don't know, but it seemed to work with Hatzimichaelis.

"*Kyrie* Hatzimichaeli. My name is Inspector Petros Zimaras."

The man looked at him and then looked at me. His eyes had hollowed out but were as black as onyx with dashes of white, a sign of cataracts. Petros did not introduce me.

"Is there something that I can get you? Water, perhaps?"

"A glass of water would be good. Thank you."

"No problem. Stauvro, ask the constable to bring us a jug of water, please."

I went to the door, knocked, and when the guard opened the door, I passed on the request. Then after the door was closed, I went back to the corner that I was leaning against.

Petros took out his cigarettes. "Do you smoke?" he asked, and when Hatzimichaelis nodded, he tapped the box and offered the cigarette that protruded from it. He took one too, and taking out a lighter, he lit both cigarettes.

Hatzimichaelis drew deeply on the cigarette and then let the smoke out slowly. Petros did the same. They sat there smoking, saying nothing.

The guard entered the room with a tray, a pint pitcher of water and three glasses. Petros poured, filling all three glasses, and then pushed one gently towards Hatzimichaeli. My leg was aching, so I took out two Aspros and swallowed them. I leaned over and took my glass and drank some water.

"Is there anything else that I can get for you?"

"No, this is fine."

"Well, we might as well start. *Kyrie* Hatzimichaeli … this is a formal interview. We need to ask you some questions. Only you are aware of some things that we are interested in. I cannot force you to tell me – in fact, there is no way that I will force you. But I want you to help me understand something. It has nothing do with your case, but it does have something to do with your friend and comrade, *Kyrios* Neoptolemos Papageorgiou."

The name registered a flick in his eyes, but Hatzimichaelis just sat smoking and looking blankly at us. He said nothing.

Then, after an uncomfortable silence, "Neoptolemos? He was killed last year."

"We know that," said Petros, knocking his cigarette against the ashtray. "What we need to know is if you know why he was killed," said Petros, depositing the long length of ash in the ashtray.

"All I know was that he got caught in some fighting on the western line." Hatzimichaelis mimicked Petros and deposited his ash in the ashtray.

"Well, that is possible, but that is not how we see it." Petros opened the file he was holding and pushed forward a photo of a dead man. "We think he was executed."

Then he put forward another photo where the top half of a half-turned handsome man was spoiled by two wounds to the heart.

"You can see the powder marks. So there is no doubt."

"Well, he did have quite a few enemies."

"Yes, we know that. We also know of his collaboration with the late Polycarpos Georghadjis."

"Yes, Neoptolemos was an attaché with our embassy in Athens."

"We know that, as well."

"It is not a secret."

"*Kyrie* Hatzimichaeli, as I said, you are the only person that we know who can help us understand … Please be assured that we are not trying to trap you. You must know that what I say about his death is true. You must have thought of the possibility. All I want to know is if you have a theory."

"What sort of theory?"

"A theory of why he was killed. As you can see, he wasn't wearing a uniform. He was wearing just a sports coat over a shirt and tie with his suit pants. His shoes were polished. We found a couple of magazines for an automatic pistol in his coat pockets. Although his pistol is missing, his wallet wasn't taken. So it wasn't a robbery. What do you think? Just your thoughts, if it is at all possible." Petros' tone became even more sympathetic, less earnest but still pleading. "It is important because there is something happening at the moment, which is very perplexing, and we think it connects back to him. We found a dead young man, and later we found *Kyriou* Papageorgiou's address and phone number in his house."

"Who?"

"Modestos Kali." Petros obviously, up to now, hadn't wanted Hatzimichaelis to know of Modestos' death.

Hatzimichaelis frowned.

"We found him in Astromeritis …"

We could both see that he knew the name.

"… Dead."

To give himself time, Hatzimichaelis lifted the glass and drained it.

381

Petros refilled the glass.

"Do you know what it could possibly mean?"

"No."

"*Kyrie* Hatzimichaeli, it is important that you help us. You see, there's a bunch of thugs who are going around executing people. We simply need your help. Have you got any idea why such a wasps' nest has been building here in Cyprus? Give us anything please, and I will do my utmost to ensure that your stay here is a little more pleasant."

"Like what?"

"Well, you name it."

"You'll get me some books?"

"What sort of books?"

Hatzimichaelis thought for a moment.

"Callinikos. Theodoulos Callinikos … his psalms. I would like his anthology. He collected all our Cypriot chants and I would like to follow his notations … to chant properly at church."

I had no idea what sort of book he was talking about but Petros obviously knew it.

"I think we have a copy at home from my grandfather, my mothers' father who was a priest. I think it's a fifties edition."

"It doesn't matter when it was published. I'd like to be of some use when I get out, and it gives me something to engage my mind."

"Well, that will not be a problem."

"Also, if you don't mind, can you bring me a copy of *The Iliad* and *The Odyssey*, and also my volume of the poetry of Palamas? I only have our Bible here. You can ask my wife for those."

"Yes. Is there anything else?"

"Can I have some more water, please?"

Petros got up and went outside. We heard him order some more water. He returned and sat down, waiting until a constable brought in another pint pitcher. The constable filled the empty glass, took the empty pitcher with him and left.

"Would you like another cigarette?" asked Petros.

The man nodded and Petros gave him his packet of cigarettes. Hatzimichaelis took one and put it in his mouth. Petros took out his lighter, leaned over and lit it. Hatzimichaelis picked a bit of tobacco off the tip of his tongue.

He then drew a deep breath. "Right. But you will have to be patient with me, Inspector.'

"Fine."

"So. Have you heard of the Black Hand?"

"The Black Hand? You mean the precursor of the Mafia in Chicago?"

"No. The Serbian one. I don't think they were related to Chicago or the Mafia."

"No. So what is it?"

"Well, as I said, they were Serbian. A military cabal, a sort of secret society. It was formed in 1911 by officers of the Serbian Army. They wanted to unify all the territories inhabited by Serbs like Garibaldi did with Italy. You must have heard of them because they were involved in the assassination of the Austrian Archduke Franz Ferdinand and his wife."

Petros shook his head. "I only know of the duke and his wife ... they were shot ... by an anarchist?" he offered.

"Yes, Gavrilo Princip – as you say, an anarchist. Princip, though, was a member of the Black Hand. I know many think that was the cause of the First World War, but I think different – but we won't go into that. Anyway, the Black Hand quickly faded away after the First World War but re-emerged in 1938 to overthrow the three-member Serbian regency that was set up until such time as the young prince, Peter II, came of age. The Black Hand was organised at the grassroots level with cells of three to five members, supervised by district committees and by a central committee in Belgrade, whose ten-member executive committee was led, more or less, by Colonel Dragutin Dimitrijević." He coughed to clear his throat. "Dimitrijević's code name was "Apis". The Black Hand was his inspiration ... as I said, that was in 1911. To ensure secrecy, members rarely knew much more than the members of their own cell and one superior above them. It is my theory that Georgios Grivas became aware of them through his association with Serbian army officers either before or during the Second World War and used a similar structure with other right-wingers to set up X, a stay-behind army in Greece, to face the Soviets in case of an invasion. Then Grivas used the same structure for EOKA in the fifties."

Suddenly, what Terry told me about stay-behind army units started to gain more credibility.

"What's a stay-behind army, *Kyrie* Hatzimichaeli?" asked Petros, who had never heard of the term.

"It's what it says. It's an army that stays behind … goes underground if a country is invaded and then carries out sabotage and guerrilla attacks and assassinations … basically making the life of the invaders difficult, like the resistance in Crete or France against the Germans."

Petros nodded, but I could see he was becoming impatient and beginning to show it.

Picking on Petros' body language, Hatzimichaelis apologised. "Sorry, I didn't mean to be so long-winded, but that history is important when I tell you that it was resurrected … the Black Hand … by Polycarpos Georghadjis as a front for his espionage activities in Greece and the Balkans. It was a blind front. He set it up to take the blame for Colonel Papadopoulos' assassination by Panagoulis in August 1968. Unfortunately, Panagoulis stuffed up the assassination attempt and he was captured. He was extensively tortured, and it's said that he didn't give anyone up, although if he did, he couldn't have given Georghadjis up because his knowledge of Georghadjis and the new Black Hand was limited. The team that undertook the assassination attempt was isolated from the instigator of the plot. Loukas was part of that team – the ones who took the explosives in a diplomatic pouch to Athens in Greece for the assassination. I had arranged for the explosives charges to be assembled, the wiring and the firing mechanism to be made, and drove Neoptolemos to the airport. Then I put them in the diplomatic pouch. There were two other cells below me.

"Georghadjis was a real *mangas*. Sometimes I thought he was mad. But I think because he had survived so many escapades, he started to believe his *Houdini* nickname and became blasé. And his relationship with other intelligence services gave him such confidence that even M16 were wary of him. He also, I think, worked for the CIA.

"Just before the coup, I heard that a couple of *malakes* – wankers – *Calamarathes* from ELDYK were running around trying to recruit soldiers to a secret organisation. This was after Georghadjis' assassination. I admit I was against Makarios by then, but I saw them running a similar ruse as Georghadjis was running against the Greek security services, but this time against KYP. Anyway, I arranged a meeting in a restaurant and lost my temper, confronted them and we came to blows. One of their henchmen's mates, another Greek officer, pulled a knife, and in the struggle, he got killed. It was really self-defence, but they tried to convict me of murder. I pleaded guilty to manslaughter, and that is why I am still here."

"So, you were here during the coup and the war?"

"Yes, and when Nicos Sampson took over, I had a chance to break out with all his supporters, but I chose not to – although when the Turks started to bomb Nicosia, I thought I had made the wrong decision. Those of us who stayed had some narrow escapes. More than one Turkish jet thought we were an ELDYK military base. A couple of bombs were dropped and missed the prison. Someone said they were fifty pounders … so we cashed in a lot of blessings that day. I volunteered to put out fires and generally to run guns and munitions to the policemen and soldiers who were defending the prison against the Turks. After the ceasefire, we went back to our cells as if nothing happened. A couple of months ago, someone sent me a letter and in it was a folded sheet of white paper and it had a black handprint on it and the word *KLISTO* underneath it."

"Have you still got the paper."

"Yes. It's in the Bible in my cell. Under my command, I had two other associates and one of them had been killed during the invasion. He was Alexis Kantou. The second, who survived, was called Savas. Savas Spithas. I heard he works for KYP now. I have also heard that he is hanging around with a *leshi* – dirt bag – called Christodoulos Prokopi. Prokopis is a gun for hire and is acting as a mercenary, or at least a pointsman, for other terrorist groups. He is also an enforcer for the Limassol mafia. I think Modestos worked with him. I think Spithas is using the Black Hand acronym to lay a trail of either credibility or confusion for those thugs.

"Why do you say that?"

"Well, as you well know, Cyprus is a small place, but without someone with local knowledge, one can easily get lost even here. From what I remember, Spithas used to be a car rally driver and so he knows all the back roads of Cyprus. He took part in the first Cyprus Rally in 1970 and would have won it if his back tyre hadn't blown and the irreparable damage took his car out of the race. His co-driver was Prokopis, who apparently now also does contract work for KYP."

I vaguely remember that there was an international rally when I came to Cyprus in the summer of 1973. That would give Prokopi the chance to get to know all the back roads that he used when we came across him. Although Petros was a good driver, he didn't have a chance against Prokopi. Thank heaven for the bus.

"So this Black Hand organisation was the precursor of ESEA, EOKA B's political wing?" ESEA stood for Committee for the Coordination of the EOKA B Enosist Struggle.

"Yes. But ESEA didn't have a chance or credibility because Grivas refused to give them any authority, let alone the autonomy Makarios had given EOKA during the revolution. Grivas kept them under a tight rein. It looks as if Neoptolemos pushed his luck with someone and that someone shot him. Or, like Georghadjis, maybe some junta officers saw the war as an opportunity to take him out. People use a war as an opportunity to get even. Neoptolemos was a religious fanatic …" said the man that Karageorgis described as one too.

"Isn't it strange that some men work all their lives to attain power so they can kill on behalf of God as if God is a helpless old man who cannot do his own killing. Then they say that God chose them to do this or that deed, but in reality, they chose themselves. They cannot see how delusional that is."

I was amazed at how an obviously intelligent man had no self-awareness: he was the mirror image of what he described in Neoptolemos Papageorgiou. This was not the first time, though, that I had come across this phenomenon ... your friendly and devout Christian psychopath.

3

After we left the prison, Petros told me that the Christodoulos Prokopis, who Hatzimichaelis mentioned, was probably the Takis that Spithas had mentioned in the conversation Karageorgis overheard at the cafe. He said that Takis is a diminutive derived from Christakis but can be also derived from Christodoulos. Well, Takis, or whatever his name was, was no more. He went through the windscreen of the BMW on the Nicosia to Troodos road. He wasn't someone that I would lose any sleep over. Nor for his mate Stelios.

*

A few hours after the prison visit, Alexandra and I met at the Botanical Gardens, a block from the hospital, after she finished the day's surgeries. We drove to Larnaca in the Morris and walked along the *Phinikoudes*. The promenade was busy but not frenetic, so we sat down at a seaside restaurant, and I enjoyed a cold beer and she a 7 Up. I was building up the courage to talk to her about my feelings for her.

However, she was obviously upset and very angry. It took a while before she told me about her day. When she told me, I understood why she was upset. Apparently, she had been working on women who sustained horrific physical injuries when they were raped during the war.

"I volunteered to help burn victims, and now I end up working on rape victims," she fumed.

I said nothing.

"What fuckin' savages you men are," she suddenly shrieked. Then she shook her head, took a deep breath and collected herself. "I am sorry, Stauvro. I don't mean you … I mean rapists, men who rape … God, help me … I have no problem with doing the operations … but some of those women will never have children, Stauvro. I also helped repair a couple whose abortion had gone wrong. Imagine … the poor souls had to get dispensation from our Church to get the abortions done. But there were also two or three men – and the doctors told me that there were more – who were raped but have hidden it because they fear that their wives will leave them. It's a stupid, patriarchal thing …

389

you know ... Who is this man who is protecting me when he cannot even protect himself? The local doctors shunned the men as if they were pariahs and they left it to me, a woman, to do it. I had to get the poor souls knocked out for the procedure. Madness!"

After the Turkish invasion, I had reported on one occasion about the Church giving dispensation to the women having the abortion procedure and to the doctors aborting the foetus of rape victims ... but I let Alexandra fume and kept quiet. It was an area that I largely stayed away from during the war, except to report the numbers given to us journalists by the United Nations' CID. From what I had picked up during my time as a foreign correspondent, rape is a way by which soldiers humiliate their enemy, and they do it by raping their women. But as Alexandra pointed out, it happened to men as well. There were many rapes in Vietnam that were not reported but we got to hear about them. From what my godfather told me during a drunken rage at one of our Christmas parties – when he got into his melancholic moods – there were rapes during the Second World War over the whole war front. He witnessed such episodes after the battle of Cassino.

The most famous mass rape I had learned of was when women were raped by the Japanese in Nanjing in China. Reports suggested a quarter of a million died but many were raped before they were killed. In Europe, it was also part of the killing and revenge by both the Russians and the Allies. My godfather said many on our side still hated the Germans and Italians for what they had done and they, in turn, did things to them that later they were ashamed of. It wasn't until 1949 that the Geneva Convention was revised to make it clear that rape was a war crime.

After Alexandra vented her anger, she seemed to relax. Towards the end of the evening, we talked about our families, and I told her briefly about

Elizabeth and her suicide. Then I told her about Melani and how I missed the possible signals that she still had feelings for Gerald, and finally, what a fool I had made of myself by knocking Gerald out.

"Jealousy is a powerful emotion," said Alexandra.

"Jealousy?"

"Yes. They don't call it the green-eyed monster for nothing. It's like gunpowder. I saw how you bristled the other day."

I ignored the latter part of her comment by changing tack.

"You know what you were talking about, that second cousin of yours who had an affair with your husband? How long was it before you found out?"

"Not very long. I think it was because she wanted me to find out. She's one of those people who has always been jealous of me for achieving so much when she never even finished university. When we were young, she'd do spiteful things, and if I caught her out, she'd deny it, and even my mother would take her side because her persona would change. Everyone other than the people she hurt would think that butter wouldn't melt in her mouth. I think she is sick. When I was at medical school, we were taught about different mental disorders so that we could differentiate people who were narcissists, hypochondriacs, or suffered from conditions like mithridatism or Munchausen syndrome."

My curiosity was piqued and anything not to get back to the rape discussion. "I've heard of Munchausen and the others but what is mithraicism?"

Alexandra took a sip of her 7 Up. "Mithridatism … It's named after an ancient King of the Pontus region to the east of the Black Sea, Mithridates the Great. What is interesting about him is that he apparently knew twenty-five languages, and he butchered over 80,000 Romans in Asia in just one day. Mithridates took a little poison every day to become used to it so his mother, who favoured his brother, could not poison him. It's now applied by people who work with poisonous snakes and need to be sort of vaccinated against their bites."

"Like journalists sipping a whisky to become immune to politicians, eh?" I said, smiling. She frowned, finding my analogy strange. "Did Mithridates survive because of it?"

"He did, but he came a cropper when he took on the Romans. After three wars, he was usurped by his son and had to commit suicide to avoid capture and humiliation. He took poison, but because of his immunity he needed his bodyguard to finish him off with a sword."

"So, why do you think your cousin was doing this?"

"I really do not know. It could be something to do with her parents, not giving her enough or too much attention."

"So, you think that jealousy is a powerful force?" I asked, casting my mind back to what Father Sosimas's parable was about and what Terry and I were talking about concerning different motivations for terrorism.

"God, yes! I wanted to kill my arsehole of a husband when I found out about his affairs, but luckily I drank a bottle of wine, threw up and passed out.

"After that, I learned to live with the rage … but it was a powerful force. Never felt it before. I totally understand crimes of passion now. A madness takes you over. It's probably what something like that does to your own self-esteem. It's instinct. You lash out to defend it."

*

Then Alexandra began by telling me that her family came from *Agios* Theodoros at the bottom of the Karpas Peninsula, which is now occupied by the Turks. Her grandfather was called Christos Abraham. She confided in me that one of her family's long-held secrets was that they were *Linobambaki* and she explained to me what that meant.

I knew that in Cyprus, family secrets are rarely divulged to anyone. Blood disorders like thalassaemia and haemophilia are never discussed as it affects the family's fortunes and the marriage prospects of the family's children, even if they are not afflicted. Maybe Alexandra's sensibilities were tempered by her experiences as an immigrant caught between two worlds in the UK. However, despite that possibility, I knew that by telling me this, Alexandra was actually indicating that she trusted me. Something that I did not take lightly.

"*Linobambaki*," she said, "comes from *lino* – linen – and *bambaki* – cotton – and describes Catholic Venetians who were left behind after the Ottomans took over Cyprus. They were linen, that is Muslim, on the outside of the duvet and cotton, Christian, on the inside, a metaphor that they chose to describe themselves by." Her grandfather's name was a combination of a Greek name *Christos* and a Muslim name *Ibrahim* – Abraham – drawn from the Old Testament into the Koran, and it was a clever construct that allowed *linobambakous* to recognise each other and retain their former Venetian identity. Her own father's name was, in turn, reversed to become *Mosha* – Moses – perpetuating a tradition set for 300 years – to keep their identity alive.

393

When the British took Cyprus over, her family then reverted to Christianity. Many other *Linobambaki* did not apostatise and, with the Turks that stayed behind, became the core of the Muslim minority of Cyprus. In addition to political and religious pressure under the Ottomans, there was economic oppression that included onerous taxes and removing their rights to own property. The Catholic inhabitants affected by these coercive acts were the Latins, Venetians and Genoese minorities. The Maronites, who were Arab Christians, and the Armenians, who were Greek Orthodox Christians, were also affected. The latter were especially targeted by the Ottomans, and they quickly converted to Islam in order to avoid the merciless oppression they were destined for. Eventually they also became encapsulated by the name *Linobambaki.*

Alexandra said that the *Linobambaki* did not entirely convert to traditional Muslim life and only demonstrated religious practices and beliefs that would gain them advantages only afforded to Muslims. For example, they frequently consumed alcohol and pork and didn't attend religious services: traditions similar to the continuing Turkish Cypriot culture of today. Many of the *Linobambaki* villages have Christian saint names that begin with *Agios* – Saint – to indicate their Latin Catholic origins. "*Linobambaki's* cultural roots and history can be found throughout Turkish Cypriot life and literature," she said. "For example, two of the most prominent main characters from Cypriot folklore are Gavur Imam and Hasan Bulli. One was a leader of a successful revolt against Ottoman taxes in 1833 and the other was a Robin Hood type of character." She said that *Linobambaki* became a part of the majority of all uprisings and revolts against Ottoman rule and other local government bodies on the island.

Later I found out that according to the Greek Consul's Report of 1869, the numbers of *Linobambaki* were stated as 10,000 to 15,000. Once Cyprus became part of the British Empire, the majority of the *Linobambaki* reintegrated into the Christian Orthodox community of Cyprus while the remaining maintained a permanent Muslim status.

"My father claimed that many of our men joined EOKA in the fifties to shrug off the label and prove our patriotism," added Alexandra. " He said that some of the bravest and most brutal fighters were *Linobambaki*. I don't know how true that is."

*

What happened between Alexandra and me that night stays between Alexandra and me. Suffice to say that early in the morning, I turned on the side lamp to smoke a half cigar. Alexandra was awake, curled up next to me. Scipio was asleep between our feet. Alexandra touched my wounded leg with some concern – at one stage I couldn't help but flinch when she had put her weight on it. Then she asked if she could have a puff of my cigar.

As we smoked, she suddenly turned to me. "Are you left or right?" she asked.

"Right, but I can be ambidextrous," I replied, slightly puzzled by the question.

"I mean politically."

"Oh!" I was surprised by the question as no one ever asked me that before. "Left, I suppose. Actually, socialist with a touch of anarchism."

"Good answer."

"Did you ask your husband that same question?"

"Yes. He said that he was a communist. It turned out that he was one of those communists whose heart is in their left pocket and their wallet in the right."

"Yeah, an interesting combination," I said.

"Except his heart was made of shit," she said with some venom.

We lay there, me smoking, her looking at the ceiling.

"Did that help your self-esteem?" I asked.

"What, me venting against my husband?"

"No, what happened before."

"Yes, it did Stauvro *mou*. What about your self-esteem?"

"Fully recharged and ready to go."

4

Alexandra came around the following evening after she had gone back to her hotel to have a nap and a bath. I had prepared a potato salad and was frying two pieces of fish.

"Sorry, Stauvro, but I had to choose between you and a long bath, and I am afraid the bath won," she joked.

"I don't blame you," I replied, laughing. "It was one of my few pleasures in Vietnam and it's the same even here. Sometimes, before I found the sauna down the road, I would book into a hotel to have a bath. When we were kids, we only had one bath a week. After Friday night shopping when we got home, our Mum would run the bath for both my brother and me. We shared the hot water. Now, if I have the chance, I bathe every day. The luxury of modern life, eh?"

She had brought a plastic shopping bag with her that held something heavy.

"I've brought dessert," she announced. She asked me where my plates were, and she chose two soup bowls. She took out an aluminium pot with a lid on it, much like those used by workers to take their soup to work.

"I went and bought this pot for it so that I could carry it," she informed me.

A very distinctive aroma arose from the pot when she lifted the lid. I suddenly felt faint and almost overwhelmed by the discomfort that it caused me.

Alexandra did not notice as she chirped on. "I couldn't resist it. I loved *mahalepi* when I was a child. Mamma always bought it for us when we came into town. It's not even fully spring and someone was selling it in Metaxa Square, and I couldn't resist it. I got the seller to put lots of *rothostema* – rose water – with it. I remember Mamma used to put *rothostema* into a cologne container and spray me when I was a girl … it was a sort of poor man's perfume. It brings nice memories back. I hope you like it with sugar. If not, I'll scrape it off for you."

I didn't say anything.

I just sat there, mute. The hairs were doing a dance at the back of my neck and suddenly, out of nowhere, a series of olfactory memories popped up. They were probably hidden in some deep recess of my mind and they came flooding back. Someone said that some memories are like bullets ... when they miss you, you are left shaken, but when they hit you, they tear you apart and leave you crying for your mother.

However, thinking about it again, there were probably several things that conjugated to create that moment.

There was the talk with Alexandra of the rape-repair surgery the previous night. Then the revelation the previous year that my mother, as a young woman, was raped at the village before she married my father. Then that incident at the Vũng Tàu brothel – down the road from the beach resort set up by the Australians for R & R in Vietnam – where I had actually walked out on a girl. Then the image of our babysitter Auntie Loulou naked that had got mixed up in my Vietnam dreams lately.

Alexandra finally noticed that something was up.

"What is wrong, Stauvro?" she asked, with more than some concern.

"Nothing," I replied.

"No, there's something wrong. What is it?"

I sat there prevaricating. Was this something that I wanted to discuss? I realised that I was somehow ashamed to talk about what had happened between Auntie Loulou and me. I was also aware that Alexandra had confided a family secret to me, something that took considerable courage and resolve and meant that she trusted me. I finally decided that if there was going to be anything serious between the two of us that this was something that needed to

398

be aired … or as Delphinidis advised, it was something that I had to divest or unburden myself of.

"Let's eat first and then I'll tell you," I said, to give myself some more time to recover.

We ate in silence. After, Alexandra cleaned up the dishes and then came back and stood looking at me.

*

"Well, it's the aroma of the rose water,' I said tentatively. "It's brought back some memories. Some are … not nice memories. I mean …"

"What?"

"I don't know … I…"

"I can throw it out." Alexandra volunteered, obviously shocked that something innocent as *mahalepi* would have such an impact on me.

"No. It's something that I have to deal with. Just leave it for the moment. Come and sit down, eh." Alexandra pulled one of the chairs and sat close to me with concern in her eyes. "You know what you said yesterday, about those men that were raped during the war … that you had operated on … and how our machismo culture stopped them seeking help … and they only came to the hospital when they were in excruciating pain, and even then, our doctors and nurses treated them like lepers …"

"Yes."

"Well, the smell of the rose water *mahalepi* brought things back to me. One particular thing that I have, to some degree, never talked about to others and really almost totally suppressed ... Well, I suppose ... I reconstructed what happened so that I didn't need to think about it."

Alexandra sat there, then leaned over and took one of my Il Moro cigars out of its packet and lit it. "Go on," she urged.

"I am actually really quite embarrassed to talk about it, but with what's happened to me over the last year or so ... and us talking about Elizabeth and other things, it seems that various things have come to the surface."

Alexandra reached out and touched my arm.

"Go on ... tell me," she urged in a gentle tone.

"Well ... When Peter and I were growing up, our parents owned and worked at a fish and chip shop to make sure that we had all that we needed. My father used to get up at five in the morning to go to the markets and buy fresh fish when it was available. He and our mother would drop us to Auntie Loulou's, a Greek woman who used to look after us. She was our babysitter. I don't remember much about her except that she worked at a sweet shop at nights, making sweets with an old Greek man who had a shop in Wellington. She used to bring us Turkish delights that smelled of *masticha* and rose syrup ... But I remember she used to play with us and cuddle us when she gave us baths, and she'd coo 'What a little *koroú* you have.' Then she'd rub our penises. 'Are you a *pustouthi*? Are you a *pustouthi* – a faggot?' she'd repeat and tickle us until we collapsed with laughter.

"I must have been about four or five years old when she suddenly disappeared off the scene, and what was worse, we weren't allowed to talk about her. Now I realise that our parents had got rid of her because my father hired someone to help him at the shop and insisted after that that our mother stayed at home until we went to school. For months after she disappeared, I used to have dreams, powerful, erotic dreams of me naked, lying on top of her, and in the dreams I could see her vividly: breasts … everything. You work out the rest. Then I started getting into trouble. Other mothers would complain to my parents that I had been playing husbands and wives and doctors and nurses with their young daughters. My mother and father would apologise and keep me at home. From what I now remember, my brother seemed to stay away from those games. Why, I don't know, because we never talked about things like that

"When I went to secondary school, I was sent to a boys' college, but I remembered going up the hill that backed the school at lunch break with my friends to look down at the girls sunbathing around the swimming pool at the neighbouring college, which was for girls only. My mother and father disapproved of us having *Playboy* centrefolds on our walls. They said it degraded women. In my sixth form year, I was in a musical called *Salad Days*, and the dance teacher, a gorgeous blonde who was brought in to teach us the dance moves throughout the rehearsals, seduced me. She was the first woman I had sex with. Well, knowingly, I suppose. In the seventh form, there was a string of girls from a really posh school that was our sister school, and by the time I went to university I was a raging little Lothario … I never stayed with the same girlfriend very long. It seemed that one went and another was there to take up from where she left off. Then I met Elizabeth in Auckland after I started at the *Auckland Star*, the evening newspaper up there. I fell for her and we started living together. Both our parents disowned us for a couple of months. She was a virgin when we met and we moved in together. But after a year she committed suicide. I found her dead in our bathroom with her wrists slashed. Elizabeth had a Jehovah's Witness background – although her parents left, but her mother went back after the divorce. Elizabeth was sexually repressed, and now I realise that I must have seen her in some convoluted way as pure and that was one of the things I liked about her, other than her amazing intelligence. I know it sounds stupid, but I think that is what happens when the marrying of a virgin is drummed into you from an early age ... Even by my mother. Elizabeth was head girl and dux at her school and a top student at university. After she died, I lost the plot.

"After work, my editor and I would always end up at the pub, and I would always get home drunk as a skunk. One day I woke up and found that I did not like what I had become, and like many lost guys who join the Foreign Legion, I did something similar ... except what I did was actually different. I chose Asia, the most dangerous part of the world that I knew of and headed there to become a foreign correspondent. I remember in Vietnam, I virtually lived the life of a monk. One day some of my Kiwi army mates persuaded me to go to a whorehouse with them. I was ready to do the deed, but something happened, and it made me get up and walk out. Now I finally realise that it was something that I have never thought about before."

"What?"

"It was the smell of rose water. The girl, well she was more of a woman, really, was virtually swimming in it, for obvious reasons.

"Last year, my friend Petros and I worked on a murder case that happened in Mpalloura, where my parents come from. It's now occupied by the Turks and all the villagers are refugees. Through the case, I found out that my mother was raped by someone who held a torch for her, to force her to marry him. He did it because my mother had chosen to become betrothed to my father. Needless to say, that came as a shock to me, and it must have been

402

awful for my mother to write and explain things to me. The whole thing became public knowledge because the guy was killed in the village *kafenio*, and during that case … the rape came out. You don't know how much more I love and respect my father now for not abandoning my mother, especially since it's possible that he is not my true father.

"Since I came to Cyprus, as I told you, I met Melani … She was a widow and I used to write letters in English for her. Her husband died in 1963 in a deadly skirmish with the Turks. She was my neighbour *Giagia* Androutsou's niece. Her brother arranged a meeting, which led to an engagement to an English soldier who served in Dhekelia. Her fiancé had lied to her that he was divorced, and after they got betrothed, he had left her and had gone back to his wife. To cut a long story short, the war threw us together. I decided to marry her. I took things really slow, afraid to ruin things, but after the war her ex turned up, having got a divorce, and she chose to go to London with him. She said that she was doing it for her son. Now I realise that Melani used to douse herself with rose water as a cologne, like you dab a little perfume behind your ears. So where one half of me wanted a relationship, maybe the other half didn't … I don't know, but it must have had some bearing on why she and I didn't really gel enough … otherwise she wouldn't have gone back to the Brit when he showed up again.

"Last night, you talked about the men and women who got raped … but it was what happened to the men that hit a chord with me. Not that I don't feel for the poor women, but it's what you said about how the men were forced because of their position in a patriarchal society not to talk about what happened to them, although I can't imagine that it is any easier for the women. I suppose they had to seek help earlier because they could have been pregnant. It must been awful for them to be caught in such a bind. Then tonight, you brought the *mahalepi* … and the scent of rose water … well, it set all this off. I

403

suppose … I must have seen it being sold in the streets, but it's probably why I never had *mahalepi* before, as well. Now I know why."

I took an Il Moro from the packet and lit it. We sat there in total silence. Then Alexandra stood up and put her arms around me and gave me a long hug. Then she turned and guided me to the bedroom. She spent the night clinging to me and me to her. That was the most loving thing she could have given me.

*

The next day we were having breakfast and coffee. Alexandra leaned over and touched my hand. "You know, Stauvro, what that bitch of a babysitter did was steal your childhood. She damaged you."

"What?" I looked at her, trying to work out why she said that. Then I realised she was angry on my behalf.

"I am serious … she damaged you."

"Well, to be totally honest, Alexandra," I said, "as a teenager for a long time, I saw myself as fortunate that I was already sexually awakened. But I am now really ... sort of conflicted. It's hard to change your mind about a belief that you have had for such a long time. I don't really know … You may be right … but now it's hard to get an accurate perspective on it … I feel sort of guilty and because of it, I suppose I feel ..."

"Listen to me, Stauvro *mou*. Children should be allowed to enjoy their years of innocence … it sets us up for the cruelties of adulthood, which is a lifetime. In London, you hear horror stories of Indian and Pakistani girls being betrothed at ten or twelve. Even among the Greek Cypriots there – who live twenty years in the past. One of my friends told me at school what her brother used to do to her when she was a child. A friend who is a GP told me similar stories. You hear of fathers also doing it to their daughters. Mothers to their sons. Cousins to cousins. It happens even here. Some say it's mainly curiosity, sexual experimentation, and in some ways it is, but whatever it is, it's kept secret within the family. I don't understand it. I suppose I was blessed. Nothing like that happened to me … except for my bloody husband."

5

Being a Saturday, the open-air farmers' market at the Costanza Bastion carpark next to the Bayraktar Mosque was in full swing. Although not in use, the mosque had been sealed and protected from desecration by the Greek side. I had arranged to see Petros at the nearby newspaper kiosk because he said he was bringing Eleni over to do her shopping. I left Alexandra sleeping, and I sneaked out to have a quick chat with Petros, get a paper at the kiosk in front of the market and also go into the market to pick some pastries for our coffee.

The stalls had early spring vegetables and citrus of all varieties. Of course, there were potatoes and fruit, like bananas from Africa. The smell of vegetables, fruit and the dug earth on the potatoes was something that I embraced, picking up goods and smelling them just for their aroma.

I had no idea that someone had been following me until I saw an effeminate man in a dark suit and with a cherub face staring at me from the other side of a stall. It was unusual to see someone so well dressed in the market. I did not recognise him. What alerted me was that when my eyes fell on him he turned quickly, and then to cover up he engaged an old woman, bargaining with her for something. When he continued to follow me around, I knew that I had a tail.

So I went to the kiosk, ordered a coffee and sat down outside, waiting for my cousin.

Imagine my surprise when Petros turned up, pushing the man I spotted in front of him.

"*Kalimera*, cousin," he said. "Did you know that this *kyrios* was following you?"

People moved, making way as if a wild beast was on the loose. My cousin was the beast and he was furious.

I said nothing.

Then gaining control of his anger, "I don't think you have made the acquaintance of *Kyrios* Pyros Patroklos. One of KYP's minions and their very own philanderer extraordinaire," he said, his sarcasm grating. "Hands behind your back," spat Petros, and Patroklos reluctantly complied. It was only then that I saw Petros' revolver. "Don't try anything because on the grave of my parents, I will shoot you. Now stay still." Again, Patroklos complied. Petros handcuffed him.

"Inside," he ordered, pushing him into the kiosk. The proprietor, who was sitting inside sipping a coffee, jumped up to protest, but after he saw the gun and the warrant card stuck under his nose, he obeyed Petros' stern nod towards the door. The man scarpered outside, closing the door. Petros then reached over and disarmed Patroklos, pocketing the automatic that he was carrying.

"So, cousin. Have you any questions to ask this creature that calls himself a public servant?"

I didn't need a second invitation.

"Why are you following me?" I asked Patroklos.

"I wasn't following you. I am here doing the shopping for my family," he said angrily.

"Yeah, you are just doing your shopping," scoffed Petros. "I saw you following Stauvro, and you weren't doing a very good job of it. C'mon, why were you following Stauvros, or should I take you down to the station, throw you in a cell and ring your boss to come and get you?"

Patroklos realised quickly that my cousin was serious. So he changed tack, adopting a reasonable tone.

"I just wanted to see what you looked like," he said, looking at me and smiling.

"What the fuck for?" spat Petros.

"To size you up, whether you were the real thing … I mean, the journalist thing …" Then, looking at Petros, "Or, if he is playing you."

"You are the one being played, Patroklos," said Petros rather spitefully. "That German bitch had you by the cock and was dragging you wherever she wanted. She was using you."

"No, she wasn't," said Patroklos rather feebly, like a child caught misbehaving. "I was under orders … to make contact."

"What … to fuck her?"

"If need be."

"And what have you managed to find out?"

"Not much, really. Just the usual crap. Embassy stuff. Anyway, why do you care? This has nothing to do with you."

"Yes, it has everything to do with me *vre vlaka* – you idiot. My cousin and I were nearly killed by those *sarandasporous* – forty seeds – that you have running around the island and your two stooges, Spithas and his mate Politis. Have you heard what happened to Politis? He and another of your supermen mixed it up with us and he had an accident. You and your boss have been played and you are running about chasing your tails."

"It's under control."

"Under control. God help us. Did you kill her?"

"Fuck, no. What the fuck do you think I am? I was fucking her, okay? But I did lose my cool with her when she started badgering me about the murder in Agia Napa, and so I told her that we needed to have a break. She just laughed and said that she had someone better to see to her needs. So she latched on to Sava. Then after a few days, she left Sava and came back to me."

"Why?" asked Petros.

"Why do you think? Savas wasn't up to it," he said, straightening his tie and throwing his shoulders back. I couldn't believe that the guy was boasting about his sexual prowess with what was now a dead woman.

"I saw your cousin here visiting her at the embassy. Maybe he was fucking her too," Patroklos said spitefully, hoping that Petros did not know this.

"That was when I turned up to rattle her cage," I said. "I told you …"

"Yes, you did," said Petros. Then turning to Patroklos. "What the fuck do you do at KYP anyway?"

Patroklos weighed up the question and was probably thinking that he'd use the Official Secrets Act but decided that Petros wasn't in the mood for prevarications. "I am second in command of the Palestinian desk."

"What, you have contact with the Palestinians?"

"Sort of."

"What do the Israelis think about that?"

"There's someone in charge of the Israeli desk as well. We basically play the two sides towards the middle. The president wants to have good relationships with both."

"Do you believe those bastards, Stauvro?"

"Stuffed if I know," I said. "But makes sense … From what I hear, that's why Cyprus Airways' planes don't get hijacked —"

"Now, you listen to me and listen well," said Petros, interrupting me. "I have three murders to solve. All you idiots have done is muddy up the sewer. You and your moronic mates stay away from my investigation."

"Well, all I know is that you shouldn't be involved," retorted Patroklos. "We have taken the case over and you should stay away. You have already blown my cover, and as for your cousin, if he doesn't stop meddling in our business, we'll chuck him out of the country … and now I hear that you are bargaining with the terrorists that shot at your cousin."

"How the fuck do you know that?"

"I know about Agia Napa too. The deal you have made to let that terrorist go. We are not idiots. This whole thing is a little beyond your plodding abilities, arsehole."

By now, Petros had had enough.

"God, help me, Patroklos! You stay away from Agia Napa, you hear me? If I see you anywhere near there, I'll shoot you, you hear?" Then dragging Patroklos up, he uncuffed him.

"You can pick up your toy at the Central Police Station. Now, fuck off."

When we exited the kiosk, we saw poor Eleni looking for us, and when she saw us, she was trying to work out what the hell was happening.

6

I went home and had breakfast and coffee with Alexandra. We promised each other we would meet at eight that night and go somewhere new to eat.

Patroklos, however, ran back to Special Branch and then to KYP, where he spent over an hour with his boss. Whatever they talked about, it was something another of Karageorgis' contacts was not privy to – he could not get close enough to eavesdrop. Apparently, when Patroklos left his boss's office, he gathered another man and spent some time prepping him up about something.

As this was D-Day, after his friend rang him Karageorgis spoke to Petros and then quickly arranged for two of his men to follow them. He sent another of his men in a separate car to ram them and take them out of the action outside Nicosia. They were obviously on their way to Agia Napa.

The so-called *accident* happened before the Larnaca turnoff. Karageorgis' man managed to nudge them enough that they went into a ditch on the side of the main road, leaving no chance for them to reverse and continue their journey. Apparently, Patroklos' backup got out, screaming his head off. Patroklos, who was driving, sat in the car and one of Karageorgis' men, who said that they were on their way to Limassol, had to go down and see if he was conscious because he wasn't moving. The driver who instigated the accident had driven off. Patroklos wanted Karageorgis' men to drive after him, but they insisted that their first priority was to make sure that their colleagues were all right.

7

Petros was back into his Alfa Romeo and he was coordinating the operation on his radio. He picked me up at Solomon Square outside the city's wall. He said he had two men covering Patroklos to make sure that he didn't put his nose into our business. We drove past where the accident happened and he waved at his men.

"Two can play dirty," intoned Petros under his breath, and he lit a cigarette.

*

Just after the village of Lympia, a radio call came through from Phantis. He said that Karageorgis had rung him, and he had looked into the background of my graffitist, the Manolis Karapanos character.

"He lied," said Phantis. "He has regularly been to Agia Napa and was seen there around the time of the murder. One of our boys caught up with him after he painted a lot of graffiti around Christmas. They opened a file on him. He has an aunt there he stays with outside the town. She said that he has a screw missing but is harmless. He could just be an idiot, but he could be using it as a cover for what he is doing. I'll send you a report. He may be worth picking up but ..." and then he listed my own reservations about Karapanos being the murderer.

Petros listened and after telling Phantis that he had done a good job, thanked him and hung up.

"What do you think, cousin?" he asked. "Do you think we'll get any soup out of this bread crumb?"

"I don't know, Petro. I agree with Phanti on this. He could have an accomplice in Agia Napa, though ... someone on the same wavelength as him. But why would he lie about it ... what is he hiding?" Then, in the spirit of fidelity, "What? You think the bread crumb has turned into a loaf of bread now?"

"Don't stuff around with Cypriot sayings, Stauvro. They all have a grain of wisdom in them."

"I've never heard of bread crumb wisdom, or crumb soup either," I said, goading him. "Our Italian neighbour used to put breadcrumbs in a soup that she'd made for her sons and my brother Peter and me when we went around after football … She called it *stracciatella zuppa*. But it also had beef stock, eggs and parmesan cheese in it. It's not just breadcrumbs and water."

"My God, Stauvro, sometimes I despair of you. You nitpick. It's a saying. From the time of the famine. It's …"

"All right, I get it … but aren't we stretching things here?"

"Stranger things have happened, cousin. Now let's concentrate on the task at hand."

*

We finally arrived at Agia Napa after picking up the man from Chandria. He said we could call him Tom.

If his name was Tom, my name is Aristophanes.

He had been waiting, as he promised, on the side of the road just beyond Lympia. He was in very bad shape and struggled to get into the car.

"How bad is it?" asked Petros, taking a quick long look at him.

"Well, you are a pretty good shot," said Tom begrudgingly. "One to the side through the rib and one next to my balls. You nicked the bone. I lost a lot of blood. But I should be all right if I get somewhere where I can get some decent treatment."

Petros took out a brown paper bag and handed it over. Tom took a couple of pills from one of the bottles inside it and swallowed them. "They are penicillin," my cousin informed him. "There is also some codeine for the pain, as you asked." Tom also swallowed two of those.

We drove down to the waterfront and there was an old fishing boat waiting. Tom finally managed to get out, followed by Petros and then me. Karageorgis arrived, parked his car and then came and moved Petros' car next to it. "I saw that your boy did a good job," said Petros.

"Yeah, he's a treat. I think he has the record for the most car prangs in the force. So he's an expert."

Petros went up to Tom and said something to him. As he left Tom, he turned. "Remember what I said. To the ends of the earth."

Then he came and stood next to me. "Are you all right with this? There is a risk, you know." He handed me a life jacket.

"I know … nothing ventured, nothing gained, as they say. Do you think it'll help my book become a bestseller?" I suggested ruefully.

I thought guiltily about how I had said nothing of what we were doing or of where I was going to Alexandra when she left for the hospital that morning. I hadn't wanted her to be worried. I knew that that would have to change if there was to be any mileage to our relationship.

Then feeling that I had to reassure him, "Listen … I am okay."

"Are you sure?"

"Yes, it's fine. He gave us his word that he will drop me off at the territorial limits. You can see the rubber dinghy. Just make sure that you get there in good time. I am a terrible swimmer, and although I am going to be wearing one of those," I lifted the life jacket, "I hear there are sharks around here."

"Don't worry, cousin, our *carcharies* are very choosy. They like something with more meat on them," Petros said jokingly, trying to lighten the situation.

Tom moved over to the old boat and talked to the boat owner. The man gave him some papers. Tom must have decided that Petros was honouring their agreement and gave the man an envelope full of money, and after the man counted it, they shook hands. Apparently, according to Petros, the owner was happy to get rid of it because it had got to the stage where it needed a lot of repairs.

"Make sure that you get the information about where the bomb is before they leave you."

"I will."

Petros leaned in and gave me a half hug. "May God go with you, cousin," he said as he turned to walk away.

"I don't think this life jacket can take both of us, cousin," I murmured, and Petros smiled and shook his head.

I followed Tom on to the boat. It was a ship's lifeboat that had been converted into a fishing boat: a caique named *Persephone*. It had a tiny skipper's cabin on top, about three-quarters of the way fore, in which there was a wheel and an assortment of rusting gadgets that helped in its navigation.

Another car arrived and two men about Tom's height got out carrying a holdall each and walked to the boat and threw them in. The car was a rental. Both men were well built and seemed totally focused on what they were doing. One, a blonde, moved to the skipper's small cabin while the other, with a shaved head, checked the engine and fuel gauge and then checked and pumped more air into the life raft. Then the blonde man in the cabin fired up the engine. They said nothing, but I assumed they were Tom's men. Neither looked like the man that Frank knocked out. Maybe he was the one left to set off the explosives if we didn't follow through with our agreement.

I noticed Petros taking in the new men. I am sure that his description of them would be more accurate than mine.

Tom was helped by one of the men to get into the caique and I followed. As soon as I got on board, I felt the boat moving, slowly at first, manoeuvring off the wharf and out of the small harbour before hitting full throttle.

I looked back and saw Petros going to a nearby small fishing boat and Karageorgis following him. The boat looked like a similar old lifeboat that had been converted, but whoever owned it looked after it because it was newly painted. The agreement was that Petros and Karageorgis would not follow for one hour. Tom did not bother telling them what would happen if they broke the agreement. Basically, I was the hostage, and my life depended on everyone sticking to what was agreed to.

The boat turned east, and I could see in the far distance the blonde, sun-bleached, rugged cliffs of Cape Greco as we left the land behind. The sea was choppy, but the boat seemed to be able to cut through it with no difficulty, although we did get tossed a little from side to side by a crosswind.

Without my realising, my hand searched for and found Delphinidis' wooden cross hanging under my shirt. I rubbed it several times in the form of a prayer, hoping that any evil that could befall me would somehow dissipate. I know, a big ask, given the circumstances. I also clutched on to Nietzsche's *why,* as I definitely wanted to know the reason why Mikis had died so young.

Neither the second man nor Tom said anything. They scanned the horizon in front to ensure that no one from the Cypriot side was waiting for them and behind to ensure that Petros had not broken his word. I didn't have a watch with me, but I estimated that we were making good time. My stomach muscles cramped up, and I realised it was pure and unadulterated fear. If they changed their mind and killed me and then threw me overboard, who was going to catch them? But I took some comfort from my cousin's threat when he said to Tom, "To the ends of the earth."

The sun was going down when the blonde man stopped the boat, and Tom gave me a torch.

"Just in case it gets dark before your friend finds you," he said.

I breathed a sigh of relief. If they were going to kill me, this would have been the time.

"I am sorry that you got dragged into this," he said, sitting opposite me.

"I thought you didn't do sorry."

"We actually thought you were someone else."

"What!"

He shrugged his shoulders. "Yes, an unfortunate mistake."

"I don't understand!"

"A mistake. It happens."

"Who did you think I was?"

"Urlich Fererer."

"Who?"

"In Cyprus, he went by the name Urlich Fererer."

"The one at the Agia Napa apartment?"

"Yes, but he's otherwise known as Ilich Sánchez."

"What?"

"Ilich Ramirez Sánchez."

"Who the fuck is he?"

"He looks a lot like you. Although you are skinnier. We were told by our source that he was Auguste's contact at the Helenis. We think Auguste was ready to change her identity to Madelaine Sorver. She was definitely a Baader Meinhof Gang agent carrying funds for weapons to the Middle East."

"Who told you that?"

"An informant in Cypriot Intelligence. He was stalking the woman, trying to get into her pants, and that boy beat him to it. He followed her one night back to the Helenis. He had managed to infiltrate her cell by screwing another German woman, who had also infiltrated the cell but who worked at the West German embassy."

"So, Bridgette Kessler was involved with the other German woman – whose name could be Claudine Auguste or Madelaine Sorver. Who organised the apartment?"

"Kessler."

"So, she was the terrorist's contact in Cyprus?"

"Yes. She was given a coordinator role by her terrorist handler, which was useful to KYP. She had another handler here."

"Who?"

"Someone at the West German embassy."

"And how did you find the Agia Napa apartment?"

"Our KYP contact followed her there, as I told you."

"Patroklos?"

He said nothing.

Then, "We rented an apartment opposite. That night when you broke into the apartment, we had gone downtown to get something to eat and were called back by the man we left behind. Your torch beam alerted him. Our intelligence led us to believe a South American terrorist who works for the PLFP was in Cyprus on his way to Lebanon. Now we know we missed him."

"I thought PLFP were mainly Palestinians."

"No, they have everyone with them, including Germans. Sánchez is from Venezuela. His father is a fanatic. A committed communist. After secondary school, he went to Cuba, where he was given some guerrilla training. When his mother divorced his father, she shifted herself and her children to London. His mother tried to get her sons into the Sorbonne, but Sánchez's father had other ideas and got him into the foreign students' university in Moscow. He was expelled from there. Too wound up, unreliable, a black-market racketeer, fucking everything in sight, etcetera, etcetera. It was after that he received his military training from the PLO. He was blooded in the Black September conflict in Jordan in 1970 between the Palestinians and the Jordanian army.

There he proved himself as fearless. A volatile bastard, but an excellent fighter. After the Palestinians were thrown out of Jordan, he went back to London, where he studied at the Polytechnic of Central London. It was during that time that he tried to assassinate a Jewish businessman. He also carried out a bomb attack in London and three on Paris newspapers. He then threw a grenade at a Parisian restaurant in an attack that killed two and injured thirty …"

"What you are French? Foreign Legion?" I tried again.

Tom ignored me. "Anyway, in January of this year, he fired a rocket at an El Al airliner and missed, and then a week later he did it again."

"So, you are Mossad?"

"What I am, as I said, is irrelevant. Suffice to say my comrades and I have failed in our mission. However, Sánchez … is a man with his own mission and is quickly gaining a reputation. Because of that, it was decided to stop him … before he sprouts wings. We want him dead.

"Now, I think you may have been right. Kessler infiltrated KYP by screwing …" he paused, then confirmed what I had asked just before, "… Patroklos. She broke it off with him and started going out with his mate Sava Spithas. Then she went back to Patroklos. I can't see what women see in the prick, but I think she was trying to make him jealous. When one of my boys told Sava he went crazy, and it seems he is the one who killed her. According to one of my boys, he knew you'd find her. That was why he tried to stop you and your friend on the way to Kalopanayioti. Savas is a thug. The world won't miss him if someone shoots him."

420

Then Tom said something that shook me. The shock must have shown on my face because he added, "We never thought that he was anyone of significance. As I said, we knew that the Auguste woman had been hanging around with the Baader Meinhof Gang in Berlin. That's where Kessler earned their trust. But he was not on our radar … By the way, the bomb is next to the public library on the city walls in Nicosia, where the water meter is. It has been buried so no one would see it. It's set to go off at eight tomorrow morning. You should have lots of time to get someone to disarm it. It's a simple device. No tricks."

He put out his hand, and I took it and felt his strength as he closed his fingers on mine like a vice, but he wasn't able to hold it for long. The wound must have been sapping his strength, and he quickly let go.

I climbed into the rubber dinghy that was already banging against the side. Once in, I put the rubber-coated torch on the floor and sat down. The second man cast me off, and from there, I was at the mercy of the currents … and the tide, which in Cyprus is not very much.

8

It took, according to Petros and Karageorgis about two hours to find me. I hadn't bothered rowing, although there were oars in the dinghy. There was an approaching storm and it put the fear of God in me. What seemed like hundreds of thunderbolts were falling to the west and the acetylene smell was thick and palpable in the air.

"We played it totally by the book," said Petros. "Any better idea about who they belong to?"

I shook my head and told him where the bomb was. After he radioed in the information, I also told him what Tom had said about mistaking me for someone else and who he saw coming in and out of the apartment in Agia Napa.

*

We got back to Nicosia and Petros was chomping at the bit to go for it. First, he arranged for his boss to meet us at the police station. He told him what I had learned, and by then the bomb dispersal squad had defused the bomb at the library.

Then he got his team together and briefed them on what they were going to do.

"That bomb was exactly where he told us it was going to be," said Sergeant Karageorgis. "It would have taken the whole of the municipal library out, including the city wall beneath it. Imagine the death and destruction at Syntagma Square! People would be going to work."

"So they weren't bluffing," said Petros' boss.

"No, *Kyrie*. But it was why I never told you. Stauvros convinced me that this Tom guy was the genuine package."

"Well, if we let the Palestinians hijackers go after a few years in prison, why shouldn't we turn a blind eye in this case," said the boss. "The president may not be pleased with us, though."

"We had no choice, *Kyrie*. The bomb would not been found if he didn't tell us," said Petros, "and it paid off for us in spades with what he said to Stauvros about Agia Napa."

"*Ne*. You are right. So, what is the plan?"

"We'll hit the apartment early when everyone is asleep," said Petros. "You cannot see a problem if Stauvros is there when we finish this?"

His boss shook his head. "*Pigenete sto kalo me ton Theon* – Go with God's speed. Let me know what happens."

*

I didn't tell Alexandra anything of what was happening. This time she cooked a simple, tasteful dinner of aubergines sautéed in tomatoes and olive oil. I had brought home a fresh round loaf of bread. We went to bed early and I snuck out, leaving her to sleep until her alarm went off.

I met Petros in the car park, and we went through the ID procedures before touching base with his office. Then we moved down to the assembly room where Karageorgis was sorting out the raid personnel. Pistols and automatic rifles were been handed out. Everyone quietened when we entered the room.

"To be absolutely clear," said Petros to the team. "No leaks. And I don't care who it is. I don't care if he is even your brother. Leak it and I will find out and you are out."

*

It took us ten minutes to get from the police station to the top of John Kennedy Avenue. Both Archbishop Makarios III Avenue and Limassol Avenue that it extends into had very little traffic at that early time of the day. John Kennedy Avenue leads off where the two meet at some traffic lights.

When we arrived at where John Kennedy Avenue ends and meets Nikis Avenue, we stopped. The apartment was to our left above a kiosk. No sirens were used. Another two police cars converged from both sides of Nikis Avenue.

"Right, let's go," said Petros.

We all got out and walked to the entrance of the building. Just as we arrived, the door opened, and someone came out. He was obviously on his way to work because he carried an aluminium container with his lunch and a thermos. Petros indicated for him to be silent and a policeman led the man off after he jammed something in the door to keep it open.

The whole of the squad was dispersed to cover the back and all points leading into the street. Unless someone were looking directly down, they would not have seen us, even if they were on the veranda.

Petros nudged a young policeman to lead us into the building. The young man crossed himself before he moved forward. Petros followed him and then went up to the lift and indicated to another policeman to stand guard and hold anyone who came down. Then he led the way up the stairs. He indicated to me to follow Karageorgis, who was behind him.

We carefully climbed the stairs, trying to minimise any noise. On the fourth floor, there were two doors on each side of the landing with the lift doors in the middle. The stairs leading up to the next landing were to our left. Petros took out the warrant and knocked on the door next to the lift.

He had to knock again. A young man who was rubbing the sleep out of his eyes and settling his dishevelled hair opened the door. The hall was dark. He was in silhouette as the light from a far window threw him in shadow.

"*Kalimera*, Antóni," said Petros.

Seeing the guns, the young man jumped back.

Then, recovering quickly, "I am not Antónis," he managed to splutter.

All of us looked at him with surprise.

"I am his brother."

Petros asked him to turn on the hall light. The young man was the same height and had the same facial features and cropped brown, blonde-tipped hair, but at a closer look, you could see that he was a bit older and more hardened.

"Where is Antónis?" asked Petros.

"He is asleep in his room."

"Where is that?" asked Petros, and when the young man pointed to the first door down the corridor, two armed policemen took off, pushed the door back and rushed into the room. We heard commands and then protests from Antónis.

At the end of the corridor and to the right, a door opened and a man in his fifties came out wearing pyjama bottoms and a white singlet. Behind him, I

425

saw a distraught woman sitting up in bed, trying to make herself decent. The parents.

The policemen who entered Antónis' bedroom brought him out, his hands handcuffed behind his back.

"Where are you taking him?" demanded the father.

"He is under arrest for murder, *Kyrie* Makri," said Petros in an understated way. "We have a warrant." He handed the warrant over.

By now, many more policemen had come up and were moving through the apartment to search it.

"Take him down to headquarters," said Petros to the policemen who were holding Antónis by the arms.

Then turning to the brother, he asked, "What's your name?"

"Panikos."

"*Kala*, Paniko. I am Inspector Petros Zimaras." He took a cigarette out and lit it. He took a long drag and exhaled. "I think, Paniko, I am starting to understand." Panikos looked blankly at him. He obviously had no idea what Petros was talking about.

"When you were questioned by us, did the policeman ask you for your ID card?"

"Yes, but ..." Panikos was having a problem but decided to come clean. "It wasn't mine. I didn't realise until it was too late ... We saw no problem with doing it. I had exchanged it with Antónis so that I could get into the special seats reserved for club members at the stadium. Antónis is the one registered, but he didn't mind sitting at the back of the stand. Then the policeman simply asked me where I was that night."

"Yes. And you were at the football in Larnaca."

"That is correct, *Kyrie*. I had leave from the army and we all went to support our team."

"Was Antónis with you?"

"No. He said that he was going to come later."

"Did you see him at the stadium in Larnaca that night?"

"Yes, but it was at the end of the match. He said that his motorbike threw its chain and he had to fix it."

"He has a motorbike?"

"Yes. It's an old one, but he adores it."

"When did he buy it?"

"About a month ago. It was in for repairs. He got it back a week before the match."

"Are you still with the army?"

"Yes, *Kyrie*, I have another year to go. I have to be back early tomorrow."

"You are not going back. We'll ring them. I would be very grateful if you come down to the police station and make the same statement you just gave us, please."

"What has Antónis done?"

"We'll tell you after you give your statement. One of my men will take you down. If you go now, you can be back by late morning to look after your parents. I am sure this would have come as a shock to them."

Petros indicated to the nearest policeman, who guided Panikos to his bedroom to get dressed, and then he moved up to the parents' bedroom where they were guarded by two armed policemen.

We were back at the police station by mid-afternoon and Petros led me to the interrogation room where Antónis was waiting. Karageorgis met us and was walking with us. He told us that Antónis refused to talk to the two detectives who initially interviewed him.

Petros told Karageorgis about the IDs and how he must have confused the two brothers as they looked so much alike. Karageorgis was embarrassed by the revelation, but to his credit, he said nothing to defend himself. To make it easier, Petros said, "Well, I made the same mistake. They are the spitting image of each other."

*

"*Yiassou*, Antóni," said Petros. "Please excuse us for being late. You know *Kyrion* Marango and this is Sergeant Karageorgis. You have given us a hell of a chase, my young friend."

Antónis was alert but said nothing.

"You had us chasing people all over the place. It was a perfect strategy, and I must admit you totally fooled me. My friend here, Stauvros, did consider the possibility that you had done it, but I dismissed it out of hand, and I set off

428

chasing my tail, or the tail of all those different demented hares, around this paddock which we call Cyprus, when I should been chasing a rabbit … a very small, but sick rabbit. You." He sat back to make sure that Antónis took this in, took another puff of his cigarette and continued. "It was very clever of you to return the Ruger to the woman's apartment. You must have seen her going to the apartment from the hotel. Followed her. How long did you watch her, trying to build up the courage to intercept her and make your case for her favours? Why did you chicken out? When she left the apartment to go back to the hotel, you had broken in and had a look around, and finding the gun, decided to teach your friend a lesson. What happened? Did the gun go off accidentally? You only meant to frighten them? Or was your jealousy so intense that you decided to exact some sort of revenge … to kill them both because you missed out on getting a piece of the German woman's cunt. Yes, you fooled me all right. In all fairness to myself, though, things did conspire against me … to lead me astray."

Then Petros, my clever cousin, threw the bait. It was a cunning move that over the years he had perfected to seem normal. Cunning is an attribute that the Greeks honour as a great asset in a man. Homer's Odysseus, my grandfather Sheitánis … Their deeds recalled and celebrated. My cousin had it in spades.

So, it was "Softly, softly, catchee monkey" again.

"I have no doubt you are a good lad. You will probably never tell us why you did it. More importantly, we can't make you tell us. However, I want to understand what makes such a good lad like you throw your life away."

Antónis said nothing.

"There is no hurry, Antóni. You are lucky that the death sentence for murder is not applied now. You can thank Archbishop Makarios for that." Then Petros stood up. "I am tired. I am going to take a break, go home and get some sleep, and we can talk again early tomorrow morning … if you want to, of course. So take some time to think about it. We do have enough to charge you for the crime. We have your shoe print and a partial fingerprint. You were seen entering and exiting the apartment." Here, Petros was pushing the truth because the witnesses who saw Antónis, Tom and his men, were somewhere in the Mediterranean, sailing away from Cyprus. "You were seen twice. Also, when we showed your photo to the maid at the Helenis, she remembered that she saw you in the corridor and thought you were a guest. Finally, we found that there was no way that you had enough money to pay off your motorbike. Good move, not taking all the money. So, we don't need to beat it out of you. Anyway, I don't believe in it. Coercion that is. You can tell us any story you want if we do that. Coercion never results in a true confession. Anyway, that's what I think. But who am I, eh? … Would you believe it that only recently I was told that I am just a bumbling plod."

Then getting up, he simply turned, opened and walked out the door, and I followed him.

9

Petros and I were sitting in his office, licking our metaphorical wounds. Out of desperation to do something, he searched his desk for cigarettes and finding a box of Peter Stuyvesant, he took it out, removed one and lit it.

"How the hell didn't we spot him before this?" he asked me in English, exhaling a cloud of smoke.

"Because we thought that we had bigger fish in play and we missed the spotty," I said, not wanting to revisit the fact that I had brought up Antóni as a possible suspect.

"Spotty?"

"A small fish like a *Maritha*."

He lifted his head in understanding.

"But how could he do this to his friend, Petro?"

"I don't know, Stauvro. But those kids were brought up on poisoned milk. You know the saying, if you suckle on a snake's tit, you become a snake."

I wasn't familiar with that saying … it's possible that Petros made it up.

"What do you mean?"

"Well, those kids are the products of the post-revolutionary period. Their fathers fought the British for *enosis*. Well, that's what they said they fought for. I know of several who said they were EOKA but weren't. Then when peace came, those real and fraudulent warriors of the revolution married and had kids … some before even the revolution ended. Anyway, those kids were brought up with their parents feeding them all sorts of chauvinistic garbage, which got reinforced by the Church." He inhaled the smoke of his cigarette, held and then released it. " Luckily for me, as I told you, my father was just a poor baker, although in 1952 he voted in the *enosis* referendum and was one of the ninety-five per cent of Cypriots who voted for it because it was the only way they could think of to get out from under the yoke of the British Empire. My father, though, became disillusioned when Grivas started killing members of the AKEL party, transferring all his Greek civil war vehemence against the communists to people who had very good reason to join that party – in Cyprus, AKEL was the party of the poor. My father was a centrist and a very devout Christian, so when two of his *koumparous,* two honourable men, were shot as so-called traitors, after that he didn't want anything to do with EOKA at all. Anyway, after the revolution, those in EOKA, as I told you a long time ago, they learned the power of the barrel of the gun. They set up their own gangs, armed to the teeth. Some got into positions of power, and like Lyssarides and Georghadjis, they ensured that some of the spoils of power trickled down to their supporters. Those that missed out formed their own gangs or parties. Some became criminals and, I told you, operated like the mafia, running dens and cabarets that were fronts for prostitution and gambling. Limassol is a cesspit and it wasn't touched last year by the Turks, really, other than what happened at the beginning with the coup when Makarios' supporters from Paphos marched on the city but were turned back after fierce fighting. This Antónis turd is one of them. The little asshole killed his own friend and the German woman and took just enough money to pay for his motorcycle, and we were running around blaming the terrorists. And then to cap things off, the terrorists were blaming you, and then the ones chasing the terrorist thought you were a terrorist too. This morning, someone from Antónis' suburb told us that his father is suspected of shooting someone in cold blood during the coup. Nothing to do with politics. Like his father, he learned the coercive power of the gun. So when his jealousy turned to momentary madness and he found the gun at that apartment, it was easy for him to pull the trigger. That he did it like a professional was an accident. That was of the many things that led me astray. It was very clever of him to pick up the shell casings and return the gun to the apartment. If it weren't for that guy Tom, he would have got away with it. I should have been more careful. Look at family and friends first. That's the first of the guiding principles of any investigation. However, in this case, I was blindsided by all the other bullshit that started flying."

10

Finally, KYP moved and got the Ministry of Foreign Affairs to make an official complaint to the West German government. What seemed strange, Petros told me, was that the body of the Bridgette Kessler, the West German intelligence officer, disappeared from Athens airport. When KYP followed all the leads, they finally discovered that instead of the coffin being flown to Frankfurt, it was sent to Czechoslovakia, behind the Iron Curtain, and from there, no one could find where it went. According to Petros, the speculation was that her body was repatriated to East Germany.

Manolis Karapanos turned out to be what he always was, a deluded young man with mental problems fighting shadows. On the balance of things, I did not resent him his graffiti. At least a wall defaced can be painted over, whereas a life lost is just that: lost, gone.

We never worked out which country Tom and his mates belonged to. The portable radio was US army and the Browning could have been Israeli. Tom was obviously upset by Kessler's death. Maybe it was one of those "My enemy's enemy is my friend" things. Maybe. That, to some degree, was partly substantiated by the arrival of some bigwig policeman from Munich and some notes and money transfers that Special Branch found in her apartment, which confirmed that Kessler was much more than what she made out to be. There was the contract for the apartment in Agia Napa that the owner said was signed through intermediaries as he never met her. She had a large amount of cash in different currencies that she kept in a cake tin in the pantry in her Agia Napa apartment, and my copies of the Conrad and Grivas books were among others that she had gathered from second-hand bookshops. As I suspected, she was killed before she could return them. Why she took them, despite Ari's theory, I have no idea.

Patroklos was oblivious that she was playing him, but it was Savas Spitha who took her up to Modesto Kalis' house in Kalopanayioti, where she was killed. Maybe they had an argument and he lost it.

The Black Hand was, as Hatzimichaeli said, a cloak and dagger ruse. Its Cypriot version was set up as a false flag, and after Giorgadjis' death, it lost traction. It popped up again briefly during the coup, and hopefully, now it has evaporated into the ether of subterfuge and the rubbish bin of history.

Modestos was also a double agent but did not know it, thinking that he was working for KYP when, in fact, he was hijacked by the hit squad through the Kessler woman.

Tom and his team were sent by someone to eliminate the terrorist cell, their main target being Ilich Sánchez. Patroklos must have deliberately worked with the hit team. Maybe he thought he was infiltrating them, when in fact, he was the one being played. He committed suicide soon after the whole thing blew up, although Petros was sceptical about the death. Maybe, like King Mithridates, Patroklos decided that he would get no mercy and took the honourable way out. He was probably under orders, but with his death, no one would know whose. There must be someone else within the KYP loop to have allowed that to happen.

The fly in the ointment was really the Cypriot contribution to all those teams that were either being misled or were playing their own double game, mainly motivated by the idea of gaining promotion or greed or both.

When agent Tom and his team saw Antónis going into the apartment they were watching, they assumed that he was somehow connected to their terrorist target. Apparently, Antónis finally confessed that he got into the apartment by waiting until the owners were working in their garden. He sneaked in through their downstairs apartment and then to the hallway through the connecting inner front door. His shoe prints matched the prints in the dust that Petros spotted. It's possible that he took the Judas door key and replaced it when he brought the gun back. Also, he took just enough money to pay off his motorbike. So there was a robbery component to Mikis' and Auguste's murders. For some reason, Antónis somehow resisted the temptation to take all the money. As Petros said, another good move.

When I broke into the apartment, the hit squad thought that I was Ilich Sánchez, who later in the year was dubbed "Carlos the Jackal". He was given that nickname by a journalist who saw a paperback of Frederick Forsyth's *The Day of the Jackal* in his apartment. When I saw several photographs of him, I thought I looked nothing like him. However, I never saw the photograph that Tom and his mates had. Carlos must have been very important if Bridgette Kessler was covering for him and the hit squad were under orders to kill him. This was the difficult part. Was Kessler part of the hit team or an accidental collaborator? But whose? If Kessler was Stasi, it's possible that the hit team were Stasi, too, but why? Maybe they were Russians taking care of someone they saw as an embarrassment. More likely they were Israeli. Terry did that a new counter-terrorist squad had been formed the previous year. For their own reasons, Tom and his mates hadn't told Patroklos or *Fraulein* Kessler that they had the apartment under surveillance.

The killing of Mikis and the German woman by Antónis must have thrown a spanner in the works and put the hit squad under pressure … and they simply misread the signals and because of it miscalculated. Patroklos told them about the Helenis and supplied my name and address to them after I visited the hotel. Agent Tom, still believing that I was Carlos, decided to visit me and take me out of the equation. At the same time, on her own initiative, Bridgette Kessler decided to snoop around and see who I was. Probably she initially thought that I was her equivalent, a talented Cypriot or British agent. She eventually told Patroklos, who told Modestos or Sava, that I was just a journalist who worked for Reuters. Word was finally passed on to Tom, who thanks to my cousin, was by then carrying two serious wounds.

The Claudine Auguste woman's body was repatriated to West Germany and handed over to her parents for burial. Her real name was Hanna Hoffmann. Apparently, many people turned up to her funeral, and some of the messages on the wreaths, according to *Der Spiegel*, confirmed her revolutionary status.

Of all the players, Bridgette Kessler was the smartest, really. She played Patroklos and KYP and the West Germans – who she had probably infiltrated years before under instructions from the Stasi. A real secret agent, but not as good as Pham Xuan An, the *Time* desk Vietcong spy. Bridgette miscalculated when throwing a tiff and leaving Patroklos for Savas Spitha and then Spitha for Patroklos. Hubris is not a quality to be overused in spy craft. Spithas killed her in a jealous rage but didn't know who she really was. The Cypriots say *Theos makarisi tous* – God bless their souls. I don't know, though, if the cantankerous Old Testament God would be generous enough to allow his name to be invoked in such a way. But his gentler, kinder son definitely would.

*

And what of the primordial waterfall in New Zealand's Fiordland that flows backwards? Easy. No miracle, really. It's just an illusion. Heavy rain and melting snow swell the waterfall and the force of the falling water is so powerful that in strong winds, it blows back … upwards. And as for cupping, as well as being used for a back massage, it can be used to drain the pus from a boil. And what is a better metaphor than a boil to describe all the ill that has befallen Cyprus in the last couple of years? The outpouring of poetry, as Petros mentioned, is the balm that will cure them.

11

The feature article I wrote on terrorism was finally published in a London paper in two consecutive Sunday supplements. I only include here some excerpts that may or not be relevant to the reader.

*

You Reap as You Have Sown

Terrorism, as a descriptive noun, in its final form comes from the French *terroriste* and was first used in 1794 by the French philosopher François-Noël Babeuf … It is defined in the Oxford Dictionary as: "The unlawful use of violence and intimidation, especially against civilians, in the pursuit of political aims." However, terrorism as an issue is much more complex, and it takes a multifaceted approach to make any real sense of this phenomenon that has plagued humans since the beginning of time.

*

437

All those who embrace terrorism, they, just like Julius Caesar, cross their own Rubicon, a line that they cannot turn back from. By crossing this symbolic ribbon of dark baptismal water, they become killers.

For a small minority, the killing spree may have begun by accident or as an act of slow-witted curiosity. Initially, it may have involved tearing wings off flies or butterflies, which then escalated to killing small animals such as cats and dogs. In some instances, the actual killing act heightened their excitement and gave them such pleasure that, like an opiate, it hooked them for life.

There are others though, the majority, who may had been influenced by careless parents, fanatical peers, their Sunday School or Madras teachers, their priests, their professors at university or a real attack such as the invasion of Poland by Germany or a false flag attack such as the Gulf of Tonkin incident in Vietnam.

*

Some individuals join the army to vent their hatred or anger against a real or imagined enemy. Others join because of some form of conscription to a national defence force – that can be quickly turned by local or international players into a lethal attack force and enlisted for nefarious purposes.

Discipline, skill and single-mindedness are instilled through rigorous and brutal training. Once instilled, the skills learned by this killer-force of obeying orders, firing on command, killing what they are conditioned to see and hate, as an inanimate thing really, an object, as the "other" rather than a living human being, leads to a myriad of unforeseen, and at times, brutal acts. Those acts in turn lead to problems that surviving soldiers have to face and rationalise when they are discharged and go home ...

So the army is, in most cases, the primary source of terrorist fighters.

*

It is said that Prometheus was motivated by a virtue: altruism. This turncoat Titan stole fire from Mount Olympus for humanity, who until then lived a troglodyte existence. Zeus, the king of the gods, punished him for his transgression by tying him to a rock where each day an eagle was sent to feed on his liver, which would then grow back overnight to be eaten again the next day. Prometheus was really an archetype, the forerunner of the rebel. He resisted all forms of institutional tyranny represented by Zeus. And Zeus was, according to the Greek myths, a tyrant, and like all tyrants, he ruled by mustering and dispensing punishment through the terror and brutal force of his thunderbolts. To the ancient Greeks, Zeus' thunderbolts were as terrifying as hydrogen bombs are to us today.

The Thracian mercenary, slave, gladiator and revolutionary Spartacus did not rebel against a god. He rebelled against a brutal empire that had built its success on the labour and deaths of a myriad of slaves. He and his co-conspirators wanted the freedom to be the masters of their own destiny. With 70,000 men, they wreaked havoc on the Roman army. Spartacus did not, in the end, succeed, but he did vent his spleen, and although he lost the war and 6,000 of his followers were crucified between Rome and Capua, history has never forgotten him.

*

There is, in humans, an impulse that, once activated, is tough to contain. This is a quality that we humans treasure and it is the stuff of legends. That impulse usually has its roots in some form of injustice, and when an individual or a group seeks to address that injustice and they are brutally put down, then the survivors find any way that they can to gain advantage and deliver, invoking their own moral right for, restitution. That they are terrorists is only because they are described as such by their enemies, but to their own kind, they are heroes.

*

Terrorism is a strategy of the weak and the vengeful. According to the historian Josephus, the Sicarii, a Jewish extremist sect, similar to the Zealots, who also opposed the Roman occupation of Judea, initially carried out guerrilla acts of terror by stabbing Roman soldiers or Hebrew Roman sympathisers with sicae, small daggers. They would then withdraw and disappear into the crowd. Eventually, after the fall of the Second Temple, they left Jerusalem and captured the fortress of Masada, a rocky mesa 1,500 feet above sea level, where they withstood a three-year siege. At the end, 960 of them suicided rather than surrender. Similarly, in 1803, sixty Souli women who, with their menfolk, rose up against the tyranny of the Ottoman Empire, did the same in the village of Zalongo in northern Greece after they were overrun by Ottoman Albanian forces. They threw themselves and their children off a cliff face rather than face rape and death at their enemy's hands. Similar events occurred on the island of Okinawa after the American invasion and in Germany after the Nazis lost the war.

This indefinable impulse can, as indicated, lead to self-destruction. The Masada mass suicide of the Sicarii was carried out by the defenders drawing lots and killing each

440

other in turn. The only man to actually commit suicide was the last man standing as Rabbinic Judaism prohibits suicide. The same edict against suicide applies in Greek Orthodoxy. The Greek women who were totally committed to their cause, though, were cast in heroic terms, even by the Church. Their self-sacrifice shamed the rest of Europe into helping the Greeks to eventually gain their independence. The Sicarii were also cast in heroic terms, and although some see them as religious fanatics who murdered their wives and children, others see them as revolutionaries who had no other alternative than to die for their God and their cause.

*

Active members of terrorist groups are a minuscule percentage of the total population. Yet in small numbers, there is strength if they are well organised, well trained and well directed. They become difficult to detect and capture, as demonstrated by the Cypriot Nationalist group EOKA lead by George Grivas against the British from 1955 to 1959, where at one point, 30,000 British soldiers were chasing 600 guerrillas.

In 1945 fifty Jewish survivors of the Holocaust, who called themselves *Nakam* – Avengers – planned to poison the water of four German cities and to kill six million Germans. They were driven by their doctrine of an eye for an eye. And although the saying is popularly attributed to Judaism as the phrase is used in the New Testament (Matthew 5:38–39), it is a paraphrase of Hammurabi's Code from the Mesopotamian culture. Basically, it promotes revenge. That the Avengers did not succeed in realising their revenge was a matter of chance.

The Red Army Faction had a core of about twenty young Germans and they were led by Andreas Baader and Ulrike Meinhof. They, too, were driven by a sense of injustice

441

when they saw former Nazis who had brought a catastrophe on the German people returning to the corridors of power. They sought revenge for being disenfranchised from shaping their own future.

*

The Alexandrian Greek poet Constantine Cavafy in his poem *Waiting for the Barbarians,* describes a poignant scene in a Greek city-state whose leaders, for political expedience and social control, stoked their citizen's fears. They did this by creating an imagined threat – the ultimate bogey – encapsulated in what became the pejorative word *barbaros* – barbarian – which is an amorphous pronoun descriptor for "the other". Cavafy also describes what happens when there is an awakening self-realisation of the citizenry to this manipulation.

> *... (How serious people's faces have become.)*
> *Why are the streets and squares emptying so rapidly,*
> *everyone going home lost in thought?*
> *Because night has fallen and the barbarians haven't come.*
> *And some of our men just in from the border say*
> *there are no barbarians any longer.*
> *Now what's going to happen to us without barbarians?*
> *Those people were a kind of solution.*

As Cavafy hints, sometimes we need those bogeys, those barbarians, because they allow us to dig ourselves out of a hole that, for a variety of reasons, we have dug ourselves into. Winston Churchill called it "the rut of inertia", others simply call it boredom .... Then, all of a sudden, BANG! ... We are hit by the sudden comprehension

442

that we are under attack. Immediately an inner response is sparked: our sympathetic nervous system is activated … There's the flush of adrenaline … It gets us going … gives us momentum, which then is harnessed to give us direction and, because of it, purpose … At first, something intangible and small, but then something bigger, larger than ourselves, something that will extend us, test our mettle, our intellect … Something like a journey or maybe a search … a search for the source of a river or a conquest … a conquest of a high peak or even something grander or imaginary like … like … like a dragon … Yes, a big, fat, scaly, multi-hued dragon … maybe scores of dragons … Or maybe, scores of giants … huge, ugly, demented giants … to stalk, charge and slay. But as Sancho Panza found to his consternation, his deranged master Don Quixote's giants were just a bunch of ordinary, run-down windmills. That it is a delusion … it's obvious. The idea of a quest, though, must not be underestimated, even as a delusion. It is a powerful and enticing motivational force, especially when also invoking God, for Christians to kill Muslims, for Catholics to kill Protestants and vice versa.

*

The IRA (Irish Republican Army) and other nationalist terrorist groups have political wings that represent them in the public forum. Those politicians, just like those that represented the Israeli Irgun terrorist group (National Military Organization in the Land of Israel), justified those terror attacks using a flamboyant and passionate nationalist narrative. The Irgun group went on to bomb the King David Hotel in 1946, killing ninety-one people of different nationalities, including Jews, and carried out the massacre at the village of Deir Yassin in 1948. Depending on who you believe,

443

between 107 and 254 Palestinians were killed, including women and children. This act was aimed to sow terror so that the Palestinians, who had lived in the area for thousands of years, would flee for their lives. Like their European terrorist equivalents, the Irgun discovered that instilling fear into the heart of your enemy is essential in order to achieve your end goal – in their case, a new homeland. So terrorism still remains an option in the arsenal and repertoire of the patriot-inspired killers such as the Maquis, who fought the Nazis to restore liberty to France and the Mau Mau or KLFA (Kenya Land and Freedom Army), who fought the British Empire for their country's independence.

*

It is most likely, though, that every politician, in the beginning, is driven by that initial Promethean altruist impulse. They want to serve; they want to do good. That they, in one way or another, are corrupted and cling on to power using dark tricks seems inevitable nowadays. But the question must be asked ... did Prometheus go on his fire-stealing quest for humanity as a benefactor or because it simply gave him something to do? Or was he harnessing humanity for a more perverse quest? Maybe he was forming an army to liberate his kin, the Titans, imprisoned in Tartarus and to overthrow the Olympian Gods and was simply just grasping for power like a neophyte politician.

*

In their ascent to power, politicians use bogeys. They demonise their opponents and play what basically is a primitive but effective wild card, and the pejorative list of nouns they collect and recite is long. Words like Jews, Blacks, Foreigners, Gypsies and

Barbarians are pulled out whenever required to become "the other" ... But those politicians are only grasping at straws because all the time the hole that has been dug is still there, waiting to be filled ... and that is when they announce through blow-horns: that a sacrifice is needed.

In *Iphigenia in Aulis*, by Euripides, Agamemnon says to his daughter, "there is not a power of arriving at the towers of Troy, unless I sacrifice you ..." because, he explains, he was commanded by the goddess Artemis ... and concludes how terrible it is for Greeks "... to be plundered perforce of our wives by barbarians." Agamemnon invoked and blamed a deity for his misfortune and obliquely demonised "an other", the Trojans. And as he implies, for the enterprise to succeed, a sacrifice is needed ... a human sacrifice ... his daughter.

Buried in the human psyche there is a deeply ingrained, abhorrent, prehistoric memory that has, over the ages, gained indelible traction and, remarkably, is still practised today. Human sacrifice was common until the end of the Neolithic period. Then animals began to be sacrificed instead. In the Old Testament, God demands a human sacrifice from Abraham as a test of his loyalty. But Isaac, Abraham's son, is spared by God and instead, a lamb is placed as a sacrifice on the pyre. In ancient Japan, a legend describes *hitobashira* – human pillars – in which maidens were buried alive near the base of some constructions to protect them against disasters or enemy attacks. This is also more starkly encapsulated by a famous Greek folk ballad, *The Bridge of Arta*. The ballad tells the grim and horrifying tale of the sacrifice of a master mason's wife, who was buried in the pillar foundations of the stone bridge that straddles the Arachthos river, west of the city of Arta, to appease a supernatural force that kept tearing it down.

In the New Testament, the parents of Jesus sacrificed two doves, and the Apostle Peter performs a Nazarite after Jesus' death. To conclude this ritual, a lamb is sacrificed as a burnt offering, a ewe as a sin-offering and a ram as a peace offering. Even Buddhists, who abhor the killing of any sentient being, still turn a blind eye to the act of animal sacrifice by one of their sects in North Sikkim, a leftover ritual from their pagan past. This sacrificial animal ritual still occurs. In Cyprus, I have witnessed a rooster being killed and its blood squirted over the building site to ensure firm foundations. That the rooster is consumed at a feast does not detract from the symbolic overlap of two religious traditions.

Christ is referred to by his apostles as the Lamb of God (John 1:29). According to the penal substitution theory of atonement, though, Christ's crucifixion is comparable to an animal sacrifice on a larger scale because his death serves as a substitutionary punishment for all of humanity's sins. And as terrible as it seems, modern politicians still sacrifice human lives – their soldiers and their civilians – and cast the deaths in heroic terms and other sanctimonious hyperbole concocted to justify them ...

"Those who can make you believe absurdities, can make you commit atrocities," said Voltaire.

*

We, humans, are social animals. After the initial evolutionary period of interpersonal cooperation, when numbers grew, people began to form tribes. Those tribes, for a

446

variety of reasons, began to attack each other. Because of this, each group developed the capacity to recognise the tribes that were a threat to them as different, as "the other". This allowed them to stay safe. Eventually, this learned attribute was passed on to future generations. It also allowed them to go on to develop societies, a grouping of tribes. This coming together, this grouping, is hardwired into us and sometimes, for reasons that we cannot fully understand, in order to belong, we are even prepared to surrender our free will. This can be for one's nation but can also be for something as mundane as belonging to a football club, a motorbike gang, a cult or even a choir.

*

We invent methods of governance for our groups, and democracy is one of the most successful forms of such governance. In a democracy, we elect our politicians and parliament is supposed to make decisions on whether to go to war. Just war theory – *jus ad bello, jus ad bellum* – is a military ethics construct that ensures war is morally justifiable between countries through a series of criteria: *jus ad bellum*, the right to go to war and *jus in bello,* the right conduct in war. That is why countries invented what now is termed "a false flag incident" to justify pre-emptive attacks.

Modern terrorism, though, is not encompassed by the just war doctrine because it works outside the rule of law by attacking lawful governments. When those lawfully created states fall victim to terrorism, there is despair and a response is strategised. When terrorism is state-sanctioned, though, one country covertly overthrowing the head of state of another, for instance, one also despairs. Such an act was carried out on the Prime Minister of Iran, Mohammad Mosaddegh, in 1953 by the United Kingdom and the United States. And in 1973, President Salvador Allende was overthrown by a

447

military coup supported by the United States. When such acts occur without a declaration of war, it is beyond the pale. It is outside the perimeters of a just war and demands condemnation, justice and restitution. If not, as we have seen, the consequences can be disastrous.

*

We humans must recognise that we all harbour deep inside us the seeds of a killer, and we must also acknowledge that we are all capable of killing. We choose to remain ignorant of all the bacteria and other forms of life we inadvertently kill in order to exist, which is an irony, really, as that ability is probably what has enabled us to be successful as an animal species.

Many cultures very quickly realised this inherent violent streak and introduced taboos that became prescriptive. A notable example is the Ten Commandments, the sixth of which clearly states, "Thou shall not kill." This is part of the moral code given by Moses, the leader of the Exodus, to the Israelites. What Moses really meant, though, was: "Thou shall not kill your own kind."

You judge people by what they say or do.

*

All human creations are organic. Society is organic … a reflection of its creator. And like its creator, it breathes, eats and thinks. Like all living organisms, it self-dissolves and self-regenerates and sometimes self-destructs, as when a tumour arises from within it and the cancerous cells fight for supremacy. Most of the time, the organism's immune system attacks and destroys the cancer. When the immune system fails to respond to this danger, the organism withers and dies. If it is a society, as when a person develops a gangrenous limb, the diseased appendage is severed to ensure survival.

It is a nature-given right for all organisms to defend themselves and find the equivalent of a vaccine to eliminate the threat posed. Sophisticated societies ostracise harmful individuals by exiling them by a popular vote – even people who have led them to victory against "the other", like General Themistocles, the mastermind of the Athenian navy's defence and victory at Salamis who saved Athens and perhaps the Greek world from the Persians. In other societies, individuals who pose a threat or danger to society are excluded and killed through autosuggestion, exemplified by the pointing of the bone in Aboriginal societies in Australia, or voodoo deaths in Haiti. In many societies, they are tried and executed. In a few humane societies, miscreants are de-radicalised and rehabilitated.

Unfortunately, the same biological analogy is also used for dealing with "the other" … exemplified by the exterminations carried out by the Turkish republic's Young Turks or by the Nazi state.

*

And what of peace? In New Zealand, there is the cautionary lesson of the Moriori people of the Chatham Islands. Because of bloody and savage intertribal fighting, they established Nunuku's Law, named after the pacifist chief Nunuka-whenua. This law forbade "cannibalism and killing in any form". Unfortunately, they paid a heavy price for this fervently held custom because they were nearly wiped off the face of the earth by another mainland Māori tribe that had no such sensibilities. As Black Panther member

George Jackson said of the non-violent tactics of Martin Luther King Junior: "The concept of non-violence is a false ideal. It presupposes the existence of compassion and a sense of justice on the part of one's adversary. When this adversary has everything to lose and nothing to gain by exercising justice and compassion, his reaction can only be negative."

So, maybe it is advisable that we keep the killer on a short leash, and – as the Latin phrase that gave the Parabellum ammunition brand its name – prepare for war ... and unleash the killer through a democratically elected, state-sanctioned authority, when we require him ... and only for self-preservation.

But just as states can unleash killers, so can amorphous but disciplined terrorist groups of varied sizes motivated by a range of ideas. Those ideas are not usually too complex. But they explain complex events, biographies and histories through a simple and narrowly focused narrative. Such a narrative motivated the Gun Powder Plot of 1605 when a group of thirteen English Catholics attempted to blow up the Protestant King James I and the Palace of Westminster, the English seat of Parliament. The man caught guarding the powder kegs for the plotters was named Guy Fawkes, and subsequently, he loaned his name to the day of the plot's demise, which is celebrated every fifth day of November with the lighting of bonfires. Fawkes was a Protestant who converted to Catholicism. Like many proselytised converts, he was driven by a burning religious zeal and sought revenge for the injustice that he felt was done to the Catholics by Protestants in England. After being blooded fighting on the side of the Catholic Spaniards in the Eighty Years' War, he returned to England, where he joined the plot to blow up the "heretic" King James I and replace him with a Catholic head of state. The conspirators were found guilty and the court was told the condemned would, among other things, have their genitals cut off and "burned before their eyes, and their bowels and hearts removed". They would then be decapitated and the dismembered parts of their bodies displayed so that they might become "prey for the fowls of the air". Their grisly death added to the heroic narrative. And such narratives can be seductive and highly motivational. They can activate a movement that can easily become violent. It is possible that the Guy Fawkes narrative eventually perhaps led to the creation of the IRA, which is also a religious terrorist organisation. The causes for terrorism can, as in those examples, be obvious, but they can also be enigmatic, and neither wealth nor poverty, ignorance nor education is a defence against them.

*

As long as there are humans, there will be some people prepared to break the rules and kill for their ideas or self-interest. And their self-interest may be simply *cupio dissolve* – "I wish to self-dissolve" – which is spurred on by Sigmund Freud's coined word *todestrieb* – the death drive. And the ritual steps they undergo to finally arrive at that point are well known ... as every sergeant major knows: "What about 'Thou shall not kill', Sergeant Major, sir?" "What are you drivelling on about, you snivelling piece of shit ... You are in the army now, private. Forget all that bullshit, you hear me! You are here to do just that. Kill!" ... and eventually, they coldly pull the trigger to take a life, several lives ... many lives, and then finally, maybe, even their own life.

*

The only way to try and vaccinate against terrorism is to listen to the malcontents' viewpoint, if they are not irreparably damaged or fatally deranged, and then try to

451

appease them by making sure that they have a stake and a voice in the society they are living in through meaningful education, employment and accessible health and political structures.

Fortunately, there is hope on the horizon as non-violent revolts of resistance seem now to be more successful. Those peaceful revolts are more likely to result in real change, and they are less likely to degenerate into civil war. Gandhi's passive resistance and non-cooperation movement – inspired by the 1849 essay of Henry David Thoreau *Resistance to Civil Government* – is still a good exemplar. Although, to Gandhi's consternation, it did eventually lead to the bloodied Pakistan/India divide. It seems, though, that when people rely on peaceful civil disobedience, their size grows exponentially. In the Soviet Union, civil resistance is used by intellectuals such as Andrei Dmitrievich Sakharov, a nuclear physicist, dissident, and activist for disarmament, peace and human rights. Novelist, historian and short-story writer Aleksandr Isayevich Solzhenitsyn, who is an outspoken critic of the Soviet Union and communism, helped to raise global awareness of its Gulag forced labour camp system. And when large numbers of people, including the middle class, withdraw their cooperation from an oppressive system, the odds in their favour increase.

It is not an exaggeration to say that terrorism other than for nation-building fails to achieve its goals most of the time – if it has any goals – and, tarnished with the mark of Cain, ends up self-destructing. It becomes an ouroboros, a snake that eats its own tail or a King Erysichthon, who fell foul of the goddess Artemis ... She cursed him to be driven by insatiable hunger and he ends up devouring himself. And of course, King Agamemnon, the King of the Greeks, the victor of Troy, got his comeuppance after his military sojourn when he was butchered in his bath by his vengeful wife's lover. Don't they say: As you sow, you shall reap? Maybe.

12

Like a good socialist with a tinge of anarchy, I placed my desultory mystical awakening on halt, banked my cheque for the newspaper article and bought Scipio a tin of tuna to celebrate.

Yeah! It's your payday too, my loyal, furry mate – bon appetit!

*

The second to last night before Alexandra left to return to London, we arranged to have dinner together in my apartment. I had given her a key and went off to do the shopping. I was happy and even whistled on my way home. The street was dark, but the streetlight in front of my house was repaired. I was quite chuffed about that because I had personally gone down to the council on two occasions to get it fixed. Maybe things were changing in Cyprus.

As I was about to open the front door, someone rushed me from behind. He grabbed me around the throat with the crook of one arm and stuck an automatic to my forehead. The pressure on my throat forced me to stand on tiptoe. Then a voice that I recognised as Savas Spithas' started berating me, warning me that he was going to shoot me like a dog if I struggled. From the smell of his breath, he was drunk. His subsequent tirade included a range of profanities, crude epithets and threats to my whole family if I didn't do what he told me to do. He said that he wanted me to move with him to his car, which

453

was about five yards away with the boot open. He and I were going to have a talk, he said. I knew that everyone, including KYP, was looking for him. I also knew that if he got me into the car, it would be curtains for me. He pulled me back, but I resisted as best as I could by letting the air out of my lungs – creating a dead weight – and then dropping my *ki*, my centre of gravity. However, he was strong and he had me off balance. So I attempted to turn us around by trying to get a foothold to push him back against the wall.

Suddenly there was a crash and I was free.

Spithas had collapsed in front of me, out cold. There were the remains of a flowerpot and its geraniums scattered around his head. Blood began to flow from a deep head wound.

"Stauvro! Are you all right?" It was Alexandra. "Have I killed him?"

I bent down and felt his pulse. "No, he's alive, but he'll have a hell of a headache. Good aim. Was that part of your medical training?"

"Thank you, Stauvro *mou*. No. It was part of my jilted wife training."

"I must remember that. The blood is pouring out of him," I said.

"Head wounds always bleed."

"He needs a hospital."

"Well, it's more than he deserves, but he'll get a doctor first and then a hospital. Give me a minute."

*

The police charged Savas Spithas with kidnapping, murder and attempted murder and bundled him up and took him to Nicosia General Hospital. Petros and Karageorgis arrived, too, and were anxious to facilitate our extraction from the paperwork as quickly as possible.

Petros locked eyes on Alexandra and I introduced them. Petros looked at me and gave me a sly smile and a nod. "Good choice, cousin," he said. "Let's see what Eleni says."

13

Alexandra and I spent our last night together at the Hilton Hotel, care of whoever was paying for her accommodation. We had dined at Petros and Eleni's. A sumptuous feast of all foods Cypriot.

Eleni loved Alexandra.

The next day I drove Alexandra to the airport, and we awkwardly stood around, waiting until it was time for her to go.

We had agreed that I'd fly to London and spend more time together before we decided on anything more. Eleni had already said that she'd gladly look after Scipio, and I think she was relieved that a woman had finally latched on to me.

Alexandra held on to me and me to her until the last minute.

As she went through the departure gate, she turned around and mouthed the words. Two Greek words ... they are similar to two words in English ... that now have special meaning to me.

After Melani, Petros, to ease my confusion and distress had said to me, "Don't the English say, cousin, there are lots more fish in the sea?"

I remembered my reply, which I am still proud of. "Yeah, that's what the English say, cousin. Unfortunately a shark only mates with a shark."

Notes

Black Hand: This Serbian secret society actually existed as well as its pre-Mafia Italian extortion racket namesake in Chicago. However, its connection to Georgios Grivas is speculation, and to Polycarpos Georghadjis, pure fiction.

Delphinidis: The character of Delphinidis is a construct based loosely on the life and work of Stylianos Atteshlis, and I hope this portrait does justice to his memory. I have never met Atteshlis, but my father once accompanied his friend Father Sosima Gavriel (the priest of Patriki) to seek his counsel. If the reader wants to read more about Atteshlis, refer to Kyriacos C. Markides *The Magus of Strovolos*.

Pham Xuan An: An actual major historical personality who was a South Vietnamese journalist and correspondent for *Time*, Reuters and the *New York Herald Tribune*. He was stationed in Saigon during the war in Vietnam while spying for the National Liberation Front. After the war he was made a general and awarded the "People's Army Force Hero" by the Vietnamese government on 15 January, 1976.

Savitri Devi Mukherji: A real historical figure who was formerly known as Maximiani Julia Portas. Her biography seems to be somewhat patchy and probably modified to fit her political beliefs.

The Massacre of Thessaloniki by Theodosius I: Church historian Theodoretus puts the figure at about 7,000, saying:

> "... by unsheathing the sword most unjustly and tyrannically against all, slaying the innocent and guilty alike. It is said seven thousand perished without any forms of law, and without even having judicial sentence passed upon them; but that, like ears of wheat in the time of harvest, they were alike cut down."

Recent archaeological excavation of the mass grave has raised the figure to 17,000.

Aesha Ozan is a construct based on the life of Türkan Aziz, who was the first Turkish nurse to be appointed as Chief Nurse at Nicosia Hospital. She died at 101 years of age in 2019. *The Death of Friendship: A Cyprus Memoir* is part biography and part polemic, the ideal construct of effective propaganda. Aziz was a graduate of the American Academy in Nicosia and studied nursing at the American University of Beirut. During her studies, she worked in university hospitals. She continued her education in London, where she researched thoracic disorders and tuberculosis. Her father, Mehmet Aziz, was responsible for the eradication of malaria in Cyprus. Normally I would attribute a real historical character their true name. However, in this instance, I found it difficult to separate the real Aesha Ozan from the one she constructed as a Turkish nationalist. In 1963 Harry Scott Gibbons, a reporter in Cyprus at the time, reported the murder of twenty-one Turkish Cypriot patients from the Nicosia General Hospital on Christmas Eve. This is taken as a fact in the Turkish Cypriot narrative, perpetuated by Türkan Aziz, but not in the Greek Cypriot narrative. Rebecca Bryant and Yiannis Papadakis in their book *Cyprus and the Politics of Memory: History, Community and Conflict* note that an investigation of the incident by a "highly reliable" Greek Cypriot source found that three Turkish Cypriots died, of which one died of a heart attack and the other two were shot by a "lone psychopath".

Bibliography

Books

Arnett, Peter, *Live from the Battlefield*, Simon and Shuster (New York,1994).

Azinas, Andreas, *Fifty Years of Silence*, Airwaves (Nicosia, 2001).

Bryant, Rebecca; Papadakis, Yiannis, eds. *Cyprus and the Politics of Memory: History, Community and Conflict.* I.B.Tauris. (2012).

Barker, Dudley, *Grivas – Portrait of a Terrorist*, The Cresset Press (London, 1959).

Drousiotis, Makarios, *Cyprus 1974 – Greek Coup and Turkish Invasion*, Mannheim und Mohnesee: Bibliopolis (2006).

Foley, Charles, *Island in Revolt*, Longmans (London, 1962).

Henn, Francis, *A Business of Some Heat: The United Nations Force in Cyprus Before and During the 1974 Turkish Invasion*, Pen & Sword (2004).

Kevork, Keshishian. *Romantic Cyprus*, Mark & Moody (1963).

Kolokotronis, Theodoros; Edmonds, Elizabeth M. (trans.), *Kolokotrones. The Klepht and the Warrior. Sixty Years of Peril and Daring. An Autobiography*, T. Fisher Unwin. (London, 1892)

O'Malley, Brendan; Craig, Ian, *The Cyprus Conspiracy*, L.B. & Tauris & Co. Ltd (London, 1999).

Wikipedia Sites

'Akrotiri And Dhekelia', Wikipedia. (n.d.), Retrieved from https://en.wikipedia.org/wiki/Court_of_the_Sovereign_Base_Areas

"Byzantine Iconoclasm', Wikipedia. (n.d.), Retrieved from
    https://en.wikipedia.org/wiki/Byzantine_Iconoclasm

'Chandria', Wikipedia. (n.d.), Retrieved from
    https://en.wikipedia.org/wiki/Handria

'Deicide', Wikipedia. (n.d.), Retrieved from
    https://en.wikipedia.org/wiki/Deicide

'French Revolution', Wikipedia. (n.d.), Retrieved from
    Wikipedia.org/wiki/French_Revolution

'Iphigenia', Wikipedia. (n.d.),
    https://en.wikisource.org/wiki/Iphigenia_at_Aulis

'Just War Theory', Wikipedia. (n.d.), Retrieved from
    https://en.wikipedia.org/wiki/Just_War_theory

'Jehovah's Witnesses', Wikipedia. (n.d.), Retrieved from
    https://en.wikipedia.org/wiki/Jehovah's_Witnesses

'Linobambaki', Wikipedia. (n.d.), Retrieved from
    https://en.wikipedia.org/wiki/Linobambaki

'Taalat Pasha', Wikipedia (n.d.), https://en.wikipedia.org/wiki/Talaat_Pasha

Further Online References

Burke, Jason, 'Sri Lanka Attackers', The Guardian (2019), Retrieved from
    https://www.theguardian.com/world/2019/apr/25/why-sri-lanka-atta
    ckers-wealthy-backgrounds-shouldnt-surprise-us

C. P. Cavafy, *Waiting for the Barbarians*, Poetry Foundation. (n.d.).
    Retrieved from

https://www.poetryfoundation.org/poems/51294/waiting-for-the-bar
barians

Heraclides, A., Bashiardes, E., Fernández-Domínguez, E., Bertoncini, S.,
Chimonas, M., Christofi, V., … Cariolou, M., 'Y-chromosomal
analysis of Greek Cypriots reveals a primarily common pre-Ottoman
paternal ancestry with Turkish Cypriots', *PLoS ONE*, 12(6),
e0179474, https://doi.org/10.1371/journal.pone.0179474

Patterson, Eric, 'Just War Theory & Terrorism', Providence (2016), Retrieved
from
https://providencemag.com/2016/11/just-war-theory-terrorism/

Varoufakis, Yanis, 'Marx Predicted Our Present Crisis and Points the Way
Out …', The Guardian (2018),
https://www.yanisvaroufakis.eu/2018/05/15/marx-predicted-our-pre
sent-crisis-and-

'Speech by Hitler on the invasion of Czechoslovakia', Alternative History,
https://althistory.fandom.com/wiki/Speech_on_the_Invasion_of_Cz
echoslovakia_by_Adolf_Hitler_(Fall_Gr%C3%BCn) An example
of rhetorical hyperbole.

'Which Revolution(s) Established Long-Lasting Democratic …', (n.d.).
Retrieved from *https://brainly.com/question/2428072*

www.ingramcontent.com/pod-product-compliance
Lightning Source LLC
Chambersburg PA
CBHW020827030726
47496CB00001B/128